The Masked Kingdom: Nights of Betrayal

The Masked Kingdom: Nights of Betrayal

S. Eang

To order additional copies of this book, contact:
Xlibris
844-714-8691
www.Xlibris.com
Orders@Xlibris.com
833806

Contents

For my grandparents

Acknowledgments

Thany Por
Ron Por
Cameron Por
Hien Nguyen
Lisa Prak
William Conroy
Lindsey Prak
Charley Sang
Rossa Mara
Steven Iang
Donna Del Core
Nina Pennacchio
Eric Luther Ingram
Jose Guzman
Dillan Nguyen
David Nop

Prologue

Standing on the cliff of the Golden Falls, glancing across the golden waterfall to the Forest of Despair stood Vesak Dragrose, an old man in his midsixties with gray hair that was tied back into a tight bun, listening to the waterfall crashing down to the golden river below. A former commander for the Kimsu clan, he committed treason by freeing twenty prisoners he said were innocent. He had five sons, including the great hero Kilyu Dragrose. All died during the fifth era war, famously known as the Lost Generation War. Now, the last of his family name.

"My sons," said Vesak, looking up to the purple moon as the rain hit his face. "Sixty-five years I lived, and for fifty years, I served the gods as their warrior. I withstand the death of all five of you, your mother, and my siblings. I walked this dreaded world we call home alone long enough." He smiled at the sky. "Will you all accept me with all the sin I come with?"

"You'll die as a traitor, Vesak," reminded Ausra, a former student of Vesak, a member of the famed Kimsu clan, the black demon of the eastern kingdom. He had long dark hair with his right eye blue and left black. There was no emotion upon his face as he held his single-edge sword in his left hand tightly. The sword named Life, the blade had two phoenixes on each side carved into it.

"Ah, Ausra. I am glad it is you that will send me to my family," said Vesak without turning around to his prized student. He shut his eyes and remembered all the good and bad times in his life. He recalled memories of his five sons then remembered the first day he met his wife. He wanted to enter the heavens with all the bad in his life forever gone.

As Sukro Kismu approached his cousin Ausra from behind, he said to him, "Lord Vesak, you don't have to die. Please, I beg of you, just confess your treason and maybe Uncle Aerin will forgive you."

There was a young man the same age as Ausra and Sukro named Torshen Iceben who stood atop a tree branch and watched over the area. He had short white hair with eyes that resembled ice. In his hand, he held an ice arrow formed out of snow, awaiting to shoot Vesak if he were to make any sudden moves.

Sukro looked up at Torshen and Ausra with disbelief in his eyes. "What's with you two?" asked Sukro. "He may be a traitor, but he is still our teacher."

"Do not worry, Sukro. I am ready to accept my fate. There is no place in this world for this old man anymore." He turned his eyes to the sky and shouted, "I am proud and honored to be the teacher of Seven Demon Dragons. My final quest for all of you is to find the truth of this world and free yourselves from the cage of Telamis."

Suddenly, Ausra quickly charged toward Vesak. Sukro tried to stop him but was too slow. Torshen shut his eyes to avoid seeing the death of his teacher.

Vesak never turned around to see his three students. Ausra's sword pierced through his spine. He looked down at the sword with his own blood dripping from it and smiled peacefully as his life ended. No longer did he have to live with the sin of a warrior anymore. He can finally feast with his sons, tell his war stories with his father, taste his mother's cooking, and love his wife again.

Ausra pulled his sword out and watched as Vesak fell to the wet ground. With a blank stare at his teacher's lifeless body, he could sense the sadness coming from Sukro and Torshen. As far as he was concerned, Vesak was nothing more than another victim to his sword. As he wiped the blood from it and sheathed it, he looked up at the sky, allowing the rain to run down his face.

Chapter One

Kingdom of Tigara

Aerin Kimsu watched proudly from the grounds of the Demon Palace, as his three youngest children rode their clouds above in the autumn sky, kicking blue fireballs at each other. A smile came over his face as he watched the enjoyment in their eyes.

Aerin had distinctive dark eyes with his hair tied in a tight bun. He had a small black goatee that symbolized the strict look of the Kimsu Clan, but on this particular day, he didn't display the dark and cold look of the clan. After hearing the good news that his prized son was returning home, all he could do since the morning was show a proud smile.

Riding with confidence and waiting for the fireball to approach her was Kiri Kimsu, a young lady with looks similar to those of her father. She had ocean-blue eyes and dark hair down to her shoulders. As she intensely watched the blue fireball, she feverishly bit the bottom of her lip. Within seconds, the fireball came flying toward her; and with a loud thrust, she quickly kicked it away.

The fireball then flew to Isa, the youngest of the Kimsu siblings. As the fireball neared him, he quickly ducked, nearly falling over his cloud. Afraid of the fireball, he wimped as he ducked and covered his head. At ten years old, he still hadn't mastered the art of fire like his older siblings. He peeked down to Aerin and saw a slight disappointment over his face.

Isa resembled Aerin from the eyes down to the smile.

Luckily, behind Isa, there was Lehue. At twelve, he was a year younger than Kiri. Although a bit chubby, he was very agile. Lehue didn't have many of his father's features but portrayed dark eyes and dark hair. He too kicked the fireball above then smiled at Isa.

Kiri quickly flew to the fireball and dribbled it with her feet. "Isa, stop ducking and kick it back!" yelled Kiri annoyingly.

"Give him a break," defended Lehue calmly.

"If he wants to unlock his flames, he need not be afraid of a fireball," argued Kiri.

"It's just a game, Kiri." Lehue turned to Isa and smiled at him. "Stop playing with the ball and kick it back already," he replied.

Each time Kiri and Lehue kicked the ball, their aggression increased. Kiri became more and more excited while Lehue tried to maintain the same level of intensity that Kiri had.

Isa, on the other hand, while afloat and sitting still on his cloud, could only watch cowardly as his siblings showed off their strength to Aerin. Again, he looked down. The disappointment continued to be expressed on Aerin's face while staring back.

All of a sudden, the disappointment on Aerin's face vanished and turned into a smile. A light-blond-haired woman with blues eyes that reflected against the sky approached behind him. She was an enchanting woman to the eye. The woman was Maenellia Kimsu.

On her shoulder was a blue-flame bird the same size as an adult hawk. It had blue feathers and a blue-fire tail.

Maenellia smiled gently toward Isa, giving him confidence. "They're having fun." Maenellia smiled at Aerin.

"Yes, they are, but Isa is still weak. The gods have cursed him," said Aerin disappointingly.

"Perhaps he's a late one. I feel that the gods have something great in store for him. We can only wait, my love," suggested Maenellia.

"However long I must wait, the boy must show his fire. The demon of the east must stay on top of the mountain."

Maenellia's smile disappeared as she listened to Aerin's words. As his wife, she supported his ambition, but deep down in her heart, she couldn't bring herself to accept his strong ambitions. "My brother wants to visit soon," she said while trying to sway Aerin's mind from thinking about his idea. "He wants to give our three young ones a gift."

"He'll be traveling from the south. It will be a long journey for him as we shall gratefully welcome him when he arrives."

Maenellia's younger brother was the head of the Ma clan in the southern kingdom. Just like the Kimsu clan, they controlled fire, but the flames were blue. The Kimsu clan controlled the black flames.

Of the children from Maenellia and Aerin, only Iszra and Ausra could control both the blue and black flames. The others could only control the blue flames.

"We must be ready for our rise," said Aerin, reverting to his plan. "I sense the land changing . . . I wish Iszra was by my side, but with Chenpu, Indris, and Ausra, I believe we can break from the kingdom of Tigara."

"Why must we rival the royal clan?" asked Maenellia. "We're at peace, and the land of Telamis is also at peace."

"I'm not rivaling the Cai clan. All I want is what my clan rightfully deserves."

Maenellia grabbed Aerin's hands and rubbed her thumb gently over his knuckles. "Whatever your plan, I will stand by you, but our children must not be harmed. They are our soul. Their life must not end before ours."

Suddenly, a guard approached Aerin and Maenellia. He was tall and muscular and had dark hair that was tied in a tight bun. He had a trimmed sharp beard and a chiseled face. He wore black steel armor with the demon sigil on his right shoulder plate. The man was Jen-Song Bore.

As he approached with his head bowed, he reported, "My lord, Lord Bloben of the Smok clan have arrived."

"Let him wait at the garden," grunted Aerin, who was not very pleased to hear about Bloben's arrival. "Maybe the scent of flowers will give him some sense of respect when speaking to me."

"Understood, my lord," said Jen-Song while bowing his head and leaving Aerin and Maenellia.

Maenellia, who also didn't like Bloben, found him to be a very disgusting man. "He wants to offer his son in marriage again." This disgusted her.

"His son will never marry any of my daughters," Aerin replied angrily. "He's afraid to lose his clan which is slowly dying off and thinks that marrying his cowardly son to one of them will breathe life and bring fame back into it. What he fails to realize is that as long as I'm alive, none of my daughters will marry his son."

Aerin looked back up to the sky and watched his three children riding on their clouds. As the blue fireball was being kicked back and forth by Kiri and Lehue, he spotted seven death birds high above the sky. These birds were gray with black snake eyes. "Ausra has returned," he uttered proudly.

*   *   *

With his hand over the back of his head and a pout face, Nisu Tavamin complained, "Why must we wait so long for Lord Aerin?" Nisu had short dark hair and golden skin with perfect features that made any woman fall for him.

The Seven Demon Dragons waited for Aerin at the great hall. The hall was dark and gloomy. The ceiling was high, and there were four pillars on each side of the hall. Hanging from the pillars were red banners with the demon sigil on it. The sigil symbolized a demon sitting on a throne. Leading to the high chair were ten steps. Behind it hanging from the wall was a giant banner of the Kimsu clan.

With a mysterious face and the eyes of a fox, Nagen Susamagi, the leader of the Seven Demon Dragons, asked Nisu, "Do you have somewhere better to be?"

"Why yes, I do. I'd much rather be at the tavern drinking my youthful life away," replied Nisu with a smile.

A tall muscular man with furious eyes and long, dark wild hair like that of a lion mane known as Kaiso Fire-Beast annoyingly grunted, "That's pathetic."

"What's the matter, Wild Beast?" Nisu asked Kaiso.

"How can you drink over our master's death?" Kaiso questioned Nisu.

"I'm getting drunk for Lord Vesak."

Kaiso rolled his eyes and crossed his arms.

"May I remind you that our dead master is a traitor," said Nagen. "He doesn't deserve any respect or honor from us."

"He's still our master. Are you forgetting everything he taught us?" Nisu asked Nagen.

Nisu hated Nagen. He saw Nagen as an egotistic and heartless man. Ever since their childhood, he always had a bad taste about Nagen. Now that they were seventeen, he still tried to find something to like about him but just couldn't. To him, the leader of the Seven Demon Dragons was a man with a hollow heart.

He looked around, hoping that others would defend their master's honor. "Are we going to allow him to speak ill of our master?" He looked to Kaiso, then to Leonaris Bellwood, a tall slender man with sharp features and short brown hair. He then looked back to Ausra, Sukro, and Torshen. All of them were avoiding eye contact with him. "You all are quick to forget our master already." He looked down sadly with concern in his eyes. "I was ten, an orphan with no future and eating nothing but dirt. Lord Vesak didn't see an orphan in me. He rescued me from my given future." He looked back up and eyed each member of the dragons with confidence. "He saved all of you, and yet you all can't respect him." He then shouted out with pride, "I will go to the tavern and drink till I fall for my master!"

The others all stayed silent.

Ausra was annoyed by Nisu. He hated when anyone showed any kind of emotion around him. He was always taught by his grandfather and father to never show his own emotions, especially to his enemies. The last time he cried was when he was seven. A man attempted to kidnap his older sister. He cried not because he couldn't save his sister, but because he killed the man with his black flames. He burned the man alive as he screamed in agony. At thirteen, he led his first army during the fifth era war. He was also the one to end the war.

"Lord Vesak certainly deserves all the respect and honor due to him," said Aerin, who calmly and proudly walked to his high chair from the back entrance of the hall. Ecstatic to see the dragons back from their mission, he felt unsafe when they were not around. They were the strongest warriors in the eastern kingdom. Ausra was believed to be the strongest warrior throughout the land of Telamis.

Aerin counted each step as he climbed to the chair. In his mind, the high chair was a throne. He sat down on his chair and faced the Seven Demon Dragons. They all bowed their heads to him.

"Where is Lord Vesak buried?" Aerin asked. "I wish to pay my last respects to him."

Nagen replied, "He's buried in the Forest of Hope, near the Golden Falls under a tree with seven stars carved in it."

"Ah . . . good. Did he die quietly like he always wanted?" asked Aerin.

"I killed him," Ausra said bluntly.

"Such a shame." Aerin shook his head. "He was a great and loyal man, yet he was cunning. I pray he enters the heavens and feast with his five sons."

Ausra saw the lie in Aerin's face.

Aerin didn't care about Vesak at all. Once Vesak stopped running with the demon, he became the enemy of the demon clan. This was especially the case with the Black Heart Demon of the East.

"What's next?" asked Nagen. "Now that the traitor is gone, shall we end the Men of Hate?"

Aerin took a moment to think as he remembered that Lord Bloben was waiting in the garden for him. He uttered to himself, "Lord Bloben has returned to offer his son's hand again. He is such a nuisance. That fat disgraceful man is a pawn to the royal clan." He chuckled. "All of you should go and rest. The rain will fall soon."

The Seven Demon Dragons all bowed their heads to Aerin. Nisu headed straight to the tavern to drink his afternoon away. Nagen traveled to the city center to buy some steam bun. Torshen went to the Lucky River to fish as Kaiso decided to go home to rest his anger, as he was still affected by Vesak's death. Leonaris headed to the library to invest his mind in new tales and stories while Ausra and Sukro stayed behind.

Sukro had a burning question he wanted to ask Aerin. He looked to Ausra and nodded at him to let him leave.

Ausra shrugged his shoulders and departed from the hall.

Sukro felt his hand sweating as the dreaded question burned inside him. He doesn't know why he wanted to ask the question now, but since Vesak was dead, he felt lost.

"Nephew, what is bothering you?" asked a concerned Aerin.

Sukro gulped and looked straight into Aerin's eyes. He was a confident man, but the burning question killed his confidence inside. "Uncle," he hesitated, "I think I'm ready . . ."

"Ready?" a confused Aerin answered.

"I'm ready to know who my father is and why he killed my mother," Sukro asked nervously.

Aerin just stared at Sukro, rubbing his chin as he measured him. "Does it bother you not knowing who your parents are?" asked Aerin.

Sukro unconvincingly looked at Aerin and replied, "No, not really. I have no memories of them, therefore it doesn't bother me."

"That's good because you were still new to the world and this world was quick to be cruel to you. Your mother was my dear little sister, stubborn and always going against our father's wishes. All three of us warned her not to anger our father and to stop seeing your father. Yet she wouldn't listen. Even when our father gave her ten lashes, she still loved your father more." A small teardrop fell from Aerin's eyes. "Father slowly accepted you, even though you were born out of wedlock. You still had the blood of the demon running through your vein. I wish I knew why your father murdered your mother then fled." He wiped away his tears. "I'm sorry, nephew, that's all I could tell you. I promised my father that I'd never talk about your father to you."

Sukro bowed his head as he looked toward the stone ground. He had a disappointing look on his face. As he picked his head back up, you could see in his eyes that his confidence was growing. "Thank you, Uncle. I appreciate everything you have done for me." As Sukro turned to leave, Vesak stopped him in his tracks.

"Sukro, Don't think about getting revenge."

"Understood," Sukro replied coldly, staring darkly at the huge wooden door of the great hall, wishing he knew what his father looked like so he can imagine the millions of ways of killing him.

* * *

After leaving the great hall, Ausra decided to ride on his cloud sitting with his legs folded over each other. The gentle breeze of the autumn wind touched his face as he shut his eyes. His hair was untied as it smoothly flowed into the wind. He began to recall his memories with Vesak.

Vesak was much more of a father figure to him than his own. Nonetheless, he was the one that unfortunately stabbed his master in the back. It was all he could dream about when he slept, yet he showed no signs of it.

He slowly opened his eyes and looked down on the city. He saw the rooftops of people's houses while the people themselves looked like ants to him. As they walked on the cobblestone streets of Mersane, the Lucky River continued to flow calmly through the city. He saw Torshen fishing by the riverbank. He spotted a crowd of people, all of them bumping and pushing each other aside. Steam was coming from the steamed bun vendors. He could see the tight alleyway of the city. He spotted a man held against the wall by another man with a knife up against his throat.

The people felt jolly and carefree knowing that the Seven Demon Dragons were their shield from the villains of Telamis. Ausra hated the people. It irked him when they called him a hero. He hated being a hero to people that only see what they want to see. Their hands were never drenched in blood like his. He saw them like he saw his father.

He sighed then lay on his back and stared at the clouds above him. He wished for the day where he would never have to hold a sword ever again. "Vesak, I hate you," he said to himself with vicious intent.

Suddenly, behind the cotton clouds appeared a long ocean-blue serpent-like creature. Its body moved like a snake as it flew past, only to be shielded by the clouds. The eyes of the creature favored golden nuggets.

Ausra watched calmly, wondering why a spirit dragon would show itself in front of him. He assumed that no one else saw what he saw because there were no sudden reactions or anyone pointing at the sky in awe, shocked about what they had just witnessed.

Spirit dragons were the first rulers of Telamis. They held that honor until the rise of the winged dragons and phoenixes. It was not a common happening to see a spirit dragon roaming the skies. By chance, if one was spotted, it was taken to be a sign of good luck. Sadly, Ausra didn't believe in luck since it (luck) had already betrayed him long ago.

Ausra continued to watch as the dragon slithered away. "Ausra," whispered a wise voice.

Ausra smiled as a part of him was glad that the dragon was real. He had heard many stories about spirit dragons from his grandfather. "How tiresome," he mumbled.

He continued to float on his cloud. As he floated, he passed by others on their clouds. Some bowed their heads to him as they passed while others waved to him and told him how thankful they were for him. He ignored their cherished gestures and continued to travel within his own thoughts, imagining himself in a world where he only existed.

"Ausra!" called a loud and energetic voice.

Ausra turned around and wasn't pleased to see his brothers Airian and Kunjae flying toward him on their clouds. Airian, a year older than Kunjae, was sixteen; and like his clan, he too had long dark hair and black eyes.

Kunjae, on the other hand, had long dark hair with a single train of braided hair hanging from his left side. His eyes were blue like their mother and resembled more of a young woman than that of a young man.

The brothers flew on each side of Ausra.

"We've been looking all over for you," said Airian. "Mother calls for you."

Ausra tied his hair back. "What a pity," he mumbled.

"A pity?" questioned Kunjae with a grin. "Is my murderous brother not happy?"

Ausra ignored Kunjae since he knew Kunjae had a knack for getting under people's skin.

"I heard it was you that killed Vesak," stated Airian with his eyes wide open. He was curious to hear Ausra's story. "I wish I could be like you. I think Father is ready to let us join the clan army." He raised his fist in front of his face. "Mark my words. I'm going to be the greatest warrior in our clan!" he proudly said.

"Our clan does need a hothead as a warrior," replied Kunjae as he teased with a smile.

Airian shot Kunjae a burning glare.

Ausra lay back on his cloud and stared up at the clouds. "There's nothing special about being a warrior," he said truthfully.

The brothers flew to the Feather Field where their mother usually spent her time with Borin, her phoenix. As they flew, Ausra tried his best to stop Airian and Kunjae from bickering.

Airian kept talking about his dream of being a warrior, and Kunjae would tease him about his dream. Airian would bring up tales of great warriors, such as Gen Yu the White Horse and Janko the Eye.

As they finally arrived at the Feather Field, they spotted their mother who was with their other five siblings. They were all sitting under a giant oak tree. Green grass was shining bright as the sun covered the field. There was a slicing breeze over the grass. A single giant nest sat up under a giant oak tree.

Borin flew majestically throughout the skies with her wings slithering through the wind. The blue-eyed bird looked to stand nine feet tall with its white feathers and blue tips with a wingspan of fourteen feet wide.

The brothers slowly lowered their clouds over the grass and carefully hopped off. They then docked their clouds into the wooden tubes hanging from their waist. They made their way to their mother and siblings who were all sitting on a cloth with a basket of steamed buns. Sitting with their mother were younger siblings Kiri, Lehue, and Isa while their two older sisters, Mani and Chenpu, looked on. Mani was a year older than Ausra. She resembled their mother more so than Aerin, but her hair and eyes were dark like her father. She was beautiful and gentle with a caring heart.

Chenpu, on the other hand, was the oldest sister. She was twenty-two and the second child of Maenellia and Aerin. Her hair and eyes were dark also. She was strict, short-tempered, and always had a mean look on her face.

Maenellia smiled as her three sons approached. She loved it when all of her children were around her. It gave her a sense of comfort knowing that she could protect them under her watch.

"Finally, my sons, come sit," acknowledged Maenellia in a cheerful manner. "There are enough steamed buns for all of us."

Lehue reached over and tried to grab another steamed bun, but Chenpu slapped his hand away, making him squeal.

"You've had enough!" snapped Chenpu at Lehue with warning eyes.

Lehue looked to his mother Maenellia with a fake sob and puppy eyes. "Mother . . ."

"Go ahead, my dear." Maenellia smiled at Lehue.

Lehue turned to Chenpu, showing a sly grin. He reached slowly, daring Chenpu to hit his hand again.

Chenpu frowned, upset that her mother was being too easy on Lehue. "Mother, how is he to become a warrior when all he's doing is becoming fat?"

"He doesn't have to be a warrior." Maenellia smiled. She noticed that Ausra was still standing. "Ausra dear, do you not want to sit?"

Ausra reached into his pockets and pulled out a hard lemon candy. "I'm fine, Mother," he said bluntly as he unwrapped his candy.

"Have some steamed buns. They're still warm," offered Maenellia to her son graciously.

"They're delicious," replied Lehue as he stuffed the bun into his mouth.

"Mother, is there something you need?" asked Ausra.

Maenellia was sad. At the same time, she felt guilty for Ausra's upbringing. "Don't you want to enjoy the company of your siblings? Your travel must have been long. It must've been hard to have to take your master's life."

"It wasn't hard," admitted Ausra calmly. "The man became a traitor. I only did what I was ordered to do."

"Sit down, Ausra. We have been waiting for you," urged Mani caringly. She was once close to Ausra, but slowly, the life of a warrior has consumed him. He had become more distant from her.

"I don't want to waste my time being with people," Ausra expressed coldly. "I never know when Father will send me away again with the others." He turned to leave. "Mother, it's not your fault that I'd rather be alone." He detected a sense of guilt coming from Maenellia. "I was cursed to run with the demon." He dislodged his cloud tube and opened his cloud. As he climbed aboard, all the others could do was sit and watch as he floated away.

* * *

An angry gigantic man who went by the name of Bloben that towered over anyone that stood near him boasted the question, "Where is your father?" His stomach was round and sticking out. He impatiently waddled back and forth, waiting for Aerin at the gazebo at the center of the Demon Garden.

Each step he took felt like the ground was shaking. His legs looked as if they couldn't hold his own body weight any longer. His black beard nearly covered his face, yet he had rosy-red fat cheeks that nearly kept his eyes shut.

"My father will be here soon," stated Indris. He was the second oldest son of Maenellia and Aerin.

He had short black hair with black eyes. He a had calming look about himself as his eyes followed Bloben who paced back and forth in front of him.

"How dare he make his prestigious guest wait," angered Bloben. "You know I fought by your father's side for many years. I don't deserve his tardiness."

"You should sit and have a cup of tea," suggested Indris.

Bloben angrily turned to Indris. "I don't want your tea, boy!" He slammed his fist on the stone table, causing the teapot and teacup to jump a little. "Give me wine. Don't mock me with tea."

Indris measured Bloben. He thought to himself that Bloben didn't need wine. He was too fat, and if he were to get drunk, he would probably roll out of the city.

"I'm sorry that I insulted you, Lord Bloben."

Bloben now measured Indris. "How old are you now, boy?" he asked.

"Twenty-one, my lord," answered Indris.

"Are you married? Do you want to marry my daughter? She's fifteen and beautiful. Any man would kill for her hand in marriage."

Indris smiled. "I kindly reject your offer, my lord." He bowed his head.

"Are you a fool? She's beautiful! If I wasn't her—"

"Apologies for the wait, Lord Bloben," said Aerin who finally arrived, walking up the white stone steps of the gazebo. He purposely made Bloben wait for him to irritate the fat lord.

Bloben turned quickly and growled. He quickly sat down, causing the ground to vibrate a little. "A great hero like me shouldn't wait long."

Aerin made his way to sit across from Bloben. He quickly grabbed the teapot and poured himself some tea. He then poured Bloben's tea. "Our tea is one of the best in the eastern kingdom."

"I'm not here to talk about tea, Aerin. I have my son and daughter accompanying me during my travels. I'm here to offer you my son and daughter's hand in marriage."

"How pitiful," said Aerin. "Is this your fifth visit with the same offer?"

"Don't mock me, Aerin. My clan fought by your clan for many decades. We deserve respect."

"None of my children will marry yours," replied Aerin with a searing grin, as he blew the steam from his tea to sip it. "I will be a fool to marry my children into a dying clan."

Out of anger, an enraged Bloben violently slapped the teacup out of Aerin's hand. The teacup smashed into pieces as it hit the ground. "You must take me for a fool!" he stated at the top of his lungs. He was loud enough that it scared the birds within the trees away.

Aerin sat unfazed as did Indris also. "I don't take you as a fool, Lord Bloben. I see you as a shell of your old self," he said with a mocking smile. "Ah yes, you were once a hero, a man that put fear into the eyes of all. But as a leader, you are nothing but a drunk that is strangling your clan's existence. Oh, how ghastly you look."

Bloben reached over and grabbed Aerin by the collar of his shirt. With fire in his eyes, he stared into the cold, calm eyes of Aerin. "You dare to continue to mock me!" he raged. He looked at Indris and noticed that he was standing still. He slowly let go of the collar of Aerin's shirt and sat back down.

"You are a victim of time," stated Aerin as he calmly fixed the collar of his shirt. "The Smok clan will soon be heard only in tales and read about in books. It's a shame how your younger brother worked so hard to save his clan but was taken out by poison. Even so, I still wonder who could've done such a shameful act." His smile disappeared with a straight and dark stare that shot into the eyes of Bloben.

Bloben froze for a bit. It felt as though he was sinking into the stone seat. Instinctively, he stood up and shouted, "I did not kill my brother," but his voice did not sound convincing. He turned away from Aerin and made his way to the steps of the gazebo. "I will beg the king to force you to marry your children to mine."

Aerin sat still, not taking a glimpse at Bloben as he left. "A fool of a man he is," said Aerin.

"Father, what will we do with him?" asked Indris.

Seven death birds landed on the ledge of the gazebo. Aerin took out seven letters out of the inside of his shirt that were rolled and sealed. "His clan will soon die. I worry nothing of him. He is a fool still living his glory days. The man lives in the past, taken by the present, and will never live to see the future."

Indris knew what Aerin was planning to do. "How about the king, Father?" asked Indris.

Dark evil thoughts clouded Aerin's mind. His eyes darkened. "I do not fear the Wise Lion."

* * *

Bloben journeyed back home through Thorn Field. The sky was still blue with the clouds calmly floating. But slowly, the dreadful gray began to take the vibrant blue. Yet the sun fought to shine.

Thorn Field was where the great battle between Kriton Boisen and Ayefu Kimsu fought during the second era war. Both men killed each other during the battle. Both were found to die with a smile on their faces. The statue of Ayefu stood at the bridge of Ends, where the Thorn fields were divided by the Singing River. Kriton's statue stood at the other end of the bridge, showing both men wearing their famous armor and wielding their famous swords.

It took two days for Bloben to return to Smoke Castle, riding his horse with his sixteen-year-old son beside him, Benyae. He was tall and lengthy, his face resembling a rat and riddled with bumps.

Riding behind was Karana and Ona. Karana was fourteen and was Bloben's daughter. For a daughter of Bloben, she was pretty, but behind the looks was sadness and shyness.

Ona was Bloben's niece, daughter of his dead younger brother. She was twenty-one and looked like her life lived longer than her age. She hated her uncle and believed that he killed her father and her lover.

Bloben took five guards to accompany him on his travel, expecting that he didn't need much protection.

"You listen to me, boy," said Bloben with rage. "If I die and you ruin this clan, our ancestors will deny you entry to the heavens."

"I will not fail, Father," Benyae responded nervously.

"I despise the Kimsu clan. All of them shall suffer. When I speak to the king, one of his whore daughters will marry you, boy." He looked up into the sky and saw seven death birds flying over his head. Bloben yielded his horse, pausing everyone, leaving everyone confused.

"All of you protect me!" Bloben demanded the guards at the back.

The guards quickly left the two young women and surrounded Bloben. Their swords were drawn, and they searched for any attackers. They were confused who they were preparing for. Benyae was scared and couldn't bring himself to draw his sword. Bloben had his sword drawn.

"I should've brought more guards." Bloben was angry with himself.

A circle of black flames surrounded Bloben, Benyae, and their guards. Bloben knew exactly who it was.

On the other side of the flames were two rabbits. Suddenly, they disappeared and were replaced by Ausra and Sukro, both wearing a black hooded cloak.

Sukro could replace and teleport himself and whoever or whatever creature touched him with another creature, but he could not replace spots with a human.

Coming from the side riding their horses were the other dragons. They all hopped off their horse. Nagen was in the middle, in his hand a dagger. Kaiso had a long sword, Nisu had two short swords, Leonaris had a long sword, Torshen with his bow, Sukro with his spear, and Ausra with his famed sword.

"Well, well. Aerin wants me dead. Spineless demon! All of you are hounds!" shouted Bloben, hiding behind his guards. "I can't be killed. King Hensi will not be fond of this. When he finds news of this, all of you, and Aerin, will pay with your heads on a stake, pieces of shit!"

"Come out and accept your death," ordered Nagen.

"How about we make a deal?" Bloben suggested. "Come and serve me, I will hand you my niece and daughter."

"Don't bribe for your life. Come out and accept your death like a man."

"The king will punish all of you!" raged Bloben, his fat face turning red.

Nagen pulled a piece of paper out of his pocket. "This is a letter from the king." Nagen showed. "In the king's words, 'I have ordered the death of Lord Bloben of Smoke Castle for treason and conspiring with the enemies. He is to be killed. His children will be taken as prisoners. Lord Aerin will take control of Smoke Castle and all military affairs.'"

"Lies! I never conspire with the enemy!" Bloben pleaded.

"Are you calling the king a liar?" questioned Nagen.

"I'm loyal, Aerin is the liar!" pleaded Bloben.

Nagen ignored Bloben's plea. "Now all of you, as your captain, I demand you to kill that traitor that stands behind you," ordered Nagen.

The guards were confused; they all looked at each other and turned around. Their swords were drawn at Bloben.

Benyae hopped off his horse and crawled away, cowardly watching as Bloben was about to be killed.

"You spineless bastards!" angered Bloben. "After all the things I've done, and you all want to kill me? All of you are nothing more than a bunch of useless hogs!"

Bloben's insult riled the guards. The five of them pulled him off his horse and began to stab and cut him like a pack of hounds mauling their meat. His yell echoed the field. He lay in a pool of his blood, his mouth twitching, still trying to grasp on to his life. Suddenly, an ice arrow went through one of the guard's heads, killing him instantly. They all turned around and was surprised.

"You guys had committed treason," said Nagen.

Everyone, except for the Seven Dragons, was confused. The guards had fallen victim to Nagen's intelligence. The letter was false, and now they were all going to die. They charged at the dragons, yelling in anger. Torshen shot another guard, and Nisu and Kaiso hopped over the ring of fire to slay the rest.

Nagen walked over the fire, followed by the rest of the Deadly Wings. He made his way to Bloben, still holding on to a thread of life. He signaled Benyae over.

Benyae nervously made his way.

"Finish him. Stick it in his heart," Nagen ordered Benyae as he handed him the dagger.

Benyae looked at the dagger and then at Bloben. His eyes were begging him not to end his life. It was the first time he saw Bloben in a weak state. He felt bad for him for once and didn't want to stick the dagger in his heart.

Ona hopped over the flames and ran toward Bloben's body. She took the dagger away from Benyae's hand and pushed him to the ground. With all the hatred in her, all she could think about was avenging her father and lover. She stared madly into Bloben's shocked eyes and stabbed the dagger into his heart, pushing deep until the last breath left his body.

"He's gone. I'm free . . . I'm free!" Ona mumbled then shouted in joy.

Benyae crawled to his father and cried over the lifeless body. Ona can't believe she was finally free. Karana stood still, glued to the ground in fear, seeing seven monsters staring coldly at her father's dead body.

"There will be war," Sukro said to Ausra.

Ausra ignored Sukro and looked up into the sky. The clouds were no longer white. The blue sky was taken by gray. Rapidly, rain began to hammer down, putting out the ring of black fire and cleansing the blood on the grass and bodies of the dead. Lightning sparked the sky. Thunder roared like a lion. Behind the clouds, he saw the spirit dragon again flying by unnoticed.

"Ausra," whispered a voice between Ausra's ears.

Chapter Two

Kingdom of Enstra

Overseeing the Silent Sea was the city of Godfree, the capital city of Enstra, the western kingdom of Telamis. The great city was divided into three levels, separating the social class of Godfree. The first level, upon entering, met with the poor, sick, and thugs of the city. The smell of human feces filled the harsh air, burning the nose. The sight of rotten rodents dead on the street cursed the eyes, the ground so muddy, making traveling a trial.

A great wall divided the first level from the second level of the city, where the famous market street stretched from the beginning of the second level to the end. Traders all over the land came to sell their goods. At the center of the second level was where the horn heads were sold to be slaves.

Then there was the third level of the city. From the elegant white stone ground and fairy sculptures to the prestigious Godfree Academy, the third level was home to the high and minor clans, the rich, and the king's officials. Strangely, it was more guarded than the third level. Sitting at the end of the city, overseeing all levels, was Fairy Palace. The massive bluestone palace stunned the eye with amazement. It made the crudity of the first level an imagination. Visitors would stand and stare at the palace from afar. It was home to King Euren and his Fairy clan.

Training on the ground of Fairy Palace was a fifteen-year-old, Princess Emmillda Fairy. Sweat over her forehead, every breath she took felt like her last, her long light-blond hair messy, nearly becoming untied, exhausted from the intense training. The heat after spring rain did not help the matter. She lifted her sword over her head and swung it wildly, nearly stumbling to the ground like a fawn trying to walk for the first time.

The Fairy clan were magic users mastering at fairy magic, a type of defense magic created by Chanfer Fairy. They were never known to be warriors.

Emmillda wished to break her family chain and stray from their born ability. The various stories she heard and read of warriors inspired her. Their trial and tribulation sparked her imagination. She wanted to be a warrior like the heroes in the stories.

The story of Norisis Marl was her favorite, a fearless captain of the Ma clan during the fourth era war, a talented naval captain that led two hundred ships to the island of Sun, remembered as the Battle of Will. Two days at sea and four days on land, she won the battle courageously, massacring every Sun man and enslaving their wives and children.

Emmillda swung her sword wildly again, nearly tripping to the ground. Her stance was clumsy and weak, making her wish she was born into a clan of warriors and not a clan of magic users, like the Kimsu or Ta-Nore. In her belief, magic users were weak and just good for support to the warriors during battle.

Training Emmillda with a disappointed look across his face was Lumen Glasor, a dark-skinned man who wasn't impressed with her.

A warrior and captain of the Fairy clan, he was in his late twenties and wore a silver steel armor with a butterfly sigil on his right shoulder plate, the Fairy clan sigil, which meant for beauty and peace. His hair was dark with long braids. He had a broad chin with a stern look. Because of his father and older brother, he was disliked throughout the western kingdom.

His father was Jamen Glasor, a former captain and adviser to King Euren until he formed his rebellion group called the Forgotten Servants. They tried to overthrow the king but failed. Jamen was executed for his crime, his head decapitated in front of the gates of Fairy Palace. Thousands of eyes watched as his head rolled to the ground with blood creating a trail.

Lumen's older brother was Endward Glasor, the man that set forth the fifth era war. Resentful at how people spoke ill of his father and family name, he stole the Fairy orb and tried to summon the fairy beast. But he was killed by Ausra Kimsu before the great beast could be summoned to reign terror over Telamis. His body was left on the battlefield for scavengers to feast on and rot.

The people of Godfree distrusted Lumen, predicting that he would betray the kingdom like his father and brother. They whispered curses onto his name, treating him like an outcast and leaving him in a dark hollow cave alone, refusing to recognize his accomplishment and triumphs. Many were afraid to confront him or speak to him.

Lumen shook his head as Emmillda swung weakly again. "Why do you see yourself as a warrior?" he asked. "Your clan are magic users. There's no purpose in becoming a warrior."

Emmillda rolled her eyes in annoyance. "I want to become a hero and have my stories told throughout the land."

Lumen chuckled deeply. "Not all warriors are heroes. We live by a code written on nothing," he added.

Emmillda stopped her training. "You don't have to be here."

"I promised the king I will watch over you," replied Lumen. Even though he was hated by the people, he stayed loyal to his king, never thinking of betraying Euren because he respected him. Before Euren's wisdom was stolen by madness, he made Lumen Emmillda a personal protector. "I must follow my king's order until he says otherwise."

Emmillda made a fist and lifted it in front of her face with oozing confidence all over her sweaty face. "When I become a warrior, I won't need any protection." She then lifted the practice sword in front of her face, gazing her silver eyes down the sword. "There's a warrior I wish to meet."

"Who is this warrior?" asked Lumen.

"The man that killed your brother—the Silent Demon."

Lumen's blood began to boil like a pot of beef stew. The nerves in his body rang, hearing the name Silent Demon. He hated Ausra, waiting for a chance to fight him for not giving his brother an honorable death. "Why? He's not an honorable warrior."

Emmillda hesitated, still admiring the sword. "He's a legend at such a young age. Our paths will cross one day. My future children will hear stories of our encounter." She turned to Lumen with a smile. "They will hear stories of you too."

Lumen was surprised by Emmillda's compliment. He exhaled. "I met Ausra Kimsu once. He was still a kid, but his hand was already dipped in a pool of blood. Nothing around him sang hero or villain." Lumen took the sword from Emmillda's hand and stared at his own reflection. "Every man and woman at that camp all feared him . . . as well as me." He reflected on the day he met Ausra. At first, it was fear during their no-communicated meeting; after, it was pure resentment toward him. "He's something out of this world. Someone you never wish to cross paths with." Lumen paused. "And he was short," Lumen finished.

"Did you witness him the dance with the sword?" asked Emmillda with excitement.

"Of course."

"Well, tell me." Emmillda was becoming more intrigued.

Lumen sighed. "Fine." He tried to recall how Ausra fought, only coming to the memory of his brother's dead body and Ausra standing over him. "He moves like the waves of the ocean."

Emmillda was confused. She didn't understand what Lumen meant. "Like waves?"

"To be a warrior, you must think like a warrior," lectured Lumen. "It's not just the sword and spear, the deeds and cheers. The truth of the warrior is in the person." He swung the practice sword in the air smoothly but fast, separating the air around him. His form was strong and perfect. "A true warrior is willing to take another life away for their own."

"Princess!" called a weak voice from afar.

Emmillda and Lumen both turned to the direction they heard the voice from. Shuffling toward them was an old lady with gray hair, bird-beak nose, and wrinkly face. Her back was hunched. She was Mai, Emmillda's caretaker.

Mai finally reached them as she tried to catch her breath. Behind her were two horn head slaves, the tip of the horn cut off to embarrass them and weaken them, their skin gray and rough like lizard scales. Their scales come in many colors. Said to be the first native of Telamis, only the western kingdom still used them as slaves. The other kingdoms had abolished slavery and allowed the horn heads to live freely among them, with some joining the army. The ones that still claimed the western kingdom home stayed hidden deep within the forests.

"Princess, what are you doing out here?" asked Mai with concern. "And why are you wearing these filthy clothes? Did that animal force you to wear it?" She hated Lumen. Like the rest of the kingdom, she didn't trust Lumen and didn't mind speaking her distrust around him.

Lumen just ignored Mai. Her insults didn't bother him since he was used to people insulting him.

"I'm training to become a warrior," Emmillda replied confidently.

"No no, my dear, the queen will not accept this," warned Mai. "Please, you must clean yourself up. The queen waits for your arrival in her study."

"No, I will go like this!" challenged Emmillda with her hands on her hips. "I will show her that I will become a warrior."

Mai looked at Lumen disgustingly. "Look at what you did. Putting foolishness in our princess's head."

"She's a woman now. If she wants to become a warrior, then let her be. I'm just her protector, not her father." Lumen turned to leave. "Emmillda, be careful with people that claim they care for you. They might turn on you in an instant."

Emmillda, Mai, and the two slaves watched Lumen leave them.

"Filthy animal," muttered Mai.

*   *   *

Emmillda and Mai walked the corridors of the Fairy Palace, Mai leading the way in a hurry while the two slaves tried to keep up. Emmillda, on the other hand, gazed into the air, walking slowly, daydreaming herself riding a white horse into the battle against the Sun men. She wondered why her mother wanted to meet her, hoping she wasn't planning to marry her off to a noble clan. Lately, Queen Facelia had been looking for a perfect marriage for Emmillda. She hated all the nobles that tried to marry their son to her. Last month, the Yanko clan offered, but their son didn't look pleasing. His head was too big for his skinny body.

There was one marriage proposal she didn't mind. It was with the Cha clan. They were a high clan and well respected in the western kingdom. They offered their third son Nezu Cha. He was a talented warrior, but a wild one.

Mai looked back, realizing that Emmillda was lost in her thoughts. "Princess, we must hurry. We don't want to anger the queen," she advised.

Emmillda shook her head out of her daydreaming and quickly made her way beside Mai.

"Princess, I wouldn't spend too much time with that animal," advised Mai rudely. "I see it in his eyes. They're like his father and brother."

"Lumen is nothing like them. He's no animal or beast," defended Emmillda. "He stayed loyal to my father and fought on our side during the war his brother started."

"I'd be careful. That mask he wears will crack and show his true intention."

They arrived in front of Queen Facelia's study. Mai took one last look at Emmillda. She licked her thumb and tried to clean a smudge of dirt off Emmillda's cheeks.

Emmillda tried to jerk away, but Mai forced herself to clean the smudge. She loved Emmillda like her own granddaughter, caring for her since she was a baby, teaching her how to behave like a princess, how to read and write, and how to cook, which still needed work.

"Look at yourself," said the disgusted Mai. "Queen Facelia will surely scold me."

"I'm fine," assured Emmillda.

Mai sighed deeply and opened the door to the study. Sitting at the center of the room at a round wooden table was Queen Facelia and Alexander Fairy.

Facelia was wearing a purple silk dress, her skin golden and hair dark and her eyes silver. She was in her midforties, a member of the Po clan, a clan known for greed and hunger for power. Their clan sigil was a toad.

Alexander was Emmillda's older brother, Facelia and Euren's second child. He was two years older than Emmillda. He looked noble and had short light-blond hair with silver eyes. He spent most of his days trying to improve the clan military since a lot of their captains had left to join other clans.

Standing beside Facelia was Manji Tomro, Facelia's personal servant. Not much was known about her, only that she comes from the Wind Tribe, a tribe of trained assassins from the Windy Mountain in the northern kingdom. She had shoulder-length dark hair and white eyes like the undead.

Both Emmillda and Mai bowed their head to Facelia. Emmillda seated herself next to Alexander while Mai stood by the door.

Facelia covered her nose. "You smell unpleasant, child." Facelia was disgusted. "Mai, did you not care to wash her before presenting her before me?"

"I'm sorry, my queen," apologized Mai. "I found her training with that animal again."

"Why do you waste time playing with swords?" Facelia asked Emmillda annoyingly. "A princess should behave like a princess."

"I'm not playing with swords, Mother," replied Emmillda. "I'm training to become a warrior."

"Warriors are savages. They follow a false code that leads to their own death," disrespected Facelia.

"Don't insult the ones that protect you, Mother," defended Alexander. "They risk their lives so people like you can hide behind the wall can live." He hinted a comforting smile to Emmillda.

"There is no honor in death. The real threats are not the ones fighting on the battlefield. It's the one hiding behind the walls, lying in bed while warriors and magic users fight until their blood floods the ground." Facelia poured herself jasmine tea. "Stories of heroes are all lies," she said, looking directly to Emmillda. "We can't fascinate over the past. This world is only built for the present and future."

"There's no future without our army," said Alexander. "We're slowly falling, and it seems like I'm the only one that cares."

"They're all cowards, betraying their king once they sense weakness," insulted Facelia.

"Don't call them cowards, Mother," warned Emmillda. "They are the ones risking their lives for our safety."

"You think like a warrior, Emmillda." She looked over to Mai. "I told you to stop letting her read stories of false heroes."

"I'm sorry, my queen," apologized Mai, looking down with discouragement.

Emmillda was agitated with her mother. She wanted to slap the teakettle off the table. Reading stories of heroic warriors took her away from her dull life as a princess. She imagined herself fighting side by side with the heroes she inspired to become. When her mother shamed their name, it upset her.

"Mother, where is George?" wondered Alexander.

"George is occupied playing king," replied Facelia. She sips her tea. "Your brother has forgotten his way. He runs around the palace pretending to be king while your father is still alive, dancing foolishly in the hall. The both of you will soon choose a side. Alexander, you wish to fix our military? Then start with all those men and women that claim to be loyal to your father, their king. Punish them for betraying him. They stabbed a dagger into his spine and watched him slowly die." She looked over to Emmillda. "And, Emmillda. You need to face the truth. Becoming a warrior is nothing but a child's dream. Don't hide who you are, accept it. Become what you were born to be. A warrior desires honor and loyalty by blood and death. Your hands . . . those fragile soft hands will never be drenched in blood." She paused and took a sip of her tea again. "With your father mad, a new era will rise very soon."

"What do you mean?" asked a confused Alexander.

"Alexander, don't play stupid. You know what I mean." Facelia sighed.

Emmillda hated the aura around Facelia. Even though she was her mother, Emmillda still found her distrustful. Sometimes she would forget that she had a mother. She was close to Euren though. On the day he went mad, it devastated her. She cried for weeks, not accepting that her father was no longer the man she once knew. His body was only a vessel to a curse. She recalled the day she tried to hug him, an attempt to bring him back from his endless madness. Instead of receiving a hug back from him, she received a strangle, his hands no longer gentle as the rough, sharp skin of the hand tightly wrapped around her small neck. Her eyes filled with tears as she stared at her father's lost and scared eyes while all his weight sat on her. Luckily, Alexander was there to pull their father off her. After that day, she could never see her father again.

Facelia sipped her tea again. "I know that the dragon bone throne belongs to George. But there is no way he can rule the kingdom when he knows so little about it."

"There's going to be no new ruler of the west," promised Alexander. "Father is still alive. The seven protectors will release him out of his curse soon."

"Stupid boy, do you not know the severity of using the forbidden fairy magic? There's no escape from madness after that magic is used," reminded Facelia.

"I believe Father will come back to us," said Emmillda with confidence.

"Oh, do you? Do you remember the day he strangled you? Was that your father?" Facelia waited for Emmillda to answer, but there was no response. Realizing the pained look on Emmillda's face, she said, "No, my dear daughter. That was a madman using your father's corpse as its instrument. And you think your father is still in there. Shame on you."

"Why are you reminding her of that day?" Alexander defended Emmillda. "And if I recall, you stood and watched while father choked her. If I wasn't passing by, she would've been dead."

"What can I do? I would've been dead myself if I intervened."

"I see where you stand, Mother." Alexander sighed.

Alexander grabbed Emmillda's wrist and helped her stand. He stared coldly at his mother while she sipped tea nonchalantly. Like Emmillda, his relationship with his mother was strained. She never took care of them when they were younger, leaving them in the hands of Mai. Without saying anything to his mother, he turned to leave, pulling Emmillda with him and leaving Facelia to her tea.

Mai followed the siblings out, worried that they were hurt by their mother. She saw the unlove they received from Facelia. Even though they were royalists, it felt like they were orphans living in the palace.

Euren would ask Mai to give reports on them since he was always busy with his king's obligations. Nevertheless, he always tried his best to spend time with them, even if it was for a short while.

* * *

George stood by the doorway behind the dragon bone throne, his silver eyes watching embarrassedly at Euren dancing in the middle of the throne room on the marble floor with his nightwear still on while his clueless lavender eyes lost in the air.

King Euren was once a respected and loved king, known as the Great Mind, now secretly known as the Broken Mind, a talented magic user that slayed the dragon Ahoria, the Village Burner of Mount Aha in the northern kingdom. The bones of the dragon were added to his dragon throne and the scale forged into his armor.

On the day he decided to use the forbidden fairy magic to show him the future, but in return, he will lose his mind. Now he spent his days needing assistance, unable to speak to his wife and children. Sometimes he would violently yell at night. He once murdered a slave by smashing his head repeatedly on the stone walls of his private chamber and ate the brains and eyes out.

George was the first to see Euren gone mad. He was close by when he heard a loud yell from Euren's study. A violent yell echoed the halls of the Fairy Palace. The scream sounded like someone was being burned alive. He rushed to the yell to see seven moths dancing in circles around Euren stealing his knowledge and sanity. He knew Euren had used the forbidden magic.

The throne room had light rays from the sun, passing through the glass windows from the side. A blue carpet led from the steps of the throne, all the way to the two giant white stone door. The walls of the room had carvings of great Fairy clan members, including the great Chanfer Fairy, the God King, the first king of the west. The man was considered to be the eight protectors of heaven.

A skinny man approached George from behind. Two slaves were followed nervously behind the skinny man. Both looked tired and abused. He was Jensu Wisefool, an adviser to the king. He looked sly and had an untrustworthy grin.

"Your mother is having a secret meeting with your siblings," whispered Jensu.

"Of what sort?" asked George.

"I wish I know. But strangely, they excluded you?"

"It is strange," wondered George angrily. "She is a Po. They only think of power and greed." He looked back to his father. *Am I the only one that worries for my father?* he asked himself. As nights and days changed and season passed, he watched his father dance in the throne room alone, flailing his arms like a jester trying to impress a king. He wondered if he was waiting for Euren's death or him to return to his old self.

"Order the guards to remove my father. And bring me my lovely mother and siblings. I have the right to know what they're speaking of," ordered George.

* * *

George comfortably sat on the dragon bone throne. Beside him was Jensu, and the other was Edsu Wisefool, Jensu's older brother and also part of the king's council. He was skinny like his brother with an untrusted aura. They waited for Facelia, Alexander, and Emmillda's arrival.

Three slaves were chained and kneeling before them, a mother and her two sons. All three were scared and confused. The mother was in the middle; both of her young sons tried to get as close to her as possible. Her arms around them acting as a shield to them, the mother felt weak and humiliated.

"Ugly creatures," insulted George. "Pathetic horn heads. Do you know why you are all chained?"

The slaves stayed silent, afraid that their answer will cost them their life.

"Silent. I will answer my question since you all want to play mute." A sinister smile came across his face. "I am going to have you guys killed. Not because you have done something wrong. In this world of men, there's division between humans and creatures. Us humans are selfish beings that crave power. We are willing to do anything for our selfish ambition, as history shows. Creatures like you guys are only pawns in our game. Now, unmute yourself and answer me. Why shall I spare your lives?"

The slaves stayed silent and looked at each other. "Because life is precious," said a slave boy nervously.

"Smart horn head," applauded George. "How old are you?"

"F-fifteen, my prince," stuttered the slave.

"Do you like being a slave?"

"N-no, my prince."

"An honest horn head. Sadly, you must die today. I was kind of fond of you."

Facelia arrived from one side of the room while Alexander and Emmillda arrived from the other side. Both siblings refused to look at their mother. It didn't bother Facelia, but only made her smirk. Manji wasn't by her side. She wasn't pleased to see George sitting on the throne and even more displeased seeing Jensu and Edsu, the two men that wanted her gone from the kingdom.

Emmillda's attention was quickly focused on the three slaves, wondering why they were chained before George, trying to figure out what he had in store for them.

Alexander was also confused. Once close to George, their close bond drifted apart when their father went mad seven months ago.

"What are you planning to do with them?" Emmillda worryingly asked.

"Don't worry, little sister," replied George with an evil smile.

"Then unchain them at once!" Emmillda demanded.

"Now, little sister, are you trying to make me angry? First a secret meeting and now ordering me around, where is the respect toward your elder?"

"George—"

"Shouldn't you play soldier somewhere!" George cut Alexander off.

This upset Alexander. He stormed out of the throne room in a fit of rage. Emmillda tried to stop him, but he refused. He hated being talked down to by George, especially when the matter involved him trying to save the clan military.

George sat and watched with a smirk. He cared little for his brother's feelings. He doesn't see Alexander and Emmillda as his siblings. Unlike the two of them, he had love from both of his parents since he was the firstborn.

"What do you want, George?" asked Facelia.

"Mother, do you think I'm stupid?" questioned George. "I know your intention." He mockingly looked to the three slaves. "Don't make me do something evil. Tell me what you were talking about at that meeting with my siblings!" he ordered angrily.

"I can't have tea with my children?" lied Facelia.

"Who are you kidding?" retorted an annoyed George. "You don't even love them."

"Stupid boy, do you not trust your own mother?"

"I'll never trust anyone who tries to take away what's rightfully mine." George looked back at the slaves. "Mother, I'll give you a glimpse of what'll happen if someone breaks my trust," he said with evil intent in mind, his silver eyes glaring heinously at the slaves.

"Please, my queen, help us!" cried the mother of the slaves. "Spare my sons and take my life, I beg of you!"

"Ugly bitch! Now you want to talk. Should've grown a spine like your son," barked George.

"Free them!" Emmillda demanded again, hoping her brother will spare the slaves.

"Order me one more time and I will have Mai's head on a stake," threatened George.

Emmillda stopped, feeling helpless. She wanted to run up to her brother and punch him square in the nose. She looked at the slaves and saw the fear in their eyes. They did nothing wrong, but because they were slaves, it didn't matter if they died. She questioned herself, debating how she can be a warrior if she couldn't save them.

"The slaves do not concern me. Kill them if you wish," dared Facelia. She looked to the mother horn head. "Shame on you for giving birth to children you can't protect," she mocked. She then glared toward Jensu and Edsu. "Did those two snake brothers fill your heads with lies? I can't wait till you become their puppet."

"We only say what is right. We know you want to rebel," exposed a smirking Edsu.

"I will never rebel against a kingdom I was raised in," argued Facelia.

"Your clan lives on greed and hunger for power," Jensu reminded Facelia.

"They're right, Mother. I can't trust you. When Father leaves us, I will be the one sitting on the throne, and you'll be thorn I must get rid of," added George.

"Stupid boy. You can play king all you want. Nobody will follow a toy king."

George chuckled. He stood up from the throne and fixed his clothes. "Guards, kill these filthy horn heads," ordered George. He left the throne room.

Jensu and Edsu both followed, both with a smirk across their faces. They peeked at each other and knew that they had George in the palm of their hands. The crows fly over the western kingdom as the butterflies slowly die.

Five guards wearing purple armor surrounded the three slaves, all wielding spears. The slaves all fearfully looked at the guards as their life was coming to an end. The mother tried to shield her children while they hid under her in a cradle position. She begged and begged to only cold stares shooting down at her.

The guards violently stabbed the slaves, blood leaking from the holes of their wounds and onto the marble ground. The mother of the slaves tried to keep her children shielded but failed. The begging and crying echoed the room, bouncing from wall to wall. Then the mother's eyes fixed on Emmillda's silver shocked eyes as the stabbing continued. Reaching her hand for help, her mouth opened wide. Her children were already gone while she kept the fight for life. Reaching for Emmillda as the breath slowly pulled away, her voice became voiceless as her life became dark as night.

Emmillda watched in terror as the family was being murdered before her eyes. Her legs were glued to the marble, the voices in her head urging her to run. This was the first time she witnessed death. It wasn't like the stories she heard and read about. This death was more horrific and gorier, their crying forever living in her head, begging and suffering as a family.

"If you want to be a warrior, then get used to seeing this," Facelia said to Emmillda, walking away and leaving her alone.

Emmillda couldn't hear her mother. All she heard were the ghostly cries of the slaves. Suddenly, she was saved from her mindless travel into horror.

Lumen approached from behind and swooped Emmillda from her feet and carried her out of the room, enraged with what she had witnessed.

*　*　*

Facelia stormed into her study. She was followed by Manji. Angry at the two snake brothers for controlling her son, she filled her teacup with jasmine tea to the rim and angrily threw the cup at the stone wall. "How dare that boy challenge me!" angered Facelia.

"What shall we do, my queen?" asked Manji.

"George cannot be the one to sit on the throne. This kingdom doesn't need a puppet king. Look at what happened to the southern king. He was weak and got assassinated. George doesn't stand a chance ruling this kingdom. Once he becomes king, the other kingdoms will laugh at us. They will invade us, and the west will be no more. I can't stand to let this boy crumble the kingdom I love," expressed Facelia.

"He doesn't picture the same world as you, my queen," consoled Manji.

"He listens to those coward brothers, letting them whisper lies in his head. Euren should've had them killed when he had a chance . . . weak man!" she spit. She had never loved Euren ever in her life, marrying him because he was the heir. She wanted power and had seduced Euren. He was going to marry a female warrior that he loved, Jilliana Sun of the Sun clan.

"There were other men I could've married," confessed Facelia. "I chose Euren because of his title. A stupid girl I was back then. I wanted people to bow to me and envy me. Now, look at me. Gave birth to children I don't see as my own. Fighting with my son for a throne I have no claim for. A fool for marrying a man I don't love."

"We must change the old ways. You're more fit to rule than the prince," added Manji.

"Indeed," agreed Facelia. "My children, they're like their father—fools. They were trained without knowing the truth of this land. As a mother, I failed. I spoiled them behind these palace walls—no, Euren spoiled them. He allowed them to feel protected and clueless to reality. Alexander talks of restoring the military that was once formidable. He's blind to what they want, a bunch of disloyal men and women who crave fame and riches. And Emmillda, such a foolish girl. She believes in overtold stories of warriors. Thinks she knows so much, but what does she know? That slaying a dragon lizard will bring honor?" She laughed to herself. "Foolish children of mine."

"Your children are not like you, my queen."

Facelia made her way to her window and stared at the outside world, watching the afternoon clouds drifting east. "I need an army. Loyal ones."

"Yes, my queen," said Manji.

Facelia thought about clans she could recruit to fight by her side. She wanted to avoid war, but George made it difficult for her. To create her kingdom, she needed to get rid of the Wisefool brothers controlling her son. Then get rid of George.

"Send letters to all the noble clans in this kingdom," ordered Facelia.

"What do I say?" asked Manji.

"Tell them to side with me, their queen, if they want to avoid bloodshed. Tell them of Jensu and Edsu."

"If they refuse?"

"Then blood will drown the soil of Enstra," finished Facelia confidently.

Chapter Three

Kingdom of Summan

Midmorning in the southern kingdom of Summan in the capital city, Sentra, the air was hot and suffocating like a winged dragon's burning breath. Despite the sweltering heat, the city was magnificent and pure, like life returning to a dead rose. It sat on the calm and singing waves of the Weeping Sea. From the Summer Palace, the seaport can be seen when peering out the window.

Home to the Sanila clan, a royal clan that ruled the south, their sigil was a dagger pointing downward, signifying that they were the law of the south. Most of the clan members were all warriors while some chose the magic path.

Surrounding the beautiful city was the Endless Desert, a desert that many dreaded to travel. Still, the people of Sentra continued to enjoy life. During the day, the air was warm; when night came, the air was cool from the waves of the crying sea. The houses and buildings were all made of clay, the stone streets crowded with people wearing straw hats to block the beaming sun. People's skin color in the south was either tan or dark. At night, the city was lit by light orbs from lampposts, showing the enchanting nightlife of Sentra. Some taverns and shops were opened in the city, some unique and some simple. Some shops sold special mushrooms from across the Weeping Sea; some shops sold books that taught blood magic.

Inside a windowless private room, with light only coming from a single torch, stood the twenty-five-year-old King Giovanis Sanila II, leaning his back against the cool, smooth stone wall. His skin tan and his hair short and dark, he wore a fine golden silk top and a golden crown with seven points and red rubies embedded into it. Loved by his people for his charisma and donations, he was first to lend his people a hand when there was a problem. He once donated two thousand summer coins to the orphanage, even finding his way to feed the poor and the sick.

He had only been king for two months, handed the crown after his father, King Geolana II was assassinated two months prior.

Unlike Giovanis, Geolana was weak and didn't have the respect as his son did. Still, he was kind to his people and tried his best to maintain the kingdom. People couldn't see his will to be a great king, only seeing a man who became king because both of his older brothers had died.

Sitting at the round wooden table at the center of the room was Prince Benavis, Giovanis's fifteen-year-old brother. His eyes were scared and lost like he had encountered a cursed ghost. The image of his father's death still haunted him. He was the only one to witness Geolana's murder. He remembered leaving the city at dawn, horse backing through the desert, only to be stopped by a sandstorm, when the unforgettable happened. Seven men appeared out of the sand. All seven of them were wearing a golden mask with a third eye on the forehead, surrounding him and Geolana.

For two months, Benavis still couldn't speak of that horrific day. He refused to remember, but the memory was vivid to him. Every time he tried to forget, the more it crossed his mind, replaying his father yelling as they stick a dagger into his heart, forcing him to feel the pain as they decapitated his head with another dagger. After they finished, they turned into crows and flew away, disappearing behind the summer clouds. All he could do was watch cowardly.

Sitting across from Benavis was Ocrist Dyu. A man in his early forties, head bald and bright, he served as an adviser to the king. He was talented in curse magic, a magic that could only be taught by the Sleeping Monks of High Mountain in the western kingdom. He was a former monk but had escaped the temple to become a scholar. Instead, he found himself serving as an adviser to the southern kings.

"My prince, you must speak on that day," urged Ocrist. "It's been two months, and you still refuse to talk."

Giovanis worried for his younger brother, hoping his brother would finally speak, wondering why his father decided to venture out of the city at dawn with no guards. Even though his father was weak and unfit to be a king, he still loved and respected him. Devastation hit when a merchant crossing the desert reported the king's lifeless body and a speechless prince in the hot golden sand.

Giovanis couldn't believe he lost both his father and mother within the same year. His mother, Queen Maji of the Wuju clan, had died from an illness that caused her to cough blood and bleed from her ears and nose.

"Please, brother," Giovanis pleaded to Benavis. "Tell us what you remember so we can find the monsters that cursed our family and avenge our father."

Benavis stayed silent, his mind continuing to replay the tragic moment, eyes gazing at the wooden table.

"Say something, brother," begged Giovanis, "for the sake of our clan. For the sake of our kingdom." He made his way to Benavis and gently placed his hand on Benavis's shoulder. "Tell me what you remember," he pleaded again.

"His mind is filled with darkness," discovered Ocrist. "A shadow with six arms, a sword, a spear, an ax, a bow, a dagger, a crow. Eyes of hollow darkness." He stopped looking into Benavis's mind, his head throbbing. "Chaos will cover the skies of Telamis again. We ought to be ready for what's to come. The era of peace among the four kingdoms will end soon."

Giovanis looked at Ocrist confusedly. "What do you mean?" questioned Giovanis.

"A shadow guards the truth." Ocrist gave Benavis a concerned look. "Let your mind be free, my prince. Tell us what you remember. I promise we will protect you."

Benavis looked up slowly, his eyes wide and lost, eyeing his brother then Ocrist. Their faces did show worry. But he felt like they wouldn't understand what he saw. It was like the stories his mother once told him when he was a child.

"Father," mumbled Benavis. "They were monsters."

Both Ocrist and Giovanis were confused. They looked at each other and wondered if Benavis was talking to himself or them. It was the first time he uttered any words.

"What do you mean?" asked Giovanis confusedly.

"His mind is opening!" Ocrist said excitedly. "I will search again."

"Stay away from me!" Benavis snapped. "The both of you know nothing!"

"Benavis, calm yourself," urged Giovanis. "We need you to avenge our father."

Benavis looked into his brother's green eyes blankly. "Father died cowardly."

Giovanis felt confused as he stared back at Benavis. The blank look on Benavis's face scared him. He wanted to grab Benavis and shake him back to reality.

Suddenly, a knock on the door settled the eeriness in the tiny room.

"Come in!" allowed Giovanis, keeping his eyes on Benavis.

A guard wearing red steel armor with a sigil of a dagger on his left shoulder plate entered the room. "My lord, Lord Hanti and his twins have arrived, and Lord Anzoren and his grandsons have also arrived."

Giovanis signaled the guard to leave. "We'll continue again after."

"No! No one can understand what I saw," Benavis growled sharply, rocking in a chair and mumbling unknown words to himself.

* * *

"King Giovanis has arrived!" announced a guard.

The chatters in the throne room quickly stopped. Everyone in the hall faced the golden throne. Giovanis made his way to the throne and stood tall in front of the people in the hall. They all bowed their heads, and he seated himself. Just two months ago, he witnessed people bowing to his father; now they were bowing to him. He enjoyed the feeling of respect and strength. However, in the back of his mind, he was thinking of Benavis.

Ocrist stood below the throne with a receiving smile.

In the hall stood Commander Thunder Tiger Foot, a dark man in his midthirties. He had the body physique of a warrior but chose to be a magic user, being talented in using elemental magic. He had a long beard with strays of gray highlight. His hair was graying and short, eyes calm. Beside him was Dada Wuju, adviser to the king and fifth richest man in the southern kingdom, known for his greed and love for women. He was in his early fifties. He had a tiny whisker mustache and short dark hair.

Bente Tulang stood beside Dada. He was also an adviser to the king. He was bald and skinny in his early forties. He had no eyebrows and had golden snake eyes.

Standing on the other side of Thunder was Seris Culu, a tall and mysterious man with dark hair and eyes that were nearly closed.

Standing in front of them was Hanti Kazchi and his twin boys, Rogi and Renjo Kazchi, both seventeen years old. They had short dark hair and golden skin. They were fit but short. Hanti had an older son, but chose not to bring him along. Rogi, the older of the twins, looked ready to fight while Renjo looked composed.

Beside them were Anzoren Bu and his grandsons Yorsenga Bu, a tired young man with long curly black hair; Uesenga Bu, a muscular young man with his hair tied in a tight bun; Rain Bu, a calm handsome young man with short dark hair; and Ba-Ben Bu, a plain young man with his hair tied back in a loose bun. Yorsenga was nineteen, Rain and Uesenga eighteen, and Ba-Ben seventeen.

The two clans did not come to Summer Palace for a marriage proposal. The Bu clan wanted to keep their alliance with the Sanila. The Kazchi family wanted to start a new alliance, willing to give up the future of their clan in Rogi and Renjo.

"My king, I am Lord Hanti, head of the Kazchi clan of Small Castle." Hanti stepped forward, bowing his head.

"Finally, I meet the famous Kazchi clan." Giovanis was pleased. "Is the south treating your clan well?"

"Yes, my king. The kingdom is beautiful, the people are kind and generous. The weather is pleasant. I will never think of going back to the barbaric north."

"That is nice to hear." Again, Giovanis was pleased. "And those boys, the famous twins I've been hearing about?"

"Yes, my king," replied Hanti. He signaled his twins to bow their heads to Giovanis. "I trained them myself. They will serve you till the day they die."

Giovanis observed both of the boys. He liked the way they looked and the aura around them, but their height bothered him. He wanted tall warriors, capable of towering their enemy and striking fear into them. The Kazchi twins stood five feet and four inches tall. They would be laughed at by their enemies even if they were strong.

"Your twins . . . they're short," said Giovanis, disappointed.

Rogi, the hothead of the twins, was furious. His face turned red, and he clenched his teeth. "My brother and I can hold our own!" said an angered Rogi. "We don't need to serve you—"

"Settle yourself, boy," ordered Hanti.

Anzoren had a smirk on his face. "Is this how you raised your sons, Hanti? Should've known. Northerners are all headless warriors," he mocked.

Hanti laughed. "Your days are over, Anzoren. There's nothing you can do that can intimidate me."

"How about you prove it in a duel!" challenged Ba-Ben.

"I'll throw your body in a pile of horseshit!" insulted Rogi, stepping in for his father.

"You northerners should return to where you came from. There's no place for weak peasants in the south," insulted Ba-Ben.

"Enough!" demanded Giovanis loudly.

They all stopped, looking forward to Giovanis.

Bente had a mischievous grin on his face. He wanted to see the Kazchi and Bu clan fight. He wanted to see Giovanis fail as a king so he can take the throne for himself. For many decades, his family had been serving the Sanila clan as their adviser. None had ever tried to challenge their king.

"I apologize, my king," apologized Hanti.

"I am not pleased with your sons." Giovanis sighed. "My warriors need to be giants among their enemy. Not warriors that stand face to face with a child. However, there is one thing I will offer. Swear an unbroken alliance with me. Raise my banner as your own."

Hanti hesitated. "I respect you as my king . . . but what you're telling me is to betray my ancestors. I still don't understand the southerners' ways. But in the north, there's pride in our spirit. I can't give up what my ancestors built."

Giovanis smiled. "Fair enough. I will not force you. I respect that you want to stand by your belief. Don't let it come to a shock if I don't answer your cry for help," warned Giovanis.

Hanti bowed his head, followed by his twins, eyeing Anzoren before he left. Then walking by Thunder, he gave him a respectful nod, leaving the hall without looking back. He expected for the day and time where he would fight the kingdom, maybe because of his foolish pride or because of Giovanis's foolish pride.

* * *

Giovanis met with his small council in the council room. He sat at the center contemplating if he had made the right decision with the Kazchi clan. His small council consisted of Dada, Bente, Seris, Ocrist, and Thunder. They all sat around him, trying to figure out what he was thinking.

"Did I make the right decision?" Giovanis finally asked, questioning his decision.

"It was a king's decision," Thunder assured. "I will never challenge your decisions."

"I was too harsh. They lack in height, but they were talented," regretted Giovanis.

"It was a good decision," stated Dada. "No northerner should serve in our military." Dada hated the north, like most southerners. "They can't be trusted and are unreliable."

"We can't insult them. Our ancestors came to this land together," Ocrist reminded.

"Did you forget they fought on the opposite side in most of the era wars?" questioned Dada angrily.

"Don't let the past anger you, Dada," advised Ocrist.

"Yes, Lord Ocrist is right. My father allowed them to live on our land freely. We must show them respect and not treat them as enemies. They're now children of the south. Even if we're not allies, I'm still their king. I must protect them still. Like Father said, our enemies can be our friends and our friends can be our enemy."

"Well said, my king," applauded Bente. "I couldn't agree with you more."

Thunder knew that Bente was being sarcastic. He despised Bente and wanted him out of Sentra. One time, he nearly murdered him. Bente called him a weak commander and insulted his pride during a drunk night. He held Bente against the wall by his throat, readying to burn his head off his body. Luckily, Seris was there to talk some sense to Thunder.

"We need more resources. Money and food are scarce. Farmers and merchants are refusing to come to the capital. They fear that they will be ambushed like our old king," informed Seris.

"More bandits are roaming outside the capital walls. Stealing and killing merchants and farmers," added Thunder.

"The people are losing trust. They are doubting you, my king," warned Seris.

Giovanis slammed his fist on the table. "It angers me when I can't help the people I swear to protect. I wonder how my father does it, how he blocked the whispers. They don't understand the struggles of ruling an entire kingdom. I'm failing as a king." He looked at each of his advisers. "My adviser should be advising me."

"You were loved like a prince. As a king, it's different. They still love you, but they doubt you. Don't blame them. Give them time—give yourself time, and you'll rule with an iron fist," comforted Ocrist.

"I will deal with these bandits. They will not underestimate you ever again," declared Thunder.

"Good. I will be the greatest king the south had ever seen!" declared Giovanis, determined to prove his greatness.

* * *

Anzoren decided to roam the Summer Garden with his four grandsons before he left them on their own. They all walked in silence as the scent of summer flowers surrounded them.

Rain glanced around the garden. Back at his clan castle, their garden wasn't nearly as big as the Summer Garden. He couldn't enjoy the garden since he despised the royal clan for what they did to his clan, turning them into a cowardly clan and forgetting the greatness of his clan.

"Remember, boys," reminded Anzoren as he continued to walk before his grandsons with his hands together behind his back, "the four of you are what my precious sons left me. Fight in the honor of your fathers and always stay by each other's side."

"Understood, Grandpa," said Uesenga confidently.

"Grandpa, when will our clan name be restored?" asked Ba-Ben. His skin looked rough and his teeth stained with yellow.

Anzoren stopped walking. "I decided to protect our clan," he said without turning to his grandsons, staring at a patch of fire flower. "I must honor the deal I made with the king."

"You're a coward, Grandpa," insulted Ba-Ben. "Our fathers' death has taken your pride."

"Ba-Ben," said Uesenga, wanting Ba-Ben to stop talking.

Rain also wanted Ba-Ben to stop. At the same time, he agreed with Ba-Ben. He thought the same. His grandfather had given up, his will weakened and pride surrendered to the king.

Anzoren chuckled. "I am a coward. I let my four sons die before me. Remember, boys, a Bu shall never die on the battlefield."

Suddenly, the five of them began to hear the sound of a flute being played. They looked around, trying to figure out where the calm and gentle sound was coming from.

Anzoren led the way, recalling the song that was being played. It was the tune he played when he was alone. The person that was playing the flute played it much better than him, nearly bringing him to tears as the sound got closer. The song was called "The Story of an Ugly Prince."

They finally stopped at the center of the garden on which sat a giant pond. At the center of the pond was a gazebo. A wooden red bridge over the pond connected the gazebo to land. Anzoren stopped and admired the song across the bridge. His four grandsons also were taken aback by the song.

Standing in the gazebo was a young woman with wavy dark hair, like the ocean waves. She was alluring, wearing a red silk dress. The young woman was Princess Janellis. She stood still as she calmly played the flute. She looked gentle as the calming sound of the flute surrounded her, not knowing that five men were in awe of her.

Anzoren turned around to his grandsons. They all were admiring Janellis's beauty. "That is the princess, boys. It's best you all stay away from her," he advised.

"She's so beautiful," admired Ba-Ben, his mouth opened wide with drool dripping from it.

"Stay away from her," warned Anzoren to Ba-Ben sternly. He turned back to Janellis and bowed his head, then continuing his walk around the garden.

Ba-Ben grunted as he followed. Uesenga bowed his head to Janellis and followed. Yorsenga followed next. But Rain stayed frozen. He was struck by her beauty and at the same time was taken by her playing.

Then Janellis suddenly stopped playing, lifting her head and opening her eyes, showing her soothing green eyes. She stared directly at Rain as he stared back at her nervously.

Rain quickly shook his head and followed the others, hating himself for falling for the princess so easily. He took a quick peek back and saw that she was no longer looking at him but staring into the water.

*   *   *

Benavis roamed around the crypt of the palace, gazing at statues of old Sanila rulers and clan members. He made his way to his father's statue and cried. He banged his head on the stone statue, wishing it was him that was dead instead of Geolana.

"I'm sorry, Father," Benavis cried as he pressed his forehead against his father's cold stone statue. "Why . . . why did we leave? It was stupid of me to ask you to see outside the wall. Selfish of me to live. Weak of me to watch you die. I'm no man, I'm no son of yours. I allowed you to enter heaven headless. Other kings will laugh at you because of me . . . I'm sorry, I'm sorry," he cried. "You're a good man. They don't know you . . . they don't understand you. These people, they don't care that you died." He paused. "Please, Father, come back. There's so much for me to learn." He turned around and laid his back against his father's statue, slowly dragging himself to the ground. He sat against his father's statue with his head tucked between his knees. He looked up to the side of his mother's statue. "Mother, I'm a failure. I failed both of you. I shouldn't walk freely in this world."

"You shouldn't take life for granted," advised Janellis, hearing Benavis talking to their parents' statues. She didn't expect to see him crying before their parents' statues.

"Why are you here?" asked Benavis, shocked, wiping his tears embarrassingly.

Janellis looked at her parents' statues. "I want to talk to Mother and Father." She then looked back at Benavis. "I can't speak to my parents?" She waited for Benavis to answer her but to no response, as he tucked his head between his knees. She calmly walked up to her parents' statues and stood in front of him. "Is that what you feel?" asked Janellis. "You want to give up your life because you're weak?" she asked with little emotion in her voice.

"I shouldn't be alive," replied Benavis as he looked up to Janellis.

"Why?"

"Because It was my fault that Father was killed. I saw him beg for his life . . . and they still killed him."

Janellis looked down at Benavis with nothing in her eyes. "That's why you don't want to be alive?" She sighed and looked back at her parents' statues. "When Mother died, I quickly accepted her death. When my father died, I quickly accepted his death. I didn't even shed a tear for either of them. I tried to and wanted to, but something was stopping me from doing so." She turned around to leave. "I wish to cry for them one day, Benavis."

"Janellis," said Benavis. "Do you hate me?"

Janellis stopped walking. "Why do you ask such a question?" asked Janellis without turning around.

"Because—"

"Of course, I hate you, Benavis. It was your fault why Father died." Janellis cut Benavis off. "But you're my brother. Maybe one day I'll forgive you." She walked away, leaving Benavis alone in his sorrow.

Benavis tucked his head between his knees. For some reason, he could open up to Janellis even though she may come off cold and heartless. She reminded him of their mother who was always kind to him. He started to cry while remembering his parents again. Unlike Janellis, he hadn't accepted his parents' death.

* * *

Night had taken Sentra, peace and silence settling the city, people sleeping till sunset. In his room was Benavis, sleeping, cold sweat soaking his nightwear. He kept twirling around in his bed, kicking the blanket off the bed.

In his dream, he dreamed of himself alone in a forest, chased by four phantoms. They had no feet, body resembling dark clouds. Their mouths were opened wide and pitch dark, the eyes just a dark hole, the face gray and dead. Arms reached forward for him, resembling bones.

Benavis was running through the forest, trying to avoid the phantoms. Suddenly, he was shot with an arrow behind the knee. He crawled, trying to get away, only to see someone's familiar boots in front of him. He looked up and was faced with his father, a smile on his face. The nightmare was turning into a wholesome dream.

King Geolana had a caring smile. His hair was dark with streaks of gray, long to his shoulder and wavy. He had a mustache and goatee. He wore a fine silk golden shirt and black pants, the clothes he had died in, reaching out his hand to help Benavis up.

Benavis reached for the help. Suddenly, his father's hands disappeared. Turning into dust and merging with the air. He scrambled to look for his father, crawling on his knees and whaling his arms. He shouted, to hear nothing. He was then surrounded by the phantoms. They all watched as he struggled to find his father.

One of the phantoms approached Benavis. He tried to back away from the phantom, but his body was frozen. The phantom opened its mouth wide, wide enough to fit his head into it. He shut his eyes and hoped this nightmare would end.

He awakened from his sleep, breathing heavily, his heart pounding like it was going to burst out of his chest. His clothes were wet and cold. He looked forward, and standing in front of him was a shadow figure. It wore a golden mask, similar to his father's assassinators. This time, it had six arms. In one of its hands was a golden dagger. It quickly charged at him and stabbed him in the heart.

"The Curse of God," whispered the figure with the golden mask.

It was another nightmare. Benavis awoke from his sleep and felt his heart pounding fast like it was going to burst from his chest. His clothes were drenched in a cold sweat. His throat was itching and his eyes bloodshot red. He wondered what his nightmare was about, inspecting his room to make sure the golden-mask creature or phantoms from his nightmare wasn't around. He felt a sharp pain in his chest. Lifting his shirt to see where the sharp pain was, he found a handprint disappearing into his skin.

Chapter Four

Kingdom of Wintra

The cold and barbaric Wintra, the northern kingdom of Telamis, was riddled with civil war and violence. Small clans retreated from the snow for the peace under the other three kingdoms, northern citizens rebelling against northern clans. There was no such thing as peace in the north. Amid the horror, sitting on his throne and allowing the northern civil war was King Rula Diamond.

In Mirky Village, two boys circled each other at the center of the village, as villagers crowded around them. One of the boys, with short black hair and golden eyes, was Kayten Lua.

The other boy was wearing a black headband with a crow stitched at the center of it, a sigil of the extinct Kong clan. The boy had long black hair, with his shirt off, not fazed by the pinching cold weather. The boy was Jamori Kong, the last of the Kong clan.

The crowd around them cheered and hollered, as the boys waited patiently for one of them to attack first. They circled each other like two wolves fighting to be leader of the pack. Jamori had a confident look over his face, having already beaten Kayten numerous times.

Kayten wildly charged at Jamori, with his arms up and hands in a fist, hoping to maybe hit Jamori. But as he neared, he found himself on his back and sinking into the cold snow.

Jamori stood over him with a teasing grin and accepting the cheers from the crowds.

The people of Mirky Village loved Jamori since he resembled his father. Like his father, he was courageous and caring, willing to put others before himself. But ever since the Mirky massacre, the villagers had been trying to find their symbol of hope. To that, they looked to Jamori.

Kayten peeked over to a man standing with his arms crossed and wearing a wolf pelt coat. He had sharp features and a small black goatee, hair loosely tied back. Unlike the villagers, he did not cheer like them. Instead, he shook his head in displeasure. The man was Zhou Bi, a former captain of the Diamond clan. He had left the clan service to warn and save the villagers of Mirky Village of the planned massacre on them, but failed to make it in time.

Standing next to Zhou, with light-blond hair and lavender eyes, was Osa Light. He was fifteen like Jamori and Kayten and was Zhou's most prized student. He had a gentle smile that nearly made his eyes shut.

Kayten clenched his teeth together and stood back up. Seeing the disappointment on Zhou's face annoyed him. Zhou was like a father to him; he was the first person he saw when he woke from his long slumber. He balled his hand and stood in his fighting stance, trying to ignore the teasing from the crowd.

Jamori was surprised that Kayten wanted to continue to fight. It was not like him to stand up and keep fighting. So he got in his fighting stance also and waited for Kayten to attack him again, predicting that he was going to put him on his back once again.

"Give up, Kayten," advised Jamori mockingly.

"Like I would give up like your clan!" insulted Kayten loudly. He allowed himself to be overcome by anger and say words that he didn't mean. With all the people laughing and teasing him, it added to his rage.

Jamori was burning; he charged wildly at Kayten, exposing himself.

Kayten quickly saw an opening and uppercuts Jamori under the jaw, knocking him to the ground, the crowd around them gasping instead of laughing, hoping that Jamori was okay since the punch was strong.

"Enough!" shouted Zhou. "Everyone, back to work."

The crowd dispersed, some mumbling about Kayten, calling him a vile boy.

Kayten could hear them as he stood still with emotions running wild in him. He never felt that he belonged to the village. Even before the massacre eight years ago, the villagers would still try to avoid him and his family.

Zhou approached Kayten with disappointment on his face. He didn't appreciate that Kayten mentioned his old friend's family. He remembered the day of the massacre clearly, riding in the night and through the entrance of the village. The villagers were all sleeping, waiting to be awakened from the sound of the cock. What they didn't know was that their sleep was going to be endless. Instead of waking from the smell of fresh bread and chicken stew, they were awakened by the slashing of the sword, yelling of horror, and the smell of blood in the night air.

When Zhou entered the city, he was too late, fighting his way through the soldiers to make it to the Kong estate that was seen blazing in fire from afar, slashing and slicing his sword, hoping that his friend made it out of the fire. On his way, he saw dead bodies of the villagers from adults to children—eyes opened, staring right at him, spears stuck in their stomachs, limbs detached from their bodies. When he finally arrived at the gates of the estate, he saw the body of his friend, Hacori Kong, lying lifeless as an eight-year-old Jamori stood, defending the body with the clan sword, Rising Fire, as seven guards circled around him.

Kayten tried to avoid eye contact with Zhou, already knowing that he was going to scold him. Osa quickly checked on Jamori, who was whining and groaning on the ground while holding his jaw.

"I'll take him to Spinder," offered Osa.

Zhou just nodded, keeping a stern stare on Kayten.

Osa helped Jamori up, and as they walked by Kayten, Osa shook his head then walked away with Jamori.

"He's your brother," reminded Zhou.

"I know," mumbled Kayten.

"Then why did you insult his clan?" asked Zhou.

"I let my anger get the best of me," answered Kayten.

"Anger will get you kill on the battlefield." He placed his hand on Kayten shoulder. "When it's time for us to attack the king, you need to control that anger inside of you."

Kayten shrugged Zhou's hands off his shoulder. He was tired of hearing Zhou talking about assassinating the king. Every time Zhou talked about it, the more he lost hope and trust toward him. Zhou had been training Kayten, Jamori, and Osa since they were eight, telling them to be ready for the king when they attacked. At first, the revenge filled his heart. But as time continued, revenge slowly faded away as a forgotten thought.

Zhou realized the disappointment on Kayten's face. Like Kayten, he wondered when he would finally follow his words and avenge the dead. Every day he pondered the idea. He promised the villagers that he would avenge their dead family and friends. They soon took his words to heart, forging him as their leader then calling themselves the Unchained, signifying that they were no longer under the rule of the Diamond clan or any other clan of the northern kingdom.

"Don't lose faith in our goal, Kayten," reminded Zhou. "We're all fighting the same enemy."

"I know," mumbled Kayten.

"Zhou," called a voice behind Zhou.

Zhou turned around and was glad to see Gen, a former adviser to the Diamond clan. Mirky Village was his birthplace. When he found out that the king wanted to get rid of the villagers and the Kong clan, he escaped the kingdom and quickly made his way to the village. But he arrived two days too late.

"Gen," greeted Zhou.

Gen bowed his head. "The spies have returned," he reported. He looked to Kayten to leave.

Zhou nodded his head and turned to Kayten. "We'll talk again soon, Kayten."

Kayten walked away without saying a word. He wanted to know what Zhou and Gen were going to talk about.

Zhou watched as Kayten walked away. "I'm afraid the villagers feel the same way as Kayten," he worried.

"They don't have to worry any longer, my friend."

Zhou turned to Gen with hopeful eyes. "Have the spies found something interesting?" wondered Zhou.

"Yes, my friend. Shenva has finally blessed us with our wish. The spineless king will be on the Polar Path when he visits Drown Village tomorrow."

"Ah, I see the poison has worked on them. It's a shame we had to risk their lives for our goal."

"They'll understand when they see the head of the spineless king on a stake in front of the gates of Polar City."

Zhou then glanced around at the villagers working. They all had a smile on their faces, living their life in the grueling winter of the north. But deep down in their heart, they were angry. They wanted Rula to pay for his sin, the pain he caused on the innocent lives he took away and allowed to live. He ordered the massacre because Hacori refused to give up his clan banner.

"It's the perfect time to attack him. But are we doing the right thing? Is our idea of freedom right?" doubted Zhou.

"The villagers long for the day the for Rula head. The bloody night still haunts them in their dreams. Every time they walked on the soil of this ground, it reminds them of the people they loved," reminded Gen, hoping that Zhou will keep his promise. "We're children of Mirky Village, Zhou. We must avenge for the ones that can no longer avenge themselves."

Zhou nodded his head in agreement. Eight years since the day, he had waited long enough to follow the promise he made to the villagers. It was time he fulfilled the promise. He then wondered if the three boys were ready to fight. Even though he had trained them to his knowledge, he still feared that they weren't ready to fight. Looking back, he saw Jamori defending his father's lifeless body as their estate burned in the fire, with the rest of their clan members trapped inside. Then to Osa walking out of the orphanage unscathed but having the look of confusion and fear. Then Kayten, finding him hiding under the steps of his house all drenched in blood and unconscious.

"We will strike fear to the spineless king. We will avenge for the night of horror. Rula will lay in his blood by my dear friend's sword!" determined Zhou.

Gen nodded in agreement.

* * *

Kayten wandered around the village daydreaming about a better north. As he walked by, he could sense people glaring at him, mumbling curses to his name. He never felt welcomed ever since he arrived in the village with his family. Whenever his father tried to find work, he would be denied or sent away. He never understood why he and his family were never welcome. But whenever he played with Jamori at his estate, he was welcomed by Jamori's mother and father.

He missed his mother and father dearly, remembering walking between them as they held his hand when going to the village market. Even though his family was hated, they still managed to keep a smile on their face for him.

He stopped in front of a broken-down house. The roof on the house had a giant hole where the snow had fallen in. The wood on the house was falling apart with black mold on it. Tears began to form in his eyes as memories of him and his mother lying on the back deck of their house and staring out to the night winter sky and counting the stars filled him. The house was his family home. Their last moment before they were murdered by the Diamond clan soldiers.

He clutched his fist tightly as the memories still haunted him. The yelling and begging of his mother as two guards prepared to rape her. Then his father's lifeless body lying in a pool of his blood with begging eyes, staring back at him. He remembered his mother looking right at him with her eyes telling him to run away. And that he followed. He hated himself for being a coward and leaving his mother to be raped and killed, hiding under the steps of his home, hearing the footsteps of soldiers running into the home to not remembering when he passed out.

He wiped his tears and continued his walk. He couldn't forget the painful memory. Every day when he awakened, it was all he could think about. He wished to numb all his memories so he wouldn't have to remember the bad ones.

He spotted Osa sitting on the steps of a house and quickly made his way to him. When he arrived, he noticed that Osa didn't look happy to see him.

"Is he okay?" worried Kayten.

"Of course," replied Osa.

"I didn't mean to—"

"We're brothers, Kayten," reminded Osa. "We swore to never hurt each other. It was only a spar, and you let your pride control you?"

"I'm sorry," apologized Kayten lowly. When Osa was serious, everyone was afraid.

"Don't apologize to me. I know Jamori can be overconfident, but that's him. You . . . you should know better."

Suddenly, the door opened. Walking out with a giant smile was Jamori. Behind was a man limping. He was Spinder, a former healer for the Diamond clan.

"Nothing is broken," reported Spinder.

"My jaw is like steel," said Jamori proudly, standing proudly in front of Osa and Kayten.

"You boys take care now." He looked to the sky. "The night will be cold." He walked back into the house.

"I'm sorry, Jamori," apologized Kayten.

Jamori walked up to Kayten. His proud smile disappeared from his face. He looked like he was going to hit Kayten as he walked up to him. "Don't mention my clan again, Kayten," he warned. "I will restore my clan, that's a promise!"

Kayten kept his eyes to the ground. He felt the aura around Jamori. Then he saw Jamori's hand sticking out to shake. In his mind, he thought they were making truths. So he shook Jamori's hand and looked up, but was quickly met with a head-butt square to the nose. He immediately fell to the ground and started weeping, rolling in the snow as blood leaked from his nose.

Osa was still seated on the steps. "Why did you do that?" he asked Jamori calmly.

"That's for my clan," replied Jamori. "I didn't break his nose." He walked up the steps and knocked on Spinder's door.

Spinder opened the door and wasn't pleased to see Jamori. "Is it a sin to enjoy a cup of tea?" Spinder sighed. "Bring him in, I'll patch him up."

* * *

Both Zhou and Gen stood in front of a house without saying a word to each other. Zhou wanted to know the future of the north when he committed the ultimate crime. An eerie aura emanated from the house. He didn't want to walk in, but fought his nervousness and entered the home with Gen following behind him.

The house was pitch dark. Zhou felt like he was walking in an endless cave all alone, trying to navigate blindly through the house. He and Gen tried to walk lightly, but with each step, they heard the creaking of the wooden floor.

"Show me the truth," demanded a voice.

The torches in the house were lit, adding life into darkness. The house was surrounded by floating eyes with different iris colors. Sitting at the center of the room was the Man of Eyes. He was an old and pale man, nearly looking like he was dying. No one knew his age; many believed he was immortal. Exactly one hundred eyes were floating in the room. He was a sorcerer and used the eyes to help see the past and future. The eyes were those of the dead children of past and present.

"You've awakened my eyes," said the Man of Eyes, his voice frail.

"Apologies, Prophet," apologized Zhou.

"Why have you come?" asked the Man of Eyes.

"I want to know the prophecy," replied Zhou.

"Of what future you wish to see?" questioned the Man of Eyes.

"The future of Telamis, as I plan to commit a sin," replied Zhou.

"Sit," allowed the Man of Eyes.

Both Zhou and Gen sat in front of the Man of Eyes. The hundreds of eyes circled them like dancing butterflies; suddenly, one of the eyes landed on the palm of the prophet's hand. The iris of the eye was black. The prophet looked into the eye to see the future.

"Ah, chaos will reign over Telamis. The end of an era, the start of a new beginning. Years of tragedy and romance, the next will fight the war while the old watch from the heavens. The age of betrayal will soon begin. Watch for the shadow hiding behind the fire. It will be one."

Both Zhou and Gen stood up and bowed to the Man of Eyes before leaving the eerie house. Zhou understood what the prophet was talking about. His death was haunting to him. His sin will cause a break in Telamis. But it must happen. He must end the dynasty of kings. People must be free from the unfit king.

When they stepped out of the house, waiting for them outside were Kayten, Jamori, and Osa. They saw Zhou and Gen walk into the house and were suspicious of why the two of them needed to see the Man of Eye.

"Is the jaw better, Jamori?" asked Zhou. Then he looked to Kayten, whose nose looked swollen. "I don't need you boys fighting each other."

"We're sorry," apologized Jamori.

Zhou looked at each boy. Everything he taught them would finally be displayed on the battlefield. But at the same time, he was nervous for them. He grew close to each boy and saw them as his own sons.

"It is time we fulfilled our promise to the dead. I am willing to blacken my heart for the dead of the innocent."

"Are we going to finally end his life!" asked Jamori anxiously.

"Indeed, Jamori. We will end the spineless king that reign evil on our land." He paused for a second and looked at each boy again. "Are you boys ready?"

"I'm ready to avenge my clan!" shouted Jamori confidently.

"I'm ready," answered Osa calmly.

Kayten hesitated; unlike the other two, he felt uneasy and nervous.

"Kayten, are you ready?" Zhou asked Kayten.

"O-of course . . .," replied Kayten with little confidence.

Zhou nodded his head but saw on the face of Kayten that he wasn't ready.

* * *

As the day passed to the next, Zhou could only think about finally killing the king. He wanted to be the man to stick his sword into the heart of Rula. During his sleep, he had a dream of himself sitting on the bone throne in the Snow Palace, a throne made out of the enemy bones, dreaming of himself being king. It bothered him. He couldn't become the thing he was trying hard to erase from the world. But deep down inside his heart, it did make him happy seeing himself on the throne. While he was sitting on the throne, the living wasn't bowing to him. It was the undead bowing and calling him their leader.

It was morning, the plan to attack Rula set for the late afternoon. A knock on the door awakened Zhou from his sleep. A broad-faced man entered the house. He was muscular and bald and wore rough iron armor. He was Baeso Steel-Head, a former warrior that served the Kong clan.

"My lord, they're waiting for you outside," informed Baeso.

Zhou rubbed his eyes, barely getting enough sleep because of his urgency to kill Rula. "I'm no lord," corrected Zhou tiredly.

"Apologies."

"I'll be right out." It was finally the day to begin a new era. He stared at his sword and then at his armor, trying to calm his nerves and excitement. A part of him was telling him to hold off on the plan while the other told him to finish the king.

He finally stood from his bed. He washed his face from a wooden bowl of water sitting on his nightstand then stared at his reflection in the water. It was time he showed the common people the path of freedom. The chain would break, and they would roam the north freely. He would finally avenge his friends and families.

He walked out the door of his house and faced the people of Mirky Village. All was waiting for him to make his speech. He saw the fire in the people's eyes. They were ready to battle and bring justice. Eight years they waited for the end of Rula. The anger built in their souls was caged; now the key had unlocked the uncaged anger.

"It is time we end the dynasty of kings," declared Zhou. "We have suffered long enough. It's been eight years since that tragic day. Finally, we will stick our swords and spears into the hearts of those royal dogs. They will feel our anger and suffering. Rula is no king—he doesn't have the heart of Wintra. The cold scares him, he sat near a fireplace while we sleep in the cold. He's no northerner. The spineless king will die!" He raised Rising Fire in the air.

Everyone cheered and repeated, "The spineless king will die!"

Kayten standing in front didn't cheer with the crowd. He was more upset than motivated. While everyone continued to cheer, he made his way through the crowd to be away from them. He took a last look back and continued walking. The intestines in his stomach felt like they were twisting around each other, feeling like he wanted to throw up.

"Are you afraid?" asked Osa behind Kayten.

Kayten quickly turned around and tried to show that he wasn't afraid. Standing beside Osa was Jamori. "Of course not."

"We can't be afraid now. It's our opportunity to avenge our village!" said a determined Jamori, raising his fist before his face. "My father will be watching over us. Our war cry will reach the souls that were taken by that spineless king and lead us to our victory."

"After we win, what's next?" wondered Osa.

All three friends stayed silent, each wondering what was next after they finally killed King Rula. For eight years, they were trained to fight, taught to hate King Rula.

"We'll keep following Zhou," Jamori finally said. "We owe our lives to him. He saved us from drowning in a river of blood and built us up as men of revenge."

Osa smiled gently, with both of his eyes smiling also. "We're all victims of revenge," he said then walked away from Kayten and Jamori, confusing his friends.

"Osa, what do you mean?" asked a confused Jamori.

"Nothing . . . Just a thought," replied Osa.

Kayten and Jamori watched Osa walk away from them, leaving them to put pieces of his words. Even though they had been friends for a long time, Osa was still difficult to understand. He always had the same smile. He was like a locked chest with no key to unlock it.

"He's ready," assumed Jamori. "Are you ready, Kayten?"

"Y-yes," lied Kayten.

"Good. I'm ready to die for revenge," declared Jamori.

Kayten looked to Jamori and saw burning passion in his eyes. The determination was written all over his face. He felt jealous of Jamori and wished he had the same confidence as him. Just once in his life, he wanted to be better than Jamori. He wanted to be loved by the villagers like him. He was tired of being in his shadow and frowned upon.

* * *

Waiting behind the snowy bushes on the side of the Polar Path was the Unchained anxiously waiting for the king and his guards to show. Kayten, hiding with Osa, thought about the blood that would cover the snow. He looked over to Osa and saw how focused he was, gripping his sword tightly and watching the road intently.

Everyone in the Unchained were all wearing straw hats and their mouths covered with cloths to hide their breath.

Zhou couldn't wait to finally kill the king. He had brought twenty men and women with him. His idea of ending the dynasty of kings was close to coming.

He looked up at the tree above him. One of his lookouts on top of the tree spotted the king and his guards. The lookout jumped down to report to Zhou.

"There are fifty guards with him, Captain," reported the lookout.

They were outnumbered by thirty. Zhou knew his men and women didn't stand a chance with trained soldiers. He could call off the ambush, but had faith that the gods were by their side.

"Captain, I will die for your cause," declared a man.

"Me too, Captain," declared a woman.

"My sword is yours, my lord," said Baeso. "I will cut down all those royal dogs in your name."

Zhou's eyes watered; seeing his people getting behind him motivated him. They couldn't lose; their death would be told in stories and written in books. Their heroism would be sung throughout the northern kingdom.

Rula was in his wooden carriage with guards around it. The guards were wearing white steel armor with the sigil of a polar bear on the right shoulder plate. The sigil of the Diamond clan. The marching halted as a man approached them, clenching his stomach in pain. The man was an Unchained, pretending that he was hurt. He fell before a soldier's foot, acting like his life was coming to an end.

"Please," begged the man. "I'm sick. I-I need medicine."

"Out of the way!" demanded the guard.

"Please . . . I just need medicine," begged the man again.

"You ought to leave, or I'll cut you down!" warned the guard.

"Why have we stopped?" asked Rula as he stepped out of the carriage. He was a skinny and frail man, his face nearly showing bones. His hair was short and dark; he wore fine silk clothing. Around his head was a crown made out of human bones like his throne. He made his way to the front of the line to confront the problem.

"Move out of the way!" demanded the Rula.

"Please, Your Grace. I am in need of medicine . . . I'm dying," pleaded the man.

"Get out of my face! These ungrateful poor people, . . . they want to ruin my kingdom. I do something gracious once and now they want charity," said a disgusted Rula.

Suddenly, the man stood up and showed the king a dagger. Rula's eyes opened wide. He tried to run away. Then from each side of the road jumped out the Unchained, yelling and all wielding spears and sword. The man with the dagger tried to stab the king from behind but was cut down by one of his guards.

"Protect the king!" shouted a guard.

Kayten jumped out late. Once he got into battle, his legs began to freeze. He felt like he was sinking into the snow. The blood draining out of the king's guards and some of the Unchained falling reminded him of the Mirky Massacre. He saw Jamori cutting down a guard and Osa stabbing a guard in the throat. But for him, he couldn't bring himself to fight. A guard approached him. He couldn't run away as the guard lifted his sword over his head, readying to slice his head off his shoulders.

A sword pierced through the guard's stomach, and blood spilled out his mouth. He looked dead into Kayten's eyes as he tried to hold himself up. The sword was pulled out, and he fell to Kayten's feet.

Osa was the one that killed the guard. He knew Kayten couldn't find the nerve to kill, so he saved him. He gave Kayten a look to start fighting and left.

Kayten still couldn't move; he felt like a coward, looking around and seeing that they were winning. The Unchained fought like a pack of wolves mauling a single deer. The royal guards' morale was down. The eyes of the rebels showed anger and revenge. Each slice and stab was added with extra force, staring into the eyes of the dead guards to let them know that there was no heart in their murderer.

The royal guards weren't ready for the attack. Rula stayed near his carriage watching his guards failing to protect him, scared and wetting his pants. He was a coward and couldn't fight. His life was ending as the anger of the poor and common was going to kill him.

All the royal guards were killed. Blood took the white snow on the ground. Rula was alone and scared, his eyes wandering as he fell to his knees. The end of his clan was near. There was nothing he could do.

Zhou approached Rula with Rising Fire in hand, gripping it tightly in his palm. His dream and idea were coming together. With the final blow to the king, he started a new beginning. The nerves were getting to him. The people around watched. Blood was on their face, clothes, and weapons. Their eyes filled with fire as they stared at the spineless king, waiting for their revenge to fulfill their satisfaction.

"Stand up!" demanded Zhou to Rula.

Rula was hesitant, his legs shaking as he tried to stand up. "P-please—"

"Spineless bear!" snapped Zhou. "These people behind me, you made them suffer enough. The people of the north, you hurt them enough."

"I'm s—"

Zhou violently slapped Rula across the face and knocked him to the ground. The crown fell into the red snow. "I'm still talking!" he shouted. "You stay shut. Nobody wants to hear a spineless king speak. The dynasty of kings is over. It will start with you, dog. Your story will end tragically. No one will care for your death. They will drink on the spill of your blood. You brought chaos to this land and laughed at the death of the poor as the civil war brew. We will no longer wait while clans fight for control. We will stand and fight for our freedom!"

"You think killing me will end the civil war. No, no, it will only add to the civil war. Without me on the throne, then the other clans will want it. Their eyes will be blind with lust and selfishness. Spare my life and I will protect your village," pleaded Rula cowardly.

Zhou picked Rula up from the ground. "Stop begging for your life, dog," he whispered. He stepped to the side and showed Rula the eyes of the people that despised him then quickly stabbing Rula from the back and watched Rula fall to the ground, as he pulled Rising Fire out. He placed his foot on Rula's back and stabbed his sword into the snow, eyeing each of his men and women. They all fought hard and tirelessly. They looked back at him, waiting for his speech.

"The end of kings starts now!" announced Zhou confidently. "This spineless coward is only the beginning. Send letters to all the clans of the north and the other kingdoms. Tell them the Unchained is here. That we killed this spineless king and we will kill more. It's time we take our path to freedom. It's time we stand up and follow a new era, an era that we want to believe in." He picked the bone crown up and raised it in the air. His people cheered for him, including Jamori, but not Kayten and Osa.

Hiding behind the trees painting a picture of Osa was a figure wearing a golden mask. On the forehead of the mask was a third eye. The man crushed the piece of paper and turned it into dust, releasing it into the air. He then took out another piece of paper and began painting a picture of Kayten.

Kayten walked his way to Osa. "Thank you!"

"You're my brother," reminded Osa.

"Why are you not cheering?" asked Kayten.

"Why should I cheer if nothing is won? We started something we can't fix. It's our sin to be part of this rebellion. Now we're criminals to the land, declaring war on Telamis. They all cheer selfishly but don't understand the consequence. The beginning of chaos . . . You and Jamori should leave. Run away from this madness."

Kayten was taken aback. He didn't expect Osa to suggest him to run away. "How about you?"

"I can't leave . . . there's a clan I must end, and this is the only way that will bring me close to them." He looked back at the forest, already knowing that someone was watching them. "Someone is watching us."

Kayten looked toward the forest, and the figure disappeared into thin air. "What was that?" questioned Kayten.

"Something evil. It's been watching us since we left the village. There's something brewing over Telamis. Promise me you'll leave when you get the chance. Live your life and find true freedom. Life of a killer is not for you."

Kayten looked down. He didn't have the heart to take a life away, just like when his family was being murdered and him running away to avoid being murdered too.

Osa walked away, expecting that war was coming. He knew that to become the killer he wanted to be, he needed to become his own enemy, removing all the people he cared for from his life. His heart must be violent and hungry. A black butterfly landed on his shoulders. His smile went away, and vengeance filled his head. The bastard son of a king. His mother was Yuma, the Witch of Love. He wished to end the clan that caused great suffering on his mother that he had never met.

Chapter Five

Kingdom of Tigara

"Again!" Aerin demanded strongly as he unimpressively watched Isa and Kiri train on the training grounds of the Demon Palace.

The late morning day was cool, yet gentle. Autumn leaves blanketed the ground with the wind gently blowing it around. Aerin had a rigid look over his face, unsatisfied with Isa.

Unlike the other siblings, Isa showed no natural talent or ability to wield the clan flames, born during the morning when the sun woke from its sleep while the rest was born during a full moon after the sound of a howling wolf, a clan saying that a demon born in the morning is not a true demon.

Aerin remembered the birth of Isa, ecstatic that the newborn was a boy. But when he held Isa in his arms and stared into the soft and innocent face, the eyes of Isa were still shut, unlike the others who showed their demon eyes. He knew Isa didn't possess the demon blood. He immediately gave the child to the midwife and stormed out of the room, even questioning if Isa was his child. As Isa got older, the more of an outcast he became.

Aerin's mind was thinking elsewhere. Ever since he ordered for Bloben's assassination, he feared that his family was in danger, sending a letter to his brother, Amin, who was serving the king as an adviser, warning him of the danger that may come upon him. Amin hasn't returned a letter yet. He prayed to the gods that nothing sinister had happened to his brother.

For the matter of Smoke Castle and the Smok clan. Instead of taking the castle for himself, he decided to place Ona as the clan head, allowing her to redeem her clan name. Benyae was given to her as a prisoner while Karana was sent to the school of healing in Mount Fang.

Isa stared at Kiri weakly, his eyes pleading to her to take hold of her strength, fearing that one more blow from her wooden sword will break a bone in his body. Violent veins exposed from her forehead, angry at Isa for no good reason.

"Stand and fight your sister, boy!" Aerin ordered Isa sharply.

Isa was startled from Aerin's strict voice, legs shaking and body frozen. He looked over to his Aerin, seeing irritation over the face. He then looked over to Lehue, who stood by Aerin daydreaming. On the other side of Aerin was Kunjae with a mocking smile over his face. Airian stood near, waiting to get in on the action.

Kiri realized Isa wasn't paying attention and charged at him, lifting the wooden sword over her head and jumping toward him with fury.

Isa's eyes opened wide in fear. He didn't want to fight her. He tried to block Kiri's attack but failed, too slow to lift his sword to defend himself. As she smashed her sword onto his left shoulder, he felt the sharp pain ringing from his shoulder to his feet, feeling the intensity dwelling in Kiri. He then fell to both knees and started to tear, trying to hide his pain from Aerin.

"Stand up!" Aerin demanded Isa. "Tears are only for the dead."

Isa held his shoulder as tears continuously fell from his eyes. He didn't want to stand back up and challenge his sister. He looked up to her and saw in her eyes that she wanted to hurt him.

"How am I supposed to become a warrior when you can't fight back!" Kiri mocked Isa angrily.

"Kiri, step away from him!" Aerin ordered Kiri. "Let the boy cry." He looked at Isa shamefully. "Waste of my time."

Isa wiped his tears from his eyes. He stood up and lifted his sword.

Lehue stopped his daydreaming, intrigued by Isa's act of bravery.

Aerin had a slight smile, proud of seeing Isa finally showing heart and determination.

Kunjae noticed that Aerin was proud.

"Look at you, Father," Kunjae said to Aerin. "You're proud of the little lamb."

"I'm proud of all my children," replied Aerin.

"Who are you fooling, Father? You treat the kid like an outcast. I've never seen you hint a smile toward him before. Did the heavenly protectors touch your heart?" Kunjae teased Aerin.

Aerin ignored Kunjae, understanding that Kunjae was only trying to irk him. But it couldn't be denied. In his heart, he was proud of Isa for standing up.

Isa hinted a sign of motivation when he saw the shameful look on Aerin's face. Breathing heavily, trying to ignore the pain coming from his left shoulder, he rushed toward Kiri, shocking her. She stepped aside and tripped him, pointing the sword at his heart as he rolled over.

"It's over," finished Kiri confidently.

Suddenly, Jen-Song Bore approached Aerin with a head bow. "My lord, a young woman wishes to speak to you."

"Her reason?" asked Aerin.

"She will not tell," replied Jen-Song.

"Then show her out of my palace," dismissed Aerin.

"Understood, my lord," Jen-Song responded, leaving the training ground.

Aerin waited till Jen-Song was gone from his sight. He dismissed his children to leave also but wanted Kunjae and Airian to stay behind. He felt like it was time to tell them they were ready to join the clan army. He measured each boy as they stood before him, remembering when they were both kids pretending to be warriors. Now their pretending was becoming reality. Airian was confused and anxious while Kunjae stood calmly.

Aerin remembered the day his father made him heir to the clan over Amin and Akin. He accepted his destiny and ran his family into greatness. Married the most beautiful woman in Telamis, he fathered talented warriors. He never questioned the gods nor went against them. All his ideas only benefitted his clan, even if it means drawing blood to keep them on top of the mountain.

"It's time you two become warriors," said Aerin strictly. "Time to run with the demon."

Airian quickly became overjoyed; ever since he was a kid, being a warrior was all he dreamed of. He wanted to burst up into the air with his arms up, yelling joyfully so everyone in Mersane could hear. He yearned for the day his father to call him a warrior. Now he could ride into battle and slay the enemies in the name of the Kimsu clan.

Kunjae, on the other hand, didn't care much. He did not react to his father's gift. Unlike Airian, he never dreamed of becoming a warrior. Instead, he was more curious why people like his brother were willing to risk their own life for pointless trophies. Why risk their lives for people that can't defend themselves?

"Kunjae, are you not satisfied?" questioned Aerin.

"Why should I be satisfied with dying?" questioned Kunjae as he walked away.

"Do you fear death, Kunjae?" asked Aerin curiously.

"I fear nothing, Father," replied Kunjae as he continued to walk away.

"How about you, Airian? Do you fear death?" Aerin asked Airian.

"No!" Airian replied confidently. "I will serve my clan till the day I die!"

"Are you afraid to be a thief of life?" asked Aerin.

Airian hesitated to answer. He didn't know how to respond to his father. He was ready to be a warrior, but not ready to take or steal life. He didn't know how it feels to stick a sword into the chest of a breathing person.

"Are you ready to take life away because you were told to? Are you ready to kill the innocent you see as your enemy?" pressured Aerin.

"I-I don't know!" doubted Airian. His head throbbed and his body felt warm, cold sweats throughout his body.

Aerin placed his hand on Airian's shoulders to calm his nerves. "You will learn that there are no friends on the battlefield. That pride is in death. The land is changing. We must change with it. We must stay on top of the mountain. We can't fear nothing . . . Grab death by the throat and strangle it." He lifted his hand off Airian's shoulder. "There will be a time that I will go and serve the gods. You all will live to see the changing world, and you all will face it."

Airian didn't understand his father, as he stood clueless. Whenever he saw his older siblings in their armor, he envied them, wishing it was him wearing the black armor with the clan sigil on the right shoulder plate. When he listened in on the stories of Chenpu or his uncle, Akin, he imagined it was him in their boots, fighting those Men of Hates, being showered with cheers by the villagers and city folks. He dismissed himself from his father and thought about killing, looking at his own two hands wondering if he would be able to take life away or will another take his. It was the way of life in Telamis, a country built on blood and war.

* * *

After training, Lehue, Kiri, and Isa decided to take the streets of Mersane. The streets were crowded with people heading to the city market at the center of the city with hundreds of vendors, a hotspot for merchants and farmers to trade or sell their goods. The air smelled of roast duck and chicken. Hundreds of conversations echoed the air. The sky was filled with people riding on clouds while some were standing on the ground opening their wooden tube that holds their cloud.

People walked by and waved to them; others smiled at them. The people of Mersane loved the Kimsu clan for keeping them safe since the founding of the city. The Kimsu didn't mind walking the city without any guards since Mersane was one of the safest cities in Telamis.

Kiri was leading, speed walking away from her brothers. The other two tried to keep up with her. She was frustrated and annoyed, feeling like everything was going upside down in her life. She didn't mean to let her anger out on Isa, angry that Aerin didn't recognize her strength. She hated fighting Isa because he was no match for her. Still, she was forced to spar him.

"Kiri! Hey, Kiri, hold up!" called Lehue, trying to slow Kiri down.

"What!" snapped Kiri. "Leave me alone." Her eyes were wide open.

"Aye, relax, Kiri," calmed Lehue.

"Shouldn't you two play in the dirt?" asked Kiri.

"Um, we're not little anymore," reminded Lehue.

"But he is!" Kiri insulted Isa, pursing her lips at him.

Isa looked away shamefully, afraid to stand up to Kiri. He didn't know how to defend himself, always hiding behind both Lehue and Kiri. He had no confidence and pride in him. He hated himself for being weak. Not even the lively streets of Mersane could release him from his prison.

"Why are you weak?" asked Kiri mockingly. "Where's your flame, Isa, where!"

"Aye, Kiri relax, you're going too far." Lehue was trying his best to calm the situation.

"Father will never see my strength when I'm always fighting with a weakling!" expressed Kiri as she eyed Isa down.

"He's smaller than us," defended Lehue cheerfully.

"You see, stop protecting him. He will never be strong hiding behind us." Kiri faced Isa. "Say something! Stop being silent and speak. Defend yourself for once in your life, stop hiding behind us."

"I-I'm sorry," Isa apologized lowly.

"Stop apologizing!" yelled Kiri. She turned and continued walking, leaving her two younger brothers behind, disappearing in the crowd of people.

"Kiri, where are you going!" Lehue shouted for Kiri. He waited for a response but was ignored. He then put his arms around Isa's shoulders. "It's okay, little brother. I believe in you. We don't have to be warriors like mother said."

"Thank you," thanked Isa. "But Kiri is right. I am weak, I can't be a warrior."

"Aye, that's Kiri. She says a lot of things, but nobody cares." Lehue saw the sad look on Isa's face. "I know what will cheer you up. We should ask our mother to let us ride, Borin."

Lehue and Isa made their way to Feather Field, where Maenellia kept her phoenix. They passed through the crowded Gift Street and then to the tight alley of Devil Alley, waving to the homeless as they run past by, then passing by the Willow Tower and waving to the guards. They arrived at Feather Field. The field grass was bright green and kept neat.

Maenellia was feeding Borin red berries while they sat under the giant oak tree. Borin was resting sickly in her nest.

When Maenellia died, the bird would burn itself into ashes, leaving behind three eggs. Only the Ma clan could ride a phoenix since Kay-Su Ma slayed the phoenix king five hundred years ago, leaving them the tamer of phoenixes.

On Maenellia's shoulder was her blue flame bird. It flew away when it saw Lehue and Isa approaching. Both boys made their way to their mother.

Isa had seen Borin many times but continued to be fascinated when he was around it. He loved riding Borin. In the sky looking down on Mersane, with his arms stretched out wide and the wind blowing to his face, he felt free from the world. The sky was a new world where anger, sadness, and disappointment didn't exist.

"My loves," greeted Maenellia kindly. "What brings you boys here?"

"Mother, Isa is feeling down. And I think riding Borin will bring his spirit back up," Lehue suggested kindly, looking at Borin with a smile.

"I'm sorry, boys. I'm afraid she's feeling a little sick today," denied Maenellia sadly. "I'm feeding her berries until she feels better."

Lehue placed his hands on Borin's beak and rubbed it. "Feel better, Borin," he consoled.

Borin shut her eyes and rested. Maenellia put the basket of berries on the ground near the nest and sat near it. Isa and Lehue sat in front of her. She gently rubbed her hand against the feather of Borin, gentle enough to not bother Borin in her sleep.

"What is wrong, Isa?" Maenellia asked Isa.

"I disappointed Father again," answered Isa. He felt safe talking to his mother. She was loving and caring toward him, unlike his father.

"It's okay to fail, my love," comforted Maenellia. "We all fail. Before Kay-Su slayed the phoenix king, he failed many times. But he kept returning and fighting until he finally stuck life into the heart of the evil king, freeing all the phoenixes from their misery by the tyrant king." She messed Isa's hair with a cheerful smile. "There will be times we disappoint and time we make people proud. We can't make them all happy, boys."

"Kiri will never be happy," said Isa with a depressed look. "She hates me."

"She can't hate you forever," consoled Maenellia. "It's okay to be angry at each other, even if we don't ask for it. You will all sit and laugh together again. We need the company of others to be happy, even if we don't want it."

"See, Isa? Everything is all right," chirped Lehue, slapping Isa back with a giant smile.

"Mother, I don't want to be a warrior," confessed Isa.

"You don't have to be a warrior, my love." Maenellia sighed. "This world is so vast with many mysteries. Don't take one path when there are so many."

"Stop whining," said Indris behind Isa and Lehue, holding a basket filled with red berries to give to Borin. "Crying only makes you feel bad for yourself."

"It's okay to cry," challenged Maenellia. "Everyone cries, it's a part of life. We cry for the one we love. We cry when someone breaks our heart. We cry when we laugh."

Indris handed his mother the basket of red berries and placed each hand on Isa's and Lehue's heads. "The demon blood is in us. Even if you can't use flames, you still have to run with the demon." His face turned into disappointment. "Father has already decided his next plan. Pity that both of your future has already been decided."

"Your father is only trying to protect our clan's future," said Maenellia.

"Our clan does not need protection," argued Indris. "Father is only protecting himself because he's afraid. Do you truly believe Airian and Kunjae are ready to be warriors?"

"I believe in all my children," replied Maenellia. She could never be angry at her children, even if they had done something wrong. She would continue to love them, and she would get upset when she saw them argue amongst each other. "All my children have flaws. As a mother, I must overlook the flaws and remind myself they are my children. When it's time for me to go, I will still watch over all of you, making sure you take the right path."

"You're just like Father," said Indris, thinking about going to the forest. Whenever he felt down or had a lot to think about, he would go to the Forest of Life and spend the night there.

Maenellia could see on the face of Indris what he was thinking about. "Indris, you can't hide forever," advised Maenellia.

"I'm finding peace away from the demon," said Indris.

"Aye, don't say that!" angered Lehue.

"Little brothers, enjoy life and find your future," advised Indris, leaving with disappointment over his face.

*   *   *

Ausra lay on the roof staring at the full moon in the mysterious night sky. In his mouth was a hard cherry candy. He avoided his family all morning and afternoon, spending the rest of his day on the roof of a random house, sleeping and daydreaming all day long, the air cool and calm. People below were teasing each other while some men flirted with the women they passed by, all heading to the Lurking Tavern for another night of drinking. He shut his eyes, trying to block the noise. Imagining himself somewhere with silence, wishing life was simple, where he wasn't needed to kill someone ever again.

"Found you," said Torshen, floating on his cloud.

"What do you want?" Ausra sighed, still lying on his back.

"Boredom," replied Torshen.

"Want to go on another mission?"

"It's better than getting drunk and waking up at noon."

"Why won't you bother the others?" questioned Ausra as he sat up.

"Nagen is sleeping, Kaiso is drunk, Leonaris is reading, Nisu is trying to bed whores, Sukro is with Jungy," said Torshen while he hopped off his cloud and onto the roof and putting it back into his wooden tube.

"And you chose to bother me. How tiresome."

"Yes."

Torshen and Ausra had been best friends since they were kids. They both treated each other like brothers. Sukro acted as their older brother since the two loved getting in trouble when they were young. The three of them swore to never leave each other and to always fight by each other's side. Sukro would always remind them about their oath, making sure the two don't forget.

Torshen sat near Ausra and handed him a piece of hard lemon candy. "Will there be war again?"

"Maybe," replied Ausra with a yawn then stared down at the people walking joyfully and freely below. "We may be the enemy this time around . . ."

I wonder how it feels to be a villain, thought Torshen.

Ausra thought about the possibility of him being a villain. He didn't believe he was a hero, molded to be a killer and bring pain to the hearts of families, a weapon that many feared. He reached his arms forward and toward the sky, pretending to grab the moon in his palm. There was nothing that he loved nor hated, like the emptiness in his palm as he looked in it.

Ausra and Torshen both climbed down from the roof to roam the night of the city. There were drunks on the street, prostitutes waiting to pick men up after a night of drinking passing by all of them, ignoring the noise and commotion surrounding them. This particular night was perfect for a useless celebration.

Suddenly, a young woman stopped in front of them, blocking their path with her arms stretched out wide. She had brown long hair tied in a ponytail with split bangs. Her skin was fair. She was wearing a brown torn cloak with an energetic and fierce look on her face.

"Aha, I found two Dragons!" the young woman said excitingly.

Ausra was confused and annoyed. "Who the hell are you?" asked Ausra confusedly.

"I'm the girl that will make your clan rich!" declared the young woman.

"Stupid." Ausra yawned, walking by the young woman.

The young woman placed her hand on Ausra's chest, stopping him again. She stared into Ausra's unique eyes. Unlike most people, she wasn't afraid. She looked back at them with intensity. "Believe me when I say I'll make your clan rich," repeated the girl. "I am—"

Ausra put a piece of candy in her mouth and walked away. "I don't care," he murmured as he left.

The young woman spit the candy into her palm and threw it at the back of Ausra's head. The throw was hard enough to stop Ausra, forcing him to rub his head.

He was getting annoyed with the young woman's behavior.

Torshen chuckled and turned around. "You shouldn't have done that," he warned.

Ausra turned around with an annoyed look. "Are you stupid!" exclaimed an angered Ausra, rarely losing his temper.

"Yes, I am," replied the girl proudly. "But being stupid got me to where I am now." She winked at Ausra cutely.

"Stupid girl!" insulted Ausra.

"You mean Stupid Daysa. For I am Daysa Gi-Su," introduced Daysa. "Let Lord Aerin know I will be meeting him at noon tomorrow, Ausra Kimsu. The Silent Demon . . ." She turned to Torshen. "And Torshen Iceben, the White Hair." She twirled and left.

"Bitch," mumbled Ausra.

"I heard that!" shouted Daysa.

"Boy, she's strange," said a drunk sitting on the steps of a random house.

Ausra tossed the drunk a piece of candy, and he continued his nightly walk with Torshen.

* * *

Aerin sat on his high chair in the great hall on an early cold autumn morning after breakfast. His young children had left the hall. Maenellia sat next to him. Standing below them was Akin Kimsu, Aerin's younger brother and a captain of the Kimsu clan. Beside him was Chenpu.

Standing in front of them were the other captains, including the Seven Demon Dragons and Jen-Song. There were twenty captains, all waiting for Aerin to pick his new commander. They all believed that the prestigious title was going to Akin while some thought he was handing it to Indris.

"You all know I am searching for a new commander," announced Aerin. "I need someone loyal. Someone that will lead my army to victory." Aerin looked at every one of his captains, all worthy of being a commander. "I found my commander. I spoke with my brother, and we both agreed with Cholee. Cholee Tegora will be my new commander!"

Cholee stepped forward. He was a man in his early forties. He was muscular and tall with long curly black hair, a talented warrior that fought many wars beside Akin. He was shocked to be given such a title, as with the other captains. He proudly accepted his new position and took his place below Aerin, next to Akin.

Estrey Soombe then stepped forward. He had a long deep scar running through the left cheekbone to his chin. "My lord, we found the Men of Hate camp near Heart Village. They're trying to cut off our rice supplies."

"Thank you, Captain Estrey for the report. I'll let Indris deal with the matter. And my other two sons will fight alongside him. It'll be an experience for them," said Aerin, looking to Indris.

Maenellia peeked a concerning look at Aerin, which he didn't notice. She didn't want her two sons to leave her so soon.

"Brother, is it the right idea to bring Airian and Kunjae into battle?" asked Akin.

"They have to start somewhere," replied Aerin.

"Then I'll travel along with them," offered Akin.

"Thank you, brother," agreed Aerin.

Broken Silly-Fin stepped forward, a white man whose face resembled a fish. "How about the Smok clan situation?" worried Broken. "The royal kingdom will surely punish us."

"Why would they punish their strongest ally?" questioned Aerin. "As long as my captains stay loyal to me, I have nothing to fear."

"Brother, have you heard back from Amin?" asked Akin with concern for Amin.

"Nothing yet."

"I'm worried," said Akin.

"Should we be ready for war?" asked Nellina Gray, a captain, her skin tan and her hair short like a man.

"We should always be ready for war," replied Aerin.

"If the royal clan decides to attack us, we will fight in your name, my lord," declared Cholee. "We run with the demon!"

"Yes, we have nothing to fear when we have Lady Maenellia's phoenix," added Broken.

"And we have the Demon Dragons!" included Gorl Hillytop, a round gigantic bald black man with rosy cheeks and a messy beard.

"Not even a winged dragon will dare to attack us!" said Broken confidently.

Chatters begin to break out in the hall, some fearing war while others ready for war.

"Silence!" demanded Aerin. "We must control ourselves. There will be no war in the east. Hensi would be stupid to declare war against us." He was confident with his army.

Some of the other captains didn't have the same confidence as Aerin, some peeking at each other with doubt while some were willing to fight by him no matter if his idea was wrong. Like the people of Mersane, he was loved by his warriors and magic users. Not only did they respect him, but they were also equally afraid of him.

The meeting in the hall took till noon. They mostly talked about the Men of Hate and how to stop them. Gorl suggested finding their camp and slaughter all of them, women and children included, while Estrey suggested forming a treaty with them. The Men of Hate had been an enemy to the eastern kingdom for centuries. They were wild people that could only see violence.

Aerin listened to all of his captain's suggestions. In truth, he wasn't going to use any of their suggestions. The Men of Hate were just a pest to him; his main goal was keeping his clan at the top of the mountain so everyone in Telamis could continue to fear and respect them. He wanted his children to be the greatest warriors to walk the soil of Telamis.

All the captains walked out of the hall, chatting to each other outside the Demon Palace. Some were concerned about the Men of Hate, and some were afraid that the four years of peace may end soon. To ease the majority of their concerns, the captains all left for the Wing Tavern. The dragons stayed behind to discuss other important matters with Aerin.

Indris made his way down the steps, only to be stopped by Estrey, who had a worried look on his face.

"Our lord is losing his touch," observed Estrey. "He's distracted."

"I know," agreed Indris. "His mind is not in the right place."

"I wonder where is mind is at," questioned Estrey.

"I wonder the same, Captain Estrey. I wonder the same for my mother. What hopeless idea is my father chasing? Is my mother a fool for believing in an idea so far from reality?" Indris was losing hope in his father and mother. For the past months, he found his father slowly falling apart mentally. What's protecting Aerin was the shell of his skin shielding his true intention. Pride was taking over his common sense.

"Does our lord fear something?"

Indris chuckled. "They say a demon fear nothing, but the gods . . . I guess he can sense the gods are hunting him."

"So blood will soon drown Telamis once again. And here I thought we were in an era of peace. Guess there's a price for peace."

"There's a price for everything," corrected Indris. "The cost of life is death. We live for another man's dream so they can sit proudly on their senseless chair while our body burns into ashes." He gazed into the sky. "Why must we follow the lies of this world?" He paused, trying to find his future, a life where he was not holding a sword. "Iszra, did you escape?"

"He did," said Estrey. "He escaped before the chaos begins."

"My brother was always intelligent. He knew something we don't know."

"What do you plan to do?" asked Estrey.

"Nothing," answered Indris calmly. Knowing that he was trapped in his father's ambition, with no way of escape. He continued to walk down the steps, sensing a dark cloud hovering over him.

As a kid, he always listened to his father, never arguing against him as Iszra did. He never had his own piece of mind. He never tried to impress his father, nor make him angry. Life was like a river to him, flowing till a boulder split the water in half, only to meet again, continuing the journey till it hit a waterfall, starting a new life and journey. There was no boulder or waterfall in his life, only a river flowing endlessly.

*   *   *

The Seven Demon Dragons stayed behind at the great hall. They all stood before Aerin. He felt proud of himself to have them under his command. They were his ultimate triumph card, instruments he saw toward his dream. When there was a major issue that needed to be dealt with, he would call for them. Just like when he ordered the assassination of Vesak and Bloben.

"I want to thank you guys for your undying loyalty," thanked Aerin. "Believe me, you guys are the pillars to my vision."

"We only follow your orders, my lord," said Nagen.

"The others don't understand what I'm trying to build," said Aerin, referring to his other captains. "I sense the distrust amongst them. I want you guys to watch each of the captains. Including my own brother."

"My lord, there's nothing to fear," advised Nagen. "They will understand when they see your vision blossom."

Ausra didn't believe in Aerin's idea but didn't care to say anything, feeling like it was a nuisance to him to say anything to his father. He'd much rather be napping under a tree or on top of a roof. He hated coming to official meetings and was tired of hearing the other captains complain.

Aerin pulled a letter out of the inside of his shirt. "The king has called for me." He showed it to Aerin.

He stared at the letter angrily, as the black flames from his hands slowly charred it, turning it into ashes, tossing the ash into the air, letting it scatter to the stone ground. "My brother finally answered. I didn't want to tell the other captains before I tell you guys. Hensi is not pleased with the death of Bloben."

"What will you do, my lord?" asked Nisu.

"Meet the king. What can he do? We are his strongest allies. I have the strongest warriors in the kingdom. What can that man do!" Aerin nearly showed madness in his eyes.

"He can have you killed," said Ausra bluntly.

"Have me killed." Aerin chuckled. "I must be blind for them to kill me."

Ausra looked at Sukro. Both knew that the man that had raised them was losing his mind. His touch with truth and reality was driven out by lies and false beliefs. His dream of keeping his clan superior over other clans brought only a cloud of a nightmare over Telamis. The cost of superiority would be blood and death, just like in the past. Power killed a man.

Suddenly, the wooden door opened, and in came Daysa, fierce and confident. Two guards tried to stop her, but she forced herself into the hall.

The dragons and Aerin were all confused.

Ausra wasn't too pleased to see her, still angry that she wasted his candy he gave her.

"Lord Aerin, I-I must speak to you." Daysa struggled as she tried to fight off the two guards.

Aerin watched, liking the fight he saw in her. "Let her in!" he ordered.

The two guards let Daysa through. She patted herself clean and taunted the guards like she won the fight, making her way through the dragons, ignoring their immense aura around her. She looked at Ausra and winked. He shot her a cold stare.

"Afternoon, my lord." Daysa bowed her head.

"Who are you?" questioned Aerin. "You did a number on my guards. A strong-willed girl, I see."

Daysa stood high and confident. "I am Daysa Gi-Su, daughter of Noba Gi-Su."

"Ah, the famous rogue mage. How is he?"

"Dead," replied Daysa bluntly. "The red waterfall stole his life."

"I'm sorry to hear that," consoled Aerin. "He was a great mage. I can tell you every clan wished to have him in their service, including myself. Sad he had to meet such a terrible ending."

"My father died happily. He accomplished so much. He taught me magic and showed me the great beasts of Telamis," said Daysa.

"Why do you need to speak to me?" asked Aerin curiously.

Daysa looked back at the dragons then at Ausra. She smiled at him, remembering their encounter before. He had annoyance written on his face. She then looked back at Aerin. "I want the Seven Demon Dragons to assist me on my next research," she said proudly with her chin up high.

The dragons all looked at each other, confused.

Aerin laughed. "Why would I hand you my strongest warriors?"

"Laugh all you want, but know I can make your clan rich."

"Why us?" asked Nagen.

"My father was researching this legendary beast thought to have died during the Dru dynasty. He found that it may be alive, resting in the southern kingdom jungles, waiting to be discovered again."

"What of this legendary beast you talk of?" asked Aerin curiously. "How can it make my clan rich?"

Daysa chuckled. "It's the legendary phoenix, Morfis. The golden phoenix—the sixth king."

Silence stopped the room. They looked at Daysa, shocked that she believed such a beast was still alive. Morfis was the phoenix that was never tamed by the Ma clan. It terrorized many villages and cities. Even Kay-Su had difficulty with the phoenix until he tamed the five other kings to kill Morfis, or so the story told.

"What makes you believe such a monster is still alive?" questioned Aerin.

"It was never dead," replied Daysa. "The stories of its death never made sense. A phoenix can only die when its rider dies. Who was Morfis's rider? No Ma ever tamed the beast. Kay-Su never killed it, his five kings were killed by that beast. I believe magic was used to cage Morfis in the jungle while it protects a legendary sword."

"Sword?" asked a confused Aerin.

"Yes, Silver Blood."

Aerin's eyes opened wide. He knew the sword. The sword was his family sword, last used by Dravin Kimsu, the Sun Demon who helped end the Dru dynasty five hundred years ago.

He was a talented warrior and magic user. Many feared him because of his lust for blood. As the first era war was coming to an end, the great protectors all decided that Dravin must die. They conspired with his brother, Nopen Kimsu, the Spider Demon, to kill him. He was ambushed and killed by his blood. His sword was not by his side.

"If this is true, then how did Dravin got past Morfis?" wondered Sukro. "Your facts doesn't make sense."

"Nothing ever makes sense. It's Telamis—there are always secrets hiding in the darkness of this land," said Daysa with a smile.

"That sword . . . that sword is my clan sword. It's ours, the black blade made out of the black of demon blood . . . Your claim is foolish, but if you believe your beast and my clan sword is hiding in the jungle in the south, then I will believe you. The sword will help me with my vision—the goal of keeping my clan on top of the mountain."

"Will the dragons assist me in my travel?" asked Daysa to Aerin again.

Aerin looked at each dragon. Letting them help her would leave him vulnerable. When other clans knew that the Wings were not by his side, they would try to take advantage of him. But his clan sword was more important to him now. It needed to come home and be around his waist.

"I will pay for their service," added Daysa. She made a magic portal beside her, and a treasure chest floated out of the portal. It landed in front of her with the front facing Aerin. The portal shut and disappeared. "This chest is filled with gold from my father's adventures and findings. I am willing to give you all his gold for the dragons' service."

"It means that much to you," said Aerin. He paused to think. "Fine, the Seven Demon Dragons will be at your service."

The dragons were shocked by Aerin's decision.

Ausra couldn't believe his father was a fool to fall for a lie. He didn't believe that Morfis was still alive even though Telamis was vast and still shocking to the eye. If legend holds true, a birdlike Morfis wouldn't hide. Instead, it should be burning cities and villages, causing havoc across the land.

"My lord, how about your safety?" asked a worried Kaiso.

"I can handle myself," assured Aerin. "Find me my sword and find this girl her beast."

"If the beast doesn't exist and the sword is not found?" asked Nagen.

Aerin looked coldly in Daysa's eyes, sending chills through her spine, making her confidence seem like dust. The black chilling eyes made her feel like she was in the demon's lair. She saw why he was called the Black Heart. He was true to his name.

"Leave her to fend for herself," declared Aerin.

Daysa gulped. "My research never failed me."

"What will we do if the beast is found?" asked Sukro.

"Take its eyes and kill it. I want it for my collection," answered Daysa.

"Idiots," mumbled Ausra as he walked away, putting a piece of cherry candy in his mouth.

Chapter Six

Kingdom of Tigara

Ausra aimlessly walked around the city of Mersane instead of floating on his cloud. The streets were crowded with people rushing to the city center, children running away from their mother's watch as they tried to enjoy the beautiful autumn breeze, some accidentally bumping into Ausra, forgetting who he was for a second. They were all living their lives peacefully, going through life routinely with only the thought of the present and future.

For Ausra, life was tedious. He hated being in the city. At the same time, he hated the missions. He never asked for a life of complication. Sadly, it was placed upon him once he came out of his mother womb. He wondered why the gods had cursed him with such a life.

He made his way to the candy shop. Sweet necklaces hung from the window to draw in children. Jars of candy were on the wooden shelves. Candies floating in the air. At the center of the shop was two spiral stairs leading the second floor. Children were with parents picking and buying their favorite candy. Ausra made his way to the hard candies since those were his favorite. There was a jar of many different flavors: dragon berry, hippo nut, and even lemon sweet. He decided to buy all the flavors since he had enough autumn coins.

When he stepped out of the store, he unwrapped a piece of Tiger Melon candy and tossed it into his mouth, continuing his lonesome walk.

"Ausra!" called a voice.

The voice sounded familiar. When he turned around, a lengthy, skinny man stood behind waving his hand to him. The man was a magic user named Jungy. He had a giant smile across his face showing his yellow-stained teeth. His clothes were covered in soot and dirt since he was also a blacksmith.

"Just the Dragon I was looking for," said Jungy with his cricket smile.

They sat on a bench on the side of the cobblestoned street. Ausra unwrapped a piece of hard lemon candy and tossed it into his mouth. Jungy still had a big cricket smile that wouldn't leave his face. They sat, watching people walk by them, listening to their conversations. Some people stopped to thank Ausra and Jungy for protecting them. Ausra shrugged them off, and Jungy proudly accepted their thanks. Since he had done nothing for years, it helped his ego.

"These people know nothing," said Jungy. "They will never know our struggle."

"Does it bother you?" asked Ausra, wishing for Jungy to leave him alone. He then tossed a dragon berry candy into his mouth. Immediately, he was taken aback by the spicy and late sweetness flavor.

"Yes, I am. I'm tired . . . it's not fair. I want to explore the world, discover new creatures and plants. Find hidden castles. But look at me, barely making it through the cracks. And they said the life of a magic user was magnificent."

Ausra took another candy out of his pocket and tossed it into his mouth. "You smile every day," noted Ausra calmly. "You're like these people. Waking up every morning to the sound of a cock. Walking the stone road of the city. Spending coins on food and clothes. Drinking till a fist hit the mouth. Sleeping for a new day. I'm the one spilling the blood." He thought of when he stuck Life into the back of Vesak.

"My demon friend, why won't you leave the warrior life?" asked Jungy as he patted Ausra's back with a giant smile. "You seem unsatisfied."

Ausra wondered if there was a way for him to escape the life of a warrior. The honor of being a hero was worth nothing to him. It was only a word people say to him to honor him. They called him a hero to feel safe. The word was an invisible wall that protected them until the day they have to fend for themselves.

"I heard you and the others are hunting a legendary beast," said Jungy with excitement. "I created a new invention, something that'll help you on your quest."

Ausra shrugged his shoulders. He didn't care about Jungy's inventions or ideas. He thought that they were childish and useless.

"You might like this one, my friend," assured Jungy. "I'll show you."

"No," rejected Ausra bluntly.

"I got candies. Even the new flavors, sweet ginger and red fire." Jungy knew his way to tempt Ausra.

"Fine."

They made their way through a crowd of people to a broken-down house, the windows of the house covered with wooden planks. The wood was nearly rotten with holes in it. Rats were running around the house. A strange odor could be smelled within thirty feet of the house.

Jungy opened the squeaking wooden door and entered the broken home. Ausra followed, covering his nose with his arm immediately. The house was filled with the stench of dead rotten rats. Everything in the house was nearly falling apart. The wooden floor creaked as they walk; it felt loose and unsafe. At any time, the floor would collapse under them.

"You should clean this place up," suggested Ausra.

"This filth is my home." Jungy smiled.

Jungy led Ausra to the back room and into his study. The room was clean, with many books organized on the shelves. Some books were floating around the room. There was a jar with an orb lighting in it sitting on a table. He made his way to the table, pushing some of the floating books aside, and opened one of the top drawers on his desk, pulling out a dagger.

The dagger looked magnificent. The blade was blue, made out of steel. Jungy showed the dagger to Ausra with a mad giant smile, exposing his yellow cricket teeth again. "My new creation," he proudly introduced. "This, my demon friend, is the greatest dagger you'll ever come across. I infused the dagger with moon lion blood from the southern jungle. The handle's made out of dragon bones."

Ausra was not amazed by Jungy's creation. "Where did you get the moon lion blood and dragon bone from?" asked Ausra.

"Some merchant from the market sold it to me. He told me the bones were from a winged dragon of Sunya Mountain."

"Sunya Mountain?" asked a confused Ausra, recalling that the mountain was once home to a legendary dragon. "Rainmore . . .," he mumbled to himself.

"Rainmore died hundreds of years ago. His remains are forged into the throne in Fairy Palace. Or so they told, my dear demon friend," said Jungy. "Not all his remains were taken. Some were buried into the soils of Sunya Mountain."

It was not rare to see a winged dragon flying over Telamis. Thousands of years ago, they ruled Telamis alongside the spirit dragons and phoenixes. At times, a winged dragon would terrorize a village or farm. But most of the time they're hiding behind the clouds or on top of mountains. Ausra himself never saw a winged dragon before. But he understood they were dangerous creatures. The phoenix and winged dragon were enemies. For thousands of years, they fought for the land. Even Shenva and Chenva couldn't contain the war between beasts. Until a great dragon, Dru, developed the ability to shapeshift into a human and lay with Kami, the god of love, giving birth to triplets that could control the winged dragons and the ability to wield their blood, leading to the rise of humans and the start of the Dru dynasty.

Ausra took the dagger and observed it as he felt it in his hand. The dagger was truly Jungy's greatest creation. But he did not want to give praise to Jungy. It felt strange to him to give compliments. "How did your merchant manage to get his hands on the bones?" he asked.

"He stole it from some hunters," replied Jungy with a cricket smile.

"Why did you infuse the steel with moon lion blood?" questioned Ausra.

"The blood of a moon lion is poisoning. A stab to the heart, and the beast will fall instantly. Imagine what it will do to a healthy man with a single cut," said Jungy as he stared intensely at the dagger.

Ausra handed the dagger back to Jungy. "You keep the dagger, maybe one day you might need it," he advised.

"I already have magic protecting me," said Jungy.

"I have seen you use magic, Jungy. Keep the dagger for protection."

"Fine. I have a question before you leave."

Ausra sighed; he wanted to leave Jungy's disgusting home badly. The stench was bothering him. He was also upset that Jungy had bribed him with candy and did not give him any.

"Should I worry . . . should I leave the city before something unexpected happens? I have a feeling something bad is going to happen. Everyone's been talking at the tavern. They're losing trust in Lord Aerin. I can't blame them. What was the meaning to order the death of Lord Bloben? Is he trying to fight a war we can't win?"

Ausra shrugged; he too wondered about what his father's plan was. "Leave if you want. At the end of the day, the one who dies will be the one with too much ambition," he ended, leaving Jungy guessing.

* * *

Kiri was on the training ground swinging her wooden sword into thin air. Every swing she swung was with anger. "Watch me be a warrior!" she said angrily to herself. "I'm going to train and be the greatest warrior in the clan." She ground her teeth together and breathed heavily. She swung her sword at the air again, this time yelling her lungs out, waking the birds from their sleep then scattering out of the trees.

"Let it all out, my dear," said Maenellia. She was watching Kiri train the entire time with her blue flame bird on her shoulder. "Let your anger out to the world so happiness can fill your heart."

"Mother!" exclaimed a surprised Kiri. "How long were you standing there?"

"Long enough," replied Maenellia with a gentle smile.

"So you heard," mumbled Kiri. "I'm sorry, Mother, but it's not fair. I trained countlessly every day and night, but Father never notices." She wanted to cry and let out more of her emotions.

Maenellia kindly smiled. "Your father sees your strength, my dear. He just has a different way of showing it."

"Why does he make me train with Isa? He's weak . . . I can hold myself against Airian and Kunjae."

"Is that the reason why you're mad at Isa? Because you hate training with him?" questioned Maenellia. She turned to leave. "I advise you to not stay angry at your brother too long, my dear." She started her walk.

"But, Mother!" Kiri tried calling for Maenellia.

Maenellia stopped walking but kept her back turned. "There is more to life than being a warrior, Kiri. Don't let your dream of being a warrior ruin your heart." She continued to walk away, leaving Kiri in her own thoughts.

Kiri stopped her training and made her way to the stable. She thought about what Maenellia said to her. She let her anger toward her father projected toward Isa. At the same time, she wanted a stronger challenger to show her strength. She didn't know how to apologize to Isa but wanted to.

Being a warrior was all she dreamed to become. She wasn't like Lehue, who easily swayed away from the warrior path.

When she was near the stable, she saw Kunjae petting an all-white horse while Airian was feeding apples to a black horse with white spots. The mane was also black. She approached her brothers. "Lucky," she said, leaning against a beam.

Kunjae just sarcastically smiled at her. Airian proudly stood tall, admiring that he was now a warrior and going on his first mission.

"What's lucky about dying?" asked Kunjae.

"Who said we're going to die?" questioned Airian confusedly.

"We have a better chance in dying than living, hothead." Kunjae pointed out, trying to scare Airian. "What? You think we're not going die at some point in battle?"

"How do you know?" asked Airian angrily.

"We've never stuck a sword into another human before. What if you get nervous and the enemy took advantage of you? What if you accidentally fall on your sword running into battle? What if an arrow hits you in the eye?" Kunjae said.

"Is my pretty brother afraid?" Kiri teased Kunjae.

"Silly little boy, sister. There's no reason for me to be scared. I'm just stating the possible ways of us dying during battle. Don't tell me you believe all warriors live forever?" Kunjae questioned Kiri.

"I can't die!" declared Airian. "I plan to live to tell my grandchildren of my war stories."

"Stories in your eyes. There's a different side to a story," said Kunjae.

"What do you want people to remember you as, Kunjae?" Kiri curiously asked.

"I could care less of what anyone says or remembers me by."

"Everyone is going to remember me as a great warrior. I will lead our army into battle and be victorious. They will tell stories of my victories throughout the land," proclaimed Airian proudly.

"How about your failures? We all fail too," Kunjae asked Airian.

"Stop with your gloomy talk, Kunjae. You only bring my spirit down," angered Airian, annoyed with Kunjae's smart mouth.

Kunjae shrugged his shoulders and continued to pet his horse.

Airian stopped and thought about all the possibilities that he could fail in battle. His confidence was only for show. In truth, he was nervous and afraid. He only knew about being a warrior through his uncle and older sibling stories, not understanding the hardship that comes with being a warrior.

* * *

The night air felt cool and peaceful. Street lights lit the streets of Mersane. The Demon Palace glowed brightly within the night. The great hall of the palace was filled with music. The decoration was bright and magnificent. Plates and goblets were floating in the air. The hall was lit with thousands of floating orb lights near the ceiling. Guests were dancing at the center of the hall while others drink wine till they fell. Laughter and chatters bounced off the stone walls of the hall. Tables were full of food, such as roast duck, braised pork belly, rice, fruits, and many more, a celebration for Airian and Kunjae for becoming warriors.

Aerin sat at the high table with Maenellia by his side. Sitting beside him was Airian and Kunjae. Beside Maenellia sat Kiri, Lehue, and Isa. The other children were all sitting elsewhere.

Airian was admiring the celebration, his eyes glowing as he watched people celebrate for him. Since he was six, he had been waiting for this day. He remembered watching his older siblings' training, seeing the smile they put on their father's face when they made him proud. He wanted to make his father proud like them. He wanted to be the greatest warrior in his clan, dreaming of one day leading his army into victory, coming back home to the shower of cheers from the people of Mersane. But at the back of his mind, he was still nervous.

Kunjae, on the other hand, didn't care much about the celebration. He wondered why these people were celebrating for him, why they laugh at the outcome of death. To him, all he saw was false smiles, only a drink could bring them happiness. They craved money and fame. When they can't make riches, they become depressed, shunned from the world they were born in.

"Look at them, Kunjae," admired Airian. "They're celebrating for us. This is our life now."

"They only celebrate because there is wine for them to drink, whores for them to stick their cocks in. And stupid men to fool," mocked Kunjae with a smile.

"Why can't you just take this moment in?" questioned Airian. "We trained hard to become warriors."

"This is not a moment. Look at these people, look at their smiles. Do you think they'll smile if we fail?" asked Kunjae.

"I don't expect to fail. I'm going to lead our army one day. And become a hero kids will admire to be like," determined Airian.

"No army will follow a hotheaded idiot like you," joked Kunjae.

Airian gripped his fork tightly, wanting to stab Kunjae with it, annoyed with Kunjae's rude jokes and comments. In his mind, he knew his brother was right. How could he lead an army with his anger? He calmed himself, which surprised him. Usually, he was unable to relax when he was angry.

"Airian, that girl is staring at you." Kunjae pointed.

"Who?" asked Airian excitedly.

"Angila Hu-Min," answered Kunjae, pointing directly at Angila.

Angila was sitting across the room alone while her parents danced at the center. She quickly looked away embarrassedly when Kunjae pointed at her. Her hair was long and dark with a golden sunflower pin in her hair. She was the same age as Airian, the daughter of Sasuwej and Inae Hu-Min. Her clan owned all the banks of Mersane. Her mother, Inae was a commoner, using her charisma to steal the eyes of Sasuwej. They were wealthy because of their keen mind for money.

Airian blushed when he turned to look. He liked Angila and wanted her to notice him. Every morning before he trained, he would go to the bakery, hoping to catch Angila buying fresh bread. When he saw her, he did not talk to her, too nervous to say a word. Instead, he chose to admire her from afar. The fresh bread he bought he would give to a random beggar on the street.

Only Kunjae and Ausra knew of his daily morning routine. Kunjae was curious why Airian was waking up early every morning and sneaking out of the palace. So he followed him and discovered his brother's reason. Even though he enjoyed teasing and annoying his siblings, he was good at keeping their secrets. Even if they upset him, he would never use their secret against them. He knew everything; there was nothing that could be hidden from him.

Ausra only caught Airian because he was walking by and ignored it.

"Look at her, sitting alone waiting for someone to offer her a dance," teased Kunjae.

"I can't . . . I'm to—"

"Airian, if you like her, go dance with her," advised Aerin, noticing his son's nervousness. "Don't throw any opportunities away. A life filled with regrets is not a life worth living."

Both brothers looked over to Aerin. They wondered how long he was listening to their conversation.

Airian hesitated; he fought his nervousness and stood from his chair. "You're right, I am a warrior now!" he said proudly. He left the table and marched toward Angila.

Aerin looked over to Kunjae, noticing the look of dissatisfaction on his face. "Are you not pleased with this celebration?"

Kunjae chuckled. "Why should I be pleased about death?"

Aerin leaned over to Kunjae and placed his arms around his shoulders. "You should never question death, son. Only the gods determine who lives and who dies. We only execute their order," he warned. "Enjoy this moment because you never know when the god will order for your death, son. They are sly, sitting on their thrones around a giant glass ball. Watching our every move. Choosing who to serve them next."

"My eyes see everything, Father. They know who's afraid and who's brave. I see the fear in your eyes. Did the gods order for your death?" mocked Kunjae. He stood up and stretched his back. "I need some air. The smell of drunks bothers me."

Aerin watched Kunjae walk away, his hands twitching and veins exposing from his neck and forehead. His face nearly burned, temped to burn the entire palace down with all the people in it.

Maenellia touched his hand to calm him, sensing his anger.

Ever since the disappearance of Iszra, Aerin was never the same, his anger getting the better of him. His thinking was blocked by clouds of failure and his body twitching when angry. His nights were sleepless, adding more stress into his mind. Without Maenellia, he would've killed himself. She was his backbone holding him up to continue life.

"Look at our children, all grown up walking away from us one by one," said Maenellia, trying to calm Aerin. "I wish I can turn back time and raise them differently. They don't deserve to be raised around war and blood."

Aerin took three deep breaths, trying to clear his mind. The warm and smooth hand of Maenellia was calming him. He looked over to her and showed a rare gentle smile. "You're a good mother. Thank you for raising them to be proud. I'm a lucky man to marry such a beautiful woman like you."

"And I'm lucky to marry such a heroic warrior like yourself," said Maenellia, holding Aerin's hand tightly. "Our children will create their own story. When we leave this world, our spirit will watch over them. We will follow them through their struggles and successes. We will cry when they cry and laugh when they laugh."

"Yes, they don't understand me yet. They don't know the world I'm trying to give them. A world they rightfully deserve."

Maenellia looked at each of her children. She looked at Kiri sitting next to her, pouting her face, then at Lehue stuffing his mouth with roast duck. Isa sat next to him, eyeing the ground. She looked over to Ausra sitting with the other dragons and Daysa. He was sucking on a hard lemon candy. She looked at Mani, surrounded by men like ants around a piece of bread crumb, begging her for a dance. She looked nervous and uncomfortable. Then at Chenpu talking with Jen-Song. Indris was nowhere to be found.

Tears appeared from her eyes. "They deserve everything. This world had already taken so much from me." She held Aerin's hand tightly, hoping he would never leave her. "I miss our son. He should be here celebrating with his brothers. Not lost in the world alone. When I look out the window, into the moon, I wonder if he's looking at it too, thinking about his grieving mother. Waiting for the day he returns."

"You are not broken," consoled Aerin. "Telamis is broken. Our son disappeared because of war. He will return to us when I change the land."

Maenellia nodded her head in agreement. "You're right. Look at me, I should be enjoying the celebration, not crying." She cleared the tears from her eyes. Like her children, she didn't believe in Aerin's plan. However, as his wife, she must trust him. She feared losing her children, not wanting Airian and Kunjae to take the warrior path. Even if they wanted to be farmers, she would've supported them. The warrior path only brought pain and sadness.

*   *   *

Ausra sat with the other dragons, Daysa, and Jungy. Next to him was Torshen, sitting with an uncomfortable look on his face, wishing he was somewhere else instead of this celebration. Kaiso was drinking wine till his stomach was filled. Nisu was surveying every young woman to potentially bed with. Jungy was bothering Daysa with many questions about her discoveries and research. Nagen and Leonaris were discussing their plan for their long travel.

"This golden-winged beast, how do you know it's still alive?" Jungy asked Daysa.

Daysa didn't mind explaining her father's research. She found enjoyment when people asked her questions about them. "The golden bird was my father's research. He worked day and night trying to figure out its whereabouts. On his deathbed, he told me of its hiding place. A small village in the southern jungle was destroyed. When my father adventured into the jungle and discovered the burned-down village, with the villagers all covered in ash that turned them into statues, he was able to pick up some drawings on some stone plates. It showed that the tribe has been battling with a bird that resembled Morfis. Sadly, the beast got the better of them."

"Wow, I wish I can help search for this beast," admired Jungy. "Imagine the great Jungy slaying the golden beast."

"So your facts are from drawings of a dead village?" questioned Nagen.

"Stupid," grunted Kaiso.

"Then explain how this village was destroyed, their homes covered in ashes and their bodies now statues?" challenged Daysa

"Your father must be a liar," insulted Nagen. "A giant golden bird can't hide from the eye."

"Nagen, take it easy," urged Jungy.

"My time is being wasted hunting something that no longer exists." Nagen was annoyed. "I'm a warrior, not some beast hunter."

"Are you scared?" teased Daysa. "The great Nagen afraid of a bird."

Nagen chuckled. "Better hope we find your beast." He left the table to head home.

Nisu measured Daysa. He couldn't find the right woman to bed with since some of them he had already slept with while some others looked unpleasant to him. "Do you want to lie with me?" asked Nisu.

Daysa looked disgusted. "I don't sleep with idiots." She cringed.

"We'll be sleeping with each other a lot," said Nisu with a perverted smile.

"This celebration is stupid. Lord Aerin knows better to never glorify unaccomplished feats," said Kaiso disgustedly.

"Come, wild beast, walk with me. Maybe a woman will look past your ugly face and lay with you," joked Nisu.

Kaiso gave Nisu a dirty look. "You talk a lot for someone who squeals over blood," mocked Kaiso.

"Blood is disgusting, just like your ox face," Nisu mocked back.

Daysa stared directly into Torshen's eyes, his face turning red when she awkwardly stared at him. She noticed something different about him. His ice-blue eyes were unique. She remembered her father's notes about people with ice-blue eyes. She opened a small portal and pulled a book out, amazing Jungy but not the dragons. The dragons and Jungy all watched, waiting to see what she would pull out. She pulled out a giant worn-down book and shut her portal. She scrambled through the pages intensely, passing through pages of drawings of a lion with a snake mane, a winged monkey, and even a winged man, trying to find the page she was looking for. She finally stopped at a page and scanned through it. She quickly then looked back up at Torshen and back at the book.

"Hey, what the hell is wrong with you!" questioned Kaiso angrily.

"Where're you from, Torshen?" Daysa asked curiously.

Torshen stood up quickly and immediately left the hall. He never knew where he came from and never knew his parents. He was sold to a merchant right out of the womb. The merchant sold him to an orphanage in Mersane where he was abused. He was saved by Vesak when Sukro and Ausra told him about an orphanage that abused children. Vesak stormed the orphanage and arrested the head mother. She was sentenced to death by Aerin. Torshen went on to live with Vesak.

"Keep your questions to yourself," warned Ausra calmly.

Daysa looked around the table. The dragons all glared at her coldly. She could feel the resentment coming from the dragons, even Jungy who was displeased with her. "I'm sorry, it wasn't my place to ask," she apologized, trying to hide her embarrassment, confused why asking about Torshen's past bothered them.

"Curiosity can get you killed," warned Leonaris. "Don't ever ask us about our lives. Don't think about asking us about our lives."

Daysa sank into her seat and slowly sipped her ale, avoiding eye contact with the others.

*   *   *

Ausra walked out of the hall. The chattering, laughter, and loud music gave him a headache. As well, he didn't enjoy hearing Nisu and Kaiso bickering. He sighed and was relieved that it was finally quiet.

"Ausra," said Indris, leaning against the stone wall on the side.

"I can never be alone," mumbled Ausra.

"I need to speak to you."

"What is it?" questioned Ausra. He walked over to Indris and also leaned on the stone wall, tossing a piece of candy into his mouth.

"What flavor is that?" asked Indris.

"Sour dragon berry," replied Ausra.

"Mind giving me one?" Indris chuckled.

Ausra reached into his pocket and pulled out a piece of candy, handing it to Indris.

Indris unwrapped the candy and tossed it into his mouth. "Hmm, spicy . . ." Indris tasted. "I don't understand why you like these candies."

"Don't waste it," warned Ausra lowly.

Indris smiled; then the smile turned into seriousness. "Father is going into madness, can you see it too?" asked Indris.

"I know."

Indris looked up to the stars. "Can you make a promise for me?"

"Promise?"

"Yes . . . please find Iszra. Only he can save Father," said Indris, as he clutched his fist.

"Why, can't you do it yourself?" questioned Ausra.

Indris stretched his back then turned to Ausra. "I think the gods has other plans for me," he finished, leaving Ausra alone.

Ausra watched his brother walk down the stone steps and into the darkness, not understanding what his brother meant. "Tiresome," he mumbled.

*   *   *

Before Ausra went off on his mission, he decided to walk around the garden alone in the morning after the celebration. The other dragons and Daysa were waiting for him at the city gate. He wanted to get one last moment alone before he embarked on a long journey. With every step he took, the memory of people he killed crossed his mind. Cursed with remembering all the faces of the people that fell by his hand, he wondered if he would ever live a life where he wouldn't have to kill anymore. He felt like a drifting boat waiting to land on a new world, where a new life could be started, his past erased from his memories. But he knew the gods had their way. They never favored his side and only favored themselves. They were selfish for using him to do their blood work.

He spotted Aerin sitting at the gazebo alone, drinking tea. Aerin noticed him and signaled him over. Ausra sighed in annoyance. He didn't want to see his father nor anyone else. "Father," greeted Ausra half-heartedly as he approached.

"Did you get enough sleep?" asked Aerin.

"No," replied Ausra.

Aerin chuckled. "Of course, your journey will be long. I apologize for not having the time to speak with you, son. I have been having a lot on mind." Aerin looked at the floating clouds. "Ausra, do you doubt me?"

"Yes," Ausra answered bluntly.

Aerin chuckled again. "Honest answer. Just know I am building—"

"I plan on leaving the dragons and the clan," declared Ausra calmly.

Aerin was shocked; he didn't expect Ausra to declare his plan to leave and so suddenly. "Why? You know you play a crucial part in our future!"

"It's your future, not mine," said Ausra.

"If you plan to leave, then there will be an order for your head, son. You don't want to suffer the same faith as Vesak now," threatened Aerin, hoping Ausra would change his mind.

"Threatening me won't work. Look at yourself, look at what you created—a monster everyone calls a hero. I'm tired of people calling me a hero when I'm the villain. I took fathers and mothers away from their children, and they glorified me for that. They only know me as an honorable warrior. No one truly knows who I am." Ausra stared into Aerin's eyes coldly, striking fear into the Black Heart. "Look at you, do you know me? I guess I am a caged bird. I know what you wish to become—a king. That's your selfish dream." Ausra turned to leave. "I bid you well, Father."

Ausra's statement stuck a dagger into Aerin's heart. His secret was exposed. He wanted to create another kingdom where he could rule.

Ausra was a crucial part of his dream; now it was gone as his greatest weapon had left him. Aerin had to go back to his planning and find another way to become king.

"Ausra! I will have you killed!" threatened Aerin. "How dare you stop running with the demons! Who do you think you are!" He began to look like a weak, cowardly old man.

Ausra turned back to his father. He lifted his left arm straight toward Aerin and fired a blast of black flames toward him.

Aerin quickly jumped out of the gazebo, nearly caught in Ausra flames. He watched in fear as the black flames burned the gazebo down. A signal of betrayal and a new beginning. Nobody knew what Ausra wanted.

Ausra walked by his mother, who witnessed everything. "Mother."

"You chose the wrong path, Ausra," warned Maenellia.

"Watch over Father and yourself. Pray that we will never come face-to-face on the battlefield," Ausra warned calmly, walking away without taking a final look back to his parents. The smoke from his flames ascended to the heavens, warning the gods of horror to come, telling Vesak that the caged bird was finally free.

Chapter Seven

Kingdom of Enstra

A week passed since Emmillda witnessed the death of the three innocent slaves. She sat by the window staring at the clouds from her bedroom balcony. But it wasn't blue spring sky she saw. She visualized the suffering eyes of the mother, the blood that ran out of her and her two sons' deep wounds, the last breath they took while they stared helplessly for help. Begging the guards to stop stabbing them with their spears till they became voiceless. All Emmillda could do was stand motionless and watch them die, unable to save them from their pain and suffering.

Her nights and mornings were spent alone wandering around the palace, no longer outgoing and talkative like she once was, refusing to talk to anyone, not even to Mai or Lumen. Lumen even offered to practice with a real sword, but she rejected. She would look at him with sorrowful eyes and escape to her bedroom. She couldn't bear to look at a blade because it reminded her of the helpless slaves. Her drive to become a warrior was stolen from her. When Mai baked her favorite cake, unicorn cake, she would push it aside and forget about it, leaving it to rot for flies to feast on and nest their eggs. Alexander even tried to cheer her up but failed. He would bring her butterflies he caught at the Fairy Garden, and she would release them instead of keeping them in a jar on her desk.

The clouds were peaceful as they drifted in the spring sky, floating with the wind unbothered by the conflict below. Emmillda imagined herself on a cloud lying on her back as it took her to a new world. But she knew nothing of the outside world, privileged to be protected by the walls of Fairy Palace.

As of late, she had been watching her father from afar as he danced idiotically alone, twirling around in the hall like he was in his dream of happiness. She once thought of her father as a strong and loved man, never a jester dancing for his king. She felt disgraced when she watched him dance, forcing herself to watch, trying to figure out what he was thinking, hoping that the man she once looked up to was still inside. It saddened her to see her hero weak. She wondered if this was the gods' way of punishment toward her clan for all the bloodshed they had caused. Was this the pain of all the people that suffered in the hands of her clan, finally catching them to bring curse upon the Fairy clan?

A knock on the door startled her, breaking her from her thoughts. She turned around and saw the door slowly creak open. Alexander poked his head into her bedroom. He had a big cheerful smile across his face, hoping that Emmillda would smile back.

"Feeling better yet, Emmillda?" asked Alexander cheerfully.

Emmillda ignored Alexander and turned back to the drifting clouds. She knew Alexander was only trying to cheer her up. However, she couldn't bring herself to accept his kindness. He was the only family member that still cared. For some reason, he still saw hope in the clan. But most of all, he wanted Emmillda to be happy. He couldn't bear to see his little sister upset.

Alexander entered the room and made his way to Emmillda. He opened his hand and created a tiny purple spirit butterfly. He showed it in front of Emmillda's face and let it dance on his palm.

Emmillda loved butterflies ever since they were kids, especially the ones Alexander created out of magic.

When they were young, Alexander would always show Emmillda new magic he learned. She would be fascinated by the magic he demonstrated to her. Even if he wasn't good at magic, she still thought of him as the greatest magic user. At one point, she wished to one day become a magic user just like him. As time continued and stories of warriors inspired her, filling her young mind, slowly her passion in becoming a magic user disappeared into the darkness of her thoughts. Still, Alexander supported her.

Emmillda smiled as the spirit butterfly flew across her face. She tried to hide the smile from Alexander, but he noticed. He also smiled, proud that he finally got her to show a slight grin.

"There's that famous smile." Alexander smiled.

The butterfly danced around Emmillda. She was happy to see the butterfly. Then suddenly, it disappeared into thin air, reminding her that happiness doesn't last forever. She quickly became upset again but didn't want to hurt Alexander's feelings by ignoring him and staying sad. She just couldn't talk to him or Mai and Lumen and thought that it was best if she kept to herself. She appreciated that they were trying to bring her back to her cheerful self.

She felt trapped in a dark cave that echoed millions of lies, hidden in the dark of the cave was the truth, navigating out of the cave of make-believe, trying to listen for the real of Telamis. All her life she lived in a lie shielded by the cold stone walls of fantasy. She was a princess so she had never felt suffering, pain, and hate before. Death she never understood.

Alexander realized that Emmillda was becoming upset again. He sighed deeply. "I'm sorry that I ran off." He was angry at himself for abandoning Emmillda in the throne room. "You were never supposed to see any of that. I made that promise to protect you . . . and failed."

Emmillda felt hurt by Alexander's apology, not knowing that Alexander was also hurting. She felt selfish for crying and not thinking of the people around her. "It's not your fault," she finally said. "None of it is your fault . . . or Mai and Lumen."

Alexander smiled again, happy to hear his sister's voice. "Even though Mother and George are conflicting with each other, we still have each other. Don't blame yourself for those slaves' death." He took in a deep breath. "Father always spoke to me about life and death. Life can be short or it can be long. He always told me. The ones that died earliest won the race. Nevertheless, don't win the race early, explore the field. Don't run, walk. Meet the people that walk along with you, become friends. Die happy with the people we love around us."

"But those slaves. What did they do to deserve to die? They were never running a race," wondered Emmillda sadly.

"Nothing. They did nothing to have their life taken from them." Alexander paused, trying to find words to say to Emmillda. "Living is so cruel. Our destiny is covered in dark." He pointed to Emmillda's heart. "Only you can light the path of darkness to your destiny." He looked to the sky, seeing a purple butterfly fly by. "We live in a cruel world were hate is more common than love." He sighed.

"Why can't we free the horn heads like the other kingdoms? Let them enjoy this world alongside us," suggested Emmillda.

Alexander turned back to Emmillda, showing a nervous smile. Like her, he wanted the horn heads to be free. But his voice wasn't enough to fight for them. "Father tried, but each time, the clans and advisers voted against him," revealed Alexander. "He was a man of righteousness. He never wanted to show that he had power."

"Why won't you become king?" wondered Emmillda. "The people love you. Our men and women love you. They can see that you're working hard to restore our military."

Alexander smiled. "I'm no king," he rejected.

There was a moment of silence between the siblings. Emmillda looked at Alexander and noticed that he was focusing on the clouds, seeing the sadness in his eyes. She wondered what was running through his mind. He was always honorable and caring to his people and her. She felt ashamed to never took the time to know him better.

She turned back to the window. "I'm scared," she admitted fearfully. "While I pretend to be a warrior, I was oblivious to what's in front of me. I thought everything was perfect. Mother and George I never expect to be consumed by hate. I'm scared that everything will fall apart, that everything will never be the same."

Alexander rubbed Emmillda's head, messing her hair up. "As long as I'm alive and breathing, nothing will harm you. It's my duty to protect you as the older brother. I'd lose a leg and arm for you. Whatever scares you, I'll jump in front of it and guard you."

Emmillda jumped from her chair and hugged Alexander cheerfully, pressing her face into his chest, holding him tightly so he could never leave her.

Alexander smiled again and patted the back of Emmillda's head.

"Promise me you'll live forever." The thought of Alexander's death scared Emmillda, never wanting to imagine his death. She'd never want to see Alexander in the same position like the poor horn heads.

Alexander stayed silent. He couldn't promise Emmillda a promise he couldn't keep. He had his own selfish goal, like Facelia and George. His selfish goal was to die a hero. To become the greatest magic user in all four kingdoms. A magic user better than the great Chanfer Fairy—the God King.

*   *   *

George sat comfortably on the dragon bone throne with an evil smirk, watching his mad father dance at the center of the hall, no longer embarrassed by his father's madness. He needed Euren to disappear so he can be king. All his fear and doubts went away when he sat on the throne. It gave him the feeling of power. He thought that it was meant for him to be sitting on the throne. No one was going to stop him from being king. But yet Facelia was still in his way.

Ever since he was a kid, he always wanted to be king. He had no aspiration of fighting on the battlefield. Instead of training to become a magic user, he elected to spend most of his days at the palace library reading books of wars and great thinkers, reading how conflicts can be settled with words instead of blood and war. He learned that all great leaders can speak into the minds of their people. Their words gave them their followers. Whatever they say controls the mind of the followers. So each night before he sleeps he pretends to make a speech. Imagining people cheering as he delivered and finished each sentence.

He enjoys reading about Chanfer Fairy. He helped ended the Dru Dynasty and carved way for the four kingdoms of Telamis, four hundred years ago. He was the leader that everyone feared and loved. A statue of him sat in front of Fairy Palace with his famous sword, Night. He was the light to his allies and the darkness to his enemies. No man or woman can escape the great magic he created called Black Butterflies. To this day, no one can figure out how to use the magic.

Jensu arrived beside the throne, smirking as he watched Euren dance like a fool. In his mind were evil plans to ruin the Fairy clan. Throughout the land, he and his brother were known as the snake brothers. They bounced from kingdom to kingdom finding lords to serve so they could gain power and recognition to finally landing in the service of the Fairy clan.

Jensu and Edsu were both born poor in a small village in the northern kingdom. Life was unfair for them. Their father was murdered in front of them when Jensu was six and Edsu was seven, leaving their mother alone to watch over them. They both witnessed their mother going mad as time went by, seeing her talking to people that wasn't there. She was heartbroken that her love was murdered and left them with no money. When the brothers were thirteen and fourteen, they left their mother, swearing an oath to never be poor again.

"My prince, your dear mother is trying to get the clans to side with her," reported Jensu slyly.

George chuckled, putting his forehead on the palm of his hand and mockingly shaking his head. "Mother will never learn," he said disappointedly. "Does she not know I'm the heir to the throne?" He slammed his fist on the armrest of the throne.

"She's a Po, my lord," reminded Jensu.

"I'm afraid my mother doesn't understand the consequences of treason." He looked over to his dancing father. "Why can't you be gone? Just disappear and let me be king already!" George yelled.

Jensu smirked, enjoying George's display of rage. "My prince, you need to stay calm. Showing anger will only weaken you," he advised.

"How can I stay calm when my own parents are in the way of my dream?" questioned George angrily.

"Every great king always stays calm when they're in the fire," calmed Jensu. "They stay patient, waiting to strike when the moment presents itself."

"So when do I strike? When do I become king? I don't want to pretend anymore."

"The moment will unfold itself, my prince. Let the pieces come together first," advised Jensu. "Right now, your mother is trying to steal the pieces. You must guard them from her."

George had to figure a way to get rid of Facelia. She was tugging him away from the throne so she can sit on it herself. The throne was rightfully his. There was no reason for her to shield him from it. She was the iron gate blocking his way to immorality.

The great door opened, and entered Alexander with two guards following him, storming his way toward his brother, passing by his dancing father without a single peek, his face burning with rage. His hands were clutched together like he was going to punch someone. He stood in front of his brother with a cold and resentful look.

"Remove my father!" ordered Alexander to the guards, keeping a strong stare on George.

George wasn't intimidated by his brother. He found it amusing seeing Alexander angry. "Alexander," he greeted mockingly.

"Stop with your games!" shot Alexander.

"Brothers shouldn't—"

"Silence, Snake!" Alexander violently cut off Jensu.

Jensu smiled. He gently bowed his head to George and made his way to the great door. Before he left, he stopped beside Alexander, showing his venomous eyes to him. "Don't let the snake catch you, my prince," he whispered to Alexander mockingly then heading to the door, licking his lips like a snake eyeing its prey.

Alexander paid no attention to Jensu's threatening words, continuing to have his eyes fixed on George. "What is wrong with you?" questioned Alexander.

"Nothing is wrong with me, brother," replied George with a sarcastic smile.

"Then get off that throne!" demanded Alexander. "Don't sit on it watching our father dance like a fool."

George laughed, degrading Alexander's demand. "You're a fool like Mother and Emmillda," he insulted. "Do you see Father? Do think he's still the man he once was?" He chuckled lightly, leaning back into the throne. "It's my turn now. It was always my dream to become king. You should've known that. Don't try to stop me from ruling this kingdom now!" Every inch in George's body began to fill with rage. "Every day I watched shamefully at our father dancing like a fool while you try reviving our dying army and Emmillda playing soldier. I'm the one that stays by Father. Where were the two of you!" he yelled nearly off the throne. "While I watched over him, I came to a realization—he's no longer our father. Our father died two years ago!"

"I guess you can't be saved," Alexander said disappointedly, shaking his head.

"It's not me that needs saving, Alexander. It's you . . . It's everyone in this kingdom. I'll be the savor to this kingdom."

"Save yourself first, George. No one will follow you. Mother may have her wicked ways, but I agree with Mother on one thing. You're weak just like those snake brothers. They whisper lies in your ears, controlling you like their puppet," warned Alexander.

"If you have a problem with me being king, then leave the west. Nothing will stop me. I'm willing to kill my own blood for this dragon throne!" declared George.

Alexander looked disappointed. He couldn't bring his brother back from his pretend belief. He felt like the never-ending rain of spring was going to flood Enstra, waiting to rain years of blood. He remembered as a kid admiring his brother's perfection. Now all he saw was George's downfall. The snakes lurking behind were waiting for the moment to strike their prey.

He turned to leave the hall. Before he took a step, he had one more thought in mind to say to George. "When you talk of being king as a child, I laughed. Father knew you were not fit to be king." He stared into his palm and created a purple spirit butterfly, letting it dance on his palm. "How can you rule when you can't master the simple parts of fairy magic? Sit on the throne all you want, but as long as I'm alive, you will never be called king!" said Alexander with confidence. He started to walk away.

"Stupid!" yelled George, his voice trembling in fear. "You think you can be king? You better wish Father stays alive because evil is creeping behind you. Turn around, stupid coward. I demand you to turn around and apologize to me!"

Alexander ignored his brother. The throne was his. Before, his father had used the forbidden fairy magic to see the light and darkness of the future. They spoke; Euren wanted him to be the heir to the throne. He held his father's sealed letter close to him so that when the day comes and his mother and brother fight for the throne, he'll hand the letter to the council and they will see that he was to be the king of Enstra.

* * *

Alexander decided to roam the second level of the city to clear his cluttering mind, the white stone street crowded on an afternoon day, the people wide awake going through their daily lives. He passed by merchants selling their goods on the street. On the side of the crowed street, people huddled around a man standing on a wooden crate as he preached his wild beliefs.

The crowd around the man laughed at him as he preached while some onlookers listened, fascinated by the charismatic beliefs and ideas. Alexander stopped to listen to the man, wondering if this man was mad. The man's eyes were pale and sleepless, his skin dead and his teeth yellow with some brown and chipped. He talked about the gods and their anger, telling everyone standing below him that he was a messenger for the gods.

"We will soon suffer again!" preached the man. "The gods will punish us again with war. We will all die." He pointed to the sky. "They're angry at us. We have sinned!"

The people looked at each other and laughed. They all thought he was just another crazy man trying to preach about his crazy imagination while others wondered if the man was speaking the truth. Alexander, on the other hand, only listened, not thinking much of the man's belief, only fascinated with the imagination that the man has. He didn't know what to make out of the man's words. This man was able to bring people around him and forced them to listen to him. Even if they thought he was an idiot with a crazy imagination, he wondered if he could make people listen to him like this man, disappointed with himself that he couldn't keep his high-ranked warriors and magic users to stay with his clan.

"I have seen the future," announced the man again. "I saw everything, there will be blood. Blood that will turn into an ocean that will flood the land of Telamis. The great beast will fly over the sky while we lay dead! Demons of the Forest of Despair will rule this land again!" The man spread his arms wide. "Follow me and I'll bring you all to sanctuary. I will protect all of you from the terror of war to come. Let these clans fight their war. We are not their subjects. We shall never kneel to an idiot king! We shall never worship an idiot king!"

The laughter slowly died, everyone in the crowd now listening closely; even the ones passing by stopped to listen. The man said something that intrigued them. They were common people with no story to their name. They lived their life routinely with no goals for the future, but only to survive day by day. Alexander looked around and saw hate and abandonment over their faces. They all knew that Euren used the forbidden magic, leaving them with no leader to follow.

Alexander clutched his fist tightly and continued his walk, upset that the man insulted his father. But was the man right? he thought. History had shown that kings and queens had failed to protect their people. It was a never-ending cycle of failure. His perspective of the world was changing slowly. These people saw life through a different glass ball while he saw life as a perfect lie. He was the one living in a false reality of banquets and honors while the common people were sweating and suffering to provide and feed their families. Fathers watched their children starve while mothers tried to protect them from the harsh reality.

As he continued to wander, he found himself in the third level of the city, making his way to the dangerous street of the level, Dagger Street. Drunks lay on the ground in their own vomit. Men huddled as they watched hatefully at Alexander. They hated the sight of any clan members. Especially royal ones. Alexander was not fazed by the cold stares. But it was unsafe for him to walk alone in the third level. If they attacked, then royal guards would raid through Dagger Street and kill every man and woman, forcing their children to live in an orphanage.

Alexander spotted the man that was preaching on the side of the street before. He was peeing on the side of a broken-down wooden house.

"Hey!" called Alexander, wanting to expose the man in his lies.

The man turned around and showed a cricket smile, showing his yellow decaying teeth. Pulling his pants back up and wiping his hands on his pants.

"Can I help you, my prince?" asked the man, without bowing his head.

"Why do you talk of lies?" questioned Alexander.

The man showed an evil smile. "I only speak the truth, my prince."

Alexander grabbed the man's shirt collar and held him against the wall. "What truth do you speak by speaking ill of my father!" angered Alexander. Not wanting to hurt the man, his instinct forced him to threaten the man. "My father did everything he can to protect this kingdom. And you . . . you just talk of lies."

"Look around, my prince," said the man calmly, not fazed by Alexander.

Alexander looked around and saw that all the forgotten people were watching. Some men had clubs or daggers in their hands while the women led their children back into their home to avoid seeing the bloody murder of the prince.

"You best let me go, my prince," warned the man.

Alexander slowly released his hold on the man's collar, shocked that these people were willing to risk their lives for his death.

"You see, my prince, these people are tired," said the man. "They don't want to live for the king anymore. They don't fear death anymore. We're our known protection."

"Why do these people trust you?" asked the confused Alexander.

"They're tired of lies. I will show them the truth of this world," said the man. "History only talks about the triumphs of murders, but what about the man that provided the murderer food? What about the women that nursed their wounds?"

Alexander was speechless. This man was right. Life was unfair to the common people. They were the pillar that held Telamis. Yet as the pillar falls, it will be replaced with another one, forgotten in the mix of history.

"Watch for the snakes creeping behind you, Alexander." The man smirked, walking away.

Alexander's eyes opened wide. He knew who was behind in putting hate in the common people's heads. It was the doing of Wisefool's brothers. He stood frozen and angry. Those two brothers were slowly making their way to the throne, dividing his family, trying to force them to hate each other. He sensed that it was too late to change the minds of the people.

* * *

Facelia stood out on her balcony sipping jasmine tea from her teacup, gazing across the city from the palace and imagining herself sitting on the dragon bone throne. She wanted to rule and have people bend their knees to her, bow their heads to her when she walked by. She wanted her enemies to fear her. But a wall blocked her from her dream. To break the wall, she had to get rid of the Wisefool brothers.

She was always ambitious. Since she was a little girl, she always had to be ahead of her brothers and cousins. Her father had taught her to never settle for anything less, to always rise and win. Their clan saying was, "A Po always laughs last." They were the most hated clan in the west. Other clans in the west couldn't trust them and considered them to be egotistic and heartless. During the lost generation war, they refused to help fight the war, rather hiding behind their castle walls while blood poured on the soil of Telamis.

Manji appeared behind Facelia. "My queen, the other clans refuse to help our cause," reported Manji.

Facelia showed anger on her face. None of the clans wanted to side with her. Some of them laughed and didn't care to send a letter back to her while others didn't want to get involved with the royal conflict.

"They're all cowards!" insulted Facelia furiously. "They'd rather follow a puppet than me?" She questioned the clan of the west to herself, wondering why they would follow someone like her son, who was weak and clueless about the land. She wanted answers but didn't know where to find them. She poured her tea down from her balcony and watched it slowly spill to the ground. She was disgusted and betrayed by the western clans.

"What shall we do, my queen?" asked Manji.

"Challenge my son for the throne, of course. I don't need those weakling clans' help."

Manji nodded her head. "I will fight for you, my queen."

Facelia looked across the horizon, overseeing the city. "It's a shame this city will suffer for my dream," said Facelia to herself with no emotions. "They yet again will witness death and sorrow."

"When you take the throne, they will all understand," said Manji. "They will bow to you and forget the death and sorrow that comes with your dream, my queen."

"You're right, Manji. They will understand. I will sit on the dragon bone throne and bring new order to this kingdom. No man or woman shall be poor. No child shall starve. One last suffering and then we all will meet true peace."

Facelia grinned as she thought about the world she wanted to build. Her idea was at a good place, but her heart was dark. She didn't care for the common people nor her idea. She was a Po; they only cared for themselves.

A knock on the door broke Facelia out of her wonderful kingdom. Both she and Manji turned to the door.

"My queen, Prince George waits for you at the great hall," said the guard behind the wooden closed door.

Facelia turned back around and grinned. "The boy wishes to speak to me," she said.

"Do you want me by your side, my queen?" asked Manji.

"Yes. Let him see the face of his enemies."

*   *   *

George sat on the dragon bone throne, twirling a rolled letter around his fingers. He looked proud sitting on the throne and excited from the news he read written on the letter. Beside him were Edsu and Jensu, both with a snakelike grin across their face.

"My mother is playing her own game," said George. "She tires me with her foolishness, planning in the shadows against me." He crushed the paper in his palm. "The clans have chosen their side. What does she have now? Manji? Ha, what can she do but be my mother dog!"

"My lord, you ought to make her pay for treason," suggested Edsu.

"Of course, I'll make her pay!" said George sharply. "But first, I must get rid of my father."

"May I suggest the Island of Pain, my prince?" suggested Jensu.

The Island of Pain sat on the Silent Sea and was guarded tightly by the tiger warriors, warriors with no alliance to any kingdom or clans. They were trained to kill anybody that dared to come close to the island. These were unwanted babies that were sent to the island then trained and honed to be heartless and brutal. The island jailed two of the land's most dangerous criminals, Yorensaga Ichica, the Thumb Warrior. He had traveled the realm murdering high and small clan members during the night, taking their thumbs wearing it around his neck as a trophy. The second criminal was Horse the Mage, a mysterious man that tried to summon the dead to start an uprising.

George thought about the idea. No one would dare go to the Island of Pain. Yorensaga was no man to challenge with. With Horse the Mage, magic was too powerful. Not even the Seven Demon Dragons would dare go to the island. And the tiger warriors themselves were strong. "That island is perfect. It holds so many secrets. It wouldn't trouble them to hold another." George licked his lip, sensing his time to being king was nearing.

"Shall I send a letter to the warden?" asked Jensu.

"Yes, send the letter. I want my father gone!" demanded George. "The walls that block me from this throne will crumble into pieces."

"How about your siblings," asked Edsu, "especially Alexander? The military officials will side with him if he rebels."

"I'm not afraid of my siblings," answered George confidently. "They're just insects waiting to be stepped on."

The great hall door opened, and entered Facelia, followed by Manji. She was confident entering the hall. When she looked over to see who was standing beside her son, her look became disgusted, annoyed at seeing the Wisefool brothers.

"Well, my mother and her loyal bitch has finally arrived," mocked George to Facelia.

"Watch your mouth, boy!" warned Facelia. She gave each Wisefool brother a disdainful look. "I see that those vermin brothers are still holding a string to your back."

"I am nobody's puppet!" angered George.

Facelia mockingly smiled. "Why did you call for me?" She looked around the hall. "I'm surprised no slaves are begging for their life."

George collected himself before he answered his mother. "I know what you're trying to do," he said. "It's sad that none of the clans are willing to join you. Why would they? You're a Po, you have no claim to the throne, and yet you still plan behind your son's back." He was listing his mother's weak claim to the throne. "How do you call yourself a mother? Or a wife? Do you even care for your father anymore? How about your children? I think I did a number to Emmillda's head." He grinned at his mother. "Did you know Alexander came bursting in here shouting at me, pretending to be heroic?" He chuckled lightly and rolled the letter into a ball and tossed it before Facelia's feet in a sign of disrespect. "You're a failure as mother, Facelia. Let me hit you with reality so you can understand. All three of you are nothing to me. When I'm king, none of you will share this palace with me. I'll make sure you all walk this kingdom as peasants and beggars."

Facelia just laughed, taking George's threat as a tease. "We don't want blood to spill, my dear George," she warned. "I always have the last laugh, stupid boy." She turned to leave with Manji.

George was baffled by his mother's reaction. "Don't you walk away from your king!" shouted George.

Facelia paused. "You're no king, George." She continued to walk away, leaving George in a fit of rage.

Hiding behind the throne, listening from the entranceway, was Emmillda. She came to the hall to see her father dance. But instead, she stumbled upon her mother and brother threatening each other. Her heart swelled as she listened to them wanting to pour blood over the kingdom. Her father had worked hard to clean the blood that covered the soil of the western kingdom. All that cleaning was done for nothing. All for two selfish people hungering for power. She leaned her back against the wall and slowly slid to the ground, crying in her palm, counting till the days of darkness.

Chapter Eight

Kingdom of Summan

Benavis sat still on his bed staring blankly at the stone wall. As of late, he had been haunted by the shadow figure with six arms in his nightmares. The nightmares never changed—running away in a mysterious forest from the shadow figures then seeing his father, only to wake up facing the six-arm shadow figure. Then to only realizing it was only a nightmare.

It felt like the figure had an obsession with him, stalking from a distance in the shadows. He tried to put the puzzle together what the shadow figure was, afraid and wanting to tell someone his nightmare. But he couldn't find the strength to leave his room. At the same time, he didn't want anyone to think he was descending into madness. Because of the nightmare, he hadn't stepped out of his room, even if he was starving for food.

He buried his face in the palm of his hand and started to sob, tired of the constant fear of his own nightmare that lingered in his sleep. He wished for his memories to be erased so he could no longer be reminded of the moment his father was murdered before him, frustrated that those masked figures allowed him to live with coward guilt.

Suddenly, he began to hear voices mumbling around his room. It sounded demonic and evil, bouncing off the walls and to his ears. He looked around the room, eyes darting at each corner, trying to figure out where the voices were coming from. He placed both of his hands on his head and grabbed his hair like a madman, pulling and twisting the roots of his dark hair as hard as he could. His eyes opened like a possessed man, and he rocked back and forth on his bed while the voices continued to taunt him. His head felt like it was getting squeezed, and his breath was fading out of him.

The voices were demoralizing him. He wanted someone to open his door and save him from the voices. There was something in the room that wanted him, waiting to strike when he would finally broke.

The voices stopped when the door flew open. Giovanis kicked the door open with worry written on his face. Benavis peeked as the voices faded away.

"I am you . . .," said a fading mysterious voice. They were the only words that Benavis could hear clearly.

"What's wrong?" asked Giovanis with concern in his voice.

Benavis looked at Giovanis with sorrowful eyes, finally feeling the urge to talk to his brother. He wanted to tell Giovanis everything—what he saw when his father died and the nightmare he had been experiencing. He wanted to tell him that he was afraid. "I'm sorry," he mumbled.

Giovanis was shocked, not expecting an apology from Benavis. A slight smile showed across his face. Hearing Benavis's apology eased his concern. "Why are you apologizing?" asked Giovanis kindly.

"You save me," mumbled Benavis nervously.

"I saved you?" Giovanis looked confused, wondering how he saved Benavis.

For weeks, he had waited outside Benavis's bedroom, worrying for the well-being of his brother. He refused to eat if Benavis was not sitting at the table with him. He skipped his kingly duty so he could only focus on Benavis. As the oldest brother, he felt obligated to watch over his siblings. Without their parents, he was his siblings' protector. It was the only way he knew how to make his parents proud as they watched down from the heavens.

"I'm ready to talk," mumbled Benavis again.

Giovanis's eyes opened wide; he was surprised and ready to hear his brother. "I must find Ocrist!" he said excitedly.

"No!" stopped Benavis. He didn't want to tell anybody else but his brother. "Only you . . . I will only talk to you."

Giovanis saw that the tears filled Benavis's eyes. He smiled and nodded in acceptance. "Fine." He grabbed a chair from the wooden desk and sat beside Benavis's bed.

Benavis kept his eyes gazed at the far wall across the room, gulping twice with second thoughts if he wanted to tell his brother what he had witnessed, his mind replaying the image of their father's death once again. The image of agony and fear on their father's eyes needed to be erased from his mind. "It was my fault that Father died. If I'd never asked him to take me out the city wall, he would still be alive," he confessed.

"Don't blame yourself for your father's death," consoled Giovanis. "There was nothing you could do to save him."

"I was a coward!" angered Benavis, gripping his blanket tightly. "I wish I could've saved him. I sat on the hot sand and watched Father die. He was begging for his life . . . I saw it in his eyes." He paused, realizing how much disappointment he had toward their father. "They were right. Father is weak."

"Don't call our father weak, Benavis!" defended Giovanis. "He worked hard keeping this kingdom safe."

"What, by trying to make these people happy? They don't appreciate anything but themselves!" argued Benavis.

Giovanis understood his brother's anger toward the people of the south. He too was angry but understood why the people didn't accept their father.

Geolana was never supposed to be king. That honor was supposed to be their uncle, Eltis.

Eltis was loved by the southern people, a war hero in the eyes of children and a protector to the kingdom. Known as the Warrior King throughout the land, warriors from all over the land knew of his feats and talents. They respected him and only saw good in him. Sadly, he was only able to sit on the throne for a year. His excellence and potential were taken away by a sip of a venomous wine.

The throne was then given to his second brother, Yanglous. Also loved by the people of the southern kingdom, but unlike his older brother, he was no warrior. Yanglous was intelligent and ambitious. Instead of ruling the kingdom with an iron fist, he chose to rule with knowledge and wisdom. He brought new ideas that changed the south. His words brought peace and alliance with enemies. When he was assassinated, the kingdom began to slowly fall apart.

Both brothers died with no heir to the throne. In turn, the throne was given to Geolana, the third brother. No one cared or shed tears when Geolana died. The kingdom saw him as a king incapable of ruling.

"Even though our father was weak," said Giovanis, "he was never corrupted. He always decided with his heart. Remember what Mother said—'Our heart can never lie to us.'"

"My heart made me into a coward," denied Benavis lowly. "What I saw happen to Father can never leave my thoughts. Every day I try and try to forget, but it keeps reappearing."

"Tell me what happened, Benavis," urged Giovanis. "I want to know what you witnessed. Then we can avenge our father's death."

Benavis was hesitant to tell his brother, his eyes lost as he stared at his blue blanket with golden roses stitched into it, remembering clearly from the morning to the moment his father was killed. "I woke up that morning wanting to see outside the city walls," he said like he was in a trance. "Father reluctantly said yes, so we snuck out of the kingdom with two horses and no guards. He had a big smile on his face like a child. I felt free once I stepped out of the city . . . Father was free too. Just a son and father enjoying the warm air of the south." He gulped.

"We were far from the kingdom, but Father didn't care that guards and advisers will worry. He didn't care that everyone was going to run around the kingdom searching for him. He asked me if I enjoyed life and what my dream was. But before I could answer, the ground began to shake. The horses were terrified and knocked us off. I landed on my head, then looked up to six masked figures wearing black cloaks surrounding us. They were wearing golden masks with three eyes, the third on the forehead of the mask standing straight up." He stopped because fear was choking him. He didn't want to talk about it anymore. Tears filled his eyes and blurred his vision.

"Don't stop!" begged Giovanis. "You must find the strength to fight your fears, Benavis."

Benavis turned to Giovanis and nodded. He took a big gulp and cleared the tears from his eyes. "They all had golden daggers in their hands," he continued. "I blinked once, and everything around me felt slow. They were moving fast toward father with their daggers, cutting him. He fell to his knees. All six surrounded him and just stared at him like he was . . . a dying animal. Father begged and begged, pleading and asking for them to spare his life and to forgive any evil he has done. But what evil did Father cause? He was a good man. Those six monsters were the ones that are evil. They made a king beg for his life. One of them approached Father and stuck a dagger into his heart, then another cut his head off." He choked. "I tried to yell . . . Nothing came out." Benavis stopped again to get ahold of himself.

He remembered the blood leaking from the punctured holes on his father's body. He remembered the golden sand turning to red. "He lay in his blood as his head rolled to the ground," he remembered. "It was humiliating . . . disgusting. They never looked at me once. After they finished with Father, they all turned into crows and flew away from the carnage they caused. That's all I remember." Benavis looked disturbed; it didn't feel right telling his brother of how their father was killed, feeling like something was wrong.

Giovanis fumed over the way his father was killed, wishing that he was the one that was with his father instead of Benavis. He gripped his pants tightly and kindly smiled at Benavis. "We will find these monsters and make them pay for what they'd done." He stood and headed toward the door, but stopped before he left the room.

"I need you to get well and rule this kingdom by my side, Benavis. It's what Father wanted. The Sanila clan is the hand of justice!" he declared confidently, then leaving Benavis alone in his room.

Benavis just sat on his bed. His brother was clueless; there was no way those monsters could be stopped. He felt guilty because he wasn't truthful to his brother. There was one missing piece to the story. Five crows flew away from the city, but one flew toward the city.

"I am you . . .," whispered a fading voice around Benavis.

Benavis wanted to escape the constant enemy in himself, a battle he couldn't win, with death being the only choice. He wanted to be saved, but there was no voice calling for him. The rope of life was turning into a single thread, waiting to snap into a lightless life.

*　　*　　*

Recruits trained on the training grounds of the summer barracks. Some were training with spears while others trained with swords. Archers practiced their aim at wooden targets. Some were training in hand-to-hand combat. Magic users were mastering their energy blast.

Standing near the barrel of water was Rain and Ba-Ben, taking a quick rest. Rain had been up since the break of dawn training, and still, he wasn't tired. He and Ba-Ben were sparring with each other, with him taking the upper hand on each spar.

"I can't get the princess out of my mind," drooled Ba-Ben. "She will lie with me soon."

Rain gave Ba-Ben a side eye, remembering what his grandfather told them. "Stay away from the princess. Our only purpose is to serve them." At the same time, he was taken by her beauty, still struck by her beauty, her eyes staring back at his.

Ba-Ben slapped Rain in the back aggressively. "Enjoy life a bit, Rain. Look, we're living the perfect life here. When will we go into war again? Just enjoy this moment of our life until we get old and die."

"Hey!" yelled Thunder Tiger-Foot. "Why are you two standing around!"

Rain fixed himself and returned to his training. Ba-Ben smirked at Thunder and walked away. He hated being told what to do. In his mind, the world should revolve around him. He was the controller of his destiny. Whatever he wanted he got, and no one stood in his way.

"Get to training, dogs!" demanded Thunder, angry that Ba-Ben was disrespecting him in front of the other recruits.

"Or what? You'll throw me into the jailhouse?" challenged Ba-Ben, taking in the moment as the other recruits had their attention on him. It gave him a sense of enjoyment as the focus was on him. "Do something about it, old man!" he provoked Thunder.

Thunder's face turned red with rage, and veins quickly appeared on his forehead and neck. Then a spark of lightning appeared around his hand. He was ready to send a bolt of lightning to Ba-Ben, when Eddis Dyu, the adopted son of Ocrist, stopped him.

Eddis was in his early twenties; he had a boyish look with short dark hair. He placed his hand on Thunder's shoulders in an attempt to stop him. "Commander, it's not wise to show your weakness around the recruits," calmed Eddis with a soothing smile.

The lightning around Thunder's hand disappeared. He took two deep breaths and shot Ba-Ben a warning look. Then turning around to leave, he said, "All of you, continue your training! Remember, we are the south, we bleed for the south, we protect the south with our steel and iron. We die to feast with the gods and our ancestors. We honor the code of loyalty—"

"Fuck loyalty!" interrupted Ba-Ben boldly. His eyes opened wide with the urge to fight overcoming him, eyes like a pervert seeing a naked woman for the first time. "I only fight for myself!"

Rain shook his head in disappointment, wishing Ba-Ben would keep his mouth shut. He was their grandfather's least-favorite grandson.

Suddenly, in the blink of an eye, Eddis appeared in front of Ba-Ben in a low stance, his three fingers pointing directly at Ba-Ben's belly button. Ba-Ben was shocked; he never saw Eddis leaving his position. Rain was also shocked and noticed that Eddis was going to hurt his cousin.

Eddis quickly stabbed Ba-Ben two times in his stomach with his three fingers. Ba-Ben fell to the ground clutching his stomach in pain, yelling in agony and feeling like he was stabbed by a sharp dagger. Eddis then kicked Ba-Ben in the face and placed his foot on the back of the head, digging Ba-Ben's face into the dirt in a sign of disrespect and superiority.

"I don't care for your name," said Eddis in a serious tone. "Don't ever disrespect our commander again," he warned Ba-Ben.

The recruits watching all knew to never get on Eddis's bad side since he was the strongest warrior in the southern kingdom. No man or woman dared to cross his path. His boyish features were deceiving; he was cold-blooded and calculated.

He took his foot off Ba-Ben's head. "Now do as you're told and continue your training!" he ordered. "And if any of you dare to disrespect your superior, I will not hesitate to kill you!" he warned the other recruits watching.

Rain was shocked; he couldn't move a single muscle in his body. He wanted to save his cousin, but the voices in his head stopped him. He wondered if this is what his clan had come to, to appear weak in front of the royal clan while they take the beating. He was angry at his grandfather for bowing so easily to the royal clan. It felt like a slap to the face to their ancestors, his father, and uncles.

Ba-Ben slowly stood back up in pain, dirt smeared over one cheek and arms over his stomach and clenching his teeth together. Rage was written all over his face like a starving lion that hadn't eaten in days.

Eddis turned around to Ba-Ben, amused that Ba-Ben still had pride left. "Oh, I see that you're stupid. Just like your clan—stupid and nothing," he insulted calmly.

"You hit like a bitch!" Ba-Ben taunted and stupidly charged at Eddis with his fist in the air.

Eddis three-finger stabbed Ba-Ben in the throat. Ba-Ben dropped to the ground, choking and wincing on the dirt. The healers quickly came to check on him. Eddis scoffed and walked away from the scene.

"Wait!" shouted a voice.

Eddis was irked and tired by the disrespect.

Standing in front of Rain with the back toward him, standing tall and honorable, was Uesenga. Rain couldn't believe that Uesenga would want to say something. Out of all the Bu cousins, Uesenga was the most talented fighter. He was a perfectionist and obedient.

"I can't let you beat my cousin without repercussions," cheerfully warned Uesenga.

Eddis smirked; he didn't care to turn to look at Uesenga. "Your cousin is a fool. Beating him was the only way for him to know his place."

"Turn around and fight me!" challenged Uesenga with a confident smile.

Eddis continued walking; he walked by Thunder and nodded his head. Thunder looked over to Uesenga and admired the smile. He saw something special in Uesenga, a warrior of a new era. He then looked over to Rain, who was frozen, then to Ba-Ben, a young man whose ego would be his downfall.

Both Eddis and Thunder walked around the Summer Barrack, making sure that all the men and women were doing their jobs. Lately, there had been many new recruitments. The dorms were getting crowded. These recruits were forced to join the army. Once a young man turned fourteen, they were sworn into the army. The young women had the choice to serve the army or serve as a healer. Even the horn head people were sworn into the army.

All this was putting a lot on Thunder's plate. He hasn't slept in days because of the constant worry of these young recruits, his energy gradually draining out of him. Ever since the death of the weak king, the demand for more soldiers became a major necessity.

"My father told me we're preparing for the unexpected," said Eddis. "I guess peace can't last forever." He shrugged.

"I need a drink," said Thunder. "These recruits are a headache. Half of them can't lift a sword off the ground."

"That's why we train them, Commander."

"Did you not see, none of them wants to be warriors or magic users," complained Thunder. "In my day, we had that hunger to be better than the person standing in front of us. There was no comfort and stability for the top spot. Every day, someone is proving themselves. Look at these recruits, they're scared. How am I supposed to lead a bunch of weak little . . ." He looked over the barrels filled with water and saw someone sitting beside it sleeping. "Hey, you!" he called angrily. "Why are you sleeping around!"

The young man calmly woke up from his sleep and looked over to Thunder. The young man was Yorsenga, the oldest of the Bu cousins. He was carefree and didn't like getting into conflicts. "I'm tired," he shouted back at Thunder lazily. Eddis laughed as Thunder's temper showed, and again his face turned red.

"Commander, indeed the recruits are useless and talentless, but they are special." Eddis laughed.

*　*　*

Benavis stood alone in the clan's crypt, staring at the statue of Geolana, praying to Shenva, hoping by chance his father would come back to life. The whispers continued to echo in his room. The only way to silence the voices was to leave his bedroom. Now he found himself staring at his father's statue, remembering all the good times and bad times. The stone face of Geolana resembled the face of a saddened man. Unlike the other kings, Geolana wasn't wearing a crown. The sculptor lied that he forgot to add the crown to the statue.

"Father, remember when you told me to always follow my dream?" said Benavis to his father's statue. "Well, I can't follow a dream when a nightmare is chasing me." He chuckled lightly. "Everything you told me . . . was it all a lie? I can't survive this world when I'm weak just like you!" His eyes filled with tears while emotions of anger and sadness battled within him.

He turned to leave the crypt, declaring that he had no future. What everyone said about his father was true—a weak and unruly king. The only way he could survive this cruel world was to be the nightmare that hunts dreams. It was the only way he could save himself.

Leaving the crypt and roaming the palace, thinking to himself how he could accept his nightmare, suddenly, his back started to feel cold. The hair on his body began to stand, feeling that something dark was around him. His leg felt like it was sinking to the ground through a black hole.

He looked around to see if anyone was around and saw no one. He wasn't scared anymore; instead, he was angry and annoyed. He wanted to know what was bothering him. Why did it choose him?

Suddenly, the whispers returned, echoing through the corridor as Benavis looked around with confusion and madness. There was more than one voice bouncing off the stone walls, all speaking over each other trying to let out what they want to say. It was like the ghost of Summer Palace all meeting each other for the first time.

"Stop!" yelled Benavis, pleading for the whispers to stop. The voices were taking over his life. What did that masked figure do to him? He wondered if this was a curse. He slapped his hands on his forehead and started clutching on to his hair. "Just leave me alone!" he cried. "Please." He fell to the ground on his butt and slid his way to the wall, leaning his back on it with terror across his face.

"I am you . . .," whispered a mysterious voice as it faded into the air.

Benavis was distraught; he didn't understand what was going on but could feel that there were others in him, all trying to escape their cage and rule his body. He smirked like he was a new person; then suddenly, he was sad again. A dark cloud of evilness hovered over him, slowly covering the last light of good that fought to shine over him.

Hiding on the other side of the corridor with a vile smile was Bente, the sly adviser. He noticed something wrong with Benavis and enjoyed the insanity that was taking over Benavis. He didn't care for anyone but himself. Seeing Benavis going mad lit an evil spark in him.

He was walking by to go to the throne room when he heard a loud yell echoing the halls. That was when he spotted Benavis clutching his head and pleading. Bente didn't understand what was going on.

He turned to leave with an evil grin, but first, he snapped his fingers and there appeared a horn head man, bowing on one knee. Horn heads could shapeshift into what they kill; this horn head was a fly following Bente.

"My lord," greeted the horn head.

"Gather the men," ordered Bente. "There's another secret we have to uncover." He ran his finger on the bottom of his lip. "There's another snake we have to hunt down. Send someone to the Sanila clan temple."

"Is there something you want us to look for?" asked the horn head.

Bente thought for a while. "A book."

"Understood, my lord."

"I want you to go to High Mountain and find what secrets they hold up there. And if you must, kill all those Sleeping Monks."

The horn head bowed and turned into a fly. He flew away, leaving Bente alone. Realizing his plan to destroy the Sanila clan may be nearing. His pawn was the disturbed Benavis; he was going to use Benavis against his brother. But he had to get rid of the other advisers somehow.

* * *

Bente made his way to the throne room, still thinking about the secret he may uncover. He spotted Ocrist standing outside the throne room talking to a guard. He smirked and made his way to Ocrist.

"Lord Ocrist," greeted Bente sarcastically.

Ocrist didn't look pleased to see Bente. In fact, like the other advisers, he hated Bente because he couldn't be trusted. He was always against the other advisers' ideas and was a secretive man.

"Bente," greeted Ocrist, as he dismissed the guard.

"Planning something?" asked Bente with sarcasm.

"Nothing that concerns you," rejected Ocrist, as he turned to enter the throne room.

Bente just stood still with a grin. "You can't hide your secrets forever," he warned Ocrist. "I will unmask you and show everyone your true colors."

Ocrist stopped. "Don't search too far," warned Ocrist. "It will only end with your life."

"I'm willing to gamble my life for your downfall," challenged Bente.

"What downfall do you speak of? It will be you falling to your stubbornness," said Ocrist as he entered the hall.

Giovanis was sitting on the golden throne with a scowled face as his advisers stood before him.

"My king," said Dada. "Our people are suffering. Bandits are blocking our trade route. Merchants and farmers are refusing to come to the capital. And the Ku-Ma clan are blocking the rice trade route to us."

"Why? Do they not respect me as king?" asked Giovanis.

"They don't want to lose any more soldiers," answered Dada.

"I can't let my people suffer!" fumed Giovanis, slamming his fist on the armrest of the golden throne.

"My king, some of the clans want to break an alliance with us," added Bente, "with all these rebellion groups rising." He took a peek at Ocrist. "They don't believe that the royal clan can protect them anymore. Some of the clans had taken the matter into their own hands, allying with each other. And may I add, King Rula has been assassinated."

"I do not care for the north and their useless king. Their conflict doesn't concern me. My only concern is the south. How dare they want to betray the kingdom!" said an annoyed Giovanis. He wondered if his ruling was already a failure. "I can't lose land in the south. The eastern and western kingdoms will take notice."

"My King, there's nothing you should worry about with the other two kingdoms," assured Bente. "Rumors has it that Enstra is fighting within. I don't see the Tigara wanting to disturb the era of peace. I believe the clan of Summan is only testing you, my young king."

"My king, I suggest we let those clans break an alliance with us," suggested Ocrist.

"So they can rage a war on us? Those clans ought to be taught a lesson," Bente suggested. "If we let these clans do whatever they wish, the land will be split into hundreds of small kingdoms with war spilling across. Now, do we want to keep order or let these monkeys run wild?"

Silence paused the meeting, all trying to figure out what was the best course of action in dealing with the southern clans.

"I can't put the kingdom in jeopardy," said Giovanis, "nor Telamis. I will force those clans to decide their fate. If they dare to break away from the royal clan, then they will meet their ancestors. If they stay, then they can live a long and peaceful life."

"Threatening them will only anger them," warned Dada.

"Then how do you suggest we keep an alliance with them?" questioned Bente. "I agree with our king. They need to think about their fate before deciding."

"You need to think about your fate before speaking," Thunder threatened Bente. "My king, I agree with Lord Dada and Lord Ocrist. Let them break their alliance with us. When they fight each other, they will crawl back to the royal kingdom and ask for alliance and protection."

"The south is still yours, meaning you still have some control over them," reminded Ocrist.

"There are two clans we need to keep an alliance with. The Ma and the Ku-Ma clans. The Ma clans are the strongest and the wealthiest clan in the south. They have more influence over the southern kingdom than your clan, my king. The Ku-Ma clan controls the trade route for our supplies. They're the two clans that can potentially break an alliance with us and give us concerns," worried Seris.

Giovanis took a while to think. Threatening them would only anger them, and letting them leave would bring the possibility of war. "Fine, I'll let them break the alliance. But when they need my help and protection, I will not answer their cry," declared Giovanis. "They dare to break from the law of justice, then I will send the troops of justice into their homes and slaughter all their wives and children. I can't be a weak king like my father. I will demand respect and be feared upon!"

The advisers bowed their heads. Bente had a grin on his face. The fate of the future was in the grasp of his hand. Nothing was going to stop him from ruling the south. He knew that whatever the king decides, there will be war. Now he must play the waiting game. When the tower falls, he will bury the crumbles of the old tower with a new one.

* * *

The sun was setting, and the mosquitoes woke to feast on blood. Standing in front of Summer Palace gates were the Bu cousins, all dressed in red steel armor with the sigil of a dagger pointing downward on their left shoulder plate. They all gazed at the giant golden gate.

Rain was still shocked when Eddis humiliated Ba-Ben and their clan while Ba-Ben was extremely angry still, imagining himself hanging Eddis over a mountain cliff and making him beg for his life to only drop him to his death.

"If I ever see that pathetic dog again—"

"You'll do nothing!" Uesenga cut off Ba-Ben, warning him to not try anything violent.

"I can't let him disrespect me," complained Ba-Ben.

"Remember our place. We are here to simply serve and take orders. There's nothing for us to pride over anymore," informed Uesenga.

"I can't take orders like a dog, especially from royal scums!" growled Ba-Ben.

"Grandpa always said that a man should always keep his word no matter what. He already sold our clan to the royal clan. We must honor it," reminded Uesenga.

Ba-Ben stormed away with frustration in his eyes. He did not expect Uesenga to accept their clan being royal dogs. It wasn't like Uesenga to allow anyone to talk down on their clan.

"I'll go with him." Yorsenga sighed, as he reluctantly followed Ba-Ben into the Summer Palace.

Rain and Uesenga watched their cousins leave. Rain wanted to shout at Uesenga for dishonoring their clan name. But Uesenga was right. There was nothing they could do but be dogs to the royal clan. He wondered what his father and uncles were thinking about in the heavens. Were they disappointed with their children for not fighting for their honor?

"We have to watch each other's back," advised Uesenga. He entered the palace, leaving Rain alone.

Rain decided to stroll around the garden instead of watching his post, which was at the west wing of the palace. While walking, he remembered a story his grandfather once told him, a story about Shugen and the warrior of dreams. Shugen was a scholar trying to find the truth about heaven. The warrior of dreams was his protector. They traveled Telamis until both were captured by the Dru clan. King Malcis, who was known as the King of Kings, ordered for the both of them to be executed. Shugen's last words were, *"There's no such thing as heaven or hell. We pray to men and women who never existed. We are selfish creatures to create lies to satisfy our reality. My whole life I wanted to discover the truth. I had found the truth, but not what I was looking for. I found the truth of life. The seven titles of life."*

Rain always loved that story even though Shugen and the warrior of the dream were met with a tragic death. Both men accepted their fate and believed in their words. He wondered why his grandfather couldn't be like Shugen, to always fight till the end. He always questioned his grandfather about the seven titles of life. But his grandfather would always tell him to discover it himself, leaving him to ponder until he can't think anymore.

Suddenly, he heard the sound of a flute. By itself, his body followed the sound, led by his ears. The sound was smooth and welcoming. The person playing sounded like they were suffering and crying. When he finally arrived at the center of the garden, standing at the center of the wooden bridge over the red-painted railing was Janellis, playing her wooden flute under the stars as they reflected the pond.

Her eyes were shut as she played her flute over the pond for the sun and moonfish to dance. She didn't notice that Rain was staring at her. She played as if her body was being controlled. The pain in her playing nearly made Rain cry.

She finally stopped and turned, but quickly became embarrassed, shocked to see Rain standing in front of the bridge. He quickly shook his head and tried to walk away.

"Wait!" called Janellis.

Rain stopped and slowly turned around as Janellis made her way to him. He kept his eyes down to avoid making eye contact with her.

"What is your name?" Janellis asked.

"Rain Bu, Princess," answered Rain, bowing his head. He blushed as he heard Janellis's voice, but shocked that she sounded cold and unemotional.

"Rain?" confused Janellis.

"I'm sorry, Princess, I must return to my post." He quickly turned around to leave, remembering that he hated the royal clan.

"Rain!" Janellis stopped Rain again.

Rain stopped and grunted, wondering why Janellis wouldn't let him leave.

"Why do you look away? I know that you stare at me from afar," wondered Janellis.

"I apologize, Princess. But a guard and a princess shouldn't speak to each other." He walked away quickly, leaving Janellis alone.

Janellis was sad but didn't show it. She gripped on to her flute tightly, only wishing for someone to talk with. She hated being trapped in the palace, wishing for the day to leave the walls of her protection and explore the vast land of Telamis. She looked back at the pond to the sight of the moon reflecting the water. The song she played that brought Rain to her was called "The Dead Moon."

*   *   *

The streets of Summan was quiet as the night covered the bright-blue sky. No drunks were roaming the street. Stray cats dashed across the street and into a dark alleyway. Benavis wore a hooded cloak to cover his identity so he could roam the silent streets of Summan. He escaped from the palace by the rear, wanting to see the streets at night.

While walking, he passed by many shops, closed till morning returned. He stopped and stood in front of one particular shop, a magic shop called Magic Magic. He looked into the glass window and eyed every herb, magic tools, staffs, and orbs. One particular staff caught his attention. It was a long staff that stood taller than him at the center of the shop. The staff was wooden and white; it had an arc shape on the top, and inside the arc was a golden glass ball.

Benavis never saw a staff this beautiful before. All he could do was awe over it since he had no magic skills. He continued his walk, wishing he had magic skills. During his nightly exploring, he wondered why he was always trapped in the palace? He felt at peace walking the streets of Sentra. The air was fresh and gave new energy.

He looked around and enjoyed the view that was given. The streets were lit from light orbs hanging from the light post on the side of the street. Also, the help of fireflies lit the city, making it glow under the night. Benavis felt free from his emotional prison. As he continued to walk, he realized the streets were getting darker. There was barely any light post on the street. The street was no longer clean, and people were lingering outside, some drunk and some keeping a close eye on Benavis, out of suspicion toward him.

Benavis had entered the poorest part of the city, the Ground, where the thieves' guilds, mercenaries, drunks, and whores called home. These people despised the royal clan, and a glimpse of Benavis would agitate them. Many believed the Ground was the true identity of Sentra, where people struggled to live and were still affected by the wars of Telamis. They were the face of suffering and hate, left in the dark while the rich and wealthy lived their life without repercussions. An invisible line divided the city, a line that split the delusion and reality.

Benavis debated if he should turn around. He did not expect to see the hidden part of Sentra. He turned back but was stopped. A man wearing rag clothing and smelling of ale blocked his escape. He had a scar over his left eye and was toothless, showing his ugly smile.

"Wwwell, I-I have n-never seen you heere b-before," slurred the man, feeling on Benavis's cloak. "I-it feels nice. Y-you rich, huh? You not around here." The man licked his lips like he had found a chest full of gold.

Benavis was afraid; he didn't know what to do. He looked around, and no one cared to help him, some either watching closely or ignoring the situation.

"Don't be s-scared, rich boy. Give me the cloak, and you'll walk free," the man intimidated while flashing a rusty dagger. "You see? I-I kill you and take the cloak. N-nobody will care if you die on the street. It's the Ground. D-death is every day, rich boy."

Benavis didn't want to hand his cloak. He knew if he revealed his identity to these people, they would turn into wolves and maul him. "Please, how about I give you some summer coins?" begged Benavis.

"B-bribing a drunk killer won't work, rich boy. Let's see your face." The man tried to grab Benavis's face, but Benavis weakly punched the man in the face and ran into an alley.

The man chased after Benavis, wobbling as he ran after him, saliva dripping from the mouth like a dog waiting for his meal. Benavis looked back, realizing how fast the man was running. The man reminded him of the shadow figures chasing him in his nightmare. He tripped to the ground and tried getting up but was caught by the man.

The man had his foot on Benavis's back. He turned Benavis around and took the cloak off him then realized that Benavis was not just a rich boy, but a prince. Benavis tried to hide his face but was too late. The man was twitching, knowing that Benavis's death would make him rich. He took his dagger out.

"Today, the gods had favored my luck," said the man. "I-I get go home with a new cloak. And make money f-for your head." He laughed heinously. "Now I won't have to starve anymore. I can stick my c-cock in any whore I want. I can buy whatever I want. I will be the h-hero of the Ground. Your death will be my happiness."

"Please, I can give you summer coins. Take the cloak and let me go free. I'll make sure you'll get what you want," pleaded Benavis.

"No, no. Y-you must die. You'll suffer like the rest of us. A-all you royal rats will pay!" the man showed his dagger to stab Benavis.

Benavis shut his eyes and continued to plead. He cradled himself, waiting in fear. He never expected his life to end in such a way. There was so much to learn and discover. Now he'd be another corpse on the Ground.

As the man settled in to stab Benavis, a shadow figure standing seven feet tall appeared behind the man, hovering over him like a rain cloud over a village. Benavis opened his eyes and was terrified of the shadow figure. It had no eye, but six arms like the shadow figures that chased him in his nightmares. But it did not have the golden mask.

The man turned around to the horror of the shadow figure, like he had seen a ghost of his past. The man dropped the dagger with his mouth wide open. The shadow figure stared down at the man then violently grabbed the man by the neck and viciously threw him against the wall. Then it floated to the man and picked him up by the neck, pinning him against the wall. With the other five arms holding shadow daggers, it stabbed the man with all five daggers in the stomach. Blood dripped down the man's mouth like a waterfall. Veins appeared on the man's forehead, his face turning blue as the shadow figure choked him. The shadow figure squeezed the man's neck tightly till his head flew off his body and let it roll onto the ground. His body dropped to the ground with blood leaking out of his headless body.

Benavis was terrified to run. It was like his father's death all over again. The shadow figure turned to him and floated to him. It stared down at him. Benavis prayed that the shadow figure wouldn't kill him.

"I am you, Benavis," said the shadow figure as it floated into the wall.

Benavis just sat still on the ground, frozen by the monster he saw. He still couldn't move but was relieved to be alive. He looked over to the headless man's body and started to vomit from the goriness of the man's death.

A golden three-eye masked man observed from the roof of a house. He created a shadow crow and placed a note under its talons. The shadow crow flew away, and the masked man stood up and removed his mask to show his identity to be Ocrist. The look on his face was cold and vile. He turned to leave but took one last look at Benavis. "A new era starts with you, Benavis," he said to himself before he turned into a crow.

Chapter Nine

Kingdom of Tigara

"Ausra will pay," expressed Aerin to Maenellia, a look of distress on his face even though the air felt nice, the grass field around them was bright green, and surrounding them was high hills, with the calming wind blowing the tall grass gently in one direction. Still, he couldn't find himself enjoying the beautiful scenery around him, still bitter about Ausra.

Both Aerin and Maenellia were riding their horses. Aerin rode a black horse with a golden mane. The horse stood tall and mighty. Maenellia rode on a white horse with a pink mane. On her left shoulder was her blue flame bird. Behind them were their guards and their children Kiri, Lehue, and Isa. They had enough guards to protect them if the Men of Hate decided to ambush them.

As they rode along the path, they passed by farms. The farmers would watch in awe and curiosity from their steps as the Kimsu clan passed. They hadn't seen such a large number of soldiers pass by them since the last era war, putting many scenarios into their heads. Even the children would stop playing to watch in fascination. Some kids waved to the soldiers but received nothing in return. Most of the farmer kids all dreamed of becoming a warrior or magic user themselves.

Maenellia enjoyed the ride even though she had her doubts about going to the capital. She tried to find ways to enjoy the moment. She was always taught to find the good in life. Her good in life was her children. At the back of her mind, she was worried for Airian and Kunjae. She prayed every day to the Seven Protectors of Heaven for their safety, hoping that Indris would take care of them while they deal with the Men of Hate that terrorized Heart Village.

"Time will bring him back to us," hoped Maenellia as she looked back at her children. "He wouldn't leave his siblings long."

"I hoped to see him on the battlefield one day," said Aerin angrily. "He spitted on my vision and ran away from his destiny. I never thought that I raised a coward."

Maenellia smiled. "If you want to accomplish your dream, you should avoid Ausra. Our son is dangerous."

Aerin scoffed; he looked back to Isa. "Up here, boy," called Aerin.

Isa took a quick nervous glance toward Lehue. He received a shoulder shrug in return. He rode his gray pony up between Maenellia and Aerin. Maenellia rubbed the back of his head, and Aerin stared at the road ahead.

"Listen, boy," said Aerin. "When it's time for you to become a man and become a warrior, I want you to never run from your destiny. Look behind you." He waited till Isa looked back. "See those men and women? They will follow you one day. But if you're a coward, they will leave. Do you understand, Isa?"

Isa gulped. "Y-yes, Father," replied Isa nervously.

"Don't let anyone weaken you. Don't give trust to anyone easily, even for your brothers and sisters," said Aerin strictly. "Remember, if they are not running with the demon, they are not worth the time."

All his life since he was a boy, Aerin always wanted to be king. Bothered as a child and into his adulthood when the other clans in the kingdom relied on his clan, he witnessed the royal clan begging his father for help whenever there was a matter they couldn't handle. What did his clan get in return? He thought to himself. Nothing, only a simple thank you and some autumn coins. He believed that his clan should be ruling Telamis, not the four clans that are weaker than his clan.

He felt like it was time to split from the Cai clan and build his kingdom. His plan was simple—use his clan power and influence to overpower King Hensi. It was time he followed his own rule. He had the strongest army in the east. But he had to wait until all piece came together. For the time being, he'd travel to the capital city on the king's order and play follower.

"Your decision has consequence, son. The lives of many will be in your hands. You'll wake up one day with a goal and idea in mind. Then you'll see them shattered. It's what you call life. You can't attack life alone," Aerin advised Isa, looking to Maenellia with a smile, letting her know that he needed her.

* * *

Aerin decided to hault the travel by the riverbank of the Lucky River so his men and women could rest for the night before they reached the capital city. There were white tents set up and a giant campfire at the center of the camp. Some soldiers were at the river washing their faces while some sat by the fire. The smell of roasted chicken coming from the cooks' tent filled the night air as they roasted several chickens over a fire beside their tent. Fireflies helped light the night, along with the stars from the sky. The morale at camp was carefree, but at the same time, they were on high alert for any Men of Hate attacks.

Isa was walking along the bank, wondering if he was capable of being a warrior. His father finally believed in him. But he felt something was strange. He stopped and stared at his reflection in the water. He saw a sad and clueless boy. The doubt was clouding his mind. He felt alone in his thoughts of deceit.

"Pouting won't make it any better, crybaby," teased Kiri, startling Isa and waking him from his thoughts.

"I'm not pouting," defended Isa. "I was looking at the fishes."

Kiri shook her head. "Don't lie to me," warned Kiri. "I know what was said between you and Father. I already concluded." She turned to the water and stared at her reflection. "It seems Father believes in you . . . I guess I must believe in you too."

"Kiri . . ." Isa began to tear up.

Kiri cringed with her words and the joyfulness in Isa's eyes. "Stop crying, it's embarrassing," she teased as she left Isa.

Isa watched as his sister left him, feeling a sense of relief that his sister was no longer angry with him. He looked over and spotted his mother calling him over. She was interacting with a soldier. Isa made his way to her. She had a cheerful smile over her face.

"How are you feeling, my love?" asked Maenellia.

"Fine," replied Isa with a little confidence.

"Don't lie to me, Isa." Maenellia sighed. "A mother knows when their child is upset."

Isa knew he couldn't hide his feeling from his mother. She was like an eagle watching over her children. "Mother, can I be a warrior?" wondered Isa. "I'm weak. I can't even control fire yet. No one will take me seriously . . . I'm just weak."

"You're not weak. It's a long road to discover who you are." Maenellia rubbed Isa's head to comfort him. "You know what our greatest enemy is?" she asked.

Isa shrugged.

"Our greatest enemy is not the person we hate, not the one that betrayed or lie to us." She pointed to Isa's forehead. "It's our mind—ourselves. We are the greatest enemy to ourselves. When you're alone with your thoughts, the monster of self-hatred crawls out of its cave. It's a dangerous place to be in." She knelt on one knee and stared into Isa's eyes with seriousness. "Don't ever be alone. Find friends and someone you love that will release you from your greatest enemy, my love. That monster of self-hatred will always be there. You must always fight it." She kissed Isa on the forehead. "If you ever find yourself in that place, remember the people that love you," she ended, leaving Isa alone.

Isa continued his walk alone along the river, thinking about his mother's words, shivering from the cold night but not wanting to go to his tent, observing the soldiers as they laughed and shared stories among each other. He listened in some of their conversations. One soldier talked about how proud he was to be a father, hoping to quickly head home to his newborn son and wife. Another soldier talked about his hopes of opening up his own shop selling exotic candies. All of these soldiers had something to look forward to. Even though their lives at times were at risk, they still managed to smile.

He thought about what his mother said to him again. Could his mind be his greatest enemy? he thought. He looked around again and wondered if those smiles on the soldiers were false. Could the smile just be a mask hiding their true feelings?

"Warriors shouldn't look down," said Nellina, with a cheerful smile.

Nellina startled Isa while he looked around. She had served the Kimsu clan since she was sixteen. Her father was Kren Gray, who had died during a conflict at the tavern. She stayed loyal to the Kimsu clan because Aerin looked after her like she was his daughter.

"Nellina!" exclaimed a shocked Isa.

"Why do you always look sad?" asked Nellina. "If something is bothering you, tell me."

"I know," replied Isa. He paused. "I know why we're going to the capital city. The king is angry because of Bloben's death. Why can't Father just tell us the truth? And now all of a sudden he believes in me."

Nellina just smiled. "Look at you, stressing," she joked, checking Isa's hair for white hair. She stopped then giggled. "You're just a kid. Don't indulge yourself with too much priority. Enjoy your moment as a kid because in the blink of an eye, it will vanish. If I have one regret, that'll be my childhood. I wish I had my childhood back, where life was just filled with imagination." She crouched down to Isa's level.

"Don't grow up too fast because we only have one chance in life. When it's time for you to grow up, you'll know. For now, be a kid. Run wild without thinking and laugh loud." She placed her hand on his shoulders. "Look around you. You see these soldiers? They wish to be a kid again. You think any of them want to die? They only smile amongst each other so the thought of death wouldn't cross their mind."

"Then why'd they choose to be soldiers?" asked Isa.

She took her hand off Isa's shoulder and looked him straight in the eye. "Who knows? Each of them has their reason. They all know the consequences of being a soldier. But I can tell you one thing. There's no fulfillment in being a warrior or magic user. The sword and magic were created to take life away. I for one don't consider myself a hero. To the eyes of the enemy, I am the villain."

"Then why do you choose this path?"

Nellina hesitated to answer Isa. "I chose this path because I am a victim of self-hate," she replied with a blank look.

"I don't understand! Why'd someone like you hate yourself?" wondered Isa worriedly.

Nellina remembered the time where she wanted to end her own life. She was fifteen when her mother died from an illness. Her father was absent and drunk because he was overwhelmed. Nothing was going right for her. She remembered sitting at the foot of her bed staring at the wall with a dagger in hand, pondering to slit her own throat. She never found the guts to commit the ultimate sin, but the idea still raced in her mind. She kept her feelings to herself. Her fierce persona was only a mask to cover her weak, lonely self. "There are things in life you don't understand," she finally replied to Isa. She smiled at him. "Don't worry about me, okay. Don't ever hate yourself."

"Take your advice, Nellina," advised Isa.

"It's too late for me to take my advice. I already chose my path. There's no need for me to look back and regret my decisions." She stood back up, and her cheerful smile reappeared. "Stop being sad, okay. Be a kid, Isa." She stood up. "One more thing, don't worry if someone believes in you or not as long you believe in yourself." She patted Isa's head and left him alone.

Isa could only watch as Nellina left him, wondering why someone like her hated herself. She was respected by the warriors and magic users and loved by the people. But how could she still hate herself?

*　　*　　*

Aerin and Kiri stood beside each other, staring off into the distance as the soldiers behind them relaxed. Aerin had his arm crossed with a stern look on his face, his finger tapping his arms anxiously, his mind clobbered with thoughts of his faith, wondering how he'd be welcomed once he set foot in the capital. Or will they ambush him before he entered the city?

"Are you still angry with your brother?" Aerin asked Kiri.

"Of course, Father," replied Kiri. "Because of his weakness, my strength is not recognized."

Aerin sighed and smiled. "It's never easy, you know. It's never supposed to be easy," he started. "If life was easy, then everybody will be lazy pigs. The greatest warrior was weak at one point in their life. You know what pushed them to be the greatest?" He slightly turned his head to Kiri, looking down at her.

Kiri shrugged her shoulders.

"Because they dreamt of themselves being the greatest. They let their determination push them to be better than the other warriors." Aerin stared across the field. "Only a few become great. I advise you, don't ever cry to become great. Show them your greatness! Don't worry, I see your strength, Kiri." He hinted a smile toward Kiri.

Kiri took her father's words to heart. A sense of determination sparked her spirit. She wondered what was her greatness. Being born a woman, she was expected to bear children for her husband, defend her home when her husband was not around. Tales she read of great women warriors inspired her. She wanted to write her own story, a story where mothers and sisters would tell.

"Father, this is not a dream," expressed Kiri. "This is reality!" A look of determination appeared on her face. "I don't run from greatness—I seek it. I will be the greatest warrior in our clan!" She clutched her fist and stared at the stars in the sky.

Aerin smiled, proud that his daughter was determined. Unlike his other children, Kiri understood her clan name. She was the demon that all of Telamis would fear. Her blue flames would set ablaze to her enemies. They would see a sword in her right hand, eyes of fire and the cool burning blue flames in her left hand. They would run and fear her.

After talking to her father, Kiri decided to walk around the camp in search of Lehue. She stopped a guard walking by her. "Have you seen, Lehue?" she asked the guard.

"I believe he's with the cooks, my lady," replied the guard, as he bowed his head to her.

She thanked the guard and rushed to the cooks' tent. She had to speak to Lehue. Since they were a year apart, she could tell him everything. Lehue was the only sibling she trusted the most.

She stopped in front of the cooks' tent, listening to their laughter coming from the inside. As the head chef told his story in his deep echoing voice, she could hear the slight laughter of Lehue, upset that he was wasting his time with the cooks again. She entered the tent, and the laughter stopped, none of them taking a peep at her, all acting like she was a stranger.

Lehue was seated on a stool with other cooks around. He looked suspicious and wanted to burst with laughter.

Kiri stood in the tent like a guard making sure the prisoners were doing their work. The cooks were servants to the Kimsu clan. There was a Kimsu policy where the servants of the clan were not allowed to build a relationship with members of the clan. But some clan members ignored the rule, including Lehue.

"Lehue, I need to speak to you," said Kiri.

Lehue stood from the stool with a suspicious smile. "So long, my donkey kings!" he said, bursting into laughter. The cooks all burst into laughter with him.

Kiri looked confused and annoyed. She wanted Lehue to respect his status as a high clan member.

Lehue bowed his head to the cooks and followed his sister out of the tent, still with a giant smile on his face. He didn't care about the difference between rich and poor. In his eyes, he saw happiness. He loved being social and enjoying life. He saw the struggles his older siblings went through so they could be perfect in their father's eyes. As time went by, he saw his siblings' smiles slowly disappear from their faces. Sadly, it was the same for Kiri.

"Why do you waste time with the cooks?" asked Kiri annoyedly. "They work for us, they're not our friends."

Lehue smiled. "Why does it matter?" wondered Lehue. "Because I'm a clan member, I shouldn't speak with the cooks? Why should I isolate myself from those people that make me smile?"

"Grow up, Lehue," said Kiri, jealous of Lehue for being carefree toward everything. She sometimes wished she could think like him, being more open toward the people around her and to herself. "We're members of the Kimsu clan. We're a clan of warriors and honor. Wasting your time with the cooks and their vile jokes does not benefit you," she warned Lehue.

"I don't care about the Kimsu honor." He looked up to the dark sky and watched white birds fly over his head and toward the direction of the capital city. "Why should I be trapped in the Kimsu prison like everyone else?"

Kiri stopped walking and turned to Lehue with disappointment on her face. "I only have one dream," she confessed. "That's to be the greatest warrior in the Kimsu clan." She looked away from Lehue. "All those stories of our ancestors. They were great warriors. I long to be like them and have my name spoken beside theirs." She turned back to Lehue, her eyes filled with rage. "If you plan to disrespect the Kimsu name, I will not hesitate to defend the name. I know Father's plan to hone Isa as the next heir to the clan. It's the reason why he's invested in him so much lately," she said.

Lehue was not fazed. He kept calm with a smile still on his face. "I'm not disrespecting the clan name. I want to follow my dream, not the clan dream. And if Father believes Isa is the clan head, then I believe in Isa too. I don't see my siblings as my rival like you, Kiri."

The two siblings stared at each other. A clash of personalities brewed in the air. Only the two of them could feel the rivalry boiling. Kiri wanted to follow the traditional way of the clan while Lehue wanted to break from the old tradition.

Chapter Ten

Kingdom of Tigara

The Wise Lion, King Hensi Cai, stared out the window from his bedroom from the magnificent Autumn Palace that sat on top of a cliff. From his window, he could see down on the rest of the beautiful Fall City. He smiled as he watched the white birds fly over the white stone buildings of the city. The city was built upward on a waterfall that led to the Lucky River. The river ran through the city. Houses were close to each other. There were thousands of stairs and hundreds of bridges, making Fall City a difficult city to invade.

The white clouds drifted by his eyes as he waited for Aerin's arrival, his arm crossed as he gently stroked his long gray goatee, keeping his mind clear of stress. His feet nervously tapped the ground as he waited for the woman he first loved. He tried to live life without the regret of his past. But only one regret still lingered on to him. It was when he lost Maenellia to Aerin.

Hensi was a loved and respected king. The people of Tigara all admired him. His idea of peace was taken into the heart of the people. With talent with the sword, he was also a wise man. During the fourth era war, the War of Tragic, he led his army against the Moon Dragons at the Battle of Might. The battle took five months to come to an end. Fighting beside him was Aerin. Using his wisdom, he brought his army to victory.

The doors opened, and entered a young man in his mid to late twenties. The man was Hensi's oldest son, Genchen Cai. He was tall and resembled his father but with short dark hair.

"Father, the scouts have returned," reported Genchen.

"Good," replied Hensi. "Let it be true. Are the dragons not by his side?"

"They searched the surrounding area. The rumor is true, Father," confirmed Genchen.

Hensi smiled and turned to Genchen. "His greatest weapon's not in his disposal." He felt that Aerin wasn't afraid of him, which bothered him. "He's my strongest ally, my closest friend. What he did was treachery against my honor. Do you understand, son?" he asked Genchen.

"Of course, Father," replied Genchen. "You're the ruler of the eastern kingdom, the symbol of peace. Aerin is nothing more than a piece to your kingdom."

Hensi was impressed with Genchen. He had three sons and two bastards living far from the city. The other two sons were Lucid and Envio. His first choice to be his heir was Genchen but he denied it. "Why don't you want to become king?" Wondered Hensi. "You're my eldest son. You should sit on the throne next."

Genchen kept a straight face. "A true hero doesn't shine in the light, father. It's the person that moves in the shadow that builds the kingdom." He bowed to his father and left the room. "I'm flattered that you still want me to be the heir. No disrespect to you, Father. My way of peace is different from your way of peace."

"What is your way of peace, Genchen?" asked Hensi, curious to hear his son's answer.

Genchen paused, his eyes darkening. He didn't want to answer his father since he felt that his father wouldn't understand his way of peace. "We shouldn't chat long. The demons await us," reminded Genchen.

*　*　*

The Autumn Palace throne room was bright as the sun rays pierced through the giant circlar window from the ceiling of the room. The throne was made out of gold with red rubies embedded into the armrests. Aerin looked around the room with envy in his eyes. He wanted to rewrite history and had himself sitting on the throne.

"This should be our clan home," said Aerin with distaste in his mouth. "History showed that we did all the dirty deeds. There will be no Tigara without the Kimsu!" Envy showed in his eyes as the mistreatment of his clan crossed his mind.

"My dear, you must not let your anger get the better of you," calmed Maenellia as she gently grabbed Aerin's hands.

"You're right. I must stay calm." He looked over to his three young children, wanting them to understand the mistreatment of their clan.

Kiri squeezed her fist tightly, agreeing with her father.

Isa looked nervous, not knowing how to respond to his father's claim. He looked around the castle and could only admire the throne room, from the marvelous white stones that had engravings of epic battles to the double stairs that curved down from each side of the throne. On the walls hung white banners with a blue dahlia on them. Leading up to the throne were four steps, covering in a red-and-gold carpet.

When they entered Fall City, the city was cleaned, and the people were lively. Climbing the stairs and crossing the stone bridges and listening to the waterfall, at one point, Isa stuck his hand out to touch the waterfall as he crossed the bridge, to feel the cool water touch is skin. He wished Mersane could be more like Fall City. In Mersane, the people there all cherished heroes of wars. Great warriors like Ausra and Indris were celebrated while the people of Fall City cherished the lavish life, like the arts and cultures. There were people of different colors and race that lived in the city, all coexisting with each other.

"My dear friends," announced Hensi from the top of the double stairs, his arms spread wide with a kind smile.

They walked down the stairs. He had a strange aura around him, like a predator stalking its prey. Behind the wisdom and honesty, there was a man with a serpent head.

Aerin kept a close watch on Hensi as he walked down the steps.

Hensi had a kind and smoothing smile across his face as he sat on the throne. Genchen showed a serious face, standing below the steps of the throne.

Aerin and the rest of his family bowed their heads to show respect. As Aerin looked to the ground, he clenched his teeth. Jealousy and anger ran through his body. His blood boiled and the black flames ready to blast the wise king, irked by the way Hensi sat on the throne.

"It's an honor to have a prestigious clan in my presence," said Hensi. He measured the three children. "Your young children are growing." He looked back at Maenellia. "And the Summer phoenix, beautiful as ever."

Maenellia bowed in thanks. She always knew that Hensi loved her and sensed that his heart still longed for her. No point in her life where she ever loved him back. She remembered Hensi begging her father for marriage. When her hand was already given to Aerin, Hensi became devastated. He even threatened to duel Aerin for her hand.

"Aerin, we ought to speak alone," suggested Hensi. "My guards will escort your family to the palace garden."

Guards wearing white armors with a blue dahlia sigil on the right shoulder plate entered the throne room and escorted Aerin's family out. Maenellia touched Aerin's hand, sensing something was wrong. He nodded to her to let her know to stay calm, but wary.

Aerin confidently stared into Hensi's eyes as his family left the hall. He wasn't afraid of Hensi and knew that he could easily beat Hensi. They were once best friends, but as time continued, they slowly drifted apart.

"Are we not speaking alone?" questioned Aerin, looking toward Genchen.

Hensi smiled. "Of course." He stood from the throne. "We should take a walk, my dear friend."

Aerin bowed in agreement, keeping his wits on high alert.

* * *

Maenellia and her three children roamed around the garden with guards following them closely. She didn't mind that guards were watching them closely because her attention was on her children and the flowers surrounding them. She hadn't seen these many flowers for a long time. She gently touched a sunflower, and tears nearly fell from her eyes. These were flowers of the south. It reminded her of her childhood, making her remember when she was sitting near the riverbank and Hensi was gifting her these flowers. Hensi had a romantic heart, but Aerin somehow stole her heart.

"Why are you crying, Mother?" asked Lehue.

Maenellia wiped the tears from her eyes. "Nothing important, my dear."

Lehue looked at the flower and wondered why this flower made his mother cry. "Is this flower like an onion?" asked Lehue as he observed and sniffed it. "I'm not crying."

Maenellia smiled and patted Lehue's head. "It's only a memory." She looked at her other two children. "There will be memories that will make you cry, either good or bad."

"Crying shows weakness," said Kiri.

Maenellia patted Kiri's head. "You cried the most when you were a baby," joked Maenellia.

"Mother, look, it's Prince Lucid and Prince Envio." Lehue pointed.

Lucid was tall and resembled his father; he had short dark hair and a broad chin. His brother Envio was much shorter than him. He had dark mysterious eyes that seemed untrustworthy. Lucid had a scroll in his hand. Both brothers were wearing armor.

Right then, Maenellia felt the world pause. She shut her eyes and pulled her kids closer to her. At the same, she was ready to fire her blue flames at the guards if they attacked. That eerie feeling was showing itself. "Follow their orders, children," warned Maenellia. "Kiri, keep your mouth shut if you want to live."

"Mother—"

"Not a word!" Maenellia sharply cut off Kiri.

"Lady Maenellia," greeted Lucid as he approached. He unsealed the scroll and read, "'I hereby do arrest you and your family for treason and the murder of Bloben Smok head of the Smok clan.' Do you accept your crime?"

"We're innocent!" challenged Kiri, disobeying her mother's warning to stay quiet.

Maenellia turned Kiri around and quickly slapped her across the face. She felt upset when she slapped Kiri. "This is the king's orders!" she yelled at Kiri. "If you want to be a warrior, then accept the crime and follow orders."

Tears fell from Kiri's eyes as she rubbed her red cheeks. She couldn't believe her mother had hit her since her mother had never put her hands on her and the siblings before. Lehue and Isa were also surprised, and at the same time, they were afraid.

Maenellia bowed to the princes. "I'm sorry for my daughter's foul mouth," she apologized. "I accept the crimes of my family."

The four magic-user guards surrounded the family. Magical restraint strings appeared from their hands, each string tying each member of the family's hands together like handcuffs.

*　　*　　*

Both Aerin and Hensi slowly walked the corridor of the palace. The halls felt cold and strange. Aerin felt distrust in the air. He tried to read Hensi's mind but couldn't conclude what Hensi was thinking, each step feeling like his last. He watched each corner of the hallway for any assassins.

"How long has it been since we fought beside each other?" wondered Hensi.

"Get to the point, Hensi," said Aerin. He didn't want to play Hensi's mind games.

Hensi laughed. "You haven't changed a bit. Always wanting to get to the point. You never cared about facts." Hensi eyes darkened, his face serious. "That will kill you, Aerin," he warned Aerin. "You're my dear friend, and your wife is the woman I still love. I don't want to see the both of you in pain." He scratched his head. "The both of you again putting me in a position I feel displeasure with. Why can't you guys make my life a little easier?"

"You put this upon yourself, Hensi," blamed Aerin. "I'm not making you decide anything. You want this because you're the king, afraid that I'm an enemy to your throne."

Hensi laughed again. "Ah, I am a king. The wise king. Do you think I'm stupid, Aerin? Am I a jester to you? My entire life was always in your shadow. I don't have your war accolades. I don't have a beautiful wife like you. I don't have talented children like you. But there is one thing I have over you. Something you craved that ruined our friendship. To be called king." He turned to Aerin. "It kills you inside that I sit on the throne. I'm not stupid, Aerin. You'll never be content with your life until you have what you want. Yet I'm still jealous of you for some odd reason. Why do you act like a king when you're not?" he asked Aerin. "Why do you challenge me when you have everything?"

"I don't have everything," replied Aerin. "Do you remember when we first saw Maenellia? You were the first to lay eyes on her. It was never supposed to be me, but I couldn't let you win her heart. I kept pushing and fighting for her. And you sat back, afraid to challenge me. I knew you loved her, but I loved her more." He stared straight into Hensi's eyes. "When you became king, I hated it. As great of a warrior you are, you're no king in my eyes. It's true, you are my rival, but not a friend." Anger appeared on his face. "My clan defended this kingdom, this realm, and what do we get? Nothing. We get nothing in return because we're the demons that shoot black flames. Everyone would fear us if we ruled. So they denied the throne from us. That traitor Nopen, that spider demon. He helped ambush his brother Dravin!"

"Dravin Kimsu was going mad. Nopen only did what was right and stopped his brother," corrected Hensi. "Why do you keep your mind stuck in the past where you don't exist? Come back to reality and stand by me." Hensi let out one last plea to his old friend.

"I know my reality, Hensi," Aerin said with cold and hateful eyes piercing to Hensi's eyes. "You're just in the way!"

Hensi disapprovingly shook his head. "Think about your wife and children, Aerin," he warned. "Guess my old friend is now my enemy. I tried to make it easy for you. Now I'll show you my power as a king."

Smoke began surrounding Aerin. Then two magic-user guards surrounded him, each having magic restraint strings appearing out of their hands, tying Aerin's wrists together.

"This is how it is," smirked Aerin. "My clan fought by your clan since the beginning of time."

"You're a threat to the people, Aerin. I tried to prevent this, but you made it difficult." He placed his hand on Aerin's shoulders. "Don't ever disobey me again, Aerin. Don't ever put me in a position where I have to put the two people I love in danger."

Aerin nudged Hensi's hand off his shoulders. "You'll regret this, Hensi!"

Hensi turned his back to Aerin. "I already regretted it. Take him to the palace ground and show him his surprise." He felt pain in his heart. "And it's King Hensi," he ended as the guards took Aerin away.

Hensi shut his eyes, upset that he made an enemy in his beloved friends. Their fond memories now burned away because of their selfish pride. The difficulty of being king was finally catching to him, burning his insides as he urged to fight the pain of betrayal. As the king of Tigara, it was his duty to protect the people. Aerin was a threat he didn't want to get rid of.

Aerin calmly walked with the guards to the palace ground, his eyes shut, thinking about his next plan, remembering that he doesn't have the dragons by his side.

When he finally arrived at the palace ground, he opened his eyes slowly; and to his shock, he was faced with his family. On one side was his wife and three children in a cage made out of lightning rods. And on the other side was his older brother, Amin, beaten and battered, eyes bruised and barely opened. He was on his knees and breathing heavily. Both warrior and magic guards were surrounding his family.

Aerin was furious, clutching his fist. He wanted to escape the magic restraints of the guards and save his family and brother. He tried jerking his arms out of the rope. One of the guards kicked him behind the knees, bringing him to the ground. Aerin looked up at his family helplessly, feeling restrained like a wild animal as he might watch his family murdered in front of him.

Hensi appeared behind Aerin. "Look what you made me do, Aerin," he blamed. "I knew the dragons are not with you. I know that you brought an army outside my city walls. I have eyes all over the east."

"Father, help!" shouted Kiri.

"Look, Aerin," said Hensi. "The children are scared. You only have yourself to blame."

"Leave my family alone!" angered Aerin.

"Look at you, still fired with pride when you're on your knees." Hensi grabbed the top of Aerin's head and turned it toward Amin. "Look at your brother. We beat him because of your crime. He squeals like a dying pig when the guards beat him."

"You dare dishonor my clan," challenged Aerin, "after everything we have done!"

"I'm willing to do anything to tame the demon," said Hensi. "You live in my kingdom so obey my rules like a dog."

"Hensi, is this how you show power?" asked Maenellia.

"Showing power?" repeated Hensi as he looked over to Maenellia. "I don't need to show power when I am power. A crime was committed—treason in the king's name. You murdered a clan head. How would I look like if I turn the other cheek? A coward, a spineless king who's afraid of the demon clan?"

"Leave my children out of this, Hensi!" begged Maenellia. "They know nothing. I'm begging you, please!"

"Maenellia, I wish I can free them, let them be kids. But I was betrayed. They will learn the consequences of treason."

"You're a coward," mocked Aerin. "Leave my family out of it. Take my head."

"I'm amazed how much pride you have still, Aerin. But I need you alive. I have a plan for peace and uniting the kingdom. And you're someone I can use to make my goal a reality. You see, I want us to fight side by side again."

"I will never fight by your side again," said Aerin, clenching his teeth.

"Don't make me the villain, Aerin. You're the one that murdered a clan head," reminded Hensi. "How much do you love your family?"

"What are you planning?" questioned Aerin.

"Listen first, Aerin. What's more important? Your family or your older brother? Take a nice look at them. How much do you love them?"

"How dare you make me decide!" angered Aerin.

"You made me decide your fate. I was advised to kill you. But deep down in my heart, I couldn't. I can't kill the man I called a friend. We have our differences now. However, I still respect you and want you to live."

"We're no longer friends," reminded Aerin.

"I want to fix that," said Hensi. "Now choose who dies today."

Aerin looked over to his family and saw fear in their eyes and to Amin with pain on his face. It was obvious for him to pick his family over his brother. He couldn't stand to see his brother in pain.

"Amin!" called Aerin. "I love you, brother."

"I will always watch over you, little brother," replied Amin. "Protect your family, I'll be fine. I get to see Mother and Father early," he joked.

Tears began to form in Aerin's eyes. Maenellia began to cry and so did the children. Hensi tried to hide his sorrow.

"I'm sorry!" cried Aerin. "This wasn't supposed to happen like this."

"It's okay, Aerin," consoled Amin. "As the clan head, you did what was best for the clan. I can't be angry about that. I'll tell Father that you're a great clan head. You honored the clan the right way. I'm proud of you, and I'll make sure our ancestors in the heavens are proud of you too."

"I'll make sure you'll be honored, Amin," promised Aerin. "The clan will never forget your name!"

"I'm sorry, my dear friend," whispered Hensi. He signaled to the executioner to decapitate Amin's head.

The executioner was a giant of a man with a faceless mask. He lifted the giant sword over his head and quickly brought the sword to the neck of Amin, detaching the head of Amin from his body. Aerin watched helplessly and speechlessly. Maenellia looked away and used her body to block her children's view. Amin's body slumped to the ground, blood sprinkling from his severed neck, his head rolling and twitching away.

Isa was stunned. Unlike his two siblings who looked away, he stared into his uncle's eyes. It was the first time he witnessed death. He saw his father weaken and become silent. The man he once feared was helpless. Never before did he see his mother and father in a position where they were vulnerable.

*　*　*

After two days, Hensi let Aerin and his family free. They were kept safe in a tower in the palace. The family did not eat their food. They were silent and didn't speak to one another. Amin's body was cremated and given to Aerin in an urn.

Aerin was leading his army home. Maenellia rode beside him. When he told his captains what happened, they were all enraged. All wanted to raise war against the king.

Their path home was silent with revenge on everyone's mind. They passed by farms, but no children or farmers came out to see them or wave to them. The bright green grass felt like it had blood spilled on it. The blue sky felt like the gray clouds were blocking it.

Gorl rode up beside Aerin. "What are we going to do?" he asked. "We can't let this happen. We must avenge Amin!"

"We must wait," replied Aerin.

"I can't wait to avenge your brother's death," said Gorl. "We were disrespected."

"It's not like you to be impatient. When the time is right, we'll strike."

"We must do it soon," said Maenellia with rage in her eyes. "He will pay for putting fear in my children's hearts!"

"He will pay," assured Aerin. "He'll suffer even after death."

Jen-Song rode to the front. "My lord, we're far from the capital."

"Good," said Aerin. He raised his hand to stop the travel. "We'll set camp here and continue when the sun rises."

The camp was quiet. No smile, no singing, only rage and hunger for revenge. Each soldier expected that they will soon go to war with the king and his army. Aerin, Maenellia, Jen-Song, Gorl, Cholee, and Nellina sat around the fire in front of Aerin's tent. They sipped on jasmine tea.

"My lord, what will we do with the spy?" asked Cholee.

The king had appointed his nephew Sai as a watcher for Aerin. Sai had to report all doings of Aerin to the king, making sure Aerin wouldn't act out of line again.

Aerin looked over to Sai sitting alone by a fire. "Are the children asleep?" Aerin asked Maenellia.

Maenellia nodded, agreeing with Aerin.

"Good, let them relax," said Aerin. "Bring that spy over."

Jen-Song left to bring Sai over. When he got back, Sai looked confused and nervous.

"Sit." Aerin pointed. "Relax, you're part of my clan now."

"Yes, my lord." Sai sat, nervously looking around.

Jen-Song handed Sai a cup of tea, and he sipped it slowly, peeking at each person around him.

"This tea is tasty, thank you!" Sai said gratefully.

"Our tea is one of the best in the kingdom," said Gorl with cold eyes.

"How old are you?" asked Aerin.

"T-twenty, my lord," replied Sai nervously.

"Were you ever taught how to use a sword?" asked Aerin.

"No, never held a sword in my life. Spent most of my life in the books." Sai laughed, looking around and realizing no one was laughing with him. "Look, I know you all won't open up to me just yet. I'm a stranger, but I'm here to help."

"You're not here to help," corrected Aerin. "Your uncle appointed you as a watcher. To make sure I stay in line."

"I'm not a spy. I'm on your side," Sai nervously defended himself.

"How can I trust you when my brother was murdered by your uncle's order?" questioned Aerin.

"I'm sorry—"

"Sorry won't bring back my brother, kid," Aerin cut off Sai. He tossed a sword to Sai's feet. "Pick it up."

Sai looked down at the sword, confused why Aerin wanted him to pick the sword up. "I don't understand."

"I can't kill an unarmed man," Aerin calmly said.

"I'm not a fighter," Sai nervously reminded.

"Pick up the sword!" Aerin violently demanded.

Sai nervously stood and picked the sword up, his hands trembling as he tried to hold the heavy sword, his legs shaking and his pleading eyes begging Aerin. "Please, my lord. I don't want to die."

"Don't beg for your life, it's embarrassing." Aerin stood. "Look, I'm declaring war against the king. Be honor that you'll be the first to die."

"No, no. Please spare me!" cried Sai, dropping to his knees and begging.

Jen-Song stood Sai back up and gave him the sword to hold.

"In war, a warrior shall show no mercy to the enemy," said Aerin. He looked as if a demon was possessing him, raising his hand and black flames appearing around Sai and slowly consuming Sai as he screamed in agony.

Within ten seconds, Sai's flesh was burned off his bone cleanly. The flames disappeared. There was a vile, cold look in Aerin's eyes, admiring the damage he had done to the young man. His soldiers surrounded him and looked at him.

"It is time we detach our self from the king!" declared Aerin. "We have drawn first blood! My men and women follow me on a new path. Let us build our kingdom with our law. We will no longer take orders from Hensi! Tell me, who runs with the demon!"

The soldiers' morale boosted up. They all cheered and watched their great leader, Aerin, as he declared war with King Hensi. Aerin raised his hands in the air and fired black flames into the sky, telling the gods a new king was coming.

Chapter Eleven

Kingdom of Wintra

Zhou sat on his bed inside the comfort of his tent, staring intensely at the bone crown he had kept after Rula's ambush, rubbing his skin on the flesh of human bones as it reflected his eyes. When he stabbed Rula, a sense of relief was lifted off him, finally killing the man that was putting his people in distress. Even though he was proud, he still felt lost. What was next? he thought as he sat alone in his tent with the bone crown.

He felt like a wanted man in the north for killing the king. Still, he wanted to continue his goal to end the era of kings. After killing Rula, he gathered all the able fighters from the village, man or woman, and set camp in the Winter Forest near Polar City, the capital city of Wintra, so he could control and halt any supplies to the city.

Zhou placed the crown on his nightstand and walked out of his tent. It was nighttime as he stepped out. His fighters were all sitting near a fire at the center of the camp to keep themselves warm from the dreaded cold. The smell of burning wood and roasted wind turkey filled the air. Everyone was happy as they enjoyed each other's company, telling old northern tales and riddles to each other.

Zhou spotted Gen sitting alone near the entrance of his tent drinking tea with a rare smile over his face, watching as the rebels laughed amongst each other. He quickly made his way to Gen.

"It seems like we won," said Zhou as he approached Gen.

Gen gently bowed his head and quickly poured Zhou a cup of tea. "Sit, my friend," said Gen cheerfully as he handed Zhou the cup of tea. "The moon is full today, so all should be full."

Zhou took the tea and sat near Gen, taking a sip of the tea. "Mhm, ginger tea?" He loved ginger tea, believing that it'll bring him good health.

"Cold nights like these needs ginger tea, my friend," said Gen.

"I agree," agreed Zhou, lifting his tea in thanks then sipping it again. He looked at his people again. "Gen, do tell me the truth." A sense of doubt rose upon him. "Are we doing the right thing? Was killing Rula the right thing?"

Gen took his time to answer, still watching the smile on the people's faces. "Look at them," he started. "They're all merry and laughing. None of them want to go back to a time when being happy was difficult." He sipped his tea. "They love you, there's nothing you can do that'll make them turn against you. You did something that no one ever planned to do. Not even the most treacherous man will. You killed a king but in the name of unselfishness. You brought justice for these people. If doubt still bothers you, my friend, do know that all these people, including me, owe you our lives?"

"You're an inspiring man, Gen." Zhou wondered why someone like Gen was willing to follow him. "But why me? Why do you follow me? There are many clans to serve under, but you chose someone that's not a clan member."

"We are all followers. Us mortals have no sense of direction." Gen sipped his tea. "Why I follow you? We knew each other since we were kids. There was something about you that made the other kids follow you. When I finally escaped my life of poverty and served under the royal clan, I found out quickly that there was no such thing as happiness. My hard work for acknowledgment was a waste . . . But you, my friend, you lit a fire in me. That night at the tavern, I remember your speech about a new era. Your determination made the drunks sober. Everyone clapped and cheered for you. You may not know this, but you're a natural-born leader. You have direction . . . you gave me direction. You are the common people's hope."

Zhou was impressed and inspired by Gen's confession. He never once thought of himself to be a leader. It was natural for him to uplift people. He didn't have the luxury of growing up sitting on a pile of gold. Everything he earned was from hard work and dedication. As a young boy, seeing his parents struggle motivated him to never live the same life as theirs. He remembered times where he didn't eat, times where he heard his mother crying because his father was passed out outside on the steps. When he earned the title of captain under the Diamond clan, all his past struggles finally disappeared.

"We were raised under the dirt," said Zhou, "growing up and seeing the difficulties of my parents' lives. I didn't want that life for myself. I feared failure. I refused the taste of ale. I have taken all the sorrow in me and locked it away. Now my life is for the common people. With you by my side, with the spirit of my people, I'll end the era of kings."

Spinder approached the men with a wary look over his face. In hand was a note he had received from a messenger owl. "Zhou, I have news from the king's advisers," he reported.

"What of it?" asked Zhou. "Will they finally surrender?"

"No, they wish to see you," replied Spinder.

"I don't trust them," worried Gen. "It could be a trap."

"I agree with, Gen," said Spinder. "We don't know what they're planning."

Zhou thought for a while wondering if he should pay a visit to the royal advisers or listen to his two most trusted allies. He thought about all the scenarios that could happen. There was a possible chance where they think that he was an idiot and meet them, just to get himself ambushed or imprisonment. Then there was a chance where they want to make a deal so no more blood could be spilled.

"If they want to see me, then I'll present myself before them," said Zhou as he finally made his decision. "Death does not fear me. If I'm killed, then my men and women will avenge me!"

Both Gen and Spinder had a concerned look on their face. They both remembered how the royal advisers operate. All the advisers had a sense of dishonesty around them. There was something always planning by the king's advisers.

"I don't trust them," worried Gen. "There's always something brewing in the ice palace."

"I'm not worried," assured Zhou. "I'm willing to die for justice."

"I'll go with you," suggested Spinder.

"No, I'll go alone. If anything does happen to me, then you two will lead the rebellion." Zhou stood and drank his tea as it started to cool. "I shall leave when the sun rises."

"What do we tell the men and women?" asked Spinder.

"Tell them the truth," replied Zhou. "For now, keep it between the three of us. If anybody else hears of this, they will try to stop me." He looked to his people. "Allow them to enjoy the moment. They deserve to laugh and celebrate after what they had been through."

Zhou left Spinder and Gen to head back to his tent. He wondered if it was a good idea to meet the royal adviser, if it was worth his life. He wanted to build a new era in the north to then expand it into the rest of the kingdom, where everyone could roam freely and peacefully around the land, where power was equal and where the common and the poor were not forgotten.

* * *

As the night got quieter and the air became cooler, many of the Unchained began to wearily escape to their tents after a long night of eating and drinking. The stars in the sky were bright, giving life to the dark gloomy sky. Kayten strayed away from the camp to be alone. He lay on a giant rock, staring at the bright stars, remembering the days his mother would stare at the stars with him as they lay on their back deck. The memories sadden him. He raised his arm and pointed to the stars, trying to connect the millions of stars.

He then remembered the golden-masked man that was spying on him and Osa, wondering who the person was and why the person was watching him then wondering how that person could disappear so instantly. That was the world of Telamis, with people with unusual skills. As his mind drifted away from reality and wonders took over, he remembered what Osa had suggested to him—to leave the Unchained. He tried to understand what Osa meant. The Unchained was all Kayten knew after the Mirky Village massacre. Why would he leave Zhou, his teacher, and leave everything else he knew behind him?

"There you are," announced Jamori. Beside him was Osa. "Why are you out here?" He looked up to the sky and smiled at the full moon. "Ah, it's a full moon."

Kayten sat up. "I needed to think," he answered.

"Think about what?" asked Jamori curiously.

Kayten took a glance at Osa, which Jamori noticed.

"Are you two planning something without me?" asked Jamori jealously.

"No," Osa replied quickly. "I only suggested that the both of you leave this madness."

"Madness!" exclaimed a confused Jamori. "What are you talking about?"

"Jamori, you can't be that much of a fool! Are you blind to what's happening? A king was killed in our names. Everyone involved will be punished by the gods."

"That spineless king deserved to die," said Jamori with anger. "I curse his death. I wish for him to never see the lights of heaven."

"Why should we be vile like him? The gods will not forgive us for killing a king," reminded Osa.

"He ordered the death of my clan, the villagers of Mirky Village. All of those lives that were taken never got a chance to avenge themselves. So we avenged it for them." He turned to leave, with anger running in him. "Osa, don't ever question our way of revenge again." He stormed away, leaving Kayten and Osa alone in the forest.

Osa stood still, watching Jamori leave with a smile over his face. He understood why Jamori was angry, but inside, he was upset that Jamori couldn't see the truth in reality. He then looked over to Kayten who had an upset look over his face.

"I understand why he's mad," Osa said. "He's not wrong . . ." He paused and looked to the stars in the sky. "We shouldn't become prisoners of revenge."

"We shouldn't betray the hand that feeds us," said Kayten.

"If Zhou loves us like his own sons, then he should let us decide our own faith," he finished and walked away. But he noticed that the golden-masked figure was hiding up a tree, watching them as it painted. When he looked to the golden-masked figure's direction, it turned into a crow that fled away. He turned back and smiled, not sure why the mysterious person was following him.

* * *

The Unchained's campsite was quiet since everyone was still sound asleep. The sun began to slowly rise behind the mountain to begin a new day. Zhou stared at his reflection from his bowl of water with his train of thought lost. During his sleep, he dreamed about sitting on the bone throne again. As he sat on the throne, there were hundreds of undead soldiers bowing down to him still. All had hollow eyes that placed fear in him. He wondered what his dream meant. He then focused his attention on the bone crown resting on his nightstand. Two halves of him fighting each other, one telling him to place the crown over his head while the other urged him not to.

Gen entered the tent with a doubtful look over his face. "The horse is ready, Zhou," he said.

Zhou nodded his head.

"Are you sure about this?" asked Gen, hoping that Zhou would change his mind.

"I'm sure," replied Zhou. "I must do this for our people and freedom."

"What if . . . they try to ambush you?"

"If I die, you'll lead them. I trust you the most."

"And how about the boy?"

"Kayten is important to us. He's crucial to our path toward freedom and ending the era of kings."

"I don't understand why a common boy is so important to you," wondered Gen.

Zhou chuckled. "I should get going." Before he stepped out of the tent, he stopped. "Kayten is someone that'll end everything," he finished.

* * *

When Zhou arrived at Polar City, he realized the city had changed. It was no longer that beautiful ice and white stone city anymore. Buildings looked like it was falling apart, the roads looked dead and in ruins. It felt like he was walking through a long dark tunnel alone with no sounds of life while riding through the city. The air in the city reeked of decaying bodies, shit, and piss. He wondered what Rula had done to the city. How could he let the city fall apart? The capital city now looked like an ancient forgotten city, with nature overtaking it.

Finally, he arrived outside the gates of the Winter Palace. The palace was made out of white stones. He remembered serving the royal clan and coming to the palace. The palace was always beautiful every time he was there. Looking at it now, it still looked the same. It seemed like it was the only thing that was kept.

The giant white stone gate opened. As he entered the palace ground, a guard approached him, wearing white armor with a polar bear sigil on the right shoulder plate.

"Lord Zhou." The guard bowed. "I'll be escorting you."

"I'm no lord," corrected Zhou.

The guard ignored Zhou and helped him off his horse. Zhou could feel something strange in the air. There were no servants, no advisers greeting him. Something strange was creeping around the palace. Something he couldn't see nor understand.

While following the guard through the palace, he tried to find any sound of life. The guard had a stoic look on his face. At every corner of the palace, there were guards, all with the same expressionless look, standing still like they were dead.

They finally arrived at two giant doors made out of ice and white stones. Zhou looked up at the marvelous door and remembered perfectly what this room was. It was the Hall of Law, where the king decided on his judgment, law, and punishment. He was going to stand in the center of the hall while the queen and the advisers sat up high on a balcony, glaring down on him.

The guard opened the two giant doors and led Zhou into the Hall of Law. It was exactly how he remembered it. Before coming to the center, he had to walk a long path made out of white stones. On each side of the stone was water with many snow fish swimming in it. They were pure white fish with ice-blue eyes.

Zhou looked back to see if the guard was following him. The guard shut the door, leaving Zhou alone. It was a life-or-death situation for Zhou. There was no escape for him. Walking the long path to the center, he wondered if he could turn back. But his pride kept him moving forward. He finally arrived at the center and looked around, looking up to see who was surrounding him from fifteen feet above. He had a feeling he could be ambushed at any time. Maybe archers will appear and shoot him down.

Suddenly, the room began to be lit up by light orbs floating around the room, startling him. When he looked up, to his surprise, he wasn't facing the queen nor any of the advisers. At the center sat a man wearing a white mask with only the eyes, no mouth and nose. On the left balcony sat a person with a red mask; next to the red-masked person was a person with a blue mask. Sitting on the other side was a person wearing a bronze mask, and the next bronze-masked person was a person wearing a yellow mask. All had only the eyes and no mouth and nose, all wearing the same color of the cloak as their mask.

Zhou was afraid and confused with masked people who were staring down at him. It felt like he was being looked down on by five undead people. He meddled with thoughts, trying to think of a plan or what to say to them. Where were the queen and the advisers? There should be many advisers sitting above and deciding his punishment.

"We are the five elements," revealed the white mask, the voice sounding like a man. "The true ruler of the north. I am Wind."

"I am Fire," said the red mask, the voice sounding like a woman.

"I am Water," said the blue mask, the voice sounding like a man.

"I am Earth," said the bronze mask, the voice sounding like a man.

"I am Lightning," said the yellow mask, the voice sounding like a woman.

"I don't understand," said a confused Zhou.

"Silence, human. We the elements ask the questions!" shouted Fire in an ordering tone.

Zhou was taken aback, his heart beating fast with fear. He wanted to run back and leave. But his legs were frozen to the cold white stone ground.

"You have committed a crime and must pay!" said Lightning.

"Pay with his head." suggested Water calmly.

"No, lock him in a dungeon for eternity!" suggested Earth's voice, which sounded rough.

"Feed him to the citizens of the city, they must be hungry," said Lightning.

They all mumbled in agreement.

"Tell me, how do you want to be punished, Zhou Bi?" asked Wind.

"I want to make a deal," suggested Zhou.

"A deal!" angered Fire. "Are you mocking us!"

"Stupid man," insulted Earth.

They all mumbled insults toward Zhou, except for Wind, who kept quiet. Zhou didn't know what these five were thinking since their masks were covering their faces. Suddenly Wind lifts his hand in the air to settle the other four.

"A deal?" questioned Wind with curiosity. "What deal can match your crime for the king murder?"

"I'll tell you, but you all must answer me first." Bargain Zhou.

"How dare you insult us!" Shouted Fire standing from her chair.

"Sit, Fire!" Ordered Wind to Fire.

Fire sat back down on her chair. Zhou could feel flames coming from her. Right then, he knew these were no ordinary people. They had the ability that could kill him. He had to be careful in dealing with them or his life will end. Still in the back of his mind, he wondered where the queen and the advisers were.

"Ask away, Zhou Bi," allowed Wind.

"Where's the queen and the advisers?" asked Zhou.

"Dead," replied Wind bluntly.

"How?" asked a confused Zhou.

"Enough questions," rejected Wind. "Now tell us the deal."

"I will not tell you the deal until you tell me what's going on!" demanded Zhou, finding his confidence.

Lightning nearly hit Zhou, forcing him to fall to the ground on his back. He looked to where the direction of the lightning came from and saw Lightning standing up from her chair with arms out.

"You are in no position to make demands, Zhou," warned Wind. "We determine if you shall live or not."

Chills began to ran down the spine of Zhou, confused who these people were and fearful of what they could do to him.

"We are the true ruler of the north," began Wind. "All the northern peasants serve under us. We created a war for our entertainment. Don't anger us or we'll end the war."

"Is people's lives entertainment to all of you?" asked Zhou as he stood back up. "Is our pain a game to you all?"

"The common and poor life is nothing to us," answered Water.

"You think it's funny to laugh and drink over our suffering?" asked Zhou, feeling angry that these people were insulting the common and poor.

"How valiant of you," insulted Fire. "Defending the people that can't defend themselves."

"I defend them because I know I can bring freedom and end the era of kings."

"Don't give them false hope," advised Wind mockingly. "There's no such thing as freedom. If there was freedom, then everyone will act out of order. People of the north needs to be controlled and tamed. Your king failed to control his people, so we the five elements controlled him."

"Just who the hell do you guys think you are?" angered Zhou.

"We're the closest thing to the gods. We determine the outcome in the north. But you . . . you little insect ruined everything," blamed Wind.

"How did I ruin everything?" asked Zhou.

"It's time we end this conversation. Time for you to pay for the king's death," said Wind. "You know too much. The deal you planned to offer no longer interests me. Your punishment—"

"Wait!" stopped Zhou. "You can't kill me."

"How dare you!" yelled Fire.

"It's too late, Zhou," denied Wind.

"It's not. I have someone that will favor all of you."

"I no longer care," said Wind.

"I have a boy who's a descendant of the Dru clan. His blood is pure."

"A Dru?" questioned Wind.

The rest of the four elements mumbled to each other. The Dru clan had all died hundreds of years ago. They were the first human rulers when Telmis was one kingdom. They were a clan much stronger than the Kimsu clan. They could use their blood as a weapon, as it came out of the pores of their body to kill their enemies. Their blood could be used to summon Taken, the Lord of Dragons, the strongest winged dragon of all winged dragons, a dragon that was capable of ending the world until members of the Dru family sealed him away, hiding him away in the Island of Blue Stone.

"Yes, I have a Dru in my service," confirmed Zhou. "He doesn't know it yet."

"You are lying!" challenged Fire. "The Dru clan all perished hundredths of years ago."

"This boy is pure blood! He's the main branch. Believe me, I was surprised too. The boy was drenched in his blood when I found him passed out under the stairs of his home during the Mirky Village massacre, hiding when his father and mother were being killed. The soldiers in the home were all sliced up from face to toe. Their armor looked deeply penetrated. The whole house was covered in blood. Right then, I knew that boy was a Dru. Only a Dru can control their blood as a weapon. He slept till the fourth purple moon since a lot of blood was lost. He looked dead, but amazingly, he woke up, not recalling a thing, but only crying."

"What is the boy's name?" asked Wind.

"Jamori Kong," lied Zhou.

"A Kong?" questioned Wind.

"Yes, he's adopted," lied Zhou again.

"How do I know that you're not lying?" doubted Wind.

"I'll deliver his blood," offered Zhou.

"No, bring us the boy," said Earth.

"He can't control his power yet. There's no chance the five of you will take him if he gets out of hand," warned Zhou.

"And you can?" questioned Water.

"He trusts me."

"Fine, bring us his blood. If it's true, then we'll want the boy, and your crime for the king's murder will be excuse," said Wind.

"No, I murdered the king because that's my sin for justice. I'll live with that crime. There's something else I want. My path to end the era of kings will continue. The boy is yours if his blood proves that he's a Dru. But in return, I want to be king of the north."

The five elements all mumbled to each other. Zhou stood in the center as the mumbles echoed the Hall of Law. Zhou wondered if they will take his offer. Even though he lied to them, he had a plan in mind. Kayten was important to him. The blood of Kayten was the key to end the era of kings.

"If the boy is a bloodline of the Dru clan, then you shall be king," concluded Wind. "If you are lying, then we'll send thousands of royal armies to your village and finish the massacre."

Zhou bowed. "I'll bring the blood. I'll need time to draw the boy's blood out. He can be dangerous if I draw it without caution."

"You want us to wait?" raged Fire.

"The blood acts on its own, and the boy is a bit of a hothead," said Zhou.

"Fine," allowed Wind. "But don't keep us waiting too long. There will be spies watching you, making sure you're not planning any tricks."

"I am an honest man. I'll never trick as it goes against my honor," lied Zhou.

Zhou left the Hall of Law with a hidden smirk across his face, proud that he had tricked the five elements. He had a goal to accomplish. Sacrificing one of his students was the cost of his goal, even if the student was his dear friend's son. He pictured himself on the throne and finally changing the face of the land, bringing an end to the era of kings, where he would be the king of Telamis.

Chapter Twelve

Heart Village

Indris sat alone in his room, meditating on the wooden floor, eyes shut as he eased his mind. Upon arriving to Heart Village, the villagers were all afraid, locking themselves in their homes. The Men of Hate had raided their village many times to the point where all the villagers were afraid of outsiders. The village lord decided to abandon the village and escape the Men of Hate terror. The soldiers settled at the village fortress, Full Heart Fortress.

Indris tried to clear his mind. Lately, his mind had been distressed. There were nights when he couldn't sleep and days he felt tired. He hasn't decided what to do with the Men of Hate camp near the village yet. Planning an attack on the camp was the last thing on his mind. All he could think about was the letter that was sent to him, a letter telling him about his uncle's death and plans moving forward. The era of peace was supposed to last forever, or so he thought. Then his brother Iszra crossed his mind. Was he smart to disappear? Indris wished Iszra was around, maybe then their father won't act out of ambition and hatred.

The door opened, and Akin entered the room, upset that he couldn't see his brother for one last time. He would've died beside Amin because of his hot-tempered personality. "It's time," said Akin.

Indris stood up and patted himself clean. "It doesn't feel right, Uncle," concerned Indris.

Akin took a sip of ale from his tiny glass bottle. "I don't understand your father. But right now, we have to pay respect to Amin." After finding the news that his brother was executed, Akin decided to drink his night away at the tavern then waking in the morning and drinking again.

Indris walked by Akin and had a disappointed look over his face. The stench of ale surrounded Akin, upset that his uncle was drinking to ease his pain. He walked out of the door without saying a word to Akin. Waiting by the door was Airian, Kunjae, and Estrey.

*   *   *

Indris knelt in front of the weeping tree outside of Heart Village on top of a hill, both hands resting on his thigh as he shut his eyes with his head down. Next to him was Akin, also in the same position as Indris. Behind them stood Airian and Kunjae, silently paying their respects to Amin and their dead ancestors. Standing afar was Estrey.

People came to the weeping tree to pay respect to the dead. All over the land from east to south and west to north, there was a weeping tree. The wood on the tree was white, and the leaves was golden. It was believed that the weeping trees were angels from heaven that turned themselves into the tree, used as messengers for one that is mourning to ones that are dead.

Indris stood. "We should head back. There's work that's to be done."

Akin was still kneeling before the weeping tree. "You all go on ahead. I'll stay a little longer."

Indris left with Airian following him. Kunjae decided to stay behind. He waited till others couldn't be seen anymore then stood up and bowed his head to his uncle, leaving Amin to deal with his own sorrow. He understood that happiness was rare for his clan. Everyone in his family was dealing with their own conflict. While the man was sunk in his own ambition, ignoring his own children, wife, and brother, the reaper crept behind, waiting to take them one by one. Maybe then his father would see that his ambition meant nothing.

*   *   *

When Kunjae arrived to the village, there were villagers out walking around and about. But their faces were gray and sleepless. There were some shops that were open. Most of the villagers decided to stay inside their homes. Even if the Kimsu guards were there to protect them, they were still afraid. They got used to random attacks from the Men of Hate to the point they begin to fear for their life. Every day they expected an attack from those lawless people. Every time the Men of Hate attacked them, they'd take the rice supplies. If there weren't enough rice, then they'd take their daughters or wives. Sometimes the body of the victims would be left at an open grave in the forest of Trap.

Kunjae made his way to the palace, thinking little of the villagers. He didn't like it that they couldn't defend themselves. Everywhere he turned he saw able men and women that could hold a sword and fend off the Men of Hate. But instead, they chose to be weak and relied on the Kimsu clan. He showed little sympathy toward people that couldn't fight for themselves.

As he continued to walk on the dirt streets, he bumped into a young boy that was crouched down playing with ants. He looked down at the boy with a blank look. But the boy didn't seem to be afraid of him. The boy had dirt smudged all over his face. His clothes were also dirty, riddled with holes in them. Kunjae looked around to see if anyone was around, like maybe his parents. But it was just the two of them.

"Hi, mister," greeted the boy cheerfully.

"Move out of the way, kid," Kunjae rudely said to the boy. He pushed the kid aside and continued to walk.

"Wait, mister. Are you a soldier for the Kimsu clan?" asked the boy.

"Go wash yourself, kid," insulted Kunjae, ignoring the boy's question.

The kid put his hands on his hip. "My papa thinks that we're all going to die."

Kunjae stopped walking and sighed. No child shouldn't be thinking about death. The kid looked to be around five years old. When he was five, he never thought about death. Instead, he was playing with wooden toys and rolling in the dirt.

He turned back to the kid and crouched to his level, staring into his innocent eyes. "Look, kid, go play, all right. Your father should be a man and never talk about death in front of you." He put his hand on the kid's head. "There's nothing to be afraid of." He messed the kid's hair up and stood back up, reaching into his pocket to give the kid a piece of candy.

"Are you afraid of anything, mister?" asked the boy curiously as took the candy from Kunjae.

Kunjae was stunned by the kid's question. The innocent kid seemed to love asking questions. "I'm afraid of spiders," lied Kunjae then turning to leave.

As he walked away from the kid, he felt a slight breeze hitting his back, making the little hair on his body stand. He stopped walking and turned around. The kid was no longer standing at the spot. But what was left was the piece of candy he gave. All he could do was smile and continue his walk, staring at his hand. "Interesting," he said to himself with a smile.

* * *

Inside the war room was Indris, Akin, and Estrey. They were looking over a map of the eastern kingdom. There was an X marked on the map, where the Men of Hate was camping in the forest. Indris was debating if he wanted to invade their camp or not.

"Nephew, I suggest we attack tonight," suggested Akin. "We have to finish them off quickly and head home. Brother needs us by his side."

"I agree with Akin," agreed Estrey. "The sooner we wipe them out, the sooner our rice supplies return."

"We haven't scouted the whole area yet," reasoned Indris. "They can ambush us."

"We can't wait!" argued Akin.

"I can't put the lives of my soldiers and brothers in jeopardy, Uncle," explained Indris. "If my father is more important, then you leave. Go be by his side to fight with the king."

"Are you not going to fight by your father's side, your clan's side . . . Amin's side?" challenged Akin.

"Are you questioning my loyalty to the clan and my father? This clan is my life. If my father decides to go into war with the king, what choice do I have? Right now, my priority is Heart Village and the Men of Hate. Understand, Uncle, without this village, our rice supplies will be depleted, and our soldiers will suffer."

"We know where they are hiding. So what are we waiting for? We have the seven protectors of heaven by our side. Best not waste our luck."

"You're not here to advise me, Uncle. You're here to watch over my brothers. So leave this room while I think of a plan," ordered Indris.

Akin slammed his fist on the table and stormed out of the room, grunting and mumbling as he left then slamming the door behind him. He was still grieving Amin's death, and ale in his body was making him angry.

"He's drunk," observed Indris. "He can't fight. Order the guards to watch over him. He's not allowed to leave this fort until he's sober."

"Understood," said Estrey. He noticed the distress on Indris's face. "You know Akin is right."

"I know."

"What are you waiting for?" asked Estrey.

"Truthfully, I don't know what I'm waiting for," answered Indris. "My gut is telling me not to invade, but the logical plan is to invade."

"It's your decision, Captain."

Indris continued to ponder. His gut was telling him to hold off on the attack, having a feeling something bad was going to happen. He didn't want to lead his soldiers into a trap and didn't want to put his brother in harm's way. "Fine, we'll destroy their camp tonight."

*   *   *

The sun was slowly fading away. Many of the shops in the village were closing for the day. There was unease in the air. The Kimsu soldiers were preparing to invade the Men of Hate camp. Many of the villagers prayed that the Kimsu comes out as the victor. But in the back of their mind, they thought the worst. Some refused to sleep, fearing that the Men of Hate would break into their homes and murder them.

The Men of Hate were gruesome people who hated common life. They always fought the opposite side of every war. Before the beginning of the great clans, Telamis was ruled by the Horn people, the Men of Hate, winged dragons, spirit dragons, and phoenixes. The Men of Hate wasn't called by their given known name. Before, they were known as the Moon people. They were enemies to the Horn head people and were masters of guerilla warfare. When the great clan rose thousands of years ago, the

Moon people lost their name and became the Men of Hate. Hatred brought them to be enemies against the clans of Telamis.

Kunjae watched as Airian swung his sword on the grounds of the fortress. Other soldiers were preparing for the ambush on the Men of Hate, and others were socializing with each other. Even though they were going into battle, all the soldiers all seemed calm. Airian, on the other hand, was anxious to have his first taste in battle. He waited his whole life to become a warrior; finally, the time had come. He could show his father his worth in battle.

He gripped on to the handle of his sword and stared at his reflection from the blade, picturing himself as a hero of war. The blade would soon be drenched in blood. It would no longer be a virgin to war. The sword was given to him by his father before he parted ways to Heart Village. The blade was a single edge, the handle was black, wrapped around a golden string. The pommel of the sword was a demon head.

"Look at you, hothead." Kunjae smiled. "Ready to become a hero," he teased.

Airian knew Kunjae was teasing him. "Unlike you, I have a goal."

"Tell me, what is your goal?"

"Why should I? You'll just tease me about it."

"Because I'm your brother and I'm curious," said Kunjae.

"I'm not telling you," refused Airian. "You're not worth my time."

"Don't hurt my feelings, big brother," joked Kunjae.

"Boys!" called Akin in a strict voice.

Both boys turned to Akin. Airian was excited to see his uncle. Kunjae had a nonchalant look over his face when he turned.

"Uncle!" said Airian excitedly. "I'm ready to fight by your side."

"I'm sorry, I won't be fighting by your side, Airian," apologized Akin. "Your brother has ordered me to stay behind." He was bothered that he wouldn't fight alongside his young nephews.

"Why would he do that?" asked a confused Airian. "You're a great warrior and our uncle. He shouldn't hold you back."

"I'm afraid he's right with his decision." Akin was ashamed that he let his drinking hinder his opportunity. "Since I won't be fighting by your side, remember to watch each other's back. Let your instinct take control. Don't make decisions during a time of war. Hesitation will get you kill," he advised. He reached into his pocket and pulled out two necklaces. One was of a weeping man covering his face in his hands, and the other was of a dagger. Both were carved out of tiger bones. "These two necklaces were given to me by my father. I want you two to have it." He handed Airian the dagger necklace and Kunjae the weeping man necklace.

"There's a bad meaning behind this necklace," recalled Kunjae. He stared at the weeping man necklace in his palm.

"Yes, I know the story. A father killed his own son with a dagger in battle and wept over the body when the mask was removed off the son."

"Then why should we wear it?" asked Kunjae.

"Because the father found the path of peace. So whenever you two are lost, the path of peace will uncover itself."

Both Airian and Kunjae wore the necklaces around their necks.

"Thank you, Uncle," said Airian. "I'll fight in your honor and our clan!"

"Good, I'm sorry I can't fight with the both of you," Akin apologized again.

Kunjae squeezed the necklace in his palm. Strange that his uncle gave him the weeping man. He knew the story well since his grandpa loved telling the story to him when he was younger. His uncle didn't tell the whole story. He never mentioned the part that the father and son was a Kimsu. That father was mad because he was a victim of curse magic. The son was not wearing a mask. His father couldn't see his true identity until one of them was dead. The son's killer was Taemin Kimsu.

* * *

"Captain, the men and women are ready," said Estrey.

Indris stood outside the entrance of the village. He turned around and saw sixty warriors ready for battle. Villagers were outside their home with concern and hope on their faces. The soldiers looked fearless, gripping on to their spears.

"Tonight, some of you will die and some of you will live. We are not fighting for a selfish goal. We are fighting for the villagers of Heart Village. These Men of Hate are monsters that terrorized these villagers. But tonight, we will be the monster to the Men of Hate, and we'll return as heroes!" Motivated Indris.

The soldiers started to cheer, their voice echoing to the heavens to let the gods know that they needed their protection. Airian cheered along, bloodthirsty for war while Kunjae stayed quiet. Finding that Indris didn't believe in his own speech, he stood with a smile over his face and shook his head in doubt.

"Don't cheer, hothead," advised Kunjae.

"Why? Why are you not happy we're finally fighting for our clan?"

With a seriousness over his face, Kunjae looked over to Airian. "Our leader is distracted."

* * *

Indris led his soldiers into the forest of Trap, a shared forest that stretched past the border between the north and east. They decided to walk in groups, creating distance with each other, avoiding the path and staying within the forest. Both Airian and Kunjae was grouped with Indris. They followed their brother as he navigated his way through the forest. He finally stopped and looked to the side, smelling the air that was filled with smoke, sensing that they were close to the Men of Hate camp. He looked over to both sides and signaled to each group leader to halt. He then looked forward and took three deep long breaths.

"Why'd we stop?" questioned Airian, gripping the handle of the sheathed sword tightly.

"Do you smell it?" asked Indris.

Airian sniffed to figure out what his brother was smelling. "I smell smoke."

"That means we're close," said Indris.

"Then we should attack," urged Airian as his heart began to beat. The blood in his body boiled, and warm nervous sweat dripped from his forehead.

"Relaxed, hothead," noticed Kunjae. "Indris has a plan. Am I correct?"

"No, I actually don't," replied Indris.

"I guess we're going to die," he joked.

Airian was confused, his confidence left him. Nervousness and fear took over him. He wasn't ready to fight. His hand was shaking, and sweat began to increasingly drip from his forehead. "What are you talking about no plan?" he asked Indris nervously. "You expect us to fight with no plan?"

"It's instinct, little brother," said Indris. "If you can't fight with instinct, then don't become a warrior." He stood up and unsheathed his sword; then pointing it forward, he directed his soldiers to ambush the camp.

The Kimsu soldiers all stood and charged, yelling their lungs out toward the camp, hoping to find the Men of Hate with a surprised look on their faces as they were going to die. It was the way of life in Telamis. The life of a warrior or magic user comes with the expectation of death. Fame and heroism come with a cost. All these men and women knew it. That was why they chose the path of war and fighting. They were willing to sacrifice their lives in the name of their pride. Some were forced to be warriors and magic users. Their free will was taken away from them, but there was no denying they too were hungry for the taste of victory.

Kunjae looked over to a nervous Airian, frozen and lost as the time to fight neared. He didn't charge with the others. Feeling like a lost child looking for his parents. He knew Airian wasn't ready to fight. Airian was all talk. His confidence was only a mask to hide his fear. It was a lie to his identity.

"This is what you want, hothead." Mocked Kunjae. "Charge and fight." He stood up and walked instead of charging with the soldiers.

Airian looked up and saw the back of every soldier as they were all prepared to die. He stood up and tried to find some confidence. Then suddenly out of instinct, he started to run, running and yelling right by Kunjae, waving his sword in the air like the other soldiers.

When Indris and the rest arrived at the camp, they arrived at an empty camping ground, the campfire still burning. There were about fifty tents. They all looked confused. Indris ordered his men to search the tents, and they came back with nothing. There was no one at the campsite.

"Should've had a plan," mocked Kunjae as he finally arrived.

"They should be here," said a confused Indris. "Where else can they go?"

"Captain," called Estrey. "What should we do?"

Indris opened his hand, and blue flames danced on his palm. "We're burning this camp down," replied Indris.

Suddenly, out of the forest, an arrow flew and hit one of the soldiers between the eyes, killing him instantly. Then more arrows rained out of the forest and killed more soldiers. Indris blocked the arrows by creating a blue firewall.

"They're hiding in the forest! Everyone, shield yourself!" Indris urgently ordered.

Then from the trees jumped out the Men of Hate. They wore no armor and had their face painted all white, resembling human skeletons. They all had an ax in their hand and started to cut down the Kimsu soldiers, slaughtering the confused soldiers down. Arrows were still flying out of the forest, trapping the soldiers in the camp. Some arrows even hit their own comrade. The Men of Hate were wild and ruthless.

Indris successfully fought off the Men of Hate. At the same time, he looked over to his younger brothers. Smoke filled the air, blue fire burning tents and trees. Kunjae was holding his own, shooting blue flames at the Men of Hate, while Airian stood still at the center of the battle, looking lost in the scene of horror. Indris tried to make his way to Airian but was blocked by five Men of Hate. He shot blue flames at them, but more kept on coming. He wondered if this would be the end of his life.

Blood splattered into the air. The green grass was covered in red. The trees were stained with blood. Yells echoed the forest. The dead lay with their eyes opened, staring blankly as they rested in the blood of others and their own.

A man approached Airian behind the smoke. His face wasn't painted like the others. He had a murderous expression over his face. He was muscular and extremely tall. In his right hand wasn't an ax but a giant sword. "Do you know me, boy?" asked the man with a raging voice, staring insanely into Airian's eyes.

Airian couldn't answer the man since fear had already overtaken him. He could only stare with his eye opened wide. He could feel his knees trembling. He felt belittled standing in front of a gigantic man. Suddenly, the man grabbed Airian by the neck and held him in the air. Airian held on to the man's wrist, his legs dangling in the air, hoping his life won't end.

"I'm going to squeeze your eyes out, boy!" snarled the man as his grip around Airian's neck became tighter.

Airian found himself fighting for air, praying for someone to save him, his legs becoming restless. His face slowly turned blue, the urge of living leaving his mind. His hand slowly let go of the man's wrist and slowly his eyes began to fade. Then as his vision almost turned black, the man plucked his fingers into the right eye of Airian, pulling the eyeball out of the socket.

Airian yelled horrifically as the man held his eyeball in the air for all to see. The man's fingers were submerged in blood as it flowed down onto his arms. Airian's yell screeched throughout the camp, interrupting the sound of steel hitting steel. Both Kunjae and Indris looked over as smoke slowly cleared. They were shocked by the sight of the man choking Airian out and holding Airian's eyeball in the air with the other hand.

"I am the eyeball eater!" announced the man. "I am the leader, the Bore." The man laughed loudly, dropping the eye into his mouth and chewing it then reaching for Airian's left eye.

Out of nowhere, Kunjae charged at the Bore with blue flames covering his feet and kicking the Bore in the face. The Bore dropped Airian and fell to the ground. The Men of Hate rushed over their leader's side while the Kimsu soldiers rushed behind Kunjae. Indris made his way to Airian, who was passed out, blood leaking out of his open right eye socket.

"How dare you kick me!" angered the Bore.

"He needs a healer," advised Indris to Kunjae.

"We should've had a plan," Kunjae blamed Indris. "Now look, the hothead has one eye. It's your fault, Indris."

Blue flames appeared on Kunjae's feet again. He looked over to the Bore with emotionless eyes. "Stand up, giant freak!" insulted Kunjae.

"Kunjae, stop, we have to retreat!" warned Indris.

"I'm going to kill this giant freak," insisted Kunjae.

The Bore stood up and touched the burn mark on his face. "I see that you're a true fighter," he scoffed. "Today is not the day I take your eyes, pretty boy," threatened the Bore. He turned to leave.

"The next time we meet, I'll turn you into ashes," Kunjae threatened back.

The Bore laughed as he led the men into the forest. Kunjae looked down at Airian still breathing but weakly. He then walked by Airian, Indris, Estrey, and the remaining soldiers without saying a word. The camp slowly burned by the blue flames, trees slowly falling and smoke filling the air.

The tragedy of war almost took his brother's life. If Airian lived, he'd live life with one eye with memories of the Bore replaying in his head. If he died, he wouldn't have to live life with the memories of the Bore or walk the land with the ugliness of his face.

But within the tragedy of war was born a new demon. There was Iszra, the loved and gifted demon. There was Ausra, the silent and dangerous demon. And in the midst of all the chaos, there was the genius demon, Kunjae Kimsu.

Chapter Thirteen

Kingdom of Enstra

Lumen stood before the weeping tree that oversaw the city of Godfree from on top of a hill. In his hand, he held two black roses, one for his brother and the other for his father. Both father and son did not have a proper burial. He was vexed whenever he thought about the disrespect his father and brother received. Even though both men did horrible things, they were still the people he loved.

Every now and then he would come up to the hill and stand in front of the weeping tree with two black roses, the only way he could pay respect to his father and brother. While standing, he reminisced the good in both men. His father's teachings still were embedded in his brain and heart, teaching him to never stop fighting for his dream. He looked up to his brother. His brother was always bold and confident. Both men's beliefs led to their downfall and death.

"I knew I'd find you here!" called Alexander, making his way to Lumen.

Lumen slowly turned around. "Prince Alexander," he greeted as he bowed his head.

"I have been looking for you all over the city. Why do you come to the weeping tree?" wondered Alexander, noticing the black roses in Lumen's hands.

"To pay my respects to my father and brother."

Alexander felt like he made the situation awkward with Lumen, baffled why Lumen looked emotionless, expecting to see tears in the eyes of Lumen. "Sorry for asking," he apologized.

"It's fine," said Lumen. "You found me, is something wrong?"

Alexander rarely talked to Lumen. He wondered how Emmillda was able to communicate with him since Lumen seemed to be a difficult man to talk with. "Umm, well . . ." Alexander tried to remember why he wanted to speak to Lumen.

"If you have nothing to say, then may you leave me alone?"

"Well, I want to know something," Alexander finally remembered. "Why did my father assign you to be Emmillda's protector?"

"I'm not sure myself," replied Lumen.

"My father must have his reason to trust you," considered Alexander.

"Do you trust me, Prince Alexander?" asked Lumen with a blank look.

Alexander was caught off guard. He didn't know if he trusted Lumen or not, knowing Lumen's family history in betraying the kingdom. All he wanted to know was what his father saw in him. If he went after the throne, he needed allies he could trust to be by his side. "I'm sorry. I don't know if I could trust you. I can't blame you for your father and brother's betrayal. But I can't look past the possibility of you doing the same," answered Alexander. "For now, I see you as someone important. Someone my father curiously finds important. If my father can see the good in you, then I must find the good in you."

"You're just like all these people." Lumen chuckled, turning to look over the city. "No one trusts me because of my father and brother. They walked the other way and speak badly of my name. Only your father and sister see the good in me. I suppose I should be angry for being hated. However, I'm not. I don't care what people think of me. I don't care if I'm foretold to be a traitor. The truth is, I'm only here to serve and take orders."

"Why do you let people speak ill of your name?" puzzled Alexander.

"Because karma will come back to get them. There's one thing my father always taught my brother and me—patience till the right moment presents itself. Sadly, he and my brother didn't stand by their own words, which led to their death."

"What are you patiently waiting for?"

"My greatest opponent." Lumen stopped to think of Ausra, who he considered to be his greatest rival even though Ausra had no clue to who he was. He remembered Ausra clearly, the man that killed his brother. "A warrior yearns for a great fight. We are a selfish and prideful breed. We were taught to have honor and pride. But my rival has no honor nor pride. He's the demon that haunts my dream."

"Why won't you leave and find him?"

"Because I have an order to complete," finished Lumen, turning to leave. "When Princess Emmillda no longer needs my protection, then I'll leave."

Lumen walked by Alexander, leaving him alone.

Alexander felt ignorant toward Lumen. He rarely spoke to Lumen, but like all the people of the western kingdom, from the mountains to forest people, they all know of Lumen, his father and brother's betrayal. A marked unjustified was placed over the head, leaving him in the darkness alone. Yet he didn't let the mark rule his life. He strived to be the greatest warrior in the western kingdom.

*   *   *

Lumen made his way back to his estate. He lived in the higher part of the city. While walking to his home, he felt the burning eyes glaring at him. Even the people above floating on clouds watched him with disdain. People whispered to each other, hoping that he didn't hear them calling him a "traitor blood" or "villain-to-be."

Lumen entered his home. Unlike others, he had no slaves. He lived alone in an empty house. Each room of his house was empty. Only the living space had furniture, which were just a bed, a chest, and a mannequin with his armor dressed on it. He barely spent time at home, only coming to it to rest. Most of his days were spent at the weeping tree or the palace. His life was bleak.

A knock on his door forced him to turn back. He opened the door to a horn head boy, his scales dark green with a hint of white. The boy had a letter in his hand and looked nervous when looking up at Lumen. "I have a letter for you, Captain Lumen," said the boy nervously, forgetting to hand Lumen his letter.

"Give it to me." He looked down at the horn head with a strict stare. The boy handed Lumen the letter. "S-sorry, Captain. Here it is."

Lumen took the letter, seeing the royal seal on it, curious to know why the royal clan would send him a letter. Since he spent most of his days there, whatever they needed to say to him could be said there. He unsealed the letter and read.

The letter was from George. The horn head boy tried to peek over to see but backed away when Lumen shot him a terrifying look.

"Is there something wrong, Captain?" the boy asked boldly.

Lumen tore the letter and let it sprinkle to the ground. "It's none of your business, kid," replied Lumen sternly.

"Y-you're right, sorry for asking," the boy said sadly.

Lumen measured the boy. "What is your name, boy?" asked Lumen.

"Y-yumpy, Captain," answered the boy nervously.

"Yumpy," repeated Lumen. "How old are you?"

"T-thirteen, Captain."

"About the same age as the princess," said Lumen. "Have you held a sword before, boy?"

"N-no, Captain."

Lumen reached into his pocket and handed the boy a purse of spring coins. "There are exactly three hundred spring coins in there. Take this coin and hand it to the prince. Tell him you're no longer his slave, and return here and I'll teach how to use a sword."

Yumpy took the purse of coins, confused and joyful for his freedom. "I'm confused, Captain. W-why are you doing this?"

"Don't worry. Take the coins to the prince, Yumpy."

Yumpy ran to the palace. Lumen watched him as he left, recounting what the letter said. George had requested him to leave the kingdom. Lumen didn't mind, but there was another request that George had asked him to do. A request that put his honor in question. It challenged his morals and put him in a position of betrayal.

* * *

Emmillda sat in front of a mirror while Mai roughly combed her hair, having a hard time untangling the knots. Emmillda didn't let the pain bother her as Mai tugged onto her hair. She was still disturbed about the three slaves' death. Each day, she tried to fight the horrific memory, trying her best to avoid her mother and George every day. Her days spent were in her bed or rambling around the palace garden, wasting her days away. Sometimes Alexander would cheer her, but even he couldn't help her.

"A princess should have beautiful hair," informed Mai as she continued to struggle with Emmillda's hair. "You need to take care of yourself, Emmillda. We don't want to disappoint the queen now."

Facelia had ordered Emmillda to meet her for tea. Emmillda didn't want to see her mother, feeling that her mother only wanted to scold her or mock her dream. But it didn't matter. Her dream of becoming a warrior was long gone. She felt that her purpose in life was lost. "I don't care," she grumbled.

Mai slapped the back of Emmillda's head gently. "Don't you say that!" warned Mai then continued to comb Emmillda's hair. "Why are you upset, child?"

"You wouldn't understand," refused Emmillda.

Mai stopped combing. "You know I raised you. I know when you're upset, child. Don't try to hide it from me."

Emmillda sighed. "I hate being a princess. I hate living here. I hate George and my mother!" Emmillda expressed her feelings. "Why was I burdened to be born in this clan?"

"A lot of girls wish to be in your shoes," said Mai then stroked Emmillda's hair gently and stared at the reflection of Emmillda from the mirror. "You're young, Emmillda. There'll be more disappointments coming your way, but there will be happier moments to erase those disappointments." She placed her hands on Emmillda's shoulders with a smile over her face. "I'm always watching, Emmillda. You're like a daughter to me. Seeing you upset makes me upset."

Emmillda touched Mai's hands and hinted at a smile that was lost for a while. "I love you more than my mother, Mai. I don't know what I'll do without you."

"Your mother loves you. She just has a different way of showing it."

"There's no need for you to defend her, Mai. I know who my mother is."

Mai stayed silent with a nervous smile over her face. There was no one that could be trusted in the palace. Everyone was seen as a spy, from the slaves to the king's advisers. She was afraid for her life. Any mistake she made could cost hers. Ever since King Euren went mad and incapable of deciding for himself, life in Godfree was never the same.

"You're ready, Princess." Mai smiled.

Emmillda stared at herself in the mirror. Seeing how beautiful she was, she never took the time to realize her beauty.

"Such a pretty girl," complimented Mai, realizing the lost look on Emmillda's face. "Any boy that marries you will be an honor."

"Yeah, will it be an honor to marry me or because I'm a princess?"

"It's just the world you live in, child," consoled Mai, placing her hands on Emmillda's shoulders. "There's no true love in your world." She removed her hands. "Well then, I'll wait outside your room. Get yourself a dress. The queen will be angry if you're tardy." She left Emmillda's room, feeling bad for Emmillda since her dreams were locked away.

Emmillda continued to stare at herself in the mirror. She had everything—the money, the title, the education. Yet she still felt unsatisfied. There was no enjoyment as a princess. She felt trapped in her own wealth she was born into. Unlike other girls her age, she didn't have to worry about marriage. Marriage was set for her. Her life was in the hands of either her mother or brother. And knowing them, they would marry her off to someone that could benefit their goals.

* * *

Queen Facelia sat in her private study sipping on tea, waiting for Emmillda's arrival, tapping her finger rapidly. Standing beside her was Manji. Facelia was annoyed with Emmillda's tardiness. She liked everything to be her way. She hated it when anyone challenged her ways.

"This child dares to be late!" expressed Facelia. "She hides from me for weeks, that's disrespectful." She sipped her tea. "Without me, they will never exist. I could've killed them if I would. All my children are fools." Her head began to ache, thinking about her children. "I can't stand them!" she expressed, slamming the teacup on her table.

"My queen, you shouldn't stress yourself too much," advised Manji.

"Then what should I do? How can I release my stress?" questioned Facelia angrily.

"I have good news. Maybe that can help, my queen."

"Good news?" wondered Facelia. "Well, tell me, don't just stand!"

"The Cha clan will fight by your side if the princess's hand goes to the youngest Cha."

Facelia grinned. Having the Cha clan by her side could benefit her greatly. An influential and strong clan like the Cha could create a chain reaction. The other clans would follow suit, and she would be the new ruler of Enstra.

"That's crucial to my plan," gushed Facelia with a sadistic smile. "They can help me take the throne and banish those snake brothers."

"Should I send them a letter, my queen?" asked Manji.

"Of course! Send it now. And, Manji, I want your sisters to be by my side. It's time we show my son my power."

"Understood." Manji bowed her head and left.

Emmillda finally arrived with a nervous Mai trailing behind her. She walked by Manji, peeking back over her shoulder, not trusting her. She made her way to her mother and seated herself in front of her, keeping her eyes away from her mother.

"I'm sorry, my—"

"Hush." Facelia cut Mai off. "You failed again, Mai."

"It's not her fault!" defended Emmillda.

"It's fine—"

"I said, hush!" angered Facelia, cutting off Mai again. "Another word from you and I'll make sure you sleep with the hogs."

"Don't talk to her like that!" warned Emmillda.

"Or what?" challenged Facelia. "You'll hide from me again? Look me in the eye, child, and apologize for keeping me waiting."

"I'm not going to apologize to you," scoffed Emmillda.

"I'm amazed how you can talk to your mother like that. I gave birth to you, child. Show me some respect and look me in the eye!" Facelia leaned back on her chair, calming herself. Her sadistic smile appeared again. "You know, stubbornness is what made your father go insane," she mocked. "Maybe you'll go insane like him."

"He only went insane because he had to sleep beside you every night," Emmillda insulted back.

"Ah, you have confidence again but can't look me in the eye." Facelia leaned over to Emmillda. "Do you remember those slaves' eyes when they were pierced by spears?"

Emmillda angrily looked over to her mother, her raging eyes staring into Facelia's vile eyes. They were face to face. Emmillda was running wild inside, her fist clutched. She wanted to hit her mother, trying her hardest to unrelease her anger. She wanted to forget about those three slaves.

"Oh, I struck a nerve," smirked Facelia, sitting back on her chair and sipping her tea. "You're still weak, child."

"You're a nasty woman," insulted Emmillda.

"You have to be nasty to survive in this world. There's no kindness in our world, darling. Reality is not tales you read in your books. If you want something, the evil in you must show."

"I can never be like you. I will never be evil to accomplish my dream!" promised Emmillda.

"You're right. You'll never be like me. None of my children will be like me. I find ways to get what I want. I never let anything manipulate my goal." Facelia sipped her tea again. "I'm that little mouse that never gives up. When that snake hunts me down, no, no, I don't let it eat me. I fight back. I use what I have to avoid being eaten." She poured tea into her cup. "Will you stand by me or your brother?"

"I stand by no one!" answered Emmillda immediately.

"Well, it's a shame for me to tell you, but you have no choice now. I control your life. Call it a guilty sin for being a princess. Don't get me wrong, a lot of girls wish to be in your place. They dream of boys falling for them. People envying them. Even an ugly princess has more love than a pretty poor girl. Lucky for you, you're a beautiful princess. Lines of boys and men are waiting to marry you. Tragically, you hold no power in your hand."

"What are you talking about?" asked a confused Emmillda annoyedly.

"I control you, my dear daughter. The life of a princess is sickening. You have no power in your life. You know why? Because you're a secret weapon when other plans don't work," smirked Facelia.

"I still don't understand!"

"Don't play stupid, little girl. Do you think you get to live life happily? No, no, you don't get the chance to be happy. You see, I have a goal I want to accomplish. Seeing that you're not willing to stand with me, I made the best decision for myself. That was giving your hand away."

"You can't do that!" yelled Emmillda, slamming her fist on the table.

"Oh yes, I can, my dear child," reminded Facelia. "I control you. You're my secret weapon."

"How do you see your own child as a weapon? How can you be so evil toward your own child?" questioned Emmillda.

"Oh, now I'm your mother. Before, I was a nasty evil woman." Facelia sipped her tea. "Look at you. Breaking when nothing goes your way. You're the mouse that'll be eaten by the snake." She sipped her tea again. "But don't you worry. I'm marrying you to the youngest Cha brother. At least you'll have someone strong and handsome looking after you. And make sure you give me a lot of grandchildren. I would love to send my grandchildren gifts," teased Facelia with an insulting grin.

Emmillda stood up and lifted the teapot off the table. She looked at Facelia who didn't have a single care over her face. She couldn't believe the darkness in Facelia's eyes.

"I hate you!" cursed Emmillda.

"Are you going to pour that hot tea on me?" challenged Facelia calmly.

Emmillda tightened her grip on the handle of the teapot. She wanted to pour the hot tea on her mother, wanting to make Facelia suffer. But she thought of something else. Making her mother suffer would only bring her to the same level. She wanted to prove her mother wrong. She was the mouse that kept on fighting from getting eaten.

"No." Emmillda poured the tea on the floor. "Making you suffer will only make me like you." She dropped the teapot to the floor. "I am that mouse that keeps fighting. But unlike you, eventually, you'll be eaten. But for me . . . I'll escape!" she finished, storming out of her mother's private study. Mai tried stopping her.

"Such a shame. A mother can't have tea with her own daughter," Facelia said to herself.

* * *

The stars in the night sky brought life into the darkness. Emmillda looked up into the sky, halting her walk around the higher level of the city.

As she stared into the stars in the sky, she wished to escape her life. She wasn't fit to be a princess. She didn't want to take orders from her mother nor brother. She wished for a simpler life than a royal life. Tired of all the formality, tired of people controlling her destiny, she wanted her story to be hers and not anybody else.

Emmillda had no clue how long she was walking since she was lost in her thoughts. Her hatred toward her mother controlled her. The citizens of Godfree were all fast asleep. The roads were empty and quiet. It felt eerie as the night waited for the morning.

"Dear seven protectors of the land," Emmillda prayed softly, staring at the starry sky. "I beg you all, please save my mother. Please save my father. Whatever sin my family caused, please place it upon me. I'll take the punishment for my family for them to be saved." Tears fell from her eyes. "Why?" she began to ask, thinking about the three slaves that were murdered in front of her. "Death is not beautiful. It only makes life ugly." She wiped the tears from her eyes. "Please protect the mother and her two sons. They should never have died. I'm sorry for not saving them."

"Umm, Princess?" wondered Yumpy, standing behind Emmillda with a sack full of his belongings.

Emmillda jumped, even more surprised to see a horn head roaming the streets of the higher level of the city. "A horn head!"

"That's me!" Yumpy smiled.

"How long were you standing there?" asked Emmillda.

"Not long," lied Yumpy.

"Why are you roaming the streets? It's against the law for a slave to roam the streets alone," reminded Emmillda.

"Well, the thing is, I'm no longer a slave. Well, I don't really know. I'm heading to my new home," revealed Yumpy, keeping a positive smile over his face.

"A new home?" wondered Emmillda.

"Yeah, Captain Lumen spent three hundred spring coins for me. That's a lot to spend on a slave."

"Lumen?"

"Yeah, the big guy who never smiles. He's my master now."

"I know who he is," said Emmillda.

"Oh wow! He's a nice guy. But kind of scary."

"Why does Lumen need a slave?" wondered Emmillda.

"I don't know, but I'm heading to his estate right now. Come along, we can find out together," invited Yumpy as he walked by Emmillda.

Emmillda followed him, intrigued to know why Lumen needed a slave. She was also confused with Yumpy's demeanor, wondering why he was upbeat for a slave.

"By the way, my name is Yumpy," introduced Yumpy.

"Hi, Yumpy," said Emmillda softly.

"Umm, if you don't mind telling me, were you crying?" asked Yumpy.

"No!" answered Emmillda sharply.

"It's okay to cry, Princess. It's a part of us. My mother told me it's okay to cry. When I found out that Prince George had her and my brothers killed, I cried for ten straight days."

Emmillda stopped walking. Her body felt frozen out of shock. She couldn't believe what she heard, not understanding how Yumpy could be nonchalant after what her brother did to his family. Deep down, he must hate her. No one was around; it was dark. He could kill her if he wanted to. She wondered why he wouldn't take revenge on her.

"We have to get going, Princess. It's my first day serving Captain Lumen. I don't want to show a bad impression of myself," hurried Yumpy.

Emmillda continued to follow but in silence and curiosity. Her body moved like a spirit was possessing her. She kept a close eye on Yumpy, trying to figure out how he could stay cheerful. He seemed to enjoy life to the fullest. In the back of her head, she wished to be like Yumpy, someone who could stay smiling. Yet she felt shameful for wishing her life to be like his. She had everything she wanted and he had nothing.

They finally arrived at Lumen's estate. Yumpy took a deep breath. He was nervous to start his new life. Emmillda was confused why Yumpy was nervous. He was going to be a slave again anyway. The western kingdom would never gift the horn heads their freedom. And if there was a slave that was free, they would be killed and left on the streets of the lower level of the city.

As Yumpy was about to knock on the door, the door opened to Lumen looking down at him and Emmillda.

"Captain!" exclaimed the startled Yumpy.

"Kid!" said Lumen then turning his attention to Emmillda. "Princess Emmillda?" He was confused to see Emmillda at his doorstep. "Why is the princess with you?" demanded Lumen for answers.

"I saw her crying and apologizing for my family," replied Yumpy, hinting a smile at Emmillda, letting her know that he heard everything she said.

"You lying horn head!" angered Emmillda.

"What's going on?" asked a confused Lumen.

"This horn head is a liar!" Emmillda pointed.

"I lied to you," said Yumpy, pointing to Emmillda. "I didn't lie to Captain Lumen."

Emmillda crossed her arms in disappointment. "Did you lie about your mother and brothers?"

"No," replied Yumpy, walking into Lumen's house.

Lumen stared sharply at Emmillda, trying to figure out why she was standing at his doorstep. He would be in serious trouble for having her in his house. She should be at the palace sound asleep and safe, not roaming the streets of Godfree in the middle of the night.

"Well, are you going to let me in?" asked Emmillda.

"Why are you here?" Lumen asked back.

"Let me in. It's getting cold," said the annoyed Emmillda.

Lumen looked around to make sure no one was watching. "Fine, but you're not spending the night."

"I wasn't planning to," said Emmillda as she headed into the house, realizing how bleak Lumen house looked. "Your house is like you."

"I only come here to sleep," said Lumen.

"Hey, Captain, can I have this room!" screamed Yumpy from the hall. "There's a lot of empty room in this house!"

"Why do you need a slave?" questioned Emmillda disapprovingly; she thought Lumen was an honorable man who did everything himself.

"He's not a slave," answered Lumen.

"Then what is he?" asked Emmillda.

"That's none of your concern. Why are you not at the palace?" questioned Lumen.

"That's none of your concern," Emmillda mockingly answered back.

Yumpy poked his head out from the hallway. "Hey, Captain, you didn't answer me."

"I don't care!" Annoyed, Lumen keeping a sharp stare on Emmillda.

"Sorry," apologized Yumpy, heading back to the hallway.

Emmillda walked around Lumen's living area, trying to annoy him. Her eyes wandered around the room, acting as if Lumen wasn't in the room with her.

Lumen was steaming as he watched. She was like an annoying little sister to him. She sat on his bed, still looking around the house, acting like he didn't exist.

"Emmillda, what is wrong!" yelled Lumen with aggression and annoyance in his tone.

Emmillda finally stopped. She needed Lumen to yell at her so she could let out her sorrow. Her eyes began to fill with tears. She wanted it to stop, but it kept flowing out of her eyes like a never-ending rainstorm.

"I hate her, Lumen," Emmillda finally confessed.

Lumen approached Emmillda and sat beside her, wrapping his arms around her shoulders and placing her head on his chest, trying to comfort her, regretting that he yelled at her.

"Why does everything have to be about that stupid throne!" cried Emmillda.

Lumen rubbed the back of Emmillda's head gently, feeling upset seeing her cry. Even though she was a pain, to him, she was the only person that saw him as a hero and not a villain. She had great admiration and respect toward him.

"It's destroying my family," continued Emmillda. "They can never love one another."

Lumen took a deep breath. "Do you know how I can live in this kingdom, knowing that I'm hated?"

"N-no," stuttered Emmillda.

"Because I know I can change them one day. It's natural to love. Hate is something that is taught. I know I can unlock the love they have for me that they caged. I take the mistake of my father and brother and accept the people's hate for them."

"Why do you put yourself in such a position?" asked Emmillda.

"I want to fix the pain my family caused."

Emmillda picked her head up from Lumen's chest and looked up at him, wiping her tears away. "Do you hate your father and brother?"

"Of course not. I looked up to them. Even if people hate them, despised them for what they did, I still loved them. Behind closed doors, they were different people."

"Hey, Captain," called Yumpy, breaking the moment between Emmillda and Lumen. "May I go to the slave quarters? Need to say my goodbyes."

"I don't care," allowed Lumen. He turned his attention back to Emmillda. "You should leave. I must head out soon."

"Where are you heading to?" questioned Emmillda.

"Important military situation," replied Lumen. "Kid, escort the princess back to the palace. If anyone stops you, tell them you serve under me."

"Understood, Captain." Yumpy bowed.

Emmillda followed Yumpy out of the door. She didn't want to argue with Lumen to let her stay. She had to face her fear. That was her mother and brother. Their family was getting torn apart because of that throne. They needed to find the beauty in family again.

As Emmillda and Yumpy were making their way back to the palace, they walked in silence, Emmillda behind Yumpy. She distrusted him for lying to her. Still, he had that cheerful smile over his face.

"You know, I'm sorry for lying," apologized Yumpy.

"I don't need your apology!" rejected Emmillda.

"When I saw you crying and apologizing for my family, it felt like you meant it. Why did you apologize when you weren't involved?"

"I stood helplessly and watched."

"Must be scary, huh?" wondered Yumpy.

"It was," answered Emmillda. "How come you're not mad?"

"Why should I? I already wept for them. All I could do is live my life because they would want me to. And if I was to avenge them, it would do me no good."

"How can you live life like that?"

"How can you live life thinking too much?" Yummy asked back. "We're young. Life shouldn't stress us."

"You're a slave. Your life was taken away from you."

"So what if I'm a slave? I still find happiness. That's what Brunchy taught me."

"Brunchy?"

"He's an old horn head that works on the grounds of the palace. All the slaves look up to him. At night, all the palace slaves would sit around him to hear him sing. We dance and enjoy the moment. He taught us that life is just a moment."

Emmillda reflected on moments in her life. They were memories to remember. Some were like a never-ending winter while others were like a short-lived summer. Like the moment Euren let her hold her first sword. She remembered being in awe as she gazed at it, her reflection staring back at her, the sun glistening off the blade, her little fingers not fully wrapping around the handle of the sword. The smile on her father's face as he witnessed the excitement in her eyes. Thinking of the good moments helped her see the love in life.

"Can I come?" asked Emmillda.

"Well, they're not going to be happy seeing you."

"I can hide," suggested Emmillda.

Yumpy tried to think of a way to sneak Emmillda in. He then took his cloak off and handed it to Emmillda. "Wear this and keep the hood over your head."

"Won't anyone ask questions?"

"If you stay in the back, you'll be fine."

Both Emmillda and Yumpy made their way to the palace. They snuck through the grounds of the palace and passed the stable, trying not to wake the horse and alert the guards. They made their way to the slave quarters. The light was shining through the window. Laughter could be heard coming from the quarter. They were loud and enjoying the moment.

"How can the guards not hear them?" wondered Emmillda.

"The guards don't bother to check on us. To them, we're nothing." Yumpy smiled.

They stopped in front of the door. Yumpy patted himself clean before he entered. "Okay, stay in the back, and no one will bother you. Everyone should all be focused on Brunchy."

When they entered the slave quarters, Emmillda was quickly fascinated with the festivity. The quarter was brightly lit with fireflies in floating bubbles. There were horn heads dancing, their broken tip horns touching and glowing as they circled each other. At the center of the room was an old horn head sitting on a chair. His scales were blue with a hint of red. Some were gathered around him, listening to him telling a story. His smile was gentle and protective.

Emmillda leaned against the wall at the back of the room. None of the horn heads seemed to notice her. The kid horn heads all ran to the old horn head sitting at the center and sat around him. Everyone stopped dancing and waited for the old man. She found herself waiting like the others.

Yumpy approached the old horn head and knelt to one knee, bowing his head. "Thank you, Brunchy."

"Stand up, Yumpy," said Brunchy, his voice sounding frail. He raised his hand. "Shall I start a song?"

All the horn heads cheered. Another horn head stood next to Brunchy. She had long white hair with all-purple scales. She began to play the flute, her eyes closed as she let the sound of the flute control her. It was smooth and yet sad. Emmillda shut her eyes to listen, letting the tune play through her ears.

Brunchy began to sing. His voice was weak, yet peaceful and soothing. Emmillda listened closely. The words resonated with her. She looked around and noticed everyone crying, including Yumpy. She touched her cheek and felt a teardrop. She knew what Brunchy was singing about. His sad and haunting poetic lyric memorialized Yumpy's mother and brothers. The tears of blood flowing into the cracks of stone, the rose to never blossom, it was pain that all the horn heads felt when their own was taken away from them.

When Brunchy finished, they all closed their eyes. Emmillda found herself closing her eyes as well, asking for forgiveness from Yumpy's mother and brothers. When they finished, they continued to dance, the men horn heads singing their lungs out and tapping their feet on the ground to create sounds. The sound of flutes echoed the quarter. The thumping of drums brought out the rhythm of dancing. Male horn heads danced with the female horn heads, the kid horn heads doing the same. Horn touched horn, some horns glowing red as they touched and some glowing white.

Yumpy made his way to Emmillda and stood near her. "Are you having fun?" he asked excitedly.

"Yes, it's amazing. Can you explain the dance to me?"

"It's a traditional dance. When the horn touches each other, it glows. If they're dancing for fun, it glows white. If they like each other, the horn glows red. They circle each other and follow the rhythm of the tune."

"Rhythm?"

"Close your eyes and listen to the tune, let the voice of the singing men control your spirit, then your body will move," explained Yumpy.

Emmillda closed her eyes, trying to listen to the voice of the men singing. She suddenly felt her feet tapping in rhythm with the voices and tune. Then her hips started to follow, moving from side to side. She started to feel her body losing control, letting the music take over her body. She opened her eyes to Yumpy's giant smile.

"You see, let the music take over," said Yumpy excitedly.

"Dance with me," suggested Emmillda.

"That's impossible. You don't have a horn."

"So what? Pretend I do."

"Fine." Yumpy placed the tip of his horn to Emmillda's forehead. The horn on his forehead glowed white. "Well, it worked." He was shocked.

Emmillda and Yumpy began to circle each other, horn touching forehead, letting the music guide them, their eyes connecting with each other. Both smiled as they circled each other. Yumpy grabbed Emmillda's hands and let the art of dancing take over. Without knowing they were at the center of the room, Emmillda's hood was off, and all the others stopped dancing. The singing of the horn head men faded away as they noticed the princess dancing in their quarter.

When the singing stopped, Emmillda and Yumpy stopped dancing, Emmillda not noticing the hateful eyes glaring at her. She smiled at Yumpy who wasn't smiling back at her, standing like a stone. His eyes were wide, knowing he had made a mistake.

"Yumpy, what is the meaning of this?" questioned Brunchy, who no longer had the gentle smile but a worried expression.

"I-I—"

"Why is the princess here?" yelled another horn head.

Suddenly, the room began to be filled with questions. Emmillda looked around the room, seeing the spiteful eyes glaring at her. She was not welcomed. It was their only time for freedom, only to be interrupted by their owner. She looked to Yumpy who looked dead and cold.

Brunchy raised his hand to silence the chatter. "Princess, why are you here?" he asked. "Did this stupid boy did something to you?"

"No, I asked to come. This is not Yumpy's fault," defended Emmillda.

"You shouldn't be here."

"I know. I-I just want—"

"You must leave, or your brother will kill more of us," worried Brunchy.

"I'm sorry—"

"Please leave. Our lives are already ruined. Don't ruin it even more," said Brunchy with an unwelcomed look.

"I will leave. I apologize for everything." Emmillda bowed. "How about Yumpy?"

"He's no longer allowed back here. He must leave too." Brunchy looked at Yumpy. "Go to your new home, Yumpy. You disappoint me. Don't ever show your face here again."

Yumpy ran out of the door without looking at Brunchy.

Emmillda felt guilty for ruining everything. "He did nothing wrong!" she defended then chased after Yumpy.

Yumpy ran across the palace ground and to the back gates of the palace where no guards were patrolling. Emmillda trailed behind. He stopped at the gate, his smile more forced. Emmillda stopped behind him, trying to catch her breath. She was calling for him, but he wouldn't listen.

Emmillda bent over, placing her hands on her knees, gasping for air. Luckily, Yumpy stopped; if he didn't, she would've never caught up to him. "I'm s-sorry," she struggled to apologize.

Yumpy never turned back to her. "You know what, don't be sorry. I'm not angry at all. Life is better with happiness," said Yumpy. His voice sounded like he was in a trance.

"It's all right to be angry. I ruin everything for you. That seems to be the story of my life."

"Why are you hard on yourself." Yumpy turned to Emmillda, his eyes watering. "You don't have the right to be miserable. I heard everything with Captain. You know, it's not fair. You get to complain about hate. I live with hate every day. But I put on a smile to hide my misery." He paused, letting out a small chuckle. "I did want to avenge my family. I wanted to cut the heads of the guards that gleefully stabbed them. You know, they walk around bragging about how they murdered my family. I want to see Prince George suffer like them."

"I'm s—"

"I don't want to hear it. I'm tired of apologies. I'm tired of letting everything be okay and hiding my pain. The only family I have left kicked me out. Why did I agree to let you come? What do I have? I'm just a slave . . . No, I'm a free slave. I'm just a horn head living in a kingdom that doesn't accept my kind. In honesty, when I saw you crying, I thought of strangling you. But then I heard you apologize to my family. You're just pathetic. My family doesn't need your pity. What is done is done. They have already faded into the black!"

"Please, Yumpy," begged Emmillda, trying to get closer to him.

"Stay away from me!" snapped Yumpy, running away and leaving Emmillda alone.

Emmillda watched as Yumpy disappeared into the darkness. All his pain was protected by a forced smile. Her eyes watered as she felt helpless again. She could've saved Yumpy from his hate but let him escape with it.

* * *

George stood on the beach on a cool night with the crescent moon sitting peacefully in the dark sky. He smelled the air of salt from the Silent Sea. The cool air calmed him, bringing back memories of when he was just a boy and running on the hot sand with his bare feet, his father chasing after him while he laughed loudly. A part of him wished for his childhood when life was much simpler.

Sitting on the Silent Sea was the island of Pain, a secured prison that was guarded by the tiger warriors, warriors with no alliance to any clan. He had already sent letters to the commander of the island for a third prisoner. A more lucrative and powerful prisoner.

Lumen finally appeared with a man in shackles and a sack over his head. The man was wearing a nightgown. His body looked frail as he took little steps. "Prince George, I have him here," announced Lumen.

George didn't respond to Lumen, keeping his eyes out into the sea. Suddenly out of the darkness of the sea, he could see a boat with two men rowing onto the shore. The men touched land and made their way to George. They were both tall and wore tiger-stripe armors. The helmet on both men resembled a tiger head.

"Ah, they're here." George smiled.

Both men approached George and bowed. "We're here to pick up our prisoner," said one of the men.

"Wow, the tiger warriors are amazing. Look at you two. What are they feeding you?" George tried to joke.

"We're not here to talk. Hand us our prisoner, and we'll be on our way," ordered the man.

"I apologize." George turned to Lumen. "Lumen, give them the prisoner."

Lumen took the sack off the man to show King Euren looking lost and tired, not knowing that his own son had given him away as a prisoner. It was George's plan to get rid of his father so he could sit on the dragon bone throne.

Before George handed his father to the two tiger warriors, he took one last look at his father, maybe trying to go back on his decision. It wasn't the man he once loved and looked up to. It was a different soul using his father's body as its home.

"Thank you, Father," started George. "This kingdom is in good hands. I'll make sure to follow your footsteps and build this kingdom toward greatness."

Euren was handed to the tiger warriors. They took him to their boat and sailed away. The lost and tired king looked back at George, who didn't have a sentimental look over his face but an insidious one. A teardrop fell from an eye, a hint of him knowing what was happening to him.

"I guess you're a king now," said Lumen.

"Indeed I am," smirked George.

"I won't be around to see the kingdom fall," said Lumen with a blank tone.

"What makes you think the kingdom will fall under my rule?" questioned George.

"You're not your father," finished Lumen, leaving George.

"Lumen!" called George, still facing the sea. "Why did you pay so much for a slave horn head?"

Lumen stopped. "I'll need a companion during my travels," he answered.

"Ah, and the other request I asked of you?"

"I'll think about it." Lumen continued to walk away, not sure if he was able to do the deed for George. The evil in him wanted him to commit the sinful act, but goodness wanted him to leave peacefully. A storm hovered over him, waiting for his decision.

Chapter Fourteen

The Forest of Despair

The dragons and Daysa chose to travel away from the open area, staying off the road of the forests. Instead, they traveled hidden within the Forest of Despair. The Forest of Despair was home to the many children of Chenva, spirit demons, and rare creatures. Legend has it that a three-head giant lurked in the forest, only coming out during the night to hunt and feast. Travelers and merchants tend to avoid the Forest of Despair for its legend and longevity. The forest bordered the south, west, and east. Part of the forest hadn't been discovered yet. The unknown spooked the mind of the common but excited the curiosity.

Not only did the three-headed giants haunt the forest. The ghost of twelve sisters also claimed the forest. The tale goes of twelve sisters escaping their imprisonment from Hillmont. An owl demon captured the girls and slaughtered their whole village. He found interest in the fourth sister and kidnapped her. Her sisters decided to hunt the demon owl down in an attempt to save their sister. When they found the demon owl's lair, they were quickly captured by his underling and kept as prisoners. The sisters planned an escape for the morning. When all the owl slept, when it was time, the fourth sister freed her siblings, and they all escaped. But they didn't get far; the forest tend to play tricks. The trees started to move. Their vision began to play with them. One by one the twelve sisters died, all unknowing of their own death. The last to survive was the fourth sister, finding herself near a cliff, staring across to the Forest of Hope. Behind her was Hillmont. She didn't want to live her life with a spirit demon-like Hillmont and jumped to her death.

"I hate this forest," complained Nisu to Kaiso, both walking the middle of the group. "It gives me an eerie feeling."

"Why are you always complaining?" questioned Kaiso, annoyed with Nisu.

"You complain as much as me," teased Nisu, wrapping his arm around Kaiso's broad shoulders.

Kaiso nudged Nisu arm off him. "Off of me, you pervert."

"Oh, pervert. If the owl man kidnaps you, don't expect this pervert to save you."

"Like I need you to save me," scoffed Kaiso.

Walking in front of them was Nagen and Leonaris; behind them was Sukro and Daysa. Both Torshen and Ausra were far behind slowly following the group. During the travel, the dragons barely spoke to Daysa. They had been traveling the Forest of Despair for fifteen days. The leaves on trees blocked the sky. When the leaves glowed, it was daytime. When the leaves stopped glowing, it was nighttime.

During their travel, the group experienced strange happenings. One strange moment was when they walked into a burial of wolves. The carcass of the wolves was all stacked like towers. Ausra decided to cremate the body using his black flames. The group had a feeling they were being stalked by something but didn't care. Only Daysa doesn't know they were being followed.

"My father always avoided this forest," said Daysa to Sukro.

Sukro wasn't paying attention to Daysa, thinking about finding his father and avenging his mother. He had many questions to ask, but didn't know where to find the answers.

"My father told me stories of this forest. The strange demons, creatures, and activities." Daysa cringed. Thinking of the old stories her father told sent cold chills down her spine. "Will you all protect me if something was to happen?" She waited for Sukro's response, looking over to realizing that he wasn't paying attention to her. "Hey! Are you listening?"

Sukro shook his head, getting out of his own thoughts. "Sorry, what did say?" he asked confusedly.

"Don't worry, my beautiful researcher. Sleep near me, and I'll protect you," Nisu flirted with Daysa; then swirling to her, he wrapped his arms around her shoulders.

"I will never!" said a disgusted Daysa, edging Nisu off her.

"Why don't you want to sleep with a handsome man like me?" teased Nisu.

"I will never sleep with a disgusting boy like you," insulted Daysa.

"Disgusting!" Nisu was shocked. "Did the Wild Beast tell you I was disgusting?"

"I don't have to say anything," said Kaiso bluntly.

Daysa looked back, wondering why Torshen and Ausra were so far behind. She wanted to talk to Torshen about the ice tribe, but he kept avoiding her. She was warned by the other dragons not to ask Torshen about his past. But her curiosity kept pressuring her to ask. *Why are they so far behind?* she wondered.

Nisu looked back too. "Ah, leave them alone. They're strange anyway. Plus, you don't want to irritate Ausra," warned Nisu.

"How about Torshen?"

"Little ice boy doesn't say much. It's best to leave him alone."

"Ausra is a slow walker, and Torshen likes staying by Ausra's side," said Sukro. "It was like that when we were younger. The two of them are like brothers."

"And how about you? Always watching their back?" questioned Nisu.

"Without me, they might act recklessly."

"So you're like a big brother to them?" asked Daysa.

"Sukro, you're old," teased Nisu. "You need to live life a little more."

"Is that all you think about?" retorted an Annoyed Kaiso. "Living life?"

"Why not? Life is precious. We should all live to the fullest. With all the good and bad moments." Nisu smiled.

"We only live for the bad moments," complained Kaiso lowly.

"You see, your way of thinking is wrong," said Nisu.

"That's why you're the weakest," mocked Kaiso. "Your way of thinking is too carefree. I don't want to keep saving you when you're rolling on the ground."

"Was I in the wrong?" challenged Nisu. "He was going too far!" His voice got louder.

Talking about an old mission where Nagen used his eye of truth and tortured a young boy to find his criminal father's whereabouts.

Nagen stopped walking, hearing the conversation with the other four behind him. He had an evil smile across his face, feeling the urge of the Freak coming in, what the others called him when using his eyes of truth ability. As the leader of the dragons, he needed to show that he had control and power. Nisu was always the victim to his eyes of truth, torturing the mind and finding what the person feared most.

"We should camp here," stopped Nagen. "The leaves will stop glowing soon." He turned around to the other four. "Nisu, shall I torture you again?"

"Do you want to taste my steel?" threatened Nisu to Nagen.

"Nisu, it's best if you stop talking," suggested Leonaris, sighing, foreseeing what situation it would lead to.

"No, let him speak. I'm trying to be a good leader," allowed Nagen with a mocking smile.

"I'm not afraid of you, Nagen," said Nisu.

"I don't want you to be afraid of me . . . I want you to respect me."

"I will never respect a freak," insulted Nisu.

"You called me freak?" The Freak was taking over Nagen's body, his eyes opening wide.

"We shouldn't fight," urged Sukro.

"Come on, guys. You guys are a team," worried Daysa, trying to calm the situation. She didn't know the deep hatred the dragons had toward each other.

"Stay out of it, girl, or I'll demonstrate my true power on you!" threatened Nagen.

"Leave her out of this!" defended Nisu.

"Oh, how chivalrous of you for someone as weak as you. You sure love acting like the hero," taunted Nagen.

"Shut your mouth." Nisu quickly charged forward toward Nagen. His speed was so fast that Sukro and Kaiso couldn't stop him.

Nagen stood with an evil smile, not fazed by Nisu's attack. His eyes slowly began to be clouded with blackness, the cursed eyes ready to torture Nisu's mind again. This time, Nisu had his eyes shut, not trying to make the same mistake again. Nagen noticed and pulled his dagger out. Suddenly, a wall of black flames formed between Nagen and Nisu. Nisu stopped his charge, and Nagen's eyes went back to normal, his evil self leaving his body.

Nisu was saved by Ausra. Nagen was afraid of Ausra's strength. Ausra stood calmly with Torshen by his side with an ice arrow formed in his hand. Everyone turned around to them. The wall of black flames disappeared. Ausra threw a piece of dragon berry candy into his mouth and went to lean under a tree. Torshen went off to hunt. The rest of the dragons prepared camp. Nisu stood in the center, still filled with rage. Daysa stood still, confused with the situation.

* * *

The glowing leaves were slowly fading, signaling that night was close. Daysa had finished setting up her sleeping area. After observing the dragons, even though they were powerful, she learned that each warrior was fighting their own demon, the bad side of creating a group so powerful. The time spent together made them despise each other. Their chemistry in battle was unmatched, but one hunger for power separated the group. She looked to the one that was the problem, the man that was to hold the group together. She stared coldly at Nagen who was setting up his sleeping area.

She went up to Ausra, sitting under a tree sleeping. "Wake up!" she ordered him.

Ausra opened one eye in annoyance. "What do you want?"

"Gather everyone around the fire," she demanded.

"No, do it yourself," Ausra said, shutting his eyes. Daysa slapped the top of Ausra's head. "What's your problem!" He was annoyed. He couldn't stand Daysa being around him. She was becoming a pest to him.

"I want you to gather the others," repeated Daysa, with her hands on her hips.

"Why me?" annoyed Ausra.

"Because they'll least expect it, idiot."

Ausra stood up. "The rest of the group is not here. Torshen is out hunting."

"I don't care, gather the group or I'll hit you again," threatened Daysa.

Ausra walked away mumbling words toward Daysa. For some reason, she wasn't afraid of him like normal people would. In a way, it made him feel normal himself. Usually, people would avoid him. Some would not even try to make eye contact with him. Children looked up to him, but yet they feared him. Many flustered over his skills and feats, yet they refused to know him.

"He hates you," said Sukro with a smile. "He's not going to do what you told him to do."

Both Daysa and Sukro watched Ausra walk to another tree to sit under, resting till Torshen came back from his hunt so he could eat. He didn't like being bothered when hungry, hoping Torshen would come back with something good.

"Can you gather the others?" Daysa asked Sukro.

"It's pointless." Sukro smiled, heading back to his sleeping area.

Daysa let out a loud exhale. Her work was cut out for her. The dragons were going to be a difficult bunch to work with.

*   *   *

Torshen jumped from tree to tree, taking the high ground to search for the group's meal. He couldn't see against the darkness, using his ears to help him navigate. He enjoyed hunting alone since it gave him time to reflect. The dragons besides Ausra and Sukro knew little about him.

He suddenly heard a girl's crying echoing the forest. The crying stopped his hunting, searching for the crying instead. Strange since it was rare to find people in the Forest of Despair. He hopped from tree to tree, following the crying of the girl, holding an ice arrow in case he had to protect the girl. The crying sounded closer as he kept hopping from trees. He sensed that the girl was alone.

He finally stopped upon an open area of the forest, standing on a tree branch looking down to a girl around his age, sitting on the ground. He couldn't see her face since it was covered with her hands. She was wearing a red silk dress with golden flower designs on it. Flying around her were hundreds of fireflies. They seemed to be protecting her, forming a circular shield around her.

Torshen was curious to know why a girl was crying alone in the middle of the forest. Thinking that she was lost, he jumped down to check on her. The ice arrow in his hand melted away in his palm. The fireflies around the girl fled away, sensing that Torshen wasn't a threat to the girl.

"Is everything okay?" checked Torshen.

The girl was still sobbing. "Who are you?"

"Torshen Iceben," answered Torshen. "Why are you crying in the middle of the forest?"

"An Iceben?" the shocked girl exclaimed. "You're part of the Ice tribe of the north."

"What are you talking about?" Torshen acted confused, wanting to avoid talking about himself.

The girl removed her hands from her face and turned to Torshen, showing her beauty to him. She had a small beauty mark over her left eye, her eyes drowned with tears like she had been crying for hundreds of years, her face pale and depressed. "Please help me. Save me . . . Get me out of this forest."

"Okay, but who are you?"

"I'm Ren Luo, the fifth Luo sister. My other sisters are lost in this forest too."

"Wait, there's more of you here?"

"Yes, there's twelve of us. The demon owl kidnapped my fourth sister. We tried to save her and now we're all lost."

"Demon owl . . ."

"Yes!" Ren was becoming scared. "Please help me."

Torshen began to hear owls hooting from the trees. He looked around but couldn't see them. Then looking back to Ren who looked frightened, he formed an ice arrow and prepared himself for an attack.

"They've found me," cried Ren into her palm.

"Who?" asked Torshen.

"The demon owls," replied Ren. "I can't escape the owl eye."

Suddenly, six owl men jumped down from the high trees, their legs covered in feathers. The feet resembled owl talons, their arms like a human and wings like owls from their back. They didn't have ears like a human. Their mouth and nose were replaced with owl beaks.

Each owl wielded a crescent sword. They flew in a circle above Torshen and Ren.

"The owl king will kill all who disobey," warned one of the demon owls then flew right for Torshen.

Torshen quickly dodged the owl demon attack. Then another one flew from behind. He jumped away from the attack. The demon owls were too fast for him. Surveying the environment around him, his only choice was to separate the demon owls, knowing that fighting them in an open field would give them a higher advantage.

He looked over to Ren and grabbed her wrist, pulling her deep inside the forest. "We have to separate them."

"They will kill us," doubted Ren.

"No, they won't," assured Torshen, noticing that one of the demon owls was trailing him. He quickly created an ice wall behind him, and the owl collided with the ice wall, killing it instantly.

Then quickly, another demon owl charged toward Torshen, giving him little time to create another ice wall. He used his bow to slap it away and started to form five ice arrows, now ready to shoot the owl when they attacked, sensing that they were watching him, figuring that these demon owls had similar behavior to a normal owl. They were hunters by nature. He was stuck; he couldn't leave Ren's side and climb up the trees. The only advantage he got was the tight environment, understanding that the demon owls wouldn't attack him at the same time. But they were patient creatures, waiting for the right time to attack him again.

"We can't escape them," doubted Ren again.

Torshen ignored her and closed his eyes, blocking all the noise surrounding him, listening to the breathing of the owls. Holding his breath and keeping his eyes shut, he pointed his arrow to the east and above and fired. The arrow flew faster than the blink of an eye and hit one demon owl fifty feet away from him. Then another demon owl flew toward him. He dodged with his eyes closed and shot back at the owl, hitting it on the back. There were three left. He held his breath again and patiently waited, noticing that one of the owls was flying quickly toward him from behind. Instead of dodging, he quickly turned around and shot the owl between the eye, as it was getting close to hitting him. He waited for the other two, hunting for them with his ears. He pointed two arrows in front of him and fired; the arrow flew thirty feet straight on, hitting an escaping demon owl in the back, then shooting up and hitting an owl demon flying above him.

He let out his breath and opened his eyes again, looking behind to see if Ren was okay. When he turned to his side, Ren was gone. Torshen looked around, but she couldn't be found. Suddenly, it hit him that the girl Ren was a spirit of the forest. She was one of the twelve sisters that Hillmont, the owl king, had killed. Now, he wondered if the sisters were killed or if they were trapped in an endless illusion.

"Thank you," echoed Ren's voice in the forest.

Torshen felt a kiss on his cheeks. A ghost has thanked him for helping her. Still, she would be chased by the owl demons. He wondered why he was able to see her.

He looked around and saw that all the demon owls he killed had turned into normal owls.

* * *

Back at the camp, fireflies gave little light as they danced above the camp. The group was patiently waiting for Torshen to return with their meal. The dragons and Daysa all sat around the fire to keep themselves warm, except for Ausra, still sitting under a tree sleeping. It felt like winter during the night.

Daysa noticed that all the dragons were staring in the fire. They were in their own thoughts. None of them hadn't said a word. Not even Nisu felt the urge to say anything. For some reason, they all seemed at peace. "Does anybody have stories to tell?" she asked, trying to break the silence.

All the dragons looked at Daysa like they didn't want her around. Daysa looked away, embarrassed by the way they looked at her. They made her feel like an idiot. She was talkative, so the silence made her feel out of place.

"Tell us your story," said Nagen. "Who are you?"

"I'm just a researcher," answered Daysa.

"I think you're lying," challenged Nagen with an evil grin.

"What is there for me lie about?" Daysa said, realizing that Nagen's evil side was showing again.

"You're a skilled magic user. There's no way I will believe you're just a researcher."

"My father taught me everything I know," defended Daysa. "He was a skilled magic user."

"If he's so skilled, how did he succumb to the red waterfall?"

"It's a deadly disease," answered Daysa with distrust toward Nagen.

"I'm going to warn you. If I think that you're lying, I will kill you," warned Nagen. "You'll suffer by my eyes." He looked over to Nisu. "Ask him how it feels."

"Shut your mouth, freak!" angered Nisu.

"Everyone should calm down," urged Sukro, trying to keep the peace.

"There will be a time when we'll split," said Leonaris. "When that time comes, I wish for us to split peacefully. Master Vesak will be upset if we split and become enemies."

"Master Vesak is dead. Stop talking about the traitor like he's still alive," reminded Nagen sharply.

"Don't talk about our master like that!" angered Kaiso.

"I can talk however I want about him," Nagen defended himself.

"Nagen, he taught us everything we know," Sukro tried to remind Nagen.

"All his teaching was all a lie." Nagen felt angry at Vesak for betraying him. Like the other dragons, he looked up to Vesak. When Vesak betrayed the Kimsu clan, his trust toward Vesak broke. Soon after, his evil side was taking over his body and mind. "This will be our last mission together. We'll separate and follow our own path." He looked to Daysa. "Better hope that your golden phoenix exists. If it's not, then I'll kill you myself."

"I'll protect her," defended Nisu.

"You think you can stop me?" Nagen challenged Nisu.

"Shut up!" yelled Ausra calmly. "There's enemy coming our way."

The rest of the dragons stood up and waited for the attackers to come. Daysa stood in the center, with magic lightning coming out of her hands. She looked over to Ausra, still sitting under the tree but his eyes opened.

Suddenly, out of the darkness came demon black bears. Even though the fireflies gave some light, it was still hard to see the black bears. But Daysa could recall her father's drawing of them.

The demon black bears were gigantic like a normal bear, had the face of a bear, the body of a human with black fur. Their hands and feet resembled bear claws. There were at least twenty of them surrounding the camp.

"Our king smelled fresh human meat and a beautiful girl. We want her and we'll kill the rest of you," threatened one of the demon black bears.

Then behind the demon bear came out a much bigger demon black bear. He had more fur than the others. The face resembled a human with the ears of a bear. His nose resembled a bear and black fur covering around his face. He had a golden ring around his head. "I am the king of the black bears, Gonfu!" announced Gonfu. "The strongest king in this forest! Don't fight me and accept your death, intruders! And I'll take my wife and she'll carry all my children."

Daysa nearly threw up. Gonfu was hideous. At the same time, she was afraid. She didn't trust that the dragons will protect her.

"For an ugly creature, you talk a lot," mocked Nisu.

"Maybe he's just talking," joined Leonaris.

"We don't like ugly creatures like black bears," Nagen chimed in. "Look at yourselves, who goes into battle half naked?"

"You dare mock us?" angered one of the black bears.

"Ha, you filthy humans will feed my whole tribe! Men, charge at our meal and retrieve my wife!" Gonfu ordered.

Daysa looked over to Nagen and saw that he was excited. There was a cocky grin over his face. She then looked over to the other members and saw the confident look over their faces. Sukro suddenly disappeared, and a wall of blue flames circled around them. The blue flames lit the forest up, and she could clearly see the face of the black bears. They were indeed ugly creatures. A firefly flew in front of her eyes, and in the blink of an eye, Sukro was in front of her. Under his arms were all the weapons of the dragons. Ausra was still outside of the blue firewall.

"Stay back if you don't want to die," Nagen warned Daysa.

The blue firewall died down, and the black bear demons quickly charged at them, their claws out like a bear and roaring like one. Gonfu stood behind and watched as twenty of his demons attacked. He noticed an unbothered Ausra still not moving from his post and walked over to him, angry that Ausra wasn't showing any fear.

"Stupid creatures," grunted Kaiso.

The dragons all charged forward, each easily cutting down the demon bear as Daysa watched. She was amazed at how easily they handled themselves, none of them showing fear. They were scarier than the demon black bears. They worked so well with each other. It was like a string was attached to them to synch them together.

One black bear managed to get to Daysa. Luckily, Nisu saved her and gave her a wink. She looked over to Ausra, now standing and facing Gonfu. He looked unfazed and emotionless as the massive black bear towered over him.

Gonfu clawed at Ausra, but he dodged smoothly behind the king of the black bear. His left hand was submerged in black flames, and he shot the black flames at the back of the bear's head.

Gonfu roared in pain and turned to claw Ausra again. This time, Ausra stepped to the side and jumped to blast blue flames out of his right hand to the face of the bear, dropping the king black bear to the ground. Again, the bear roared and quickly stood back up to charge at Ausra, only to run into a wall of blue-and-black flames merging in together. Suddenly, his sword, Life, broke through the wall of flames and stabbed Gonfu in the stomach. The wall of flames died out as Ausra stepped over, pushing the sword deeper into the stomach of Gonfu.

Gonfu tried swiping his claw at Ausra but felt his swinging getting slower. Ausra dodged all the attempts and continued to push the sword into him. Gonfu felt his leg weakening and knelt to the ground. He was still able to look down at Ausra. He saw a monster, a cold-blooded monster, in the eyes of his killer.

"I can't die." Gonfu struggled. "What the hell are you?" he questioned Ausra.

"Everyone dies. You chose today to be your death," said Ausra with stillness. "I'm just the person who gave you your wish."

"W-what the h-hell you talking about," stuttered Gonfu. The sword pushed deeper into his stomach.

"Look around you," said Ausra. "All of your underlings are dead. Killed by mere humans."

"N-none of y-you are h-humans," said a scared Gonfu.

Finally, the guard of the sword touched the stomach of Gonfu. Ausra looked up at Gonfu, his face showing no sympathy. He twisted the sword up. "Life is precious. Yet it is taken for granted." He quickly brought the sword up and sliced the top of Gonfu's body in half then wiped the blood off his sword and sheathed it back around his waist.

Daysa was horrified. She didn't expect Ausra to be a monster. The way he fought was beautiful and smooth. It was like watching a bird flying in the sky. His emotions never changed while he beat his enemy. It was best for her to steer clear of the Silent Demon. He showed calmness on the outside. But his blood ran wild with the rage of a demon.

"I guess we all fought demons." Torshen arrived, dragging six owls.

Chapter Fifteen

Kingdom of Tigara

The calm clouds peacefully sailed in the sky. The smell of early morning steamed bun scented the market of Mersane, the sounds of cleaver hitting wooden chopping board echoed the air. The citizens' eyes focused on the sky as they stared in awe at Borin. The wings of the mystic bird spread wide, slicing the wind. Even the ones floating on clouds stared with disbelief. Though it was not rare to see Borin soaring in the sky, swirling into clouds and back. It still amazed them to see a great bird, the feathers pulling back and the sight of the magnificent color of blue-and-white feathers.

Maenellia, riding on Borin, flying beside them was her blue flame bird. A saddened look had taken over her face after learning that Airian had lost an eye. Not knowing if he was dead or alive greatly bothered her, burning her inside, wishing to be beside him. She sent many letters to Indris, but nothing returned. The urge to fly to Heart Village consumed her.

As of late, she felt like she had failed as a mother. Her three younger children saw their uncle executed before them. At the same time, they were part of a cruel decision if they'll live or not. She felt helpless after her protective shield over her children was shattered.

For a while, she had violent thoughts to burn Fall City down, picturing herself riding over the city and burning all the people alive. She didn't care about the people of Fall City. They were supporters of King Hensi.

Whatever he said they believed and followed. She wanted to tie Hensi up while he begged for his life and watched his sons' life taken before his eyes then leaving him in prison to rot. All this was in her imagination built out of anger and revenge.

To release the distress in her mind, she had to fly. Being in the sky helped her think. It gave her an escape from the upside-down world. All her doubts, failures, and disappointments were all left behind on land. She was angry at Aerin for only having one concern. She didn't care about his goal and ambition. All she worried about was her children and their safety. Her greatest fear was having one of her children taken before her.

She finally landed on Feather Field, hopping off Borin and feeding the bird red berries from her pocket. She gently petted Borin's head then touched her forehead to Borin's forehead. Pulling a sealed letter out of her pocket, she whistled her blue flame bird over. The bird landed on her shoulders, and she too petted its head.

"I'm going to need you to find the dragons," she said to the blue flame bird kindly then putting the letter under the talons of the bird.

Maenellia watched as the bird fled away, hoping the letter would reach the dragons and force them to return. Or at least for Ausra and Sukro to return. Even though Aerin thought he didn't need Ausra, in truth, without Ausra fighting by his side, there was no way the Kimsu clan could win against the eastern kingdom.

"Mother," called Mani.

Maenellia turned around with a false smile over her face, not wanting to have her children seeing her upset. Borin made her way to her nest to rest.

Both Mani and Chenpu were worried about Maenellia. They waited for hours for her to finish her flying. Chenpu had her hands on her hips with an unconcerned look, compared to Mani with her hands together and thumb rubbing against each other with concern. The two sisters were the complete opposite.

"You didn't join us for breakfast," said Mani.

"It was nothing good anyway. Rice porridge and dried fish," added Chenpu.

"I wasn't hungry," answered Maenellia.

"Are you doing well, Mother?" worried Mani.

"Of course," lied Maenellia. "What makes you think I'm not?"

"You seem upset," said Mani.

Maenellia hesitated, her mind at ease for a while, forgetting about Airian and her short imprisonment. "Did the two of you check on your father?" she asked, avoiding answering to her daughters.

"He was at breakfast. Seems to be fine," answered Chenpu.

"He's more concerned with the war," added Mani sadly, wishing her clan won't go to war with the kingdom, fearing that it would only split her family apart.

Maenellia had a sour taste in her mouth, irked that Aerin didn't care about their children as she did. She was fed up with him, wondering if his true intention was showing.

"Mother, do we stand a chance against the entire eastern kingdom?" questioned Mani worriedly.

"Of course, we stand a chance," said Chenpu confidently. "We're the Kimsu clan. Our flames will burn the enemies that stand in our way!"

"Is that what you think, Chenpu?" asked Maenellia with seriousness, challenging her daughter's confidence. "Because of our name and our ability, we'll win?"

"Our fire will burn until we become the victor!" Chenpu replied overconfidently.

"Being overconfident can ruin you," warned Maenellia.

"You believe we can't win?" said Chenpu with disappointment.

"I stood by your father for a long time. This time, I wish to not fight by his side. I don't believe in us winning this war." Maenellia stopped to think if she regretted marrying Aerin. "I'm heading back to the palace." She walked by both her daughters.

"Mother, do you still run with the demon?" asked Chenpu.

Maenellia stopped. "I don't run with a blind demon." She continued her walk, only thinking about confronting Aerin.

Chenpu and Mani stood and watched.

Mani thought about chasing after her mother.

Chenpu was disappointed that her mother was against the clan. She had a hunger to be a strong warrior. She envied Iszra and Ausra whenever their father praised them. Even though Iszra was gone, Aerin still talked highly of him in front of her. She really hated being ignored. Her goal was to be the clan head.

"Mother is right," agreed Mani. "We can't run with a blind demon."

"If you agree with Mother, then leave!" angered Chenpu, storming away from Mani.

*   *   *

Mani decided to roam around the city. It was still morning, and the people of Mersane were merry. Their life was carefree and thoughtless. Everyone got along; the poor and rich lived peacefully together, people singing loudly and beautifully on the cobblestone street. A crowd stood at the center of the market. She was curious and decided to see what the clapping and cheering were about. She bumped and forced her way to the front, saying "excuse me!" and "sorry!" When she arrived to see the excitement, she unexpectedly saw a giant wooden dummy wearing the Cai clan colors. The crowd was throwing a ball of rice, fruits, and some throwing feces.

Mani was disgusted. She couldn't believe how the people were behaving. These people were ready to fight. They all listened to her father's insane ambition, not caring that the chance of living was far more unlikely than the chance of dying.

Mani turned back and continued her disappointing walk around the city. She looked around again. For the same, she saw that people were happy, enjoying life as it should be. But they did not know that life was not meant to be enjoyed. To the eye of the clans, the people that control the land, the common people, the freed horn heads, were nothing more but a shield protecting the important people hiding behind the stone walls.

She finally ended her walk at the Lucky River that cut through the city, sitting on the stone ground with her slippers off then placing her feet into the cool water. The gentle autumn air felt nice. The green clear water flowed gently. The river was home to many fishes, mainly the cloud fish and greenback fish. There were fishermen on their boats wearing straw hats. There were people over the bridge. Children fed fishes with fresh pieces of bread. It was soothing and peaceful.

Mani stared at her own reflection, touching her own face, running her fingers down her cheeks. She hated herself; she hated her beauty and her privilege, thinking that people only loved her because of her beauty. She hated being envied by other girls since it came with hatred. At Mersane Academy, where she was learning to become a healer, the other students wouldn't talk to her. They didn't want to be friends with someone that had a better life than them.

She thought that asking her father to allow her to attend the academy would help her make friends. After days of begging and asking, Aerin finally gave in. But she was wrong; she had a hard time building a friendship with the other students. Even at the palace, the servants were afraid to speak to her. She felt like Aerin ordered a guard to secretly follow her everywhere she went.

"Mani . . ." called a soft distant voice.

Mani broke her thoughts and looked around, trying to figure out who called her. As she looked around, everyone that was around was gone. An eerie whistle rang in the air, forcing her to cup her ears. Then a roaring sound of men crying echoed in her ears, followed by the neighing of horses and hooves banging the ground. She wondered if the sounds were coming from her own thoughts.

"Mani, Mani!" called out a voice as it was getting closer to her. "Mani, Mani, Mani!"

"Who's there?" called Mani.

"Mani!" The voice sounded like it was drowning.

Mani looked at the water, not seeing her present reflection, but herself when she was nine. Taking her feet out quickly and leaning her face over the water, she was stunned that she was staring at her younger self. Then a hand popped out of the water and grabbed her by the face, pulling her in. She didn't know how to swim. Trying to fight her way back to the surface, she felt like the hand was around her ankles, pulling her deeper into the water. Water filled her throat, choking and slowing her down. Looking up to the surface with every image of reality fading away, she saw her younger self staring down at her with no emotions.

Mani shut her eyes to appear in a dark room with a single door. To her confusion and distress, she believed she had died. She opened the door; to her surprise, she stood in front of a forest with snow covering the ground. Surrounding the forest was dark-gray smoke. As she stepped out and looked around, she was surrounded by dead soldiers wearing her clan colors. The scene horrified her. Trying to turn back, she found that the door was no longer there.

It was just her and the body of the dead in the forest surrounded by dark-gray smoke. The blood looked fresh as it leaked out of the dead, staining the snow on the ground. Some of them were pinned against a tree with a spear, some with arrows penetrated into their bodies while others were headless. As she continued to walk, trying to avoid the dead around her, stepping over the bodies on the ground, the smoke began to clear; but the more it cleared, the more corpses she saw. Her eyes were peeled back to the corpses, forcing her to see the horror.

She finally stopped to a state of terror, falling to her knees to the sight of both of her parents' heads on a spike, posed in front of their clan temple. Their eyes were clouded, staring back at her, the mouths opened wide as flies and spiders crawled out of them. Around the decapitated heads were the dead bodies of her siblings, all piled on one another lying in a pool of their own blood.

Mani tried to cry out, but no sound came out, crying her lungs out till her throat was strained. She begged the gods to take her. Why was she punished with the sight of her family's death? Then five black phantoms wearing a golden mask floated around her. They had no legs, only two arms, a body, and a head. They held a pike in their hand. These creatures were the underlings of the God of Death, Chenva, creatures he created to challenge his brother, the God of Life, Shenva, and heaven's angels.

The demon phantoms all raised their pikes in the air, preparing to stab Mani. Mani tried to look away, but forced herself to look back to them. She turned pale as she stared at death. The pike came down at her; but before she was stabbed, behind the phantom, up in the night sky, went a purple moon. Then everything turned into black.

* * *

Lost in a trance and swinging her sword vigorously was Kiri. With every swing, she imagined the king's guards, still disturbed by the sight of her uncle's execution. Watching her while sitting on the ground were both

Isa and Lehue. The three were not asleep when Aerin burned the nephew of King Hensi alive. They saw everything when they peeked out of their tent, from him yelling as the fire of hell consumed him to their father declaring war against the king.

Kiri knew she had to be strong and get used to seeing people dying. She swung her sword again, this time with more force and anger, gripping the sword with both hands as tightly as her small hands could. Her teeth clenched, and her eyes filled with hate, the veins from her wrist showing themselves. The slap from her mother opened her eyes. The weakness she saw in her father gave doubts. If she wanted to be like her heroes from tales she read and stories she heard, then she must turn herself into a pure demon. A demon that no one in the land had ever seen before.

"Why are you swinging with much aggression?" asked Lehue.

"How you can forget?" Kiri asked back. "We could've died if Father didn't choose Uncle Amin."

"Of course, I remember. But I'm not going to let it bother me," said Lehue.

"You're stupid," Kiri insulted Lehue. "And you, Isa. You should be training if you're going to become a warrior."

Isa woke from his daydreaming. He wondered why he didn't look away when his uncle's head rolled to the ground and faced him. "I should . . ." He attempted to stand, but Lehue pulled him back down.

"Don't listen to her if you don't want to," advised Lehue.

"Then be weak!" exclaimed an annoyed Kiri.

A guard approached the three siblings. "Lord Aerin calls for the three of you," reported the guard.

"Guess the war meeting is over," thoughtfully said Kiri.

"He wants you guys at the war meeting," corrected the guard.

Kiri immediately was overcome with excitement, dropping her sword and sprinting off the palace ground. Both Lehue and Isa walked after her.

The bloody storm was nearing. Aerin could sense the need to train his children quickly. When the night of crows and parasites feast, it will be the night a victor will be crowned.

The three siblings made their way to the war room. Kiri couldn't contain her smile. Finally, her father saw her worth. She was tired of being forgotten and overlooked. Lehue was more suspicious why their father wanted them in the meeting.

"Finally, Father realized I'm ready!" said Kiri excitedly.

"I won't be too excited," said Lehue. "Heard these meetings are long and boring."

"I don't care. I waited for this opportunity my entire life."

They stood in front of the wooden door to the war room, Kiri jogging in place. She wanted to yell and jump with excitement. Once they entered the room, their whole life will change. Life will no longer be simple and easy. It would be a blazing wave of fire, a powerful wave of reality, and a world where it sometimes could be upright with flowers and sunshine. And at the same time be downward with blood and rain.

Lehue tried to open the door, but Kiri slapped his hand away. She wanted to be the one to open the door to the start of their new life. She tried to fix herself and get rid of the smile on her face. She didn't want her first impression to be a joke, taking four deep breaths and shutting her eyes before entering the room.

The door creaked open slowly. The three siblings entered the room, feeling like thousands of eyes glaring them down. At the center of the room was a table that sat the map of Telmis. It seemed like they had interrupted a conversation. Standing at the center was Aerin, smiling proudly as his three young children entered the room. The other high officials were confused to see the children. Even Chenpu was lost.

"What's the meaning of this!" questioned Chenpu angrily. "Children shouldn't be here!"

"I invited them," answered Aerin.

"With all due respect, my lord," said Gorl, "I don't think children should be here."

"It's fine," assured Aerin. "We're at war with life and death. It's important that my children learn the process of war early. I don't want them to fail like Airian."

The three siblings walked toward Aerin to stand by him.

Kiri was fascinated with the map on the table, the vast and unknown land of Telamis.

"Shall we continue?" asked Aerin.

"My lord, I think we will be at a disadvantage without the dragons on our side," worried Gorl.

"I agree," said Broken.

"Father, we don't have any allies. I suggest we heighten our defense," suggested Chenpu.

"Hmm, I know all of you are concerned," said Aerin, hand rubbing his chin. His attention was on Fall City on the map. "We're starting a war that we may not win. I'd like to thank you all first for staying and running with the demon." He pointed at the Fall City on the map, where the goal was the capital. "Invading it will be difficult. Hensi has influence throughout the kingdom. If the dragons were fighting by our side, our victory would be inevitable. But they're not here." He looked at each of his high officials. "I trust all of you to bring me my victory. We're going to control this war. Patience will bring us to the light!"

"What do you suggest, my lord?" asked Gorl.

"First, we need to build our army," said Aerin. "Since Indris is already in Heart Village, he'll recruit young men and women to fight by our side. And with Heart Village, our rice supply shouldn't be a problem. Then we'll claim nearby villages."

"My lord, are you suggesting we kill innocent villagers?" questioned Broken.

"No, of course not. The villagers are crucial to us," answered Aerin. "Hensi will not dare to harm the people. We'll use them as shields. Every village we take will raise the Kimsu clan banner."

"How about the Men of Hate?" asked Cholee.

"They're not just our enemy," said Aerin. "The kingdom has a problem with them too. We can use them to our advantage."

"What do you mean?" asked a confused Nellina.

"I'm suggesting to side with the enemy," said Aerin. "They'll be useful for us during the war. When other clans are distracted, they will never expect us attacking them from behind."

Suddenly, the war room door flew open. A guard rushed in, his face in a state of shock and concern, breathing heavily like he was running up a hill. All the officials were startled and angry that guard had interrupted their meeting.

"My lord—"

"What is wrong with you!" angered Aerin. "How dare you interrupt a war meeting!"

"M-my lord. I come with b-bad news," the guard struggled to say, nervous to announce the bad news to Aerin. "L-lady Mani was found unconscious near the Lucky River."

Aerin's eyes opened wide in shock. The daughter he had tried so hard to protect was now harmed. He backed up, feeling like he was going to pass out, thinking the worst had happened to his daughter. Kiri grabbed hold of his arms, helping him stand. He mumbled words that didn't make sense.

"Where is my sister!" demanded Chenpu with a worried look, her fist slamming the table.

"S-she was brought back to the palace by Jungy. There was a needle in her neck," reported the guard.

Aerin rushed out of the room, forgetting the war planning, hoping that his daughter will survive. His heart ached in pain, blood rushing to his head as millions of thoughts mixed in his mind, wondering if the season of darkness would come upon his family early.

He finally made it to Mani's private chamber. Servants stood in front of the door. Aerin moved them aside and entered the room to see a healer healing his daughter's neck. A string of blood floating with spots of dark purple poison floated out of her neck and into the bucket. Maenellia was kneeling by the bedside, holding their daughter's hand with her head pressed against them, praying that Mani would live. Standing at the footrest of the bed was Jungy watching urgently. All he could do was stand motionless at the door.

They all noticed Aerin. Maenellia picked her head up, tears flowing down her face. "T-they hurt our daughter," cried Maenellia. Again, she felt like she had failed as a mother.

"I'm sorry, my lord," apologized Jungy.

Aerin ran near the healer and grabbed his daughter's hand tightly, not knowing who could've poisoned his daughter. Then thinking it was all King Hensi's plan, his grip tightened. Revenge clouded his mind. Hensi wanted him to suffer.

"My lord, she'll survive. Jungy managed to take out enough poison to not hit her vital organs. I placed my tracking worm in her to search for any stray poison," said the healer. "It's best if she rests."

"Just continue to take out the blood," said Aerin as he let go of Mani's hands. "Jungy, where is the needle."

Jungy reached into his pocket and pulled out a needle that was one inch long and had a red ruby on the top. "It was in her neck, my lord." He handed the needle to Aerin.

Aerin investigated the needle. The needle was no ordinary needle, from the red ruby to the length of the needle. The culprits were not just an ordinary assassin. They were members of the Sulin-Wu clan of Fool Castle in Tilton, the clan of elite assassins. He squeezed the needle in his palm and burned it.

"They will pay!" determined Aerin to himself.

"How can you think of revenge when our daughter is lying in bed hurt?" questioned Maenellia angrily.

"I must. They attacked my children. I'll burn their clan out of existence!" Aerin argued back.

"Can you forget about revenge and just worry for our children?" Maenellia stood up, her built-up anger coming out. "I don't want to fight if it means seeing my children all getting hurt. Did you ever think about Airian? How about Kiri, Lehue, and Isa, do you not care for them? How selfish are you, Aerin?"

"I'm going to war for my clan. I want my children to have what's rightfully theirs."

"Stop thinking about the past!" yelled Maenellia. "We're living in the present." Maenellia stormed out of the room, tears flying back.

Aerin stood in anger. He was not thinking about the present. He was looking toward the future, when Telamis would run with the demon. He called for a guard and ordered the guards to heighten the defense in the city then telling another to let all the captains start recruiting young men and women for the military. The haunting of Telamis would reign terror with the Black Heart Demon of the east as the head of the serpent.

Chapter Sixteen

Kingdom of Wintra

The midmorning winter sky cooled the air. Back at the Unchained campsite, most of the rebels were sitting around the fire, some staying in their tents for warmth. A sense of annoyance and anxiety was felt around the campsite as they waited for the next plan, some wishing to return to Mirky Village and back to the comfort of their homes. The coldness was starting to affect the rebels. Food supplies were nearly at the end. Some rebels were dealing with fever. At first, they celebrated their victory, now they're overcome with regret.

Trying to build the rebels' morale up was Gen. After Zhou came back from the Capital City, he started acting strange, escaping into the forest with Kayten, Jamori, and Osa. For some reason, he started to train them intensely.

Gen was curious to know what happened in the city, but Zhou would change the subject whenever asked. However, he knew that rebels were becoming wary of him.

Gen walked to the fire where five men were sitting on logs, their hands over the fire and each with thin blankets over their shoulders, trying their best to keep warm. He tapped one of the men's shoulders gently and stared into the fire. He saw his own face burning in the fire staring back at him. He then looked in the direction of Polar City, sensing an uncomfortable aura looming over the rebels. The last time he ever felt something uncomfortable was when he served King Rula.

"Lord Gen," said one of the men with red hair. "How long must we wait?"

Gen didn't have an answer to the man. He wondered the same himself. "We must trust Zhou," he urged.

"We do trust him. But why does he hide in the forest?" asked another man.

"I left everything to fight for justice," said the third man. "It seems like I made a foolish decision."

"I will speak to him," promised Gen trying to ease the men's stress. "We fought hard and should be rewarded." He looked around the camp, seeing the struggle on the rebels' faces. "The winter death is coming for us," he whispered to himself, referring to the God of Death, Chenva.

The Unchained feared they were being punished by Chenva, haunting over them with his sinister grin, entertained by their struggles while slowly deteriorating the morals of the rebels. It was their punishment for killing a king. The four kings of Telamis were considered to be the servants of the Seven Protectors of Heaven.

Gen continued his walking, thinking about the sin they had committed. A sin he considered to be a justified one. The fool that ruled the north was no longer sitting on the throne. The north lived too long under the rule of the Diamond clan. Even though there were good rulers in the Diamond clan, still, the era of the Diamond clan had to come to an end. The endless civil war had to finally stop. Nights of blood spilling on the grounds of Wintra must come to a rest so that Wintra could blossom once again.

Gen wanted the north to be united as one, believing that unity between the other rebels, surviving clans, and villages would lead toward stability.

"Lord Gen!" called Spinder with a concerned look.

Gen turned around and was glad to see Spinder. Spinder had all the information throughout the north. Even though he seemed like a man who didn't possess any skills, he was gifted by the gods with exceptional skills as a healer.

"Lord Spinder," greeted Gen.

Spinder took a long, deep breath. He looked like he had run up a hill and back down several times. "I have news from the city," he finally said.

"Tell me," said Gen.

"I ran into a runaway while I was harvesting some herbs." Spinder took a giant gulp. "We need to leave immediately. The queen and her children are longer alive. The advisers are all gone."

"Make some sense, Spinder," said a baffled Gen.

"We have to leave, Lord Gen. The city is dead . . . Zhou is hiding something from us. I fear we will be victims to the hand of the unknown."

"If what you say is true, then who shall fear? If there is no queen nor advisers, then why are we not attacking? Who sits on the bone throne?" wondered Gen.

"We shall find out," said Spinder. "Zhou must tell us the truth."

Gen nodded his head in agreement. "He's hiding in the forest with the three boys."

The two men left the camp to search for Zhou, both trying to piece the puzzle in Zhou's head, wondering who sat on the bone throne and what happened to the queen. Gen was worried that Zhou was straying away from justice.

*   *   *

In the middle of the forest wincing in pain as the cold sharp air stung the tip of his nose and ears was Kayten, kneeling to one knee and clutching his stomach. Standing before him was Jamori, waiting for Kayten to stand so they could resume their training. Watching the two boys train was Zhou with Osa and Baeso standing beside him. Zhou was unimpressed with Kayten for showing no improvement in his strength.

Zhou pondered in his thoughts, trying to figure out how he could draw Kayten's blood for the five elements since finding out that the bone throne had no ruler sitting on it. He believed he could be the one sitting on the cursed throne. Even though the thought went against the rebels' idea of no kings, each day he thought about himself as a king. In the world of Telamis, there must be a ruler. He came to the conclusion that ending the era of kings was impossible. The Unchained already saw him as their leader, so why not take the throne for himself?

"Kayten, how do you wish to improve if you keep falling to Jamori?" asked Zhou sternly.

Kayten grunted. He slowly stood back up and charged at Jamori. Jamori moved to the side and kneed Kayten in the stomach then maneuvered behind Kayten, wrapping his arm around the neck. Using Kayten's weight against him, he flipped him from his back and to the stomach.

Kayten ate snow as he lay on the ground, slowly trying to stand up, sensing his anger coming in. He hated training with Jamori because usually, he ended up losing. He could feel the oozing disappointment coming from Zhou. He stood back up and spit on the ground, raising his fist in the air, then wildly charged forward to Jamori.

Jamori grinned, knowing that he was going to win again. He moved aside and tripped Kayten then placed his foot on the back of Kayten, making sure that he wouldn't stand back up. Their strength was at a different level. The fighting came naturally for Jamori. It also helped that he was a quick learner.

"You can't win," taunted Jamori to Kayten.

Then with rage boiling in him, Kayten forced himself up. Jamori smiled because he struck a nerve in him.

Kayten went for a punch, only to miss.

Then Jamori punched him in the stomach, followed with an elbow to the upper back. This time, Kayten didn't fall. Letting instinct take over, he went for a combination of punches.

Jamori effortlessly dodged. Out of boredom, he slapped Kayten across the face.

Kayten stopped and felt his cheek, shocked that Jamori slapped him. He looked to Jamori and saw his cocky smirk, hating him even more, his blood boiling. "How dare you!" he yelled.

"Enough!" ordered Zhou.

The two boys stopped. They turned to Zhou and saw the annoyance on his face.

"Brothers don't disrespect each other," reminded Zhou. "I raised the two of you better than that."

"I was only trying to help," argued Jamori. "Maybe if he's angry he'll actually beat me."

"You know better, Jamori, to never use childish tactics," said Zhou.

"I'm sorry, next time I'll try a different tactic," grunted Jamori, crossing his arms in disappointment.

"Enough training for today," said Zhou. "Come gather around me. I have something important to say." Zhou eyed each boy as they waited for him to talk. "I never got the chance to express my thank you to you boys. I thank you boys for seeing the same vision as me. We have created chaos in the north. I do not know what punishment will come for us. But I do not fear the storm that's chasing us. As long as I have the loyalty of my people, I fear nothing . . . not even death."

"I also fear nothing!" said Jamori loudly. "I will avenge my clan, build the great name back from the ashes."

Zhou just nodded his head, understanding the anger coming from Jamori, the same anger that everyone from Mirky Village had, the tears and suffering that ran in their blood. The three boys had no clue that Zhou was planning to sacrifice Jamori for his own good.

"From this day forth, I will need the trust from the three of you," declared Zhou.

"Of course you can trust us," said Jamori. "We owe you our lives."

Osa sensed that something was wrong, but chose to not say anything, keeping a close eye on Zhou. The mask was slow cracking. There was a dark cloud hovering over Zhou. Only he could see it.

"What is the next plan, Zhou?" asked Gen with seriousness, as he approached with Spinder.

Zhou was surprised to see Gen, noticing that Gen didn't look thrilled. "Gen?"

"We need to know about the next plan, Zhou," asked Gen calmly again. "Do you not notice that everyone is losing their patience? Where have you been? Our food supplies are nearly gone. People are sick. The cold is cutting them . . . us. Everyone wants to go home, Zhou."

"Yes, I have been absent. But not blind. I know that everyone is suffering. But we have to be patient."

"We can't be patient anymore," worried Spinder. "Stop avoiding us and tell us the truth, Zhou."

Zhou sighed. He was against the wall. He had no choice but to tell the truth to Spinder and Gen to ease their concerns. "If I must tell the truth, I did not meet with the queen nor the advisers. As a matter of fact, I do not know what has happened to them. But I was met with five powerful beings. I do not know if they're humans or demons."

"What are you saying?" asked a confused Gen.

"I think the Diamond clan is no more."

"Who are these five powerful beings you speak of?" asked Spinder.

"Each controlled five elements. The one that holds wind is their leader."

"Do you expect us to believe you, Zhou?" questioned Gen. "Why would you withhold such information from us?"

Zhou stopped to think. He didn't want to tell them his plan to sacrifice Jamori. They would be against the idea. "I should've informed the both of you sooner." He put on a deceiving apologetic face. "I was only trying to protect the people. We have stayed on course to our goal." He bowed his head to both Gen and Spinder. "You two are my trusted allies. I should've never acted alone."

Both Gen and Spinder were skeptical, debating if they should trust Zhou or not. The act he put on was believable. He had Kayten, Jamori, and Baeso falling for it.

Osa was the only one that saw through the smoke, sensing that Zhou was planning something sinister. Unlike the others, he refused to be fooled by Zhou, shocked that Gen and Spinder can't see through his lie.

"Fine, what will we do about the people?" asked Gen. "They can't live like this any longer."

"I know," agreed Zhou. "But I need them to hold on a little longer. I promise we'll reach our peace." He paused for a second, looking at the group around him. Inside, he was straying away from himself. He could feel the waves of evil snatching him away from good. "We should all head back to camp. I'll ease everyone from their worries."

Everyone else nodded in agreement. Gen felt comfortable again, Spinder no longer in a panic. Jamori and Baeso were confident with their leader. Kayten was still fighting inside himself and nodded, not knowing the conversation. Only Osa didn't nod.

* * *

Osa decided to stay behind as everyone left. The air was getting colder as the day continued. Black butterflies danced beautifully around him, acting as a protective shield to him. He noticed the masked figure hiding behind a tree but didn't bother to attack.

"He speaks of lies," exposed the masked figure. The figure had a man's voice.

"I know," agreed Osa.

"Why follow him?" asked the masked man.

"I do not know why I continue to follow him," wondered Osa.

"Do you know your identity, Osa?" asked the masked man. "A boy like you should never follow a man who was raised from poverty."

"Of course I know who I am. I'm the bastard son of Euren. That's why you follow me?"

"Ah, you're a smart boy, my prince."

"I'm no prince. That man does not know of my existence."

"But we do, my prince. Us the Gods' Hands know of you. Follow us and we'll lead you to the truth. Don't follow a liar."

Osa looked to the sky. His mind was clouded with many thoughts. He didn't know why he continued to follow Zhou. He saw through Zhou's mask and his true intention. Then going back to his initial goal, he wanted to kill Euren for abandoning him.

"What are the Gods' Hands?" asked Osa.

"We serve the gods and keep order in this land," answered the masked man.

"What happens if I join? Will anything change? Or will this cruel land still be ruled with unfairness?"

"It's Telamis. This land is controlled by the clans. But we the Gods' Hands are not ruled by any clan nor king. We are the answer to our own destiny."

A black butterfly landed on Osa's finger. The black symbolized the ending of life. Ever since he was a kid, he wondered why the black butterfly followed him. It came naturally to him to use fairy magic, a power he greatly despised but couldn't avoid. "I try so hard to escape who I am. I hated my father and mother even though I barely knew them," he expressed. "The snow wolves were supposed to feast on me, but what kept me alive was these black butterflies." He let the butterfly fly off his hand. "Why do I follow a man like Zhou?" he asked himself, watching the butterfly fly away. "Because I myself don't know who I am."

"Join us and we'll help you discover yourself."

Osa smiled. "I don't wish to discover myself. My existence in this world is nothing. I was born as nobody . . . Just another flower in the ground."

The masked man showed himself. "The gods created us to be nothing. We live because they allow us to." The masked man stuck his palm toward Osa, showing a flower with seven petals tattooed on the palm.

Suddenly, black butterflies began to dance around the masked man.

Osa stood with a black energy orb in his hand. He wanted the masked man to show himself so he could finally kill him. But what he told the masked man was true. Every word that was said came from the heart. "You know, I wished to hear my mother and father's voice," he said calmly. "Sometimes I imagine a happy life with my parents, even if didn't know how they looked and sounded like. The pain of abandonment still hurts. I knew of my mother because Andrena spoke to me after I murdered the guards at the orphanage with these black butterflies." The orb in his hand got bigger. "It doesn't matter what you want with me. But leave Kayten alone."

"You protect a Dru? A monster?" asked the masked man.

"No friend of mine is a monster."

"Oh, prince, there's no friendship in this world."

Osa threw the black orb at the masked man.

The black butterflies scattered, and within an inch of getting the masked man, he had turned himself into a crow. Then flying toward Osa with its beak charging at his chest, he managed to dodge, and the man fled away.

Osa turned back to the direction where he threw the black orb, seeing he had knocked down a line of three. If the man didn't move away, he would've been dead instantly. He felt the extent of his power and ability in him.

* * *

Zhou sat in his tent staring at the bone crown in his hand, again imagining himself wearing the crown. He was slowly becoming fixated with the crown to the point where we didn't want it to leave its sight. While training the boys in the forest, he worried for the crown, afraid that someone might sneak into his tent and steal it. After easing the people at the camp, he hurried back into his tent for the night.

The crown was trapping him, strangling him until he became one with it. It felt like vines looping around his neck, suffocating him until he allowed it to overtake him.

Jamori entered the tent.

Zhou had asked him to come to meet him to discuss something important. He rested the crown back on the nightstand beside his bed, running his finger across the surface for one last time.

"Zhou, you call for me?" questioned Jamori.

"Yes," answered Zhou, his eyes drifting back to the crown. "I have an important task for you."

Jamori became thrilled, raising his chest and standing straight, showing that he was ready for any challenge. "You can count on me."

"I know I can." He paused. "But can I trust you?"

"Of course you can! I'm loyal to the end," expressed Jamori confidently.

"Good, I'm going to put a tasking mission on you. It will prove your loyalty to me." Zhou stood from his bed and paced back and forth. "Do you consider Kayten your brother?" he asked.

Jamori blinked in confusion. "Of course, occasionally we fight. But still, he's my brother till the end."

"That's good. I taught you well." Zhou smiled and continued to pace back and forth. "Remember the story of the two brothers?" asked Zhou.

"Yeah, the younger brother killed the older brother because he possessed powers greater than the gods," recalled Jamori.

"Right." Zhou stopped pacing; he turned to Jamori with a serious expression on his face. "What if I order you to kill your brother because he possessed the power of evil?"

Jamori was baffled. He couldn't believe the words coming out of Zhou's mouth, hoping it was only a sick joke he was playing on him. "I will never kill my brother!" expressed Jamori.

"I know. What I asked of you is difficult. But sometimes it's important to put the greater good over the people you love." He walked over to Jamori and placed his hands on his shoulder, showing a fake caring look. "We have a common goal, Jamori. And that's to end the era of kings. Kayten is a liability to our goal."

"Kayten is part of the goal. We all witnessed the same horror together. He deserves to see the end of our goal together!" Jamori explained with confusion and anger.

"He's not like you and me. He doesn't see the same goal we see."

"Why must we kill him? Can we just kick him out of the Unchained?" argued Jamori.

"No, he's not going to survive alone." Zhou stopped to think, finding it hard to convince Jamori. "Let me tell you the story of the wolf and her weak pup. The weak pup was holding the pack behind. And you know what the mother did? She committed the greatest sacrifice. For her other pups to survive, she left the weak pup to die." He turned Jamori to where Rising Fire was resting on a table. "That sword is yours if you choose to take Kayten's life."

Jamori made his way to the sword, his body moving by itself like a ghost was forcing him to hold the sword. Finally, he could hold the sword that was meant to be his. He picked the sword up and unsheathed it, seeing his own reflection on the flat of the sword. The edges of the sword were sharp. It felt light as he held it in his hand.

"For us to prosper, we must allow ourselves to break from the weak ones," finished Zhou.

Chapter Seventeen

Heart Village

Sitting under the weeping tree was Kunjae on a night when the purple moon sat still. Ten days passed since their battle with the Men of Hate. Everyone at Heart Village had been uneasy since their loss.

Kunjae looked over to the village wondering why these villagers couldn't defend themselves. If they were able to defend themselves, then Airian would've never lost an eye. He shut his eyes and tried to remember days when life was much simple. Aerin didn't see him as a weapon as he saw in Ausra. He was much freer. Sadly, as he got older, he realized his clan's truth, something that none of his siblings couldn't see but him. As a kid, he loved to spy on his siblings.

There was one particular day where his spying went too far. He recalled that night perfectly at the time he was still young, not knowing what was right and wrong, peeking through the crack of his grandfather's door, hoping to hear another story from him. They were close to each other. Whenever he was feeling down, So-Yen would bring him to the candy shop. The two were inseparable. He loved listening to his grandfather playing the flute; it was peaceful and soothing. And stories made him feel like he was a part of it.

But on the night So-Yen died, he could not erase it from his memories. All he could do was tuck the memory away, but sometimes it would reappear, peeking through the cracked door and witnessing someone wearing a golden mask with a third eye on the forehead standing at his grandfather's bedside. Hands hovered over the body as the soul left the body. Also standing beside was Aerin with an emotionless look over his face, watching as his own father die.

Kunjae ran away from the sight, stunned and heartbroken that his grandfather was killed by Aerin. From that day on, he hated Aerin, keeping what he knew away from his siblings. His calm demeanor masked his truth. His life was like a never-ending winter, waiting for the sun to melt all his dark memories away.

He opened his palm and allowed a small blue flame to dance on it, staring at it till his eyes burned, coming to the realization he was no different from his siblings. Unlike them, he had nothing to prove to his father, but he was still trapped in Aerin's game. He closed his palm to put the flames out and stared into the purple moon in the night sky. The moon was said to have borne many legends. But whoever was born on the night of purple would likely die young. If they made it far, then they had done something great with their life.

He reached his arms out to the purple moon, trying to fit it in his palm, trusting himself to be the one to end the Bore. Avenging Airian was his secret goal. When he had the chance to kill the Bore, he let him free. The next time they meet, one of them must die. Though he rarely showed that he cared for his siblings, deep in the depths of his heart, he worried for them.

Akin climbed up the hill and approached Kunjae, mad at himself that he wasn't able to protect Airian. He couldn't bear to see his nephew hurt and disappointed that he couldn't follow his one order. He spent all morning recruiting new soldiers to the clan. Villagers were skeptic to join but folded when they realized they had no choice. Mothers were afraid to lose their sons and daughters, fathers planning for their family's future.

"There you are," said Akin.

"Uncle."

"Why are you up here?" asked Akin.

Kunjae took a while; he wanted to be alone, away from the havoc and have time with his own thoughts. Since the battle, he hadn't had time for himself. He had been tasked with the recruiting process. If he was not recruiting, he was learning under Akin, teaching him how to lead and the philosophy of war.

Kunjae shrugged his shoulders and looked down at the village. "The village bores me," he replied back.

"What do you expect? The villagers have been suffering for months."

"That's their own fault." Kunjae paused. "They should learn how to defend themselves."

"Is that how you feel, Kunjae?" questioned Akin.

"If these people knew how to defend themselves, then the hothead wouldn't have lost an eye," replied Kunjae.

"Airian lost his eye because I wasn't there to protect him," regretted Akin. "I made a promise to my brother to protect his sons and I failed. That's my guilt." Akin also turned to look at the village below. "Tell me, what do you suggest we do?"

Kunjae took a while to state his opinion. In his head, he already had an idea of how to deal with the situation in Heart Village. But his idea didn't fit the mold as a warrior. "I say we abandon the village. We lost a lot of men and women in the first battle. What makes the new recruit any better? The result will be the same. If it's true that we're preparing for war with the king, then we shouldn't waste any more pointless men and women. This village is the king's village, not the Kimsu clan village, which makes them our enemy."

Akin chuckled, knowing that Kunjae was right. There was no point for them to defend the village. But it challenged his code as a warrior. Even if they follow the king, they were still innocent people. "Your thinking is straightforward, Kunjae. Sometimes having a little imagination will help." He turned to Kunjae. "I want to ask… what are you afraid of?"

"What is there for me to be afraid of?" wondered Kunjae. "Am I supposed to be afraid of death? It's too late for me to be afraid of anything, Uncle. I may be young, but I know what my life is. I have to accept my destiny even if I don't approve of it."

"You're a smart kid, Kunjae." He rubbed the top of Kunjae's head, messing up his hair. "I hope someday the sun will set on you, nephew." He left Kunjae with his parting words, remembering the day his own father asked what he was most afraid of. His greatest fear was seeing the people he loved most dying. Hence the reason why he refused to have kids of his own. When he saw Airian and Kunjae, he saw them as his own sons.

Kunjae stared back at the moon, wondering what his uncle meant. Why should he be afraid, he wondered. The world of Telamis was filled with fear. The four kingdoms of Telamis was built on fear and ambition. He had his fear, but not his ambition. In truth, he was afraid. Deep down, he was terrified of dying, hiding his fear with his calmness and sarcasm, knowing at some point there will be a time where his fear will present itself.

Kunjae left the weeping tree and wandered around the village, electing not to see Airian, guessing that Airian may still be sleeping or staring at the wall because of shock. While walking the village, the streets were empty. It felt that spirits were watching him within the darkness. But the emptiness was peaceful for Kunjae. The orb lights lighting the streets gave a calming atmosphere. The day was long for him. Nights was the only time where he had time for himself.

He enjoyed himself walking the streets. The villagers were too afraid to roam the night. Even the local taverns were closed. The homeless hid themselves in the alleyways. Drunks were now sober. Muggers stole from themselves.

Kunjae spotted an old lady sitting by herself during his wandering. She had a gentle smile over her face, staring right at Kunjae. He tried to avoid the old lady, but curiosity brought him to her. It was strange to see an old lady sitting by herself under the moon. She wasn't counting stars nor enjoying the fireflies. She was just staring right at Kunjae.

"Why is an old lady sitting by herself?" asked Kunjae as he approached when he got a better look at the lady. She reminded him of someone he knew, but couldn't wrap his mind around it. She had a green apple in her hand.

"I sit alone because the night is cool."

"Are you not afraid of what could happen to you during the night?"

"What is there for me to be afraid of? An old lady like me is not afraid of anything. I already accept what I fear most," said the old lady.

Kunjae was intrigued by the old lady. "What did you once fear?" he asked curiously.

"Life is meant to travel. What I once feared I learned to accept through my travels, through the children I once bore and abandoned, but watched from afar"—the old lady teared up—"I learn to accept death."

"Of course you have to accept death," said Kunjae. "Everyone dies."

"Child, I see through you. I know what you fear."

Kunjae chuckled, thinking the old lady was a fool. "You're just an old lady waiting for her time to pass." He turned to leave. "I wasted my time talking to you."

"Kunjae, you are no different than your siblings. Your memories hold the key to the Kimsu clan's truth."

Kunjae stopped, the nerves in his body ringing throughout, baffled by how the old lady knew in the past when he saw his grandfather's death. He sensed that she was reading him.

"I know a lot, child. I see a lot," revealed the old lady. "It's a curse that I can read the memories of people."

"So you sit around intruding people's memories?"

"Yes, I like to know what darkness people hide," replied the old lady. "It's harmless but yet so evil of me."

"You find pleasure in this?"

"Truthfully I don't, that's the reason why I abandoned the man I loved and our children. Like I said, life is meant to be traveled. I traveled the four kingdoms and gathered many memories. It is silly what kind of memories people hide. Even funnier how people hide the good memories."

"Are you some kind of demon?" asked Kunjae.

"Silly child, I'm no demon. I'm just an old lady waiting for her moment."

Kunjae turned back around to the old lady, to see her no longer sitting on the bench. He looked around confusedly, trying to figure out where she went, wondering if he was talking to himself. Suddenly, a black crow flew by him and off to the night sky, leaving him alone with his confusion. He stood on the lit street, trying to figure out who the old lady was. For an unknown reason, the old lady looked familiar to him. He looked at the bench and saw that she had left the apple.

Suddenly, that same boy with dirt all over his face appeared beside him. "She left me an apple." He picked up the apple and turned to Kunjae. "Should we split it?"

Kunjae just chuckled and walked away, ignoring the boy's offer to share the apples shaking his head and telling himself that he wasn't crazy.

The boy didn't look upset that Kunjae denied him. He just watched with a smile, and slowly he began to fade away and dropped the apple to the ground.

* * *

The morning in Heart Village was bleak and tiring. Some villagers elected not to work. Shop owners chose to keep their shop close. Even the homeless kept themselves hidden from the public eye. The streets were quiet as if a ghost of silence has taken the village.

Airian sat on his bed staring straight at the wall, woken by his nightmare of the Bore gouging his eye out. He slowly moved his hand to feel the eye patch over his right eye, ashamed of himself for being weak. Both Kunjae and Indris barely visited him since they were busy with recruitment. Sometimes during the day, his uncle would come to see him. He could see the hurt and shame on Akin's face.

In truth, Airian wanted to be alone. He barely stepped outside his room. Sometimes he would read letters his mother would send him. Even though her letter was refreshing, he still felt hopeless. When he stepped outside, he felt like people were laughing at him, poking fun at his failure.

A young girl entered Airian's room with a bucket of water and a white cloth. She was about the same age as him and was unhappy when she entered the room. The girl was Liana Fong, daughter of a farmer and healer. Her mother was Tenju Fong, a healer who was caring for Airian. Placing the bucket beside Airian's bed and peeking over to him to see the lost and anguished look on his face, she did not pity him but instead seeing him as a pathetic clan member.

"The water is beside your bed, Lord Airian," said Liana. She quickly turned to leave, not wanting to be in a room with his negative energy.

"How is it out there?" asked Airian, still with the lost look over his face and feeling the eye patch over his right eye.

Liana stopped. "I wouldn't know. I have been stuck caring for you." She left the room but was blocked by Kunjae standing in front of the doorway. "Lord Kunjae." She bowed.

"Somebody's not happy." Kunjae noticed with a smile. He peeked over to Airian. "I see my idiot brother still sits on his bed." Then he looked back at Liana. "The healers of Heart Village are doing a terrible job." He insulted Liana's mother as a healer.

Liana was irate but kept a calm expression. "He is healing, but we can't fix a mind that's broken," she insulted back then moved Kunjae aside to leave. "I can't believe that the Men of Hate is stronger than the great Kimsu clan."

Kunjae smiled, liking that Liana was standing up for herself. "Common girl like you should watch their mouth," he warned. "If it was my decision, I would let this dead village burn." He leaned over to Liana's ear. "Your brother got recruited to be a soldier for the Kimsu clan," he whispered then stepped into Airian's room.

Liana stood in anger. Kunjae had gotten into her head. She wanted to turn back and continue to fight back with him. But her mother told her to respect them and to hold her tongue. Her mother hoped that by helping them, she would be able to attend Mersane Academy and study to be a healer.

Kunjae sat on the chair beside the door. He saw that Airian was in a dark place in his own thoughts. He had no clue on how to save his brother. That once brash and hothead of a boy was now a quiet little child.

"Feeling pity for yourself will not bring your eye back," said Kunjae.

"I disappointed Father," said Airian.

"Why does it matter what he thinks?" questioned Kunjae.

"I'm a disappointment to the clan." Airian ignored Kunjae's question. "I can never be a warrior. I'm too afraid to kill." Tears dripped from his left eye. "I'm a weakling. Father will banish me for sure."

"Stop worrying," suggested Kunjae. "He wouldn't be a great father if he banishes his own son for being weak." He stood up. "Our life doesn't revolve around his hot head." He left the room calmly, feeling his brother was only lost because he was afraid of their father.

Airian sat still on his bed, thinking of why he revolved his life around his father. Ever since he was a kid, he wanted to impress his father. But it seemed his father was never impressed by him because he wasn't Ausra or Iszra. He clutched his blanket tightly with pain in his head. Why did he work so hard for a one man's approval? Missing out on the importance of his life. He let out a loud cry that could be heard through the hallway, a yell of pain and self-hate to finish off with tears filling his face, hiding his pain in the palm of his hand.

Kunjae turned around after hearing the loud cry echoing the hall, looking at the door to Airian's room with a smile on his face. The only way for his siblings to be happy was to release themselves from their father's web. He held the weeping man necklace in his palm. To him, his father was no different from the man who killed his own son. Instead of killing them physically, their father was killing each of them with his ambition. Their father was the monster that haunted their dreams.

He made his way to the war room of the fortress where Indris, Estrey, and Akin was waiting for him.

Indris had been pressured by their father to finish the mission quickly and return to Mersane.

Kunjae took time making his way to the war room. The fact was, he didn't like the war room. He hated listening about the plan of attack and defense tactics. All he wanted was to go back to Mersane, to sleep on his bed and live a lazy, carefree life.

While walking the hall, he can feel a cool draft coming from behind him. The fortress felt eerie and haunted to him. For some reason, he feels that the stone walls had eyes that were watching him. At the same time, he sensed that something was following him.

He finally arrived to the war room. Taking a couple of breaths before he indulged himself in boredom. Ever since he hinted at potential against The Bore, he has been treated differently by Indris. He didn't mean to show his potential but he had no other choice. If he wouldn't have done something, then Airian would've been dead. Now both Indris and Akin are involving him more in the strategies.

He pushed opened the wooden door and entered the unexciting room. Indris was standing at the center staring at the map on the table. Akin at one side of the table and across him was Estrey. Kunjae made his way to the end of the table, looking across to Indris.

"You're late." Annoyed Indris.

"I went to visit, hothead," said Kunjae.

"How is he?" asked Indris.

"Hopeless," answered Kunjae.

"I ought to check on that boy," said a concerned Akin.

"Please, Uncle," agreed Indris. "It's not the time for him to be weak."

"I think it's best to give him time," suggested Estrey. "The young lord did lose an eye."

"How much time does he need?" questioned Indris.

"However long," replied Akin. "As his protector, I forbid him to fight this battle."

"This battle?" asked the confused Kunjae.

"Yes, we're attacking the Men of Hate again," confirmed Indris.

"What is the plan, Captain Indris?" asked Estrey. "We can't fall for the same mistake again."

Indris took a while to think. He doesn't know what to do. Since Aerin was pushing him to finish the Men of Hate quickly, he couldn't think of anything. Lately, his mind had been drifting since his first attempt to get rid of the Men of Hate failed.

"How're the new recruits?" questioned Indris.

"They're not ready. We can't bring little boys and girls to a fight," answered Akin.

"It's not like we have a choice, Uncle."

"If we put them into battle, they'll die, and the result will be the same," argued Akin.

"Then what do you suggested, Uncle?" challenged Indris.

Akin looked at Kunjae who looked distant from the conversation. "Kunjae, what do you think we should do?"

They all looked to Kunjae. He was unfazed by their eager eyes. At the same time, he could see that their eager eyes were lost. They had no direction and answer of their own. He then focused on the map on the table. "I would let this village burn," he started. "That's thinking long term. In the end, we're going to kill these people when we go into war with the kingdom." He paused for a second. "But since we want to be heroes, we can fight like the Men of Hate."

"What do you mean?" asked Indris.

"The Men of Hate are masters of guerilla warfare. The forest is their strength," answered Kunjae. "You see, they're intelligent. That's why they attack at night, where they can be free. They're not going to challenge us out in the open. So we should use what we have to our advantage."

"What is it?" asked Estrey.

"Old people are not smart at all. Our advantage is fire. We can burn the forest and trap them. Then attack them as they attack us."

"I'll send a hawk to find their camp," said Estrey immediately, liking Kunjae's plan.

"No need, they know we are looking for them," said Kunjae. "The Bore wants his match against me."

"They're stupid enough to camp at the same spot?" questioned Indris.

"If someone is hungry, they don't wait, brother. I kept the Bore waiting. He's starving to cut my head off. I can sense him licking his lip and waiting for my arrival. The giant freak is not going to hide from his meal."

"I'm not going to let you fight the Bore, Kunjae," denied Indris. "I will not let what happen to Airian happen to you."

"Whatever you wish, brother," said Kunjae. "Better for me if I don't have to do too much work."

"Then it's decided, we're going to trap them with fire."

Suddenly, the door flew open and in rushed Airian in his nightgown, sweating waterfalls as he entered like he was running from a bear, breathing heavily and trying to hold himself up. The expression on his face was filled with confidence.

Airian looked up, confused eyes staring at him. He slightly found himself again. After his yelling and crying, he found some of his strength. But a part of him was still weak, trying to force him back to his room. "I'm ready!" he yelled.

"Ready for what?" Confused Indris.

"I'm ready to fight again," said Airian with little confidence.

"No, you're not," rejected Indris.

"Yes, I am!" argued Airian. "I can fight."

"Airian, enough!" yelled Akin. "You're still weak. Acting with little confidence and no plan only makes you look like a fool."

"Uncle—"

"You're not ready," insisted Akin.

"Hothead, I have to agree with Uncle," agreed Kunjae.

"Please! Give me another chance," begged Airian.

"Be grateful that you have a chance to live," said Indris. "The truth is, there is little to no chance when in battle."

"Lord Airian, with all due respect, the gods gave you a chance to live. It's best to not waste their gift to you," advised Estrey.

Airian felt like a fool. His confidence was gone. Again, he was lost trying to figure out if he was a warrior. "Then when will I fight again?"

"When the gods gift you with confidence again," answered Akin.

Airian walked out of the war room. The door shut behind him, tears falling from his eyes. He let a loud painful yell, upset that he couldn't redeem himself.

* * *

Kunjae tightened his boots while sitting on a stool at the barrack. The new recruits between the age of thirteen to forty looked nervous as they prepared for battle, praying that the god of war would be by their side. For Kunjae, he wasn't afraid or nervous, only his second time going to battle. He still kept the same emotion. Eyeing the room, he wondered how these inexperienced fighters and magic users will act in battle. Some will hide or run away while others will let their instinct take over.

After finishing tightening his boots, he walked out of the barrack. Looking up at the sky. It was almost time for them to leave, and some of the soldiers weren't ready. There were some soldiers outside the barrack, preparing themselves to march out the gates of the village. But the rest mainly stayed inside. Waiting for Indris to give them orders.

"Kunjae!" Called Indris from behind.

Kunjae sighed, he wanted some time alone before he goes into battle and listens to the shout of triumph, agony, and death. When the sound of steel hitting steel collides in the name of victory.

"I hope your plan works," said Indris. "We can't afford to lose. The lives of these villagers are in our hands."

"Why do you care so much for these people?" asked Kunjae.

Indris gazed out into the distance, seeing the laughter and anxiety in his men and women. "Even though we will soon be the enemy to these villagers, they will see our clan as villains and traitors. But at the end of the day, they're just innocent lives in the greedy war to come. As a warrior, we fight for the lives that can't fight for themselves."

"That's a pointless code to follow," mocked Kunjae.

"Codes are what keep us sane."

"Then father is breaking the code," said Kunjae.

Indris took a while to think. He couldn't deny that Kunjae was right. Their father was turning into a monster that would terrorize the eastern kingdom. He and the rest of his siblings would be the weapon to reign terror over the kingdom. "He wants to build a world that he only sees. The vision he sees is blind to reality." He placed his hand on Kunjae's shoulder.

"Why are you talking weird?" Kunjae shrugged Indris's hand off his shoulders and walked away. While walking away, he thought about what Indris just said to him. Their father only saw his own path, but was blind to his own children's suffering. But he, unlike his father, saw the suffering in his siblings' eyes. He remembered the look on Iszra's face before disappearing without a trace. He saw Chenpu yearning for recognition. He witnessed Indris's hardship to find a voice. He understood Ausra's annoyance to being called a hero. He felt Mani's urge to be involved, to Airian and Kiri wanting approval from their father, then to Lehue wanting to stray away from the clan tradition, and lastly, Isa's fears toward their father.

Unlike his siblings, he knew his father's secret, keeping it to himself so he wouldn't belittle himself to his father's power. Instead, he'd rather let hatred live inside him since the day he saw Aerin in the room with the golden-masked figure taking the soul out of his grandfather. Aerin was the villain that was pretending to be a hero.

* * *

Airian was killed inside that he couldn't fight beside his brothers and uncle. He wanted his redemption to prove that he could fight. He was suffering inside. All he could think about was him screaming while the Bore gouged his right eye out.

All day he hid in his room, watching from his window, seeing soldiers unconfidently marching out of the village gate to fight the Men of Hate again. Leading the troop was Indris who didn't have a confident look either.

"Lord Airian, you should rest," advised Tenju with Liana standing behind her. She held a cup of herbal medical tea in her hand.

"I'm useless," Airian said to himself.

Tenju handed him his tea. He took a sip and quickly spit it out. "What is this!" He was disgusted. The tea tasted bitter with a spicy aftertaste.

Liana didn't look happy when Airian spit her mother's tea out. She couldn't stand to see a high clan member in her presence. She thought of them as privileged and selfish humans.

"It's medicine tea I made myself, Lord Airian," replied Tenju kindly.

"It's disgusting," said Airian then giving her back the cup and staring back out the window.

"I'm sorry." Tenju bowed.

"I don't need to be care anymore."

"Captain—"

"I can take care of myself. I don't need anybody to watch over me," Airian cut Tenju off.

Liana was annoyed seeing Tenju being disrespected by a high clan member. "Thank you would be nice," she suggested coldly.

"Liana!" warned Tenju, hoping Liana would keep her mouth shut.

Airian turned to both Tenju and Liana. "Thank you," he thanked then turned back to the window.

Both Tenju and Liana was surprised to hear a thank-you out of Airian. They wondered what he was staring at out the window. Ever since the day they took care of him, he barely mouth a word to them. He acted as if they weren't in the room, staring at the wall and feeling his eye patch.

"Lord Airian, what is it you're staring at?" wondered Tenju.

"Nothing," answered Airian. "I wish I was fighting alongside my comrades."

Liana rolled her eyes and turned to leave. But Tenju grabbed her wrist for her to stay. Tenju had tears coming down her eyes. It was a dream for every young man and woman to bring acclaim to their family name. Taking the path of war was a game of luck and chance, where death has a higher chance than living.

When Tenju found out that her son Go was going to fight for the Kimsu clan, she was heartbroken even though Go was excited to fight. As a mother, she didn't want to lose her only son.

"My son is fighting for your clan," said Tenju. "So please, Lord Airian, don't say you wish to fight alongside your comrades. While you lie in your bed, Captain Indris was recruiting villagers to fight, including my son. You don't even know his name."

Airian was baffled; he didn't understand the feelings of others. When he saw tears in Tenju's eyes, his heart sank a little, not knowing that his brother was recruiting the villagers to fight the Men of Hate. They were asked to come and protect the villagers, not use them to fight the battle.

"Mother," said a concerned Liana, holding Tenju's hand.

"If you were my son, I would be broken to hear you wanting to die," continued Tenju. "My son is Go Fong, son of a farmer and healer." She bowed and left the room.

Liana gave a cold glance toward Airian as her mother left. "Is that what all clan members think of? Do they only worry for themselves?" she asked coldly, then leaving Airian in his own confusion.

Airian just sat on his bed, alone in his silent room. All his life he was taught about his clan. He never stopped to think about the common people. To him, they were the forgotten characters in his story.

*   *   *

The sun had fallen to a slumber. The moon wakened, lighting the streets of Heart Village. Though the sun may be sleeping, the villagers were still awake, anxious to know if the Kimsu clan were able to end the Men of Hate, hoping to see the banner of the demon clan and not the evil eyes of hate.

Parents wondered if they would see their child again. Young wives hoped to live long with their husbands. The thought of death and no longer seeing a loved one disturbed their mind.

Airian watched from his window, waiting for his brothers' and uncle's arrival. Watching ants crawling in his room, he remembered the day when he broke his arm, learning how to ride a horse. The horse threw him off and dropped him on his arm. While crying on the ground and holding his arm. Aerin told him to stand and to stop crying. From then on, he had to prove his value to his father.

As he waited throughout the night for his brothers and uncle to return, his patience became his enemy. The thought of not knowing disturbed his sleep as he paced back and forth in his room, hoping to see victory for the Kimsu clan so they could return home to Mersane.

For a second, he forgot about his eye, slowly feeling the patch over his right eye. Then there came a flashback of the Bore raising him by the neck, his feet dangling in the air, thinking that the Bore would strangle him to death but instead of getting his eye plunged out with the disgusting fingers of the Bore, he was left to live with his ugliness.

All of a sudden from outside his window, he could hear cheering from the villagers. He rushed over to see and saw that the soldiers had returned. Overcome with excitement, he ran out of his room to greet his brothers at the front gate but was stopped by a guard.

"Why are you blocking me?" asked Airian.

The guard had a sad look over his face. "You must go to the infirmary," reported the guard.

"For what?" asked a confused Airian.

"Captain Indris has been severely wounded in battle."

Out of shock and horror, Airian pushed the guard aside and rushed to the infirmary. There was no way Indris could be hurt in battle. He was supposed to be untouchable. His mind racing as he ran through the halls of Full Heart Fortress, praying that Indris would survive.

When he finally arrived at the infirmary outside the fortress, he burst into the room and saw lying on the bed with blood all over the bedsheets was Indris with a healing bubble around him. His eyes were shut tight while Tenju tried to save him, trying to stop the blood from flowing out from his opened chest. In the room were Akin, Estrey, and Kunjae. Liana stood behind Tenju watching with unease.

Tenju's magic energy wasn't enough to save Indris. Each time she tried to seal the wound, the more energy was taken away from her. The wound wouldn't shut. The cut was too deep for any chance for Indris to survive.

"No . . . no. This can't be," exclaimed a shocked Airian, staring at his brother's lifeless body, not wanting to accept Indris's death. "How could this happen?"

Kunjae stared expressionless at Indris's body, confused about how he was supposed to feel. He never expected Indris to die. During the attack on the Men of Hate, the Kimsu clan was winning. The Men of Hate and the Bore were retreating until Indris gave chase. He saw the rage and regret in Indris. It felt like Indris wanted to die.

He chased after Indris but was too late. The Bore had already slashed down on his chest, breaking his arm then retreating deep within the forest. He held Indris in his arms with blood leaking from the wound and his mouth. Indris was staring at the stars with a smile on his face. When Akin and Estrey finally arrived, they immediately flew Indris on a cloud before the others could see.

Kunjae was praying for Indris to come back alive. But he knew that Tenju's healing magic wasn't working; he had to accept the fact that he would no longer see his brother. He dropped to his knee with nothing in his eyes. His heart felt like it wasn't beating anymore. All he could do was stare at nothing.

Airian wanted answers, but everyone was speechless. All they could do was look helplessly at the body of Indris. "Someone say something!" angered Airian. He looked over to Kunjae. "Kunjae, say something stupid," he begged. "Uncle, . . . please say something. Why did you let him die?" Tears fell from his one eye, and his vision became blurry. He looked to Tenju. "Save him, healer!" he cried. He rushed over to Tenju, but Akin stepped in front of him and held him to his chest tightly.

Airian cried into the armor of his uncle. "Save him . . ." His voice sounded muffled. "Uncle, tell her to save him . . ." He fell to his knees and started to cry loudly in Akin's arms.

*　　*　　*

At the Demon Palace, looking to the night sky was Aerin, watching Maenellia flying around on Borin. He had a look of sadness over his face. A single white bird landed on the ledge followed by a shooting star across the moon. Something tragic had happened. A teardrop fell from his eyes. One of his children had fallen.

Chapter Eighteen

Forest of Despair

Still inside the Forest of Despair after weeks of walking without seeing the sun, the dragons grew tired of each other. Daysa was able to figure out enough about the dragons. There was intense hatred between Nisu and Nagen. Kaiso had a bad temper and seemed to hate everything around him. Leonaris was only into his books and didn't seem to acknowledge the other. Ausra was lazy and always finding the time to nap. Torshen was either off hunting or lingering around Ausra. Only Sukro was the only one that acknowledged her.

The dragons and Daysa had been settling down at the ruined temple that worshipped the God of Death, Chenva, for the past two days. They decided to rest longer to gather enough energy since they predicted they would be heading into more difficult challenges as they continued their quest. A giant statue of Chenva sat in the main room of the temple. The statue was made out of wood, sitting on the head of a serpent. Chenva was the god that created all demons to challenge his brother Shenva's angels, hence the reason why his temple sat in the Forest of Despair.

While everyone rested inside, Ausra sat outside under a tree to nap. Really, he was reminiscing about his childhood training under Vesak. It would be a lie if he didn't miss Vesak. But regrets of killing his teacher never crossed his mind. Vesak wanted to die. When he stabbed Vesak in the back, it felt like the old man had come to terms with death.

Ausra remembered the first time he held a real sword, standing in front of a black bear that his father had the guards captured while Vesak and Aerin watched with the other dragons to the side. It was Ausra alone with the bloodthirsty hungry beast. All his emotions had been taken away from him as he stared at the beast with careless eyes, waiting for it to be uncaged for him to fight.

When the guards released the bear from its imprisonment, it quickly charged at Ausra with the intention of mauling him to death. He did not see a bear trying to kill him. He saw a life he must kill because he was told to. He dropped his sword and lifted his left arm. Once the bear got close enough, he let out a giant blast of black flames, burning the bear to death. He remembered looking to his father and Vesak and seeing the proudness in their eyes.

Ausra opened his eyes to a blue flame bird in front of him with a letter under its talons, his memories stored back in the deepest part of his mind, locked until he revisited it again.

The seal on the letter was his clan seal. He already knew that the letter belonged to his mother. Unsealing the letter to see what she wrote to him, taking a quick glance, the words were written to him. His mother begged the dragons and him to return to Mersane. She was concerned for Aerin and worried that the clan will suffer when they go into war with the king.

Ausra sensed that his mother was afraid. But he didn't care because he was sticking to his word. Finding the golden bird would be the last order he took from his father.

Just a night ago, while he rested under the same tree, he had a strange dream. He dreamed of one of his siblings dying. He recalled the dream of him on a battlefield against the Men of Hate, fire surrounding the area. Smoke filled the air, making it difficult to see who the enemy and ally were. Then he saw Indris lying on the ground staring at the stars in the sky with a smile on his face. He then recalled his conversation with Indris when he said that he didn't expect to live long.

He stood from his spot under the tree and made his way to the ruined temple. Sitting on the steps was Nagen sharpening his daggers on a whetstone. Without saying a word to Nagen, he handed the letter to him.

Nagen also quickly glanced at the letter and followed Ausra into the temple.

Everyone in the temple was relaxing, waiting for Torshen to return from his hunt. Leonaris was sitting near the wooden statue of Chenva reading his book. Kaiso was napping at the corner with his sword leaning on his shoulder. Daysa was reading her father's research book. Sukro was admiring the painting on the walls of Chenva and his conquests. And Nisu was daydreaming because of boredom.

Ausra made his way to Chenva's statue and sat at the bottom steps.

Nagen stood in front so the rest could see him. Everyone stopped what they were doing to look up at him, except for Daysa; she still didn't understand the Dragon's way.

She was still reading her father's research, glued to the interesting facts of the beast and ancient people her father discovered. She didn't realize that Nagen was waiting for her attention. Sukro was beside her. He tapped her shoulder, breaking her from her reading. She looked up, finally realizing that the others were waiting for her. She closed her book in embarrassment and opened a portal to return then focused her attention on Nagen, not trying to make eye contact with the other dragons. She dreaded her time with the dragons.

Nagen showed the letter to everyone in the room. "Lady Maenellia has asked us to return to Mersane," he revealed. "Seems Lord Aerin has declared war with Tigara."

"We should return and fight alongside Lord Aerin immediately," suggested Kaiso quickly.

"I agree. Without the dragons, the Kimsu clan stands no chance against the entire eastern kingdom," agreed Leonaris.

"I also think we should return home," Sukro added his opinion.

Daysa was upset that half the dragons didn't want to finish their mission. "How about our agreement?" she asked. "I was promised the golden bird."

"I agree with Daysa," agreed Nisu, winking to Daysa. "Lord Aerin assigned us a mission to find his sword."

"Do you think the clan can hold the entire eastern kingdom without us?" asked Kaiso.

"We have a mission we must complete. It was Lord Aerin's order," argued Nisu.

"We swore to be warriors to protect Lord Aerin. I'm returning to the city to fight beside my lord," Kaiso argued back.

"Enough!" ordered Nagen. "Fighting and arguing amongst each other won't do any good."

The room was silent as they all waited for Nagen to say something.

Nagen also wanted to go back to Mersane, feeling that the mission was a waste of time, believing that it was impossible to find the golden phoenix. Before they left Mersane to embark on their long mission, he spent all night researching on the bird at the library, reading countless researches and stories. And they were all the same. The bird was never found after it fought the five kings. It was true that the bird was strong enough to kill all five. But it did take an amount of damage for it to die.

"Then what do you suggest?" Sukro asked Nagen.

Nagen looked over to Daysa. "Do you believe that your bird is alive?" he asked mockingly.

Daysa hesitated, seeing that his eyes darkened. "My father re—"

"Maybe your father is an idiot," insulted Nagen. "I did my own research. I don't believe such a bird exists."

"My father only writes what is true," defended Daysa.

"Your father was a fool," Nagen insulted again. "A man with such magical powers wasted on stupid, pointless researches. And his daughter trying to live his dream."

"It's my dream too," angered Daysa. "You weren't there to hear the stories and scars Father received from his travels and discoveries."

Nagen smirked; he slowly walked over to Daysa but was stopped by a wall of blue flames. He looked over to Ausra, shocked that Ausra was defending Daysa.

Daysa was also surprised that Ausra was defending her.

"I told my father I will be leaving the dragons after this mission," he revealed, shocking everyone in the room. "I don't expect to go back to Mersane. I prefer to finish this mission out and leave my clan."

"Why?" asked a confused Sukro.

"I'm tired," replied Ausra. "I'm tired of all of you. I'm tired of my father. I'm tired of Mersane and its people. I just want to leave."

Nagen chuckled. "It's not easy, Ausra. You can't choose when to leave. I don't care that you're the son of Lord Aerin. We're bound together forever—all of us. We can't escape what our destiny created for us."

"If you all stop me or stand in the way of me leaving, then I'll kill you all," warned Ausra calmly. He looked over to Sukro. "I'll kill you and Torshen if you both try to stop me." He then looked to Daysa. "If we don't find that bird of yours, then I'll kill you too."

Ausra put fear in everyone. His strength was incomparable to them. Everyone in the dragons was strong, but Ausra was different. They trained together as kids. He was trained the hardest while the others ate and rested. He was on the training ground mastering his flames with his father. If he was not mastering his flame, then he was mastering the sword with Vesak.

Nagen's eyes become more insane, his mind racing with violence. He didn't like it when his leadership was challenged. He expected that all the dragons should give him his respect. "If you plan to leave, then I'll be happy to kill you myself." He looked back to Daysa. "And you, if that bird of yours is not found, I'll gladly kill you with Ausra."

Fear stung the nerves in Daysa's body. The hair on her body stood. She was afraid for her life. Two of the dragons wanted to kill her. Her father always told her to stay strong, especially when nothing was going her way. Now she was stuck in a situation where her life was on the line.

"We need some time away from each other," suggested Leonaris, breaking the tension in the room.

"What do you suggest, Leonaris?" asked Sukro.

"This forest is huge. Maybe we should explore it a little bit," thought Leonaris out loud.

Ausra stood up and walked toward the door without saying a word. When he walked by Nagen, he didn't glance over. But Nagen had a sinister smile, eyeing him with mad eyes.

Nagen's hunger for violence and control ran in his body. He was in his mad self, the Freak.

Standing at the doorway was Torshen, holding four rabbits from his hunt. He had just arrived and had no clue that there was tension in the room. When Ausra walked by him, he dropped the rabbits and followed.

"I'm going with Ausra and Torshen," said Sukro. "We'll meet each here when everyone's mind is clear." He followed Ausra and Torshen.

Daysa stood up and followed. She didn't want to be alone in the temple. She was afraid of Nagen and didn't want to be around him, choosing to go with Sukro, Ausra, and Torshen. Even though the other two didn't like her, Sukro was kind to her.

"Wild Beast, should we explore together?" Nisu asked Kaiso.

Kaiso stood up and walked toward the door without saying a word. He gave Nagen an angry glance as he walked by.

Nisu followed him out the door. He too gave Nagen a look also as he walked by.

Leonaris and Nagen were the only two in the temple.

Nagen was slowly going back to his normal self. Deep down, he was hurt that they all hated him. He wanted to get along with them, but the voice in his head told him that they were his enemy.

"Why are you still here?" Nagen asked Leonaris.

"I don't want you to do anything stupid," replied Leonaris with a straight look. He sat back down and read his book.

*   *   *

Nisu followed Kaiso with his hands on his head and whistling a tune he had created.

Kaiso was irked that Nisu decided to follow him. He had no direction on where he was going, thinking that if he kept walking, something interesting would appear.

Nisu, on the other hand, didn't want to go with Ausra or Nagen. He hated Nagen and was afraid of Ausra. But Kaiso, on the other hand, was not intimated by him, finding him amusing to be around.

"Do you think we'll ever split?" asked Nisu.

"No, Ausra is just speaking nonsense," replied Kaiso. "Lord Aerin would never let the dragons disband."

"If we do go our separate ways, what will you do?"

Kaiso took a while to answer. He didn't want the dragons to split. The idea never crossed his mind. His whole life was loyalty to the Kimsu clan. Knowing nothing else about himself and his dream. Without the dragons, he'd be lost. "Finding my home," he replied. His reply felt like it came out by itself.

"Home? Where is your home?" asked Nisu.

"Stop asking questions," said an annoyed Kaiso.

"Just want to make conversation." Nisu shrugged. "I wonder what I'll do with my freedom," he said to himself, thinking about the many options he could choose from. "I'd probably find my parents or maybe serve another clan."

"You willing to betray Lord Aerin?" questioned Kaiso.

"Well, if the dragons are no longer going to be around, why should I stay?"

"Loyalty. Do you have any loyalty?"

Nisu chuckled. "I slept with many women. And tell many lies. I think loyalty is out of the question, Wild Beast."

"That's why I don't like you," mumbled Kaiso.

The two men continued walking, not saying a single word to each other. But both were thinking the same. What would they do with their life if the dragons split? They both needed the dragons since it was all they knew.

As they continued to walk, they could feel a warm moisture in the air. The warm air was familiar to Nisu. During his downtime, he'd either be chasing after women or spending time at the hot springs. He knew the warm, moist air meant they were close to one. Nothing was better than relaxing the body in hot steaming water.

"We're close to a hot spring, Wild Beast!" said Nisu with excitement.

"I don't care," grunted Kaiso.

"What, you don't like hot springs?" exclaimed a surprised Nisu.

"I don't like wasting my time," replied Kaiso.

Nisu placed his arm around Kaiso's shoulders. "You know why women don't like you?" he asked. "Because you're always angry . . . and you're ugly."

"I will rather be ugly than be a weak rat," Kaiso insulted back.

Nisu followed the warm steam. "Well, I'm going for the hot springs. Join me if you so choose to."

Kaiso followed because he had nowhere else to go. But at the same time, he wanted to know how it feels to sit in a hot spring. He created a barrier that protected him. He didn't want to understand the world around him, believing that it will hinder his ability to fight. There was a dark memory that still haunted him, the day he left his homeland, ripped away from his mother as his father watched helplessly. The people that took him away from his parents told them they were selling their only son to the Kimsu clan. He developed pure hatred toward his father for not showing a hint of a fight for him.

When they finally arrived to the hot springs, they found that there were ten springs of different sizes. Steam filled the air. Nisu couldn't contain his excitement, rushing his way to the biggest spring. He quickly stripped his clothes off and jumped into the spring.

Kaiso was disgusted seeing Nisu's full naked body jumping into the spring and confused about the spring. But he did feel relief by the warm stream it created. He felt his body relaxing, a feeling he hadn't felt in years.

"Wild Beast, jump in. Once your body is in, your body will never be the same again. Maybe it'll make you handsome," Nisu joked.

"Shut your mouth or I'll drown you where you sit," threatened Kaiso.

"Relax, Wild Beast. This is a place of relaxation. Release that anger you have an join me," recommended Nisu.

Kaiso took a while. He didn't want to show Nisu that he was interested in sitting in the warm steaming water. His pride didn't want to give Nisu the satisfaction of being correct. But the relaxation in his body was bothering him. In fact, he didn't remember the last time where he just sat and relaxed, always moving, never having the time to sit. Out of all the dragons, it was him and Leonaris that Nagen relied on the most.

He proceeded to strip his naked body, showing hundreds of scars that riddled his body, then slowly sat in the hot spring, the warm water healing the thousands of wounds on his body. The reason he was called the Wild Beast was because of his animal-like fighting, willing to sacrifice his body to defeat his opponent. Vesak had urged him to change his style of fighting, but he was too ignorant to listen, believing that every wound he received from battle makes him stronger.

"You see, Wild beast, it's relaxing," said Nisu.

"Shut your mouth," warned Kaiso. But he couldn't deny that Nisu was right.

"Next we need to fix your attitude. No woman likes a man that's a grouch," teased Nisu.

"Keep talking and I'll drown you," warned Kaiso again.

"It's only us two here. I'll look stupid talking to myself."

"I don't care."

"Can I ask you a question?" asked Nisu.

"I said shut your mouth!" said the annoyed Kaiso.

Nisu ignored Kaiso. "Do you trust Nagen?"

Kaiso hesitated to answer Nisu. He thought the same as Nisu. As of late, he had been losing faith in Nagen, sensing the slow decline into madness in him. Yet he didn't say anything to Nagen. Was he afraid or perhaps he wanted Nagen to suffer?

"He's our leader," answered Kaiso. "Our life is in his hands."

"Do you not notice the Freak coming out more often?"

"Of course!" Kaiso said sharply. "I know everything. He's slowly falling apart."

"What is it that he wants?" wondered Nisu.

"What everybody wants in this world—power and fame," said Kaiso.

Suddenly, the two dragons stopped talking as the sound of soft humming echoed the forest. They looked around, but the mist was blocking their vision. They did not know if the sound was far or close to them. Both men were on high alert, waiting for an attack behind the mist.

Kaiso stood from the water to try to get a better look at his surroundings.

Then coming out of the mist was four demon foxes. They had the face of a fox but the body of a human, their tails puffed liked a fox. Two foxes stood in front side by side while two stood behind also side by side. They stood as if they were protecting someone at the center of them.

"Human, you dare to stand naked in front of the princess!" warned one of the foxes from the front.

Kaiso forgot that he was naked and sat back down into the spring. "Who are you guys?" he asked the demon foxes.

"We are Princess Nen's guards."

"Princess?" Nisu tried to look behind the two foxes. From a tiny crack, he could see a girl standing at the center. "Who's the girl?" he asked the demon foxes.

"Leave, humans, or we'll take your life," warned one of the foxes in front.

"Don't threaten us," challenged Nisu. He tried to look behind the two foxes again. "Hey, pretty woman. Do you want to leave those strange foxes and sit in the spring with Nisu, the Mighty Bliss?" invited Nisu confidently.

"How dare you speak to our princess that way!" angered one of the foxes.

"This must be my lucky day," smiled Nisue

"Are all humans brash and ill-minded?" asked the princess behind the two foxes in an innocent voice.

"She can speak. There's room for you in here. Come sit with us," offered Nisu then looking over to Kaiso with an annoying smile.

Kaiso was irritated with the situation. He stood from the spring and left, walking toward his belongings. He didn't like talking and noticed that the demon foxes didn't have the skill and urgency to fight.

"You with the scar," called the princess, finally stepping out of her protection. She did not look like a fox, but more of a human. She wore a red-and-white silk dress. The only fox feature she had was the orange-and-black-striped tail behind her.

Nisu was astonished by her charming and innocent eyes. He was lost in her attractiveness and didn't expect her to look like a human. Her dark hair was long and braided.

"I-I didn't expect you to look so human," exclaimed a shocked Nisu.

Princess Nen ignored Nisu and focused her attention on Kaiso's back. "Your scars . . . why do have so many scars?" she questioned with interest.

Kaiso grunted as he put his clothes back on. "It's none of your business, fox." He looked over to the demon foxes and Princess Nen. "Don't waste my time with threats," he warned.

"Show respect to the princess, human," demanded one of the foxes.

Kaiso picked his sword up and stared at it. "You know . . . I have been itching for a fight." He turned and pointed his sword at one of the demon foxes. "Don't try to scare me with threats, you demons!" he warned.

Nisu realized that Kaiso was serious. He looked at the demon foxes and saw fear in their eyes then to the princess who wasn't fazed by Kaiso. "Umm, the wild beast doesn't know what he's talking about." He climbed out of the spring and made his way to his clothes. "Stupid, that's a princess," he whispered to Kaiso while putting on his clothes.

"I can care less," said Kaiso. "They threaten to kill us."

"Still, she's a princess." He peeked back at the princess. "A pretty one too. So calm yourself before something goes wrong."

"You dare kill the princess of this forest?" asked Princess Nen calmly.

"I'll kill anyone that threatens me," replied Kaiso.

"Idiot," whispered Nisu, shaking his head, hoping for no violence.

"Very well then," said Princess Nen.

"Very well?" Nisu said to himself with confusion.

"Guards, stand down. This human wants to kill me," ordered Princess Nen.

The four demon fox guards backed down while Princess Nen stood calmly, waiting for Kaiso to make his move. She stared into Kaiso's intense eyes. "Humans know nothing of this forest," she started. "Kill me and see the demons of this forest unit."

"Let them all come. My sword starves for demon blood," challenged Kaiso.

Nisu stood between the princess and Kaiso with his arms up. "My friend here doesn't know what he's talking about." He bowed to the princess. "I apologize for our misunderstanding."

"Stay out of this, pervert," insulted Princess Nen calmly.

"Pervert?" Nisu said to himself with embarrassment.

Kaiso sheathed his sword. "We're going now, Nisu," he said.

"Are all humans cowards?" mocked Princess Nen calmly.

"I'm not stupid. I know there's more foxes hiding behind the trees."

"So you're a smart human?" questioned Princess Nen.

"I'm not a smart human, but I know of the four protectors of this forest. The protector of the western part of the forest is the western spirit dragon, Sorun. The protector of the northern part is the tenth son of Chenva, Krean. The protector of the southern part is the monkey demon king, Woku. And protector of the east is the demon fox queen, Aesi."

"So you know."

"If I kill you, then war will break loose in the forest. Am I correct?"

"It will be thousands of years' war," said Princess Nen. "If you know so much, then why did you threaten to kill me?"

"I challenged your guards. But I see they're weak."

Princess Nen looked at each of her guards. She agreed with Kaiso that they were weak. Her guards did not know how to fight. "I have an offer for you. Train my guards how to fight."

"No," Kaiso quickly rejected.

Nisu quickly shot a shocking look at Kaiso. "What are you doing?" he whispered. "We need a place to stay. I don't want to go back to the temple."

"You can go with them," said Kaiso. "I'm leaving."

Nisu looked back to Princess Nen. "I want to apologize for my idiot friend."

"Silence, pervert," insulted Princess Nen calmly.

"Pervert again," Nisu mumbled to himself in a saddened tone.

"What is that you want?" asked Princess Nen. "Do you want gold? Food?" She looked at the scars on Kaiso's body. "Do you want me?"

"You're willing to sell yourself for your weakling guards?" questioned Kaiso.

"I'll do whatever it takes to protect the eastern part of the forest."

Kaiso pondered for a while, seeing that he only had to teach the guards the basics of fighting. Also with Nisu by his side, the training wouldn't take long. Nisu was a natural teacher and didn't mind helping and teaching. "Fine. You don't have to sell yourself to me. All I want in return is a place to sleep and eat."

"That can be arranged," agreed Princess Nen.

"I'll only teach till the fortnight. Nothing more."

Princess Nen nodded her head. The demon foxes all turned around. "It's time for me to enjoy the spring," she said, realizing that both Kaiso and Nisu didn't understand that she wanted them to turn around. "Look away so I can undress."

Both Kaiso and Nisu turned around.

Nisu was disappointed that he couldn't see the princess naked.

Kaiso, on the other hand, didn't care. All he cared about was that he had a place to stay for the time being. Like Nisu, he didn't want to return to the temple but didn't want to show it.

As Kaiso stood and waited, he felt a warm and gentle hand grazing the wounds on his back. He wanted to turn around, but his body prevented him from doing so. Princess Nen was touching his wound. She stood naked behind him, feeling the wound on his body, saddened at the damaged and hurt he had been through.

"Why do you suffer?" she whispered to Kaiso.

Kaiso didn't respond. Though he was a man that showed a lot of emotion and anger, the scars on his body sealed the pain he had been through. When his enemy cut him, the pain left his body. As the wound sealed, it covered another pain he had dealt with. But the suffering he faced was the same. His past he tried to forget, but it kept on returning, the past of being ripped away by his parents and sailed away to another world. He listened as Princess Nen dipped into the spring, wishing for her gentle warm hand to touch his wounds again.

After Princess Nen was finished with the spring, she and her guards led Kaiso and Nisu to her mother. They walked in silence; she was still guarded tightly.

Kaiso could see the other demon foxes following them behind the trees. He counted at least twenty of them.

Nisu, on the other hand, was curious as to how Princess Nen looked so human. He expected her to resemble more of a fox.

"Princess, I didn't expect you to look so human," said a surprised Nisu.

"Silence, pervert," insulted Princess Nen calmly.

Nisu turned to Kaiso. "Do I look like a pervert?" he curiously asked Kaiso.

"She's telling the truth," replied Kaiso coldly.

Nisu put his head down in shame.

Kaiso, on the other hand, was skeptic about the situation. Princess Nen was protected tightly. Even though the demon foxes didn't look like fighters, he could still sense their fox mentality. They were sneaky and would strike when the moment presented itself. He was on high alert waiting for the foxes to make their move.

"What is your name, the one with the scars?" Princess Nen asked Kaiso.

"Kaiso," answered Kaiso.

"My name is Nisu—"

"Silence, pervert," Princess Nen cut off Nisu. She noticed that Kaiso was anxious about the other foxes hiding behind the trees. "You don't have to worry for them, Kaiso. My mother is only worried for my safety."

"I still don't trust a demon. Especially a fox demon," said Kaiso.

"Have you killed a fox demon before?" asked Princess Nen.

"I wish," answered Kaiso.

"Tell me, did you receive those scars killing demons?" wondered Princess Nen.

"Don't worry about my scar. It's none of your concern."

They finally stopped at an entrance of a cave. Kaiso and Nisu looked behind to see the other guards. They resembled a fox with hands and feet of humans. Nisu was starting to doubt the offer from Princess Nen. Kaiso had his hand on the handle of his sword. Ready to unsheathed when the guards' attack.

"Are you afraid?" asked Princess Nen calmly.

"Of course," answered Nisu truthfully.

"I didn't ask you, pervert," denied Princess Nen. "Kaiso, are you afraid?"

Kaiso released his hand from the handle of his sword. "No."

"Don't worry, we are accepting toward strangers," calmed Princess Nen then entered the cave.

The cave was dark, with torches lighting the pathway. The path was wide. The stone was moist and cool. Kaiso and Nisu could hear a waterfall, wondering if the cave would lead them to a new world. The walk took them twenty minutes. When they finally arrived at the center of the cave, both men were astounded by the sight. It was exactly what they thought.

A whole new world. The cave was like a city that homed all the foxes. They looked up and could see an opening where there was sunshine. There was a river with a waterfall. The ground had dirt and on the streets of the city were stone walkways. Houses were made of stone, some wooden. There were trees. Strangely, it was a cave, but it reassembled a normal city. But the city barely had any guards patrolling the streets.

"Welcome to Foxsu." Princess Nen waved her hand to them. Breaking them from their astonishment.

"I didn't expect to see an entire city," said a shocked Nisu.

"Foxsu is a city of beauty," explained Princess Nen. "My mother built this city from the ground up. Before, all the foxes fought each other. It was only grass and trees. Now they coexist to make our city a peaceful one."

Nisu looked up at the bright blue sky. "I haven't seen the sky in months." He was amazed while taking in the sun.

"Follow me, my mother is at the palace," directed Princess Nen.

The guards all went their separate ways. Only two stayed to escort Princess Nen to her palace. While walking the stone streets, Kaiso and Nisu noticed there was a tavern and some shops. There was a city center.

At the center of the city sat the statue of a man wearing armor and holding a sword in the air directly toward the sun. Like Princess Nen, he had a tail.

They finally arrived at a staircase that led them to a palace. There were about four hundred steps. Princess Nen turned to Nisu and Kaiso. "I will inform my mother of your arrival." All of a sudden, she morphed into an actual fox. The clothes she wore fell to the ground, and she sprinted up the stairs.

One of the guards picked her clothes up and proceeded to climb the stairs.

Nisu was so shocked that he couldn't find words to blurt out of his mouth.

Kaiso followed the two guards. He knew that all the demons had the ability to shapeshift into their second form.

After hours of climbing, they finally arrived at the entrance of the palace. Both Nisu and Kaiso were not exhausted by the number of stairs they had climbed. But both were hungry. During the climb, their stomachs kept on growling. It was loud enough for the two guards they were following to hear. But they all climbed in silence.

Standing at the main door of the palace was Princess Nen, now wearing a blue silk dress. Her hair was nicely done.

Nisu was still amazed by her beauty.

Kaiso ignored the fact and continued to follow the guards. Nisu was awed at the scenery around him. The palace was surrounded by forest. The leaves on the trees were bright green. To the side of the palace was a river with two waterfalls, one coming from the giant opening of the cave, creating another river, and the other waterfall going down to the entire city.

When they finally arrived, Princess Nen was waiting for them at the entrance of the palace. The two guards greeted her with a bow. Both Kaiso and Nisu were confused if they should bow to her also. The two guards took their swords and walked away with them.

"My mother is waiting inside," said Princess Nen. "Please bow to her when you present yourself." She opened the great door that opened to the great hall. She led Kaiso and Nisu into the hall.

The hall was gigantic. The ceiling was high and had a huge opening where the sun could shine through. From the pillars to the wall, it was made out of white stones. There were ten steps that led to the throne that was also made out of white stone. Sitting on the high chair with two guards standing at the bottom of the steps on each side was a woman wearing a red silk dress and a golden crown with five points, and in each point was embedded purple sapphire stone. Like Princess Nen, she had a tail, but a black one. She resembled all the human features, but unlike Princess Nen, who had calming eyes, her eyes were more striking, her hair braided on both sides and tied back. She was the fox queen, Queen Aesi.

Kaiso and Nisu followed Princess Nen to the center of the hall. She bowed to her mother and stepped aside.

Both Kaiso and Nisu bowed and stayed at the center, waiting for the queen to say something to them.

"So you're the one my daughter awed about," started Queen Aesi to Kaiso, ignoring Nisu's existence.

Princess Nen blushed when her mother exposed her. She focused attention on the ground to hide her embarrassment.

Nisu noticed that she was hiding her embarrassment. And right away, his romantic instinct knew the situation.

"We were promised food and shelter in exchange. We'll train your guards how to fight," said Kaiso.

"My guards do not need to know how to fight. For hundreds of years, we avoided fighting. But if you insist on training them, then I'll take the offer," said Queen Aesi.

"I didn't offer. It was a promise your daughter made to me," corrected Kaiso.

"Ah yes, my daughter doesn't have the power to make offers. I see that she tricked you." She shot a strict look at Princess Nen. "It's rare that we see humans in our city. My daughter lied to the both of you for her own selfishness."

"Then I'm taking that you don't want our help," said Kaiso.

Nisu put his hand up and bowed to the queen. He turned to Kaiso. "Wild Beast, are you not understanding the situation?" he whispered. "We're not needed here. The princess is only interested in you."

"Why?" asked a confused Kaiso.

"For some odd reason, she finds you attractive."

"What are you two whispering about?" asked the annoyed Queen Aesi.

"Let me do the talking, Wild Beast," whispered Nisu. He turned to the queen and bowed. "Our apologies." He took in a deep breath. "My beautiful queen."

"I am not your queen, human," shot Queen Aesi.

"Ah yes, you're not. But I stand in your presence so that makes you my queen. But please may I speak?"

Queen Aesi took a while to think. "Say what you have to say, then leave my city."

"Fair enough, but what I have to say may interest you, my beautiful queen. You see, the Wild Beast and I are members of a deadly group. We master in the area of assassination. Maybe you know them or not, but we serve the Kimsu clan."

Queen Aesi leaned from her throne, interested to hear Nisu speak. "Are telling me that you're that famous warrior of that clan?"

"So you know us. Wow, we are famous," said the surprised Nisu.

"Of course, why wouldn't I know the boy that killed all my sons?"

Both Nisu and Kaiso were shocked, frozen to their core. They looked at each other and wondered if any of them had killed a fox before. Both were confused; none of them had ever confronted a demon fox before. They weren't even sure that the other dragons encountered a demon fox themselves.

"Don't look confused, boys. I had four sons," revealed Queen Aesi. "My sons left the cave, with their tails hidden. And only one came back but died two nights later. He said a boy with eyes of a demon and angel attacked them." She paused. "They wanted to see outside of the forest. But was confronted by a monster with black flames. He said the boy was with a man with dark sinister eyes." She balled her hands in a fist, biting the bottom of her lip. "That boy took my sons away from me. Looking at the two of you, I don't see that demon and angel eyes. But I will avenge my sons' death with yours."

"Mother!" pleaded Princess Nen. "They can help us." She was hoping her mother wouldn't hurt Kaiso.

"Silence, Nen. Have you forgotten your brothers? These two humans serve the Kimsu clan."

Suddenly, one of the guards blew a whistle, and entering the great hall were about twenty guards, all holding spears pointed directly at Nisu and Kaiso. They were defenseless without their swords with them.

"Before I order the death of the both of you," said Queen Aesi, "who's the boy that killed my sons?"

Nisu stood straight. "Let us make a deal," suggested Nisu. "We know the boy that killed your sons. As matter of fact, he's in this forest somewhere."

Kaiso was shocked that Nisu was willing to sacrifice Ausra. Kaiso was the type to never give his comrades. He would rather die than give up his comrade. He looked to Nisu and saw that Nisu was serious to give up Ausra. "What are you doing?" he whispered to Nisu.

Nisu ignored Kaiso. He was thinking about his own survival, but at the same time, he had already made a plan in his head. He had to protect them or they'll die on the spot. Even though they were stronger than the guards, cutting through hundreds of them wouldn't be a bright idea.

"The boy is in the forest?" questioned Queen Aesi curiously.

"Yes, if you spare our lives, I'll tell you who he is," said Nisu.

Queen Aesi signaled to the guards to put their spears down. "Fine, tell me who this boy is."

"The boy you're looking for is Ausra Kimsu, the Silent Demon. He's someone that you wish to never cross paths with. Like you say yourself, a monster. But if you allow us to train your guards, we'll teach them how to defeat him."

"Why should I believe you? Are you guys not comrades?" questioned Queen Aesi.

"He's a comrade, but a rat that sleeps with his friend's wife. I sat long enough while my wife and him sleep around," lied Nisu. "We both want the same thing, my queen. And it is his death. I know the secret in defeating that rat monster."

Queen Aesi took a while to think. "Fine. Teach my guards how to defeat him. But you'll be sleeping at the barrack. And don't you dare step foot in my palace," she warned.

Kaiso and Nisu were led out of the palace by the guards. Their swords were not returned to them. Watching from behind was Princess Nen, upset that her mother hated Kaiso, but still showing the calm stillness over her face.

Both Kaiso and Nisu followed a guard down the four hundred steps without talking to each other. Nisu was satisfied that he got to live and had not spilled blood.

Kaiso was angry at Nisu for wanting to help the enemy.

When they arrived at the bottom of the steps, the atmosphere felt strange. It felt like thousands of hateful eyes were burning them to the ground. The guard led the both of them through the city and to the barrack. The barrack had a huge training ground where no fox was training. There were servants but little guards. The guard led them to their room that was just an empty room with just a single window.

"When it is time to train, we'll let you out," said the guard. "The queen orders that you two spend your days in the room. You'll be fed twice a day, humans." The guard shut the door and locked it from the outside.

Kaiso couldn't keep his eyes off Nisu. He wanted to wrap his hand around Nisu's neck and strangle him.

Nisu paid no attention to Kaiso and proceeded to lie on the ground, laying his head on his hand and with one leg across over the other.

"I know that you're angry, but I have no choice," said Nisu. "We'll die if I didn't make a deal with her."

"I will never betray my comrade to the enemy!" angered Kaiso.

"Relax, Wild Beast," said Nisu. "You're as stupid as they can be. I'll never let my comrades die either."

"Then why did you offer to train them to kill Ausra?" questioned Kaiso.

"It's hard to explain because you're an idiot. But if I'm correct, then love will make people do stupid things." He smiled.

"What are you talking about!' asked a confused Kaiso who sat on the ground with his back leaning against the wall.

Both men stayed silent in the room, Kaiso trying to figure out Nisu's plan.

Nisu, on the other hand, wanted to understand the meaning of comrade. He turned to the side away from Kaiso and showed a sad look. The dragons were not comrades.

* * *

Ausra daydreamed about a world of his own creation. At a young age, he was taught to accept his fate. Unlike other children, rich or poor, Ausra had no choice. From the day he was born, his future had already been decided.

Following him through the mysterious forest was Daysa and Sukro. Torshen walked beside him. Their time in the forest allowed them to have time to reflect on their life. Each of them all dealing with their own dilemma. Including the other dragons. They all suffered from their own conflict. Torshen wanted to forget his memories. Sukro wanted to find his father and avenge his mother.

"Where do you think we're going?" Daysa asked Sukro.

"I don't know," answered Sukro. "I guess wherever this forest leads us."

"Do you think he knows where he's going?" asked Daysa again.

"I wish I know," replied Sukro. "I never know what's he thinking. It's like playing a guessing game with him."

"How about Torshen?"

"He only follows Ausra," answered Sukro.

"So those two are inseparable," Daysa said to herself.

"Do you truly believe that the golden phoenix is alive?" asked Sukro.

"Yes. My father's research is never wrong," proclaimed Daysa. "Even if he thinks he's wrong, he's right."

"You must be close to your father."

"Of course, after my mother died, it was only him, myself, and my older brother. He too suffers the same fate as my mother. My father was everything to me. He taught me everything I need to know about life. About the creatures of Telamis." Daysa paused for a second to reflect on her father. The memories of him swelled her heart. She wanted to forget the night he took his last breath, smiling at her and telling her to chase her dreams. She took in a deep breath to prevent herself from crying. "I saw countless clan heads coming to our home begging for my father's service. I never knew how talented of a magic user he was."

Sukro noticed that Daysa was getting upset. He didn't want her to cry. "If it makes you better, I'll answer one question."

Daysa became ecstatic, wiping the tears from her eyes. Finally, she could get a glimpse of the dragons, racing through her mind, trying to find the right question to ask Sukro. "Why are you guys called the Seven Demon Dragons?" she asked.

"Ah, is that what you want to know?" questioned Sukro, turning to Daysa as she nodded. "Well, it's really not that interesting. We didn't name it ourselves. It was my grandpa that gave us the name. There was supposed to be eight of us. Including my older cousin, Iszra. But he opted out and decided to join Jen-Song and Kilyu. We're called the dragons because we're the dragons that carries the demon to victory," he answered.

"Interesting," Daysa said to herself.

Suddenly, the group stopped walking. From a distance, they could hear that they were close to a river. At the same time, they could hear the soft melody of a flute being played.

Ausra continued to walk toward the sound with Torshen by his side. Sukro followed without saying a word to Daysa.

Daysa was skeptic to follow the sound of the flute.

"Should we not follow the sound of the flute?" Daysa asked Sukro.

"He's curious and maybe hungry," said Sukro.

"Is he not afraid?"

"I thought you're a researcher. Shouldn't you be fearless and curious?"

"Of course I am, but I'm not stupid," Daysa said, defending herself.

As they followed the sound of the flute and the sound of the river, they found themselves at a clear water river, where fishes could be seen swimming downstream. The sound of the flute was loud and gentle. Looking ahead on the riverbank was a wooden shack. Hanging from the ledge of the shack was dried fish. Sitting on the porch facing them was a man, his skin red like blood with the bottom fangs long up to his cheekbones. Around his neck was a bead necklace, his eyes shut as he played the flute, not noticing the curious eyes staring at him from afar.

"That's a demon," said a shocked Daysa. "It's a complete demon." It was her first time seeing a full demon. Not even her father had ever seen one.

"Are you afraid?" asked Ausra as he walked toward the demon.

"What are you doing?" asked a confused Daysa.

"I'm hungry," answered Ausra.

The others followed. Daysa lingered behind. She didn't want to bother the demon, knowing what they're capable of doing. Reading her father's research, she learned there were four types of demons. There were animal demons, half-blood humans, moon demons, and full demon. Ausra, along with other siblings, except for Sukro and Isa, was born on a full moon, meaning their blood was a pureblood demon, they're the moon demon. Full demons were demons that were a direct bloodline to Chenva. There were fifty known direct children of his.

As they approached the demon, the demon stopped playing his flute, opening his eyes and showing his pure black eyes. He had a mustache that curled up at each end. He didn't look too happy to see Ausra and the other, especially when they distracted him while he played his flute.

"You have any food?" asked Ausra directly.

"Ausra, you have to ask kindly," corrected Sukro.

"Is that how you talk to your elder?" asked the demon. His voice was deep and haunting.

"I'm sorry for my cousin, he's just hungry," explained Sukro, praying that the demon won't attack them.

"Aren't we all hungry?" said the demon. "Do you guys know who I am?"

"An ugly creature," answered Ausra bluntly.

Daysa was afraid and shocked that Ausra had little fear toward the demon. At the same time, she was embarrassed to be in the same presence as him. She wondered where he got his manners from. If her father caught her speaking to an elder like Ausra, he would for sure scold her and slap her on the back of the head.

The demon let out a loud laugh that echoed the forest, scaring the birds as they fled away from the tree branch they stood on. Some of the glowing leaves fell from the tree because of the vibration from the laugh. Once it fell from the tree, it stopped glowing.

The laugh sounded evil, but yet the demon seemed cheerful. "Been years since I saw a human. From the dark eyes on the left, I'm guessing you're from the Kimsu clan," he asked Ausra.

Ausra stayed silent; all he wanted was food.

The other, on the other hand, was surprised that the demon didn't take Ausra's comments as insulting. Instead, he looked to enjoy Ausra's blatant words.

"It's nice to see my kin. Do you know who I am?" asked the demon again.

Ausra sighed in annoyance. "You're Srey-Lau. The third child of Chenva."

"Ah, my kin know me. And I know you—Ausra Kimsu, the Silent Demon. I was foretold by Andrena that you will come and visit me." Srey-Lau laughed. He looked behind Ausra. "Are these your friends?"

"I'm actually a member of the Kimsu clan," said Sukro.

Srey-Lau measured Sukro. "You're not my kin. Your blood is not pure." He then focused back on Ausra. "Sit, my kin, let's talk."

"I don't want to," rejected Ausra.

"Ausra, you must show your manners," urged Sukro.

Srey-Lau let a loud laugh again. "She told me you'll be naïve," said Srey-Lau. "I'll feed you after we talk. In fact, I'll let you rest for however long in my shack."

After convincing Ausra. Srey-Lau managed to get Ausra to stay with the help of Sukro.

They all sat on the porch facing Srey-Lau. He made them rice and with the dried fish he had hanging from the ledge. He watched them eat like they were his own children, digging in with their hands. "What brings you into this cursed forest?" he asked.

"We're helping her find a golden phoenix," answered Sukro, pointing to Daysa.

"Ah, the golden phoenix. What a pretty girl like you want with a wretched bird like that?" Srey-Lau asked Daysa.

"I want to complete my father's research," answered Daysa.

"Ah, a daughter completing her father's dream," Srey-Lau said to himself. "I can make a song about it."

"S-so you like music?" asked Daysa nervously.

"Of course! Music is what brings life together." He turned to Ausra. "Am I right, my kin?"

"Sure," replied Ausra with a mouth full of rice.

Srey-Lau laughed again. "Ausra, you are a strange one. Let me guess, you can control the blue flame?"

"Yeah."

"Ah, you're like what she said," said an amazed Srey-Lau. "Tell me, how did you know who I am?"

Ausra swallowed his rice and looked straight into the eyes of Srey-Lau. "Because all demons know each other."

"Who are you lying to, my kin?"

"You're the demon that kidnapped the princess. The master of five flames," said Ausra.

"Ah, so you're smart. How do you know?" wondered Srey-Lau.

"Grandpa told me," replied Ausra. "Out of Chenva children, there are five with red skin. Only one hides in the Forest of Despair."

The others were speechless. All they could do was listen to Ausra and Srey-Lau converse with each other. They didn't know how Ausra could talk naturally to a demon. But then again, it was Ausra. Everything he did, from his behavior and his thoughts, was surprising. Especially for Daysa. She couldn't believe how much he knew.

Srey-Lau became serious as he watched Ausra continue to eat. "Tell me, kin. Do you believe in peace?"

"No," answered Ausra with rice in his mouth.

"I want to tell you something," said Srey-Lau. "It was fate that brought us here. Andrena had requested me to speak to you. The gods of this world watch our every move. For some reason, they're fascinated by you, my kin. I'm here to guide you. Do you understand?"

Ausra swallowed his food. "If the gods are watching over me, then why did they give me the life of a hero?"

"Ah, you still don't understand, my kin. Everything that's given to you is a lesson to learn. The goal in our life from creature to human is to find peace. You have yet to find your peace, boy, but still so young. Only time will be your enemy." Srey-Lau paused, realizing that Ausra was barely paying attention, but the other three were listening.

"I found my peace after I committed the ultimate sin in my life. I was once brash and naïve. I only cared for myself and thought of myself as equal to the gods because I was the son of Chenva. One day, walking in the city of Summan in my disguise, I spotted the princess. The youngest daughter. To me, I thought that I could have anything I want. Quickly, I fell in love with her. When the opportunity arose, I kidnapped her and brought her back to my home. In this forest. Love is a strange magic. I was blind to her feelings and fear. For months I kept her captive without knowing that she didn't love me back. Till one day the God of Love, Kami, came into my dreams and placed me in my love shoes." Tears formed in his eyes. "I was a monster—an ugly monster that forced an innocent life to love me. To make everything right, I returned her to her palace and swore to never love again. After that day, I found my peace."

Ausra finished his food and swallowed the last of it, noticing that the other three were emotional by Srey-Lau's story. "You found peace after kidnapping a princess?" mocked Ausra. "Pathetic. I will never find peace. I will never find enjoyment. From the day I was born, I was already a warrior. I kill many fathers, mothers, sons, and daughters. I ruin many families. And you still think I'll change one day?"

"Everybody changes, my kin," advised Srey-Lau.

"You're wrong. I will never change. I am what I am." Ausra stood up and tossed a piece of lemon hard candy in his mouth. "It's weak of you to say you found peace because some princess didn't love you back."

"You're not understanding, my kin."

"What is there for me to understand?"

Srey-Lau took a deep breath. "Peace . . . find your peace, my kin."

Ausra turned back to Srey-Lau. "I'll find my peace when I'm dead."

Srey-Lau sighed in disappointment. "Do you want to know about the five flames of life?"

"No."

"Ausra, show him some respect," urged Daysa. "He's trying to help you."

"I don't care."

"Ausra, listen to him!" demanded Sukro strictly.

Ausra knew that when Sukro yelled at him, it meant that he was serious. It was rare to see Sukro angry. So he sat back down with his arms crossed, looking Srey-Lau dead in the eyes. Torshen placed his hand on his shoulder to let him know he was by his side.

Srey-Lau nodded to Sukro in thanks. "The five flames of life," he began. "The first flames, the normal orange, is the flames of life." He opened his palm to show the flame dancing on his palm. "The flame that the common use to survive. Then there are the green flames." A green flame appeared, dancing on the palm. "The flame of fate, the path that's taken." Then blue flame appeared on the palm. "The blue flame, the flame of love. Everyone will find someone they love." The blue flame disappeared and showed a purple flame on his palm. "Then there's the purple flame. The flame of peace and suffering. Find the peace and avoid the suffering." He closed his palm and opened it again to show black flame. "The black flame. The flame of death. The final chapter of life." He closed his palm to see if Ausra understood his theory on life. "Andrena came to me while I was fishing. She tasked me to help a lost child understand the meaning of life."

Ausra stood up to leave; without saying a word, he walked away, heading toward a tree to rest. He was annoyed with Srey-Lau. At the same time, the words Srey-Lau spoke was true. He hasn't found his fate in life yet.

Srey-Lau could sense that Ausra wanted to understand, but was battling with himself inside. He turned to the other three. "My home is your home," he said with a smile.

Torshen stood and bowed then headed toward the river.

Daysa and Sukro stayed behind; they were intrigued by Srey-Lau and his story. He had lived for thousands of years, so his stories to tell could last for years.

"Sukro," said Srey-Lau. "Though you're not my kin, I sense you are hurt."

"We are all hurt," said Sukro.

"Find your peace," finished Srey-Lau.

Sukro struggled with his own demon. From the outside, he seemed to be the peacemaker of the dragons. There was something that kept pulling at him—a boy who grew up with no parents, only knowing that his own father murdered his mother. He could never find his peace until he found him. He wanted to complete the puzzle of his life.

* * *

Instead of staying at the temple and waiting for the others. Nagen and Leonaris decided to adventure into the forest themselves. After hours of silence, Leonaris suggested that the both of them should take a walk. He thought that maybe taking a walk in the forest aimlessly will take Nagen's mind off of his own conflict. He noticed the battle Nagen went through in his own head, which in turn affected the entire group. Leonaris did not say much, but when he needed to step in, he would. Out of all the members, he was second in command, which was given to him by Vesak.

"Do you think I'm a good leader?" asked Nagen.

"You have your own ways of leading," replied Leonaris, trying to avoid the question.

"I know I'm not well-liked," noticed Nagen. "Frankly, I don't care what the others think."

"It's important to know what your comrades are thinking, Nagen."

Nagen thought to himself, wondering if he considered himself a good leader. In his own selfish mind, he had one goal in mind, and that was to be the greatest warrior out of all the seven dragons. He was jealous of the other members' abilities and talents. Even outside of fighting, he hated when they succeeded over him. He wished to have Leonaris's intelligence, Nisu's confidence, Torshen's instinct, Kaiso's strength, Sukro's kindness, and Ausra's pure talent. As kids, when they trained, he was the weakest. The only thing going for him was his eyes of truth. Sometimes he wondered why Vesak chose him to lead the group.

"Leonaris, what will you do if we split?" questioned Nagen.

Leonaris took a while to think. He didn't know what he'd do if the dragons split. Yet there were so many options he could choose from. "The world is vast," he replied. "Maybe I'll travel."

"Do you not want to serve another clan?" asked Nagen.

"I'm tired of fighting." Leonaris shrugged.

"You can't be tired of what you were born to do," said Nagen.

"I wasn't born to be a warrior. There are many paths we can take. This path was chosen for me. If we do go our separate ways, then I'll take the path that I want."

Nagen didn't know what his own path was. His story was similar to the other dragons. Stripped of their childhood to be honed into a weapon, he was just an object in the eyes of lords, someone they could throw into the battlefield and do all the bloodshed. "I don't see my path as anything else," he confessed to Nagen. "All I know is the life I have right now."

Leonaris was observant and felt that Nagen was suffering. "Maybe one day the perfect path will present itself to you." He looked up to glowing leaves that blocked the sky, wishing to see the sky again. "Vesak always told me that life needs time. One day we'll reach our ultimate happiness." He paused. "It kills me to not know if he ever reached his ultimate happiness."

"Ultimate happiness," Nagen mumbled to himself.

As they continued to walk in silence, each thought about their ultimate happiness, having no clue what it was. But they both knew what they wanted. They wanted what was taken from them—their life. Maybe it was time for the dragons to split? All seven of them needed to challenge their greatest enemy.

Suddenly, something caught their eyes. They stopped in front of a tree. The sight they saw would make a normal person jump in terror. But to them, it was another dead body. It was a man hanging from the branch of a tree. The body looked to be hanging for at least two days.

Both Nagen and Leonaris stood staring at the body, both thinking the same thing, that this man had decided to adventure into the forest with the intent to end his own life. Judging by the silk clothes he was wearing, the man must come from a high or minor clan. Even though he was dead, they could still see the pain, doubt, and suffering the man had been through.

They thought the same: what if ultimate happiness can't be found? Then what's the point of living life in this wretched world? Do they want to suffer like the man hanging from the tree? To never find the satisfaction of life and to take one's own life because of self-hatred or failure to live.

"I guess this man never found his ultimate happiness," ended Leonaris.

Chapter Nineteen

Kingdom of Summan

"I'm nothing," said Benavis as he stared at the wall of his private chamber. "I'm weak. I'm a coward." He continued to belittle himself.

It was early morning with stars nearly fading away. Instead of sleeping through the night, Benavis sat on his bed staring at the wall with a blank look, putting himself down, still disturbed by the sight of the thief beheaded before him. Weeks had passed since the disturbing day. As of late, he had been able to hide his madness better, making it seem like he was normal once again.

Sometimes the shadow figure would appear when Benavis was alone, standing by or in front of him and staring down at him. He couldn't bear the sight of the shadow figure. It had no face, no emotions. He wondered what that shadow figure was. Why did it keep saying it was him?

He turned toward the window and realized he had miss sleep once again. There were nights when he slept like a baby and nights where he was up like an owl. All he wanted was simplicity again. Where he could just be a prince and live his life. He lay on his back and stared at the ceiling, picturing a war scene above him. He imagined an army of men and women flying on giant hawks, diving down and scooping an army of men and women riding on horses from their talons and dropping them back to the ground.

"Is that what we see?" asked the shadow figure beside Benavis's bed.

Benavis tried to ignore the shadow. Sometimes it would ask him questions, but he would avoid answering them. He continued to stare at the ceiling, not sure if he was afraid of the shadow figure or slowly accepting its presence though he did find the shadow figure to be an annoyance to him. He hated the fact that it randomly appeared when it wanted to.

"We are silent, I see," said the shadow figure. The shadow floated above Benavis and lay vertical over him. "Look at me! I am you," it urged.

Benavis positioned his body back toward the window, ignoring the shadow figure. The figure was acting like an unwanted dog following its owner wherever he went.

Benavis was pleading with himself, hoping that it would leave him alone and disappear.

The figure floated in front of Benavis and floated horizontally. "Why are you ignoring me? I am you, Benavis."

Benavis sighed in annoyance. "Leave me alone," he said, turning to the other side.

"But I am you." It floated to the other side to face Benavis.

"You're a nuisance," insulted Benavis.

"We're a nuisance," corrected the figure.

Benavis felt like the figure was mocking him, teasing him for being scared and weak. He believed that shadow figure was just another mishap in his demented existence of madness.

"I protected us from dying," reminded the shadow figure. "It is kind if you acknowledge us."

"Stop saying 'us'!" exclaimed the annoyed Benavis, getting off his bed from the other side, walking to his closet to change to his day clothes. "What the hell are you? I never ask for you to protect me," he wondered.

"Silly, like I said, I am you."

"Say that one more time . . ." Benavis took a while to think. He didn't know what he'd do to the shadow figure.

"You'll get rid of us," mocked the shadow figure, who was now floating above Benavis's bed in a circular motion like it was enjoying the time of its life. "I only act in the way of what we think."

Benavis turned around, irked to see that the shadow was enjoying its time. "What are you doing?" he asked annoyingly.

"Enjoying the freedom we have!" replied the shadow figure.

Benavis put on his boots to leave. "You stay in here and leave me alone," he ordered the figure.

The shadow figure floated to the window. "It's still dark out."

"I don't care," said Benavis as he left for the door. "Just stay in here and leave me alone."

The shadow figure floated behind Benavis. "I can't because I am you, fool," mocked the shadow. "Where are we going?"

Benavis grunted. There was no way for him to get rid of the figure. All he could do was accept its presence. "I'm going to wait till breakfast."

"So boring!" cried the shadow figure then it merged into the walls. "See, no one could see."

Benavis turned to the wall where the shadow figure walked beside him, amazed to see his own shadow but knowing that it was not him. The figure waved to him and continued to walk. He heard the figure humming in his ears as they passed the palace guards, wondering if they could hear the humming too. Instead, he saw the mockery in their eyes, hearing them mumbling lies in his name, calling him insane or strange.

He walked by and heard two guards talking, overhearing one of them saying that he was dead, that a horn head had killed him and taken his form.

"Do you wish for them to die?" asked the shadow figure.

Benavis ignored the figure. He didn't want anyone to see him talking to himself. He didn't want to feed into their rumors and beliefs. In some way, he knew that he was unstable.

He tried to act as normal as possible so he wouldn't give the impression he was disturbed. But acting normal had been difficult for him with the shadow figure pestering around him.

"They can die like the man that tried to kill us," reminded the shadow figure.

"Enough!" yelled Benavis.

Standing in front of Benavis as he had just woken from a nap was Yorsenga. He had a dumb look over his face and was confused why Benavis yelled at him. He had cut the corner and seen Benavis and was going to bow to him in respect. Instead, he was greeted by a yell.

"Did I do something wrong, my prince?" asked a confused Yorsenga.

"Nothing. Carry on," lied Benavis, walking by Yorsenga quickly and hiding his embarrassment.

Yorsenga looked back as Benavis cut the corner. "Everyone in this kingdom is strange," he sighed then continued his walk.

Benavis was irritated with the shadow figure. If he could, he would want to strangle the figure. "Why can't you stay quiet?" he muttered.

"What we think I express," answered the shadow figure.

"So what are you supposed to be the opposite of me?" questioned Benavis.

"Correct."

"I demand you to leave me alone," demanded Benavis.

The shadow floated in front of Benavis. "You don't control me. I was locked away in your body since the day you were born, Benavis. I waited for the day to be unleashed. Waited for your great suffering."

"What are you talking about?" asked Benavis, realizing the shadow figure no longer referred itself to him.

The shadow figure floated back into the wall. "If you want to know the truth, then know your clan secret."

"What's my clan secret?"

"Go find out yourself," replied the shadow figure.

Benavis finally arrived at the dining hall. He was alone in the hall and sat on the side, waiting for breakfast to be served, guessing which one of his siblings would come next. It felt eerie sitting alone in the dining hall. But he wasn't alone; for a second, he forgot that the shadow figure was around him. The figure was floating in the wall to the side.

"Do you ever sit still?" asked Benavis with displeasure.

"I'm free," answered the shadow figure.

"Do you have a name?"

"What is my name?" wondered about the shadow figure.

"I'm asking you," said the annoyed Benavis.

The shadow floated to the chair across Benavis. "I have no name."

"That's where my sister sits."

The shadow continued to float around the room. "I want a name, Benavis. Give me a name." The shadow figure floated upside down above Benavis like a spider webbing down from the ceiling, slowly coming face-to-face with him. "Give me a good name."

"If I give you a name, will you leave me alone?" asked Benavis.

The shadow floated again, going into walls and out of it. "I can't leave you alone."

"Fine, then you ought to listen to me and answer all my questions?"

"Depends," answered the shadow figure.

"It does not depend. You must promise me."

"Fine, I agree," promised the figure.

Benavis took a while to figure out a name for the shadow figure, juggling through his mind to find a perfect name for it. "How about Moon?"

"After that thing in the sky when it's black?" asked the shadow figure.

"No, after my dead pet rabbit," said Benavis.

"My name is Moon," said the excited Moon, floating excitedly near the ceiling of the hall. "My name is Moon! My name is Moon!"

"Now answer my question," demanded Benavis. "What is my clan secret?"

Moon stopped floating and headed back into the wall as Giovanis entered the dining hall. Giovanis was surprised to see Benavis at the dining table so early in the morning. In his hand, he held a book. Usually, before he ate his morning meal, he would try to get some reading in, sitting alone at the dining table before he started his long day.

"Benavis! What a surprise," exclaimed a shocked Giovanis.

Benavis stood from his chair and bowed his head. "Brother."

"Ask him," whispered Moon inside Benavis thoughts.

"Sit, there's no need for you to bow," said Giovanis, making his way to sit at the head of the table.

When Benavis saw his brother sit at the spot where his father used to sit, it reminded him of days of simplicity, wishing his father and mother were still alive so they could once again sit around the table and laugh once more.

"Why are you up so early?" asked Giovanis.

"I couldn't sleep," replied Benavis.

"Is something wrong?" worried Giovanis.

"No."

"It's fine to talk to me, Benavis," reminded Giovanis.

"Ask him," whispered Moon. "He knows."

"Um . . . there's something I've been wanting to ask you." Benavis struggled to say, debating if he wanted to ask the question or not.

"What is it?" wondered Giovanis.

"Well, I want to know our clan secret."

"Secret?" asked Giovanis.

"He's pretending," whispered Moon.

"Does our clan have any secrets?" asked Benavis again.

Giovanis looked up to the ceiling with his hand on his chin. "Secret," he said to himself then scratched his head, trying to show Benavis that he didn't know. "I don't think our clan has any secrets that are known to me."

Benavis saw the lie on Giovanis's face. "Right, sorry for asking." He was disappointed.

Giovanis realized that he had upset his brother. "Well, I do know that Grandpa was a big fan of sweets," cheered Giovanis.

"Everybody knows he loved sweet."

"Should we kill him for lying?" whispered Moon.

Finally, Janellis entered the hall. She too was surprised to see Benavis up early and ready for breakfast. She walked to her chair and nodded to Giovanis then sat down and noticed that Benavis was disappointed.

"You must be really hungry," said Janellis calmly to Benavis.

"I like her," whispered Moon.

"I had a long night," answered Benavis.

The three siblings sat quietly as they waited for the morning meal.

Moon was floating above inside the ceiling like a fish swimming in a pond.

Benavis was baffled that his siblings couldn't sense Moon floating above them.

They ate their breakfast in silence. For breakfast, they were served a simple meal of rice porridge and dried salted fish.

Benavis barely touched his food since he wasn't a big fan of dried salted fish.

"Eat," whispered Moon. "I'm hungry."

"I don't care," mumbled Benavis.

"You said something?" questioned Giovanis.

Benavis thought he had spoken low enough so his siblings wouldn't hear him. "Nothing," he replied then shoved the rice porridge into his mouth without chewing, leaving the salted dried fish alone.

"That's it," whispered Moon.

"Benavis, slow down or you'll choke," urged Giovanis.

Janellis noticed that there was something wrong with Benavis. She kept her suspicions to herself but kept a keen eye on him, sensing something dark surrounding him.

"I'm fine," said Benavis with porridge in his mouth.

Giovanis could also see that Benavis was acting strange. But he didn't want to confront him because he was happy they were eating together. But in the back of his mind, he wondered why Benavis wanted to know the clan secret. He made a promise to his father, uncles, and grandpa to keep the clan secret silent from Benavis and Janellis. They must never know about the curse shadows that hide in their body.

"When everything settles, we ought to take a vacation," suggested Giovanis. "Maybe to Clear Island, where Mother and Father used to take us."

"Yeah," Benavis agreed lowly, showing little interest to go on vacation with his siblings.

Giovanis placed his hand on Benavis's shoulders. "You'll love it there, Benavis. The beaches are nice, and the women are beautiful."

Benavis knew it was impossible for Giovanis to follow up on his promise.

Since becoming king, Giovanis's life had been in a constant rainstorm. He was left with so many problems that needed to be fixed in the kingdom. The people were growing weary of his ability to rule, some comparing him to his father.

"Giovanis, can I sit in on a small council meeting?" asked Benavis.

Both Janellis and Giovanis was shocked. Both were caught off guard by Benavis. They didn't think he was interested in the kingdom politics.

"Are you sure?" asked Giovanis.

"I am the prince. I should be more involved with the kingdom."

"All right then, if that's what you want. But be warned these meetings are long," joked Giovanis.

"Boring!" whispered Moon. "I hate boring!"

"I don't mind," said Benavis, standing up to leave. "I'll meet you at the council room."

Giovanis watched as Benavis left the dining hall. Janellis continued to eat calmly, reaching across the table and taking Benavis's dried salted fish then picking and tossing the pieces into her rice porridge.

"I'm worried for him," worried Giovanis.

Janellis finished her rice porridge and stood to leave, ignoring Giovanis. She didn't talk much to her brothers and kept her distance away from them. She loved being alone in a quiet place.

"Janellis," said Giovanis. "I'm worried for you too. I never saw you cry for Mother and Father."

Janellis turned back to Giovanis. "I don't need to mourn if I accepted their deaths," said Janellis.

Giovanis was confused by Janellis. "Do you have any dreams?" he asked.

"I dream when I sleep," replied Janellis bluntly.

Giovanis chuckled. "You and Benavis are able to have dreams unlike me. My dream was taken away from me after my father died. Now my life is invested into this kingdom."

"Then leave," said Janellis.

"If I leave, then the two of you will have to rule this kingdom." He stared across the table. "I'm willing to sacrifice my dream for the two of you."

Janellis just looked at her brother. Some part of her felt bad for him, but couldn't show it. "I want to leave this kingdom and travel," she admitted.

Giovanis turned to Janellis. "What's stopping you from doing so?" he asked.

Janellis was stunned. "I don't know," she mumbled. She turned to leave. As she was near the door, she turned back to Giovanis. Was he allowing her to leave the kingdom?

*   *   *

Benavis sat in the council room alone, staring across to the giant window where the sun's rays passed through. While walking to the council room, Moon couldn't stop talking and kept floating around. Much to his being bothersome, Moon was becoming more of a pet to him. Even sitting in the council room, Moon still floated from wall to wall.

"I want to have fun!" expressed Moon. "This is boring."

"Then leave," suggested Benavis.

"I can't leave when I'm a part of you."

"Then stay. Since I'm the prince, it's my duty to listen in on the council meeting."

"No, it's not. You asked your lying brother to join."

"My brother is not a liar," defended Benavis.

"He lied to your face. He knows the clan secret," exposed Moon.

"Maybe it's best that I don't know." Benavis watched as Moon floated above him. "How about you tell me?"

Moon stopped floating. "I'm your curse," he answered then started floating again.

"Curse?" Benavis said to himself. "What do you mean curse?"

Suddenly, the door opened, and all the five members of council entered the room. They were surprised to see Benavis sitting alone at the table. They all made their way to the table, and each sat at a chair.

Bente had a smirk on his face, sensing something strange in the room.

"My prince," greeted Bente. "Surprised to see you here."

"Prince Benavis." Ocrist bowed, sensing Moon's presence. He knew of Benavis's ability, and the Sanila clan secret.

"The bald one knows." Whispered Moon. "I don't like him. Shall I kill him?"

Giovanis finally arrived last, through the back door of the room.

All the council members stood to bow their heads, including Benavis. Giovanis sat on the main chair and the rest all followed. He sighed deeply wishing he could be somewhere else. He looked over to Benavis and smiled.

"Shall we start?" asked Giovanis.

"My king, our food supplies still suffering," reported Dada. "People are starving."

"Thunder, I thought you said you'll handle the bandit situation?" questioned Giovanis.

"My king, our recruits need more time training. These bandits have been getting the best of us," answered Thunder shamefully, his pride declining because of the losses he suffered.

"You're the great Thunder Tiger-Foot. I expect you to do better and keep your promise," said a disappointed Giovanis.

"I'm sorry, my king," apologized Thunder.

"You're losing your touch, Thunder," mocked Bente. "Maybe it's time to retire?"

Thunder shot a warning look toward Bente.

"Just a suggestion," smirked Bente.

"Without the food supplies, then the capital will suffer. May I suggest calling for the Ma clan assistant?" suggested Seris.

"No. We don't need other clans' help. This matter can be dealt within ourselves," declined Giovanis.

"With all due respect, my king," worried Dada, "selfish pride will make our people suffer more."

"I'm thinking about the kingdom," argued Giovanis. "If the people see that we need the Ma clan's help, what will they think of us?"

"I don't care what they think of us," said Dada. "As long as the people are not starving."

"I think about the people too, Lord Dada," said Giovanis. "But please believe in Thunder that he will end the matter." He gave Thunder a warning look.

"We shouldn't keep the people waiting. They'll be wary of you," warned Dada.

"Boring," whispered Moon.

An argument began to break out with Bente questioning Thunder's ability to lead the army, Seris questioning the lack of food supplies and how it affected the southern economy, and Dada arguing for the people.

All Giovanis could do was listen. His head was ready to explode from all the stress. Even though he was king, his power was limited. With all the events going on in the south, he was incapable of pushing his own ideas, from the clans wanting to break their alliance to wanting to avenge his father's death.

"Look at the fighting," whispered Moon. "Shall I end their conflict?"

Benavis sat silently listening to the argument. Being a king was hard, but he didn't expect the unlimited problem it had. A king should never let his council argue before him. Though his brother may be liked, he didn't possess the cloak of a king. He then looked across the table to Ocrist, who was staring at him with a smile that sent chills through his spine.

"I don't trust the bald one," whispered Moon. "I think he sees us."

Giovanis banged his fist on the wooden table, halting the argument echoing in the room. He was not a man to lose his temper. But as of late, his thoughts had been challenged to the point where he was angry at his father for leaving him with the daunting task of running an entire kingdom.

"Enough!" expressed Giovanis.

"He's not happy," whispered Moon.

"I'm tired of all this bickering back and forth," fumed Giovanis. "Do you all think that I like being king?" He looked at each council member including Benavis. "I never asked to be king. My father never asked to be king. We were forced to take the throne because of unfortunate events." He rubbed his forehead to relieve stress. "All I'm asking for is guidance. I know that I'm becoming unpopular amongst the people, but I need my council members to stop fighting and help me rule this kingdom." He paused then leaned back on his chair. "I can't stand this anymore. Everyone out of my face!" he expressed.

"My king, there's more we need to discuss," retorted a concerned Seris.

"Not today," dismissed Giovanis.

Dada stood from his chair and bowed his head then stormed out of the room. Seris and Thunder followed with Thunder first apologizing to Giovanis. Bente smiled and bowed after. Ocrist followed after, leaving Benavis in the room alone with his brother.

"I'm sorry, Benavis," apologized Giovanis. "These meetings tend to get a little out of hand."

"It's fine," said Benavis.

Giovanis placed his hand on Benavis's shoulders. "I wish for you to never be in this position."

Benavis nodded and stood to leave. He bowed to Giovanis as he walked toward the door. Giovanis was no different from their father. The path their father created was now being continued by Giovanis.

"He's weak," whispered Moon.

"I know," mumbled Benavis as walked out the door.

After the council meeting, Benavis didn't know what to do. His thought on the meeting didn't reach his expectation. While listening to the council members yelling at each other and seeing Giovanis struggle with settling the council down, he concluded that there was no way the south would last long under Giovanis's rule.

To the eye, Giovanis may be a great fit to be king. But the truth was, he was nowhere near a king. His heart was pure and kind, but it was his weakness.

Benavis remembered his walk to the Ground and how he was almost stabbed to death but was saved by Moon. The eyes of people of the Ground still lived in his mind. There was more hate in the south than love, a problem Giovanis was blind to.

After walking around the palace aimlessly, Moon, still being a nuisance to him, asked him when dinner was or wanted to kill every guard they passed by. Benavis could only wish that Moon would stop bothering him, still upset that Giovanis avoided answering the question about their clan secret. Not knowing of the secret made him anxious. He needed to know what his clan was hiding. He thought about asking Janellis but doubted that she knew the secret.

Benavis entered an empty throne room and walked to the center of the room, staring at the golden throne and imagining himself sitting on it, wearing the golden crown and ruling the south, believing that he was a better ruler than his brother. The aura of power surrounded him. The south needed a ruler, not a king with no spine. After all the tragedy he had been through, the suffering and sorrow he endured, he had to be king.

Moon floated beside Benavis, also facing the direction of the throne. "We will sit on the throne soon," promised Moon.

"I don't wish to be king," lied Benavis.

"I know what you want. I am you," reminded Moon.

Benavis ignored Moon and focused on the throne. He never once took the time to take a good look at the throne. It was never a thought to him.

Moon suddenly fell to the ground and swam to the sidewall, sensing that someone was coming from the side. Benavis was still fixated on the throne, not bothered by Moon's alertness. All he could see was his own imagination of him on it, a visible rope pulling him closer to the throne. A rope he hoped to never be cut.

Ocrist came from the side, spotting Benavis standing at the center of the room with the light from the sun's rays shining through the glass ceiling shining on him. He made his way beside him, seeing that Benavis was fixated with the throne. He hinted at a smirk. "The golden throne is the path to justice," he said.

Benavis broke from his trance. "Lord Ocrist," he said with a surprised look to Ocrist.

"Don't mind me, my prince. I was just passing by."

"He's lying," whispered Moon.

"Oh, am I lying?" asked Ocrist.

Both Benavis and Moon were shocked, confused if Ocrist was able to hear Moon whisper.

"He can hear me?" asked a confused Moon.

"I can," replied Ocrist with a smile. "Do you still want to kill me?"

Moon swam to Benavis's side from the ground and showed himself to Ocrist.

Ocrist wasn't afraid by the towering shadow, the monster that lived inside Benavis and the secret of the Sanila clan—the ability that was kept hidden and locked for hundreds of years, the ability that the clan called shadow of madness.

"How do you know?" asked the confused Benavis.

"Remember when I looked into your mind?" reminded Ocrist. "While searching your mind, I found the deepest part of it." He turned to the throne. "I found a locked door and picked the lock."

"Are you telling me that it was you who unleashed this pest?" questioned Benavis with anger.

"I am not a pest," defended Moon.

"I was curious. I wanted to see the power of the Sanila myself," explained Ocrist.

"I will let my brother know immediately! You'll be exile from this kingdom," exclaimed the angered Benavis.

"Should I kill him?" asked Moon.

"Why?" asked Ocrist, still focusing on the throne.

"Because you unleashed a monster in me. This shadow thing will not leave me alone."

"This shadow thing is you," reminded Moon.

"Can you shut your mouth?" annoyedly said Benavis to Moon.

"I don't have a mouth to shut," reminded Moon.

"I apologize for unleashing a monster in you. But tell your brother what I did. I believe I did nothing wrong." He turned back to Benavis. "This is your clan secret, the great power your clan holds. It shouldn't be kept hidden away in your body. The land is changing, and it's best you have that shadow protecting you," he explained.

"My name is Moon," said Moon.

"What do you mean 'changing'?" asked a confused Benavis.

"When you accept your faith, you'll know." Ocrist turned back to the throne. "There's a monster that's coming soon. And the God Hands could only do so much to fend from this monster." He paused. "I finish with these parting words, my prince. Whoever is seated on the throne controls the fate and lives of the people of the south. The chair holds the power of evil or good. Amazing what a simple chair can do." He turned back to Benavis. "The right person needs to sit on that throne, my prince." He bowed and turned his back. "Look how far you've come since King Geolana's assassination. Maybe that shadow of yours is a blessing, my prince," he finished and parted from Benavis.

Benavis stood still, debating if he should tell Giovanis about what Ocrist had done. At the same time, he wondered what Ocrist meant when he spoke about the throne. All the thinking was giving him a headache. He wished there was someone that could give him all the answers, annoyed with all the guessing and thinking.

"I don't trust that bald man, but he's right," said Moon. "The right person needs to sit on it." Then he floated above Benavis and up to the ceiling. "I think we should sit on the throne."

Benavis turned back to the throne without saying a word to Moon. Again, he imagined himself sitting on it. This time, he imagined himself with tired evil eyes with a cloud of gray hovering over him.

*   *   *

Ocrist couldn't contain himself as he walked out of the throne room, sensing that his plan was coming to fruition—not just his goal but including all the members of the God Hands. He was the Master of Curse for the secret order. After wheezing his way to be Geolana and Giovanis's trusted adviser, he found himself now siding against them but secretly. After his observation and inspecting on Giovanis, he found that Giovanis wasn't the king to rule the South. It had to be someone with great power. The person with the greatest power was Benavis.

He made his way to the courtyard of the palace where the Tree of Sanila sat under the open roof. Sitting on the bench around the tree was Bente with two horn heads knelt before him. Ocrist noticed that they were talking about something secretive and made his way to them.

Once Bente and the two horn heads noticed Ocrist, Bente signaled the horn head to turn into flies, which then flew away. He wasn't pleased to see Ocrist but showed a smile still. He considered Ocrist to be his greatest intellectual rivaled and the wall that blocked him from the throne.

"Are you doing well, Lord Bente?" greeted Ocrist.

"Stop playing games, Ocrist," denied Bente. "I know you're planning something."

Ocrist just smiled. "I know you know. That's why your spy died by the hands of the Sleeping Monks."

"He was useless anyway," said Bente. "Do you mind telling me what happened to the shadow book that was kept in the Sanila Temple?" asked Bente.

Ocrist pretended he didn't know anything. "I don't know what you are talking about."

"Don't take me for an idiot, Ocrist. My family has been serving the Sanila clan for centuries. We know about the Shadow Book," reminded Bente.

"I see that there's no way we can be friends," Ocrist realized as he turned away from Bente. "I see you as an intelligent man that rivals mine. Out of all other advisers, I only see you and myself as the only people that can save the south. You do see that?"

"Where are you getting at, Ocrist?"

"It's best we work together than against," finished Ocrist as he walked away.

Bente smirked, thinking that he was close to exposing Ocrist. "Are you afraid that I will unmask you, Ocrist?"

Ocrist stopped walking, showing a villainous smile but not turning back to Bente. "You cannot unmask the God's servant," he ended, leaving Bente to his own confusion.

Bente continued to sit on the bench, thinking of strategies to get rid of Ocrist. He thought of many ideas, but none pleased him. If they did not hate each other, they could possibly prevent the south from slowly falling. But his ego and hunger for power prevented him from doing so.

Ever since he was a kid, he saw his grandfather and father serve as the king's advisers. He witnessed the advice they gave to the king. But his family was never the one to receive the thanks and cheer. They were unknown to the public eye. He was tired of people seeing kings as the hero for their feat in battles. He wanted glory for the ones that fought with their words. They were the unsung heroes of Telamis and the true villains.

Two flies flew in front of him then morphed into two horn heads, the same horn heads Bente signaled to leave. They knelt before him, awaiting for his orders. Bente pondered in his thoughts to create a plan. He needed a good enough plan to get rid of Ocrist from the southern kingdom.

"My lord, what is the plan?" asked one horn head.

"Keep eyes on Prince Benavis," ordered Bente.

The two horn heads turned back into flies and flew away. Benavis would be his key to power.

*   *   *

Janellis sat out on her balcony watching the summer shooting stars dashing across the night sky, wishing herself to be a shooting star. At the same time, she was thinking about leaving the kingdom.

She then looked to the moon, wondering if her parents were staring down at her. She needed her mother's advice and father's words of encouragement. The rest of the days she spent alone and bored. In the morning, while her brothers were busy with the kingdom's business, she was writing her romance novel about a princess and her warrior lover then reading some of her father's writings. One of his writings stuck out to her. It was the story of a warrior who didn't know himself. The warrior saw himself as a hero, but not until he had to kill a father in front of his children. That was when the warrior didn't grasp who he was in the world.

After staring at the stars for a while, she decided to lie on her bed and try to sleep, but couldn't. Tossing and turning in her bed, her mind was bothered with many thoughts crossing. She poured a cup of water that was on her nightstand, grabbing her wooden flute that was also on the nightstand, and walked over to her balcony, taking a sip of water as she walked.

She stared back into the night sky, hoping her parents were watching as she prepared to play a song for them. She wanted to cry for them but couldn't. Each time she tried, the tears wouldn't fall from her eyes.

She placed her cup of water on the guardrail of the balcony. As she prepared to whistle into her flute, she peered below to make sure no one was around. But to her surprise, standing under her balcony and stretching his arm was Rain.

There were always new faces guarding the palace. For some reason, she always came across Rain. When she was walking the corridor, Rain would cut the corner, avoiding her. When she was sitting in the courtyard, Rain would pass by and try to keep his eyes off her.

She poured the water down her balcony and splashed the top of Rain's head, startling him and forcing him to look up. He looked agitated when he looked up and saw the smile across her face. Quickly, he changed his expression and was surprised to see her.

Janellis waved down at Rain. "It rained on you," joked Janellis. The calmness in her voice didn't fit the delivery of her joke.

Rain was confused if Janellis was trying to be funny.

Janellis leaned over the guardrail. "Why do we always come across each other?" she wondered.

"I never noticed, Princess," lied Rain.

Janellis looked back up to the stars. "The stars are pretty tonight," she admired.

Rain looked up to the stars also then back at Janellis. He was speechless seeing Janellis reflecting from the lights in the sky. He couldn't take his eyes off her.

Janellis looked back down at Rain and smiled. "Can we be friends?" she asked.

Rain shook his head and gathered himself. "A guard and a princess are not allowed to speak to each other," reminded Rain.

"I don't care. I'm asking you to be my friend."

Rain ignored Janellis and bowed to her.

"If I wasn't a princess, would you be my friend?" asked Janellis.

Rain lifted his head up. "It's pointless for a warrior to have friends."

Janellis sighed. "You're a difficult person, Rain." She looked back up to the sky. "These stars in the sky. They're lucky."

Rain was confused. "What do you mean, Princess?"

"They have freedom unlike me. I wish to be a star and be free." She sighed and picked up her flute. "Very well then, I guess we can't be friends."

"If you want to be free, then why won't you free yourself?" questioned Rain, stopping Janellis from playing her flute. "I once saw a man who longs for freedom. I saw him cry for the woman he loved as her spirits leave her body. I saw him descend into madness. Now I'm trapped with his burden." He paused for a second. "It's hard to find freedom in Telamis, Princess." He clutched his hand into a fist tightly, remembering the downfall of his father then seeing his grandpa burning their clan banners and hanging the banner of the Sanila clan as their own.

"Why live that burden?" asked Janellis. "Escape with me. Away from this city and discover this land with me."

"I can't leave what I was brought into," replied Rain.

"In twelve nights, before the purple moon, I will be waiting for you at my clan's crypt. I won't wait long, but long enough for you to come. It's your choice to escape with me, Rain. It's your only chance to escape your burden." She walked back inside, leaving Rain with his own pondering.

Rain stood alone under the night sky, wondering why Janellis was so invested in him. At the same time, he wondered why she wanted to leave a life that was already perfect. He wanted to take her offer, but his hatred toward the Sanila clan left a wound in his heart. But he could feel his heart healing whenever he crossed paths with Janellis.

Chapter Twenty

Kingdom of Wintra

Moons and months passed as winter continued to slice and sting the Unchained. Everyone at the campsite was wary, pondering if Zhou was the leader they thought he was. The days were slow and painful, food became scarce, some members had already been taken by illness, buried deep within the forest. The night before, a child was born and died that same day, buried near the river. Everyone from the camp attended but Zhou.

Zhou was slowly becoming consumed by the bone crown. Every morning when he woke up, he would stare at the crown on his nightstand. In the afternoon, he became concerned for the crown, hoping that no one would sneak into his tent to steal it. At night, he would stare at the crown till he fell asleep. The others could see the change on his face. He had dark circles under his eyes. The eyes were also wide like a madman. His face was pale as a ghost, and he looked skinny nearly to the bone.

Meals were forgotten, Zhou choosing to hold the bone crown in his hand, rubbing so graciously and imagining himself sitting on the bone throne. He did know that the Unchained were becoming unconfident and worried for him. But yet he did not want to change.

Baeso entered Zhou's tent, bowing his head. "My lord, the people are waiting outside your tent," he reported.

Zhou did not shoot a look toward Baeso, keeping his attention tightly on the bone crown. "I'll speak to them. They'll understand my goal to end the era of kings."

Baeso just bowed his head.

"Baeso, do you still follow me?" asked Zhou.

"I am loyal to the end, my lord," answered Baeso with a straight face then left the tent.

Zhou sighed and smiled toward the air, placing the crown gently on his nightstand then standing up from his bed slowly. "I will be the man to end the era of kings. They will see that the gods had tasked me in changing the land of Telamis," he said to himself before walking out of his tent.

Once he walked out, he was met with a mob of people of unrest, all angry and annoyed written on their faces.

Gau, Spinder, and Baeso tried their best to calm the people as they tried to force themselves into Zhou's tent.

When they saw Zhou, the sight of him only fired them up. They wanted to charge at him with questions.

"Zhou, why are we still here!"

"Coward!"

"You are no leader!"

"We want to return home!"

Soon, the shouts and anger began to mix in with one another, now sounding like a rumble filling the air. Zhou still stood with a smile on his face, unfazed by the people's unrest and displeasure. He raised his hand up high up in the air.

Shockingly, the people slowly stopped their questions and shouting, their eyes all focused on Zhou like a tiger eyeing its prey.

"I understand the unrest all of you are feeling. I apologize to the followers that have died because of this grueling winter. But their death will not go unnoticed. When it's time we invade the capital, the dead will fight alongside us."

"How long must we wait, Zhou?" asked a man annoyedly.

"For however long. The gods will tell us when. Patience, my friends," said Zhou.

"We need food and water. Medicine for the sick!" shouted a woman.

"We can't wait anymore!" shouted a man.

"How long must we suffer this winter!" shouted another man.

Zhou looked unbothered. "I promise we will reach our goal. We will avenge the people that were taken from us eight years ago."

The Unchained all had a scowling face, staring sharply into the heart of Zhou silently, tired of hearing the same thing. Then an old man stepped forward. His eyes were nearly shut, and he had a long white beard. He had a wooden cane to help with his limp. He was small and fragile.

"You are nothing like Hacori, Zhou," said the old man, his voice sounding old and weak. "We do not want to avenge the massacre if we have to suffer without spilling blood. When the moon returns, we either return to the village or we invade the capital." Slowly, the people began to separate. "Zhou, make the right decision," urged the old man. "Don't be a leader of nothing." He bowed his head slowly and left.

Still, Zhou was unbothered; he turned to head back inside his tent.

"Zhou, what are we going to do?" asked Gau.

"Whoever stays will witness the light I will shine over the north." He walked into his tent, leaving Gau, Spinder, and Baeso alone.

Gau and Spinder looked at each other with concern, both witnessing the change in Zhou into madness.

Watching from afar from their tents was Jamori, Osa, and Kayten. They didn't join the crowd while they surrounded Zhou's tent. They watched as their mentor tried to calm the people but failed, each of them having different thoughts toward Zhou.

Osa sensed that Zhou was slowly losing his mind, entering a weakening state where he probably would never return from.

Kayten couldn't believe how the people quickly turned on Zhou in the way he saw himself how they never accepted him.

Jamori was different while the other two eyes were focused forward. His eyes were focused on Kayten, still remembering his conversation with Zhou to kill Kayten.

* * *

Jamori roamed around the camp. He declined Osa and Kayten when asked to go fishing with them. As of late, he hadn't been himself. He was no longer talkative or confident. Instead, he was silent and mysterious.

The other two noticed too but didn't want to ask him if something was bothering him.

While roaming around the camp, he overheard conversations from different members of the Unchained, some wanting to leave and return home while some wanted to, give Zhou one more chance. He had already made up his mind, choosing to continue to fight with Zhou and avenge his father's death.

Zhou gave him time to decide on Kayten's faith. He thought that Kayten must've done something to challenge the Unchained's idea.

He continued to walk around the camp, passing by people packing their belongings to leave. There were people coughing because of the sharp winter wind. There were people sitting by the fire to warm their hands.

Finally, he made his way in front of Zhou's tent, taking three deep breaths before entering. As he exhaled, cold air came from his breath, nervous to enter Zhou's tent, wondering what Zhou would say to him when he entered.

Once he stepped inside, Zhou was staring at the crown resting on his palm. His eyes were dancing with madness as he stared graciously, drooling to the ground, not noticing anyone in the tent with him.

"Zhou," said Jamori nervously.

Zhou quickly put the crown beside him, startled by Jamori's arrival. "Jamori." He noticed the lost look on Jamori's face. "Is something wrong?"

"About Kayten. Why must I kill him? Why must I decide on my friend's faith?" confessed Jamori.

"Don't think too hard, Jamori." Zhou smiled. "If you do not wish to kill your own brother, then I'll understand. But the blood of Kayten is important to us."

"Why? He lived that terrible event with us. He should see the light too."

Zhou stood from his bed and walked over to Jamori. He placed his hands gently on Jamori's shoulders. "We live in a world with many different paths. Unfortunately, most of the path is unforgiven."

Jamori nudged Zhou's hands off his shoulders. "We're supposed to walk the same path. We're supposed to fight by each other side . . . like you said."

"Of course." He walked back toward his bed. "I will carve a new path for the future. I believe your father would have done the same." He looked over to the Kong clan sword resting on the table. "Your father was fearless and intelligent. He would've chosen what's best for the village. I want you to follow the same path as him."

Jamori looked over to clan sword. "My father will never sacrifice his friends."

Zhou turned back around. "Don't be a fool, Jamori. If you want to sit on the mountain long enough, we must sacrifice what is dear to us."

"Why Kayten?"

"For you to understand, I must tell the truth—the blood of Dru that runs in Kayten. He must die, and his blood must be drawn for peace in the north."

"A Dru?" asked a confused Jamori.

"Yes, Kayten is a Dru."

"B-but they no longer exist . . ."

"Not all of them is gone. I believe Kayten is the last of their bloodline." He stared sharply into Jamori's eyes. "Do you understand now, Jamori?"

Jamori was taken aback, frozen by what he had just learned. His grandmother had always told him stories of the Dru clan and how they were evil. Their blood was used as their weapon, coming out of the pores of their skin and slicing the enemies and allies around them. They were also the key to unlock the legendary dragon, Taken.

Zhou walked by Jamori as he stood frozen. "Take your sword, Jamori. Draw his blood and take his life for our future. For your clan." He walked out of his tent, leaving Jamori alone.

Jamori pondered with the idea of killing Kayten. At the same time, he had heard enough stories of the Dru clan. They were monsters to land. He stared at his clan sword. The urge was over. At last, he could finally claim what was rightfully his.

Listening from the outside, behind Zhou's tent, was Osa with a straight look on his face. On his finger was a black butterfly. He allowed the butterfly to fly away, and he walked away from the tent. He had overheard the entire conversation between Zhou and Jamori.

* * *

Slowly, people began to leave the camp. Some tents were taken down. Gau and Spinder tried their best to convince the people to stay. The ones that stayed could only watch as others left, some of them bidding goodbye to the ones leaving.

Zhou watched from his tent. He didn't care that majority of the Unchained no longer wanted to follow him. He smiled kindly as they waved to him, nodding gently and thanking them for allowing him to be their leader.

The old man approached him.

"It's a shame that this path must be taken," expressed the old man.

"I understand if you all no longer believe in me. I thank you for serving under me. I will pray for safe travel for all of you."

The old man bowed his head. "I hope the gods will watch over you, Zhou. I fear that you have taken the wrong path." The old man walked away.

"The path I've taken is the path that will change Telamis."

"I live long enough to see many men that have the same ambition as you. They all suffered the same faith. Please take care of yourself, Zhou. Don't be a victim of selfish ambition. I bid you well." The old man continued to walk away, leaving Zhou alone with a smirk over his face.

* * *

Osa and Kayten watched from their tent as people left. Kayten couldn't believe his eyes. He looked over to Osa, who looked calm. For the first time, people would walk by him and wave goodbye. Some told him to take care of himself. It made him smile inside.

Jamori approached Osa and Kayten with a long face. "They chose to leave," he said.

Osa noticed Jamori's clan sword. "So Zhou decided to give you your sword," said Osa with a smile.

"H-he said I was ready," said Jamori nervously. He then looked at Kayten, remembering what Zhou wanted him to do. "Kayten, we should go hunting or maybe a walk. It's better to not be here when everyone's leaving," he suggested.

Kayten looked around. "You're right." He turned to Osa. "Care to join us, Osa?"

Osa hesitated; he first looked at Kayten, who was clueless about Zhou and Jamori's plan to kill him. He then looked to Jamori, disappointed that Jamori had chosen the wrong path. He stretched his arms. "I'm staying behind." He smiled.

"Are you sure?" asked Kayten.

"You two go enjoy your walk under the stars," he teased and heading into the tent.

Jamori and Kayten both shrugged their shoulders. But Jamori could sense something wrong with Osa.

*   *   *

Kayten and Jamori walked in the forest alone. The night was cold, yet the full moon shone brightly in the sky. They both walked in silence with Kayten trailing behind.

Kayten stared up into the sky, connecting the stars to create an image in his head. He wished life was peaceful as the stars. The sound of crickets and owl hooting was the only thing heard. He didn't expect the walk to be calming, expecting Jamori to tease or talk about his dream.

Jamori, on the other hand, was thinking about killing Kayten. He had finally made his decision and chosen his path. Even if the path was wrong, all he wanted was to avenge his clan, even if it meant killing his best friend. His hand was tightly holding the handle of his sheathed sword. In his pocket were two wooden tubes for Kayten's blood. He stopped walking, and tears slowly fell from his eyes.

Kayten stopped also, wondering why Jamori was standing still, not knowing that his friend and rival was going to take his life.

"Kayten, I'm sorry," apologized Jamori.

"Why are you apologizing?" asked a confused Kayten.

"This world is cruel. I'm willing to sacrifice the ones I love for the future." He turned around and drew his sword.

Kayten stepped back in fear, stunned as to why Jamori had drawn his sword on him. He tried to figure out what Jamori meant, but couldn't put the puzzles together. He felt cold sweat dripping down his spine. His mind throbbed, as time to him felt slow. A death bird flew to a branch and watched below.

"W-what are you talking about?" asked Kayten.

Jamori's grip on the handle of his sword became tighter. His other hand was in a fist, nails digging into his sweaty palm. "Stop talking, Kayten!" he barked at Kayten. The tears continued to fall. "I must do what's right for the future."

Suddenly, black butterflies began to fly around Jamori. Both he and Kayten were confused. The black butterflies began to hit Jamori's face, which annoyed him. Then he started to swing his sword violently at the butterflies. But each time he swung, the more butterflies showed up. It started to become a pest to him to the point where he started to swear.

Osa showed himself from behind the trees. He stood behind Jamori with a straight emotionless look, watching him struggle against the attacking butterflies.

Jamori peeked back. "Osa?"

"I heard the plan. We're brothers. We shouldn't kill each other," Osa reminded Jamori calmly.

"You don't understand, Osa. I am looking toward the future." Jamori focused his attention on Kayten, but could barely see since the butterflies kept blocking his vision. "He's a bloodline of a Dru. They're monsters to this land!" he revealed angrily.

"What are you two talking about?" asked Kayten, confused, tears nearly falling from his eyes.

"I told you, Kayten, to leave the Unchained. Yet you still stay," Reminded Osa. "You're just a pawn to Zhou's true intention."

"I'm not going to leave," argued Kayten.

"You still won't leave after he ordered for your death?" questioned Osa. "Zhou wants you dead. Your blood is all he wants because you're a Dru." He turned his attention to Jamori. "You . . . you're willing to kill your own brother for nothing. The two of you should've listened and run away."

"And how about you, Osa. Why do you stay?" questioned Jamori.

"I'm staying because this is the only path that will lead me to the man I want to kill," revealed Osa.

"Who is that man?" questioned Jamori.

"That does not concern you, Jamori," answered Osa.

"Then stay out of this. I must kill Kayten."

Suddenly, the black butterflies began to fly in a circle around Jamori, creating a wall around him. All he saw was the black wings of the butterflies. "What is this?" he wondered.

Osa lifted his arms up straight. His hands opened wide. "Kayten, this is your only chance to leave. Zhou no longer wants you. Save yourself and find a better future."

"I-I can't . . . Where can I go? The two of you are all I know. I don't want to be alone. No one will ever accept me. You guys are the only ones that saw pass the hatred on me."

"They hate you because you're a Dru. They saw you as a monster. Zhou only used you . . . I myself hate you, Kayten. I pretended to consider you my brother because I felt bad for you," said Osa. A teardrop fell from his eye, hoping Kayten will run away.

"He's right, Kayten. Run. We never cared for you," added Jamori behind the wall of butterflies. His voice sounded sad and insincere.

"You two are lying!" yelled Kayten.

"If you don't leave, then I will kill you myself, Kayten," threatened Osa.

Kayten stood still and quiet. He wiped tears from his eyes. Then he ran, running by the wall of butterflies and then by Osa, tears flowing back as he sprinted. He didn't want to be killed. He didn't know where to go since the world didn't want him. His only two friends urged him to leave. The man he looked up to wanted him dead, not knowing the powerful blood that ran in him.

Osa and Jamori waited in silence till Kayten could no longer be seen. Both boys had tears filling in their eyes, blocking their vision. Both were heartbroken that their bond was broken.

"This is it," said Jamori, smiling toward the night sky, wondering if his father was smiling down at him. "I am a fool to follow a madman's orders." He fell to his knees into the snow, closing his eyes.

"I'm sorry," he apologized to Osa with sadness. "Don't cry, Osa. Do what you must. But promise me that you will accomplish what you're searching for."

"Stop talking!" cried Osa.

"I'll watch over the two of you . . . Don't cry for me." Jamori laughed. He looked around at the walls of black butterflies surrounding him. "Impressive magic . . ."

Osa shut his eyes tightly and squeezed his hand together. Then the wall of butterflies all closed in and started slicing Jamori with their wings.

Jamori tried to hold the pain, but the cuts were too much. He fell face-first into the snow. Blood leaked from his cuts. The butterflies finally stopped and disappeared deep within the darkness of the forest. His breathing became staggered, and he became weak. Slowly, he shut his eyes and into the darkness he went, hoping that his father was waiting for him at the gates of heaven.

Osa sniffled, staring at Jamori's lifeless body, angry at himself that he had to kill his own friend. He wiped tears from his eyes as a black butterfly landed on his shoulder.

"Prince Osa, the man you follow will only continue into madness," said the masked man behind him.

"I'll follow him until I reach King Euren."

"We can help you, my prince. Join us and the path to your destiny will open."

Osa hesitated and stared at Jamori's body. "If I join, will Kayten be protected?"

"I cannot make that promise."

"Promise me he will be protected."

"Accept the offer of the God's Hands, and his life will be protected by you."

"Then I'll join. I will stand before Euren and kill him."

"Good. The others will be happy to hear the news. Your first task is to kill the five elements." The masked man turned into a crow and flew off into the night sky. Osa stood alone in the dark winter forest, trying to figure out if he had made the right decision to join the God's Hands. His heart was also broken that he had killed his own friend. Now he will carry vengeance of Jamori with him, adding Zhou to the list of people he will kill.

Chapter Twenty-One

Kingdom of Tigara

The morning sunshine shone brightly over the city of Mersane, waiting till noon to come. The market didn't look lively as it used to be. Staring out the window of her chamber was Maenellia. She looked pale and lost. When the news of Indris's death came upon her, she was stricken with grief. For the past few days, she couldn't eat or bear to look Aerin in the eyes.

Indris's body was kept at the Kimsu clan temple, preserved in a preservation bubble by the temple monk so his spirit would know that he had passed.

Every morning, Maenellia would skip out on breakfast and just sit by her window and stare out into the sky, even if the days were raining. She was broken into a million pieces, feeling like each day was long, upset that she couldn't protect her son. She put Indris's death upon herself.

At the same time, she had a great amount of resentment toward Aerin. Ever since the news of Indris's death and his body still lying in the temple till the next day, Aerin still acted as if nothing had happened, focusing on the war plans against the Cai clan. She couldn't believe how selfish and mad Aerin had become.

The door opened, and Kiri entered the chamber with a concerned look on her face. She was worried for her mother and tried different ways to cheer her up. Even the other siblings would try. Isa would come in with a book and read it to her. Lehue would come in with dishes he made for her to try. But she wouldn't eat them. Chenpu would come and try to talk to her. Even Airian would come to talk. The only two that wouldn't come was Mani and Kunjae.

"Mother, how are you feeling today?" asked a concerned Kiri. She waited for her mother's response, but there was nothing.

Maenellia kept her eyes to the sky, acting as if Kiri wasn't in the room with her. The only thing in her mind was Indris, retracing all the memories she had with him, from the day he was born to the day she last spoke to him. Out of all her children, he was the least difficult to worry about, always the one to do right. Yet like all her children, she didn't know what kind of conflict he was going through.

"Mother, it's me, Kiri." Kiri wiped tears from her eyes. "I'm your child too, Mother. You have other children too. I know it's hard for you to accept Indris's death. I'm upset about it like you." She paused for a second, wondering if she would be able to get through to Maenellia. "Can you at least turn around and look at me? We all need you," she begged. "You're supposed to be someone strong. Someone we can go cry and talk to. And yet you're the one being weak."

"I'm not a good mother," Maenellia finally said as she put herself down.

Kiri's eyes opened wide after hearing her mother's voice. "You're still a good mother to me."

"No, I let my son die," blamed Maenellia. "A mother should never let her child die before her."

"He died with honor on the battlefield," explained Kiri.

"There's no honor in dying," said Maenellia. She turned to Kiri with a lost look in her eyes. "My love, please find your own future. Don't live for someone else's dream," she finished and then turned back to the window.

"Mother," said Kiri to silence in return. "Please, Mother." She sobbed. "Mother, I need you . . . We all need you. P-please come back to us." Her words were broken and sad. She sniffed and sobbed. "Am I not your child too? You're my mom too." She ran out, covering her eyes with her arms so no one could see her crying, upset that she had lost her mother.

"I'm sorry," mumbled Maenellia as she sat still on her seat, staring aimlessly out the window.

***

The early afternoon sky felt cool and eerie, still having the gloomy, uncomfortable feeling in the air. On the training ground of the demons' palace was Aerin, watching both Isa and Lehue as they practiced releasing their flames. Standing beside Aerin was Airian who still looked affected by the loss of Indris. Beside him was Kunjae who looked unbothered. Standing on the other side of Aerin was Jen-Song and Akin.

Aerin didn't look impressed while he watched Lehue and Isa. Lehue was able to release his flame, but it was weak. The blue flames danced on his palm, but it would either disappear quickly or too small.

Isa, on the other hand, couldn't release any flame. He stood in a power stance with his palm out, sweating and focusing so the flame would appear. He could feel that there were no flames running through his body. The harder he strained his body, the more pain he felt. At one point, his mind played a trick on him and made him think he created blue flames.

Aerin wasn't concerned about Indris's death or his funeral the next day, instead placing more focus on the future and his plan. He needed both Lehue and Isa to improve, but they were taking too long. When Indris's death reached him, he had already begun his next step for war. He felt mocked when the Cai clan tried to assassinate Mani.

Before he could make the Cai clan pay, he must wait after Indris's funeral. Even though he was itching to end the Cai clan, he still had to show respect for his son. His days had been stressful as he strained himself thinking about war, wondering if he'd come out as the victor. He had been avoiding Maenellia, knowing that he had greatly upset her. Looking at the officials and army he had under him, he believed that it was enough to defeat the Cai clan. He felt that they were ready to die for him. But without the dragons and to the eyes of all the eastern clan, the Kimsu clan didn't look that threatening.

"Again!" demanded Aerin angrily to Lehue and Isa.

"Aye, Father. Can we have a break?" asked Lehue.

"You think there will be breaks in battle?" Aerin asked Lehue with a strict look.

Lehue pouted his face and groaned in dissatisfaction.

"Boy!" angered Aerin, irritated by Lehue. His yell startled everyone around him. "You want to act like a child in front of me! Do you want to end up like your brother?!"

Isa was afraid; he had never seen his father yell with pure rage before. It was like Aerin was losing his mind. All the stress he accumulated was getting to him, letting the anger and emotion out on Lehue.

"I'm trying to build something for our clan. And you want to stop me!" raged Aerin. "We deserve to be seen as kings and queens . . . I deserve to be king!" His eyes were slowly beginning to fill with madness. "They all expect me to sit down as a fool. Not do anything about it. What they did to my clan. They executed my brother before my eyes, before my children and wife's eyes. They want to stop me! No no, I can't be stopped. I won't be stopped." He gave Lehue a menacing look, who in return gave him a fearful eye. He then looked around and saw that everyone else was shocked. "Do you all think it's over? You all think we're going to lose. Because the dragons are no longer by my side, that means I'm going to lose? All of you, including you, Akin, are all weak. All of you are afraid to fight and die for what's rightfully mine!"

"How selfish are you!" questioned Kunjae. "Indris died because of you. Ausra and Iszra left because of you. Mani got hurt because of you. And still, you want to think about your stupid ambition?"

"Stupid?" Aerin pushed Airian aside and got into Kunjae's face. "I'm getting tired of you, boy," said the annoyed Aerin. "You're like Ausra. The both of you think I don't care about my children."

Kunjae chuckled. "It's true, Father," said Kunjae sarcastically. "You're just a sad man with a hopeless dream."

Aerin felt the black flames readying to burst out of his body, seeing the mocking smile on Kunjae's face. All of his anger was ready to be released out of the pores of his skin. He cocked his arm back and swung with the million strength of dead warriors directly to the face of Kunjae, knocking Kunjae to the ground. Then looking down at Kunjae with black flames in his hand, Akin immediately grabbed his hand to put out the flames. If he used the flame on a defenseless Kunjae, it would end with another demon funeral.

Airian immediately checked on Kunjae who had his hand on his cheek with blood dripping down his bottom lip. Both Lehue and Isa looked at each other, shocked and afraid of what they saw. Jen-Song stood still watching, not knowing how to react. But they saw that Aerin was losing his mind.

"Wow, that was a good slap." Kunjae coughed then stood up on his own strength, staring into Aerin's dark eyes. "You're not a good father," he continued to mock.

"Kunjae, do you have a death wish?" questioned Akin, wondering why Kunjae continued to irritate Aerin.

"No, Uncle. I just want to know what happened to my father."

With anger and annoyance, Aerin quickly charged toward Kunjae, holding him by the collar of his shirt. "Boy, what did I say about questioning death!" he reminded with rage and talking with his teeth clenched.

Jen-Song, Akin, and Airian tried to pry Aerin off Kunjae, all three hoping Kunjae wouldn't continue to instigated Aerin. But seeing the smile on Kunjae's face, they all knew he wasn't done. It was like he was trying to get Aerin to kill him.

"I wouldn't need to question death when my father puts it upon me," finished Kunjae.

With all the power he has, all the rage and fire, Aerin picked Kunjae up and slammed him to the stone ground onto his back. Everyone around him was stunned. Kunjae was laughing as he hit the ground, proud that he had gotten into Aerin's head.

Jen-Song and Akin pulled Aerin away from Kunjae.

Airian checked on Kunjae again.

Kunjae stood up on his own power again with a pained smile on his face.

Airian stood beside him, trying to figure out what Kunjae was trying to do.

Kunjae was slouching, feeling the intense pain coming from his back. "I-if you're a good father, then you wouldn't put death upon your children," Kunjae struggled to say with a smile. "I-I don't want to run with the demon anymore."

"Stop . . .," urged Airian.

"No, he must know. Running with the demon is a stupid p-phrase . . ." He took a painful deep breath. "If you're such a man for the future, then worry about what your children want, Aerin." He turned to leave, limping and slouching as he went.

Aerin watched as Kunjae walked away. He lifted one arm up with black flames around his hand, aiming at Kunjae's back. Airian stood between, facing Aerin with his arms spread wide, preparing to take the blast to protect a defenseless Kunjae.

"Move out of the way, Airian," ordered Aerin.

"No," refused Airian with tears in his eyes.

"Don't be like him, Airian," warned Aerin.

"I won't let you kill another brother of mine."

Aerin put his arms down and let out a loud and stressful shout, his head throbbing with anger. There were doubts in him when he attacked Kunjae, hating himself for hurting his son. He was struggling with his own internal conflict. To the outside, it looked like he didn't care for the loss of Indris, not bothered that both Iszra and Ausra had left his side. The three sons he trusted most were no longer by his side. He felt like he was in black autumn.

"Training dismissed," said Akin, taking charge as Aerin reflected on himself.

Both Lehue and Isa quickly ran away before Aerin got his sense back. They were afraid and didn't want to anger their father anymore. After seeing Aerin hit Kunjae, they didn't want to end up like him.

"Brother, have you lost your mind?" questioned Akin disappointedly.

"What have I become?" Aerin asked himself. "I didn't mean to strike him."

"Kunjae may have a smart mouth. But he's right. Be their father first. Think about the war later. Go grieve for your dead son."

"Akin, you know I'm doing this for the clan."

"I don't care. Are you willing to risk your children for the sake of the clan?"

"The clan is my children," replied Aerin.

"I wish for you to come back to reality. But right now, I think reality has left you. The clan is not your children." He bowed to Aerin. "I'm going to check on Airian and Kunjae. Jen-Song, watch over my brother."

Akin left, disappointed that Aerin was being driven away by his own ambition, creating a wedge between him and his family, wondering if Ausra and Iszra were smart to escape.

* * *

Kunjae sat by the side of the palace and leaned against the stone wall, trying to ease the pain coming from his back, satisfied with himself for unmasking his father but at the expense of him getting injured. He was annoyed that Aerin was acting as if nothing mattered, feeling that he was the only one to see the dark path his father was embarking on.

Airian stood before Kunjae with his arms crossed, confused as to why Kunjae instigated their father to hit him.

"You stood up to him, one-eyed hothead," teased Kunjae but impressed with Airian.

"You're a fool. Why the hell did you instigate him?" retorted a confused Airian.

"It's for Indris."

"What do you mean?"

"You do not know, huh? Grandpa always told me our greatest enemy is ourselves," remembered Kunjae. "He said to never fight ourselves because that was our ultimate killer." He smiled. "Don't you see? All of us is our own enemy. Look at Mother and Father. Look at Iszra and Ausra, even the three young ones."

"I don't understand." Airian was trying to figure out what Kunjae was talking about.

"Of course you don't, one-eyed hothead. You'll never understand. But yet you also fight yourself."

"That's why you wanted to get hit?" asked Akin as he approached Airian and Kunjae. "That wasn't smart of you, Kunjae."

"That's what I said," agreed Airian.

"But I agree with you, Kunjae. I think your father is gone," said Akin.

"Uncle . . ." Airian was surprised.

"The both of you know I love guys like my own children. I'll never let anything happen to the two of you. But yet I have failed. I let you lose an eye," Akin said to Airian. "And allowed pressure to be put on you during the mission," he said to Kunjae. "I don't agree with my brother's plan at all. He believes in a false idea that our clan should be kings and queens. But he doesn't understand we are bloodlines of Chenva." He crossed his arms and shook his head. "I don't see a bright future for my brother. I see a dark and ominous one."

"Are you afraid, Uncle?" asked Kunjae.

Akin smiled. "You know why I drink?" he asked, looking at each boy as they waited for him to explain. "I drink because I want to numb my brain from reality. When I'm sober, I know how dangerous, how upside down this world is. But when I'm drunk, I know nothing. I speak nonsense without regrets. I sleep better at night. I sleep with women, not caring how they look. All it matters is that I'm away from reality for a moment." He paused and reflected on how downward his life had been. "You never know what anyone's thinking until they release themselves. The taste of wine and ale allow me to release my true self," he said, feeling upset with himself. "I'm a coward to the truth and reality."

"That's weak of you, Uncle," mocked Kunjae.

Akin laughed. "I know, Kunjae. But as you get older and life became bleaker, what do you turn to? Sadly, I turned to a bitter drink of sin and happiness. I always wanted to find the heart of gold, but never accomplished it. Living the life of a warrior never gave me the opportunity. I want you boys to promise me to find the heart of gold, to never turn to the bitter drink of sin and happiness. Don't ruin your future as I did. Don't pity yourself."

"It's not too late, Uncle," consoled Airian. "I can help you."

"Airian, that heart of yours is big, but yet you're so brash. Don't be quick to help someone find themselves when you have yet to find yourself," advised Akin.

Kunjae held and squeezed his weeping man necklace, understanding that his uncle gave up a lot for the clan, refusing to marry and have children because of the fear of losing the ones he loved. When Indris died, it was Akin who cried the most, the one who numbed his pain with wine and ale. The one that stayed beside Indris and shamed himself for letting Indris die. But what he didn't know was that Indris wanted to die.

"Uncle, thank you," said Kunjae.

"For what?" Akin was surprised by Kunjae's sudden thanks.

"For being more of a father than my own. If you had children, I think you'll make a great father," explained Kunjae.

"I'm surprised, Kunjae. I didn't expect this side of you."

"Life comes with the unknown, as so Grandpa said," recalled Kunjae.

"Ah, my father was a smart man," awed Akin. He bowed his head to Airian and Kunjae. "Thank you, boys."

"Uncle, please," begged Airian, not wanting his uncle to bow to him.

"No, I must," insisted Akin. "The future is never guaranteed. It's important to laugh and respect each other. If we fight and argue, we should always come back to love and respect." He finished then left his two nephews, thinking in his head of wine and ale, upset that he was weakened by the taste of bitterness, feeling the pain of his suffering.

Kunjae shook his head, seeing the look on his uncle's face. Seeing through the words was a weak man, still searching for his purpose in life, still in pain for his nephew. He knew where Akin was going, a place where he too often could be found—the Wings Tavern, where he could laugh with other drunks and cheer till they fell, a place where the most suffered went to ease their pain.

* * *

After his altercation with Kunjae, Aerin and Jen-Song made their way to the council meeting. Aerin was still bothered by the altercation, which Jen-Song could clearly see. He wanted to find words to encourage Aerin but couldn't think of anything. It was not expected of him to say words of encouragement anyway. All he knew was to stay quiet and follow orders.

On their way to the war room, both men walked in silence, neither wanting to say a word to each other. When they finally arrived, all the other high officials had their eyes on them, all seeing the visible anger on Aerin's face.

"Where's Uncle?" questioned Chenpu as Aerin made his way next to her.

"Akin won't be joining us today," replied Aerin in a stern tone. He looked at each of his five high officials. Even though he was there physically, his mind was elsewhere, still trying to find calmness within himself. "We must not waste any more time," he started. "The Cai clan is getting the better of us. We need to retaliate for what they did to my daughter."

"My lord, with all due respect, don't you think we should hold off on war against the Cai clan?" suggested Estrey. "The mission at Heart Village took a lot of our men and women. We need time to rebuild."

"We don't need to rebuild. I believe in my army's strength," rejected Aerin. "Broken, has the spy returned with the news?"

"All my spies are dead," answered Broken. "There's a traitor amongst us."

Aerin banged his fist on the table. "Nothing is going my way!" expressed Aerin.

"My lord, I agree with Captain Estrey," worried Nellina. "We don't stand a chance against the entire eastern kingdom."

"Yes, without the dragons, we're just a mere clan," added Gorl.

"The dragons are no longer with us!" reminded Aerin with annoyance. "We don't need them to win the Cai clan."

"I'm sorry, my lord," apologized Gorl.

"If any of you want to stop serving under my clan, then walk out of that door," challenged Aerin, trying to see if any of his top officials were loyal. "Remember, you all serve me. You all fight under the demon banner. I'm trying to build a future for my clan. If any of you don't see the same future as me, then leave. I won't be upset. But I will not hesitate to kill if I see any of you on the opposing side."

He waited for a while to see who was willing to leave. But they all stayed. Even though they stayed, he could still see the doubt over their faces. "Good. We must find the traitor amongst us."

"I'll find the traitor, my lord," said Cholee.

"Then we must recruit any young men and women that are willing to fight under the demon banner. Search the nearby villages if we must. Captain Broken, I'll leave you in charge of the recruiting process."

"Understood, my lord."

"After my son's funeral, we'll push forward into war. We attack each clan one by one within the darkness. Sulin-Wu clan will be the first. Hensi broke the war code first so we'll do the same," determined Aerin.

He dismissed the meeting but stayed behind, thinking to himself if they could actually win against the entire eastern kingdom. He had a strange feeling that a cloud of raining blood was coming. But still, he felt that his goal must come forth for the sake of his clan and children.

*　*　*

The night was closing in. The people of Mersane were all preparing for dinner. Akin was drinking and cheering at the Wings Tavern. Jen-Song was at Jungy's home observing the moon lion dagger. Nellina was at her home sharpening her sword. Gorl was at his home eating with his family. Broken was at the Demon barrack in his quarter doing paperwork. Estrey and Cholee were drinking tea at a tea shop.

Life continued in Mersane, not knowing the unexpected to come. As everyone from common to soldier to ranked officials lived life one at a time, they did not sense the darkness that was coming. The night air was cool and calm, making that night nothing special. Families enjoyed their dinner together. Children told their parents about their day. Fathers were tired from their long day at work. Mothers smiled at the company of their family. Students of the Mersane Academy skipped dinner to study for their exams.

But at the Demon Palace, it wasn't as simple as the outside. The Kimsu children were slowly drifting away from their parents, a funeral being prepared for the next day.

Maenellia stared at her black silk dressed on the wooden mannequin, a dress she would wear to her son's funeral. She never expected to ask the seamstress to create such a dress for her. While she stared at the dress, gazing her eyes at the dove design, she burst into tears, crying loudly for her son to hear from the heavens.

While Maenellia cried, the rest of her family were at the dining hall, all eating their dinner of roasted pork, steamed fish, and rice on the side without saying a word to one another.

Aerin sat at the head of the table. From his left were two empty chairs. Then sat Chenpu, Mani, and Kiri. The first chair was Iszra's chair, the second was Indris's. On his right was another empty chair, which was Ausra's. Then sat Airian, Kunjae, Lehue, and Isa.

It was a tradition in the Kimsu clan to eat dinner as a family before a funeral. Chairs were left empty for the dead ones or the ones that were not around. Only the immediate family could join the dinner table. Their wives, children, or husbands were not allowed to join.

Aerin remembered when he had to do the same for his father and sister. When his sister died, two chairs were left empty for his sister and mother. When his father died, three chairs were left empty.

He looked across the table, upset that Maenellia wasn't sitting there to show respect to their son. He then looked at the empty chair to his right, imagining Ausra sitting next to him eating. He then looked to the chair to his left, imagining Iszra when he was eight years old, his smile so bright and dirt smudged on his cheeks. Then to the chair next, imagining Indris looking back at him and giving a simple nod.

Aerin wanted to burst out crying knowing that his three oldest sons weren't with him anymore, one having disappeared, not knowing if he's dead or not, the other leaving him when he could've stopped him, and Indris, the one that had died in battle. He then looked at his other children. Who didn't look happy to be around him? He needed Maenellia since she was the pillar that held the family together. With her in her own sadness, the family slowly began to fall apart.

They all ate silently, no one making eye contact with each other. The food tasted delicious, but with all the distaste and depression around the table, not even the taste of the food could crack a smile.

Finally, Maenellia entered the hall. With red swollen eyes from crying, she walked directly to her chair and slammed her fist on the table, startling everybody at the table. She stared fiercely at the eyes of Aerin from across the table who was also shocked. The look in her eyes paralleled a mother bear protecting her cubs from hunters.

"You're a selfish man!" expressed Maenellia with grief and resentment. "Our son is gone, and yet you sit around like he doesn't exist!" She looked at each of her children and the three empty chairs. "I lost three sons because of you, Aerin. Because of you, one of them is dead! Are you going to take any more of my children?"

Aerin slammed his fist on the table, making the plates bounce. "Do you think I don't care!" Aerin yelled back. "I'm suffering like you."

"You're not suffering enough," objected Maenellia. "My child shouldn't die before me. They should be here with their mother!"

The children at the table could only sit in silence while their parents argued, all choosing their mother's side.

Mani wanted to cry with her mother since she felt ashamed for not talking to her, still recovering from the assassination attempt on her.

Kunjae gave his father a look of disapproval. His back was still in pain.

"I can't sit around and cry all day. I have reasonability. I have a war—"

Suddenly, a ball of blue flames flew by Aerin, nearly hitting him in the face. The flames hit the giant demon banner hanging from the wall and slowly burned it.

Aerin stared with fear in his eyes at Maenellia, as she breathed heavily with her arms out after firing a ball of blue flames at him.

Their kids were also taken aback by their mother's actions, all seeing in her eyes that she was willing to kill Aerin. They sat still, feeling the ground was getting warmer. At any minute, their mother would burn the whole palace down. She had the power to do so. That was why they avoided making her angry.

"How dare you put my child before your ambition, Aerin! He died because of your ambition. And you want to speak about it in front of me? What war are we talking about? For the past month, you put this family through war. Kiri, Lehue, and Isa saw their uncle's head split from his body. Mani was poisoned because of you. Airian lost his eye because of you. Indris died because of you!" she yelled.

Aerin stayed silent out of fear, not knowing what to say to Maenellia. She was right; he did ruin his family. Because he was so focused on his ambition, he didn't realize how much suffering he had caused on his children.

"No more, Aerin," finished Maenellia with tears in her eyes. Then she turned to leave.

Kiri jumped from her chair and followed her mother without giving a single look to Aerin. Lehue and Isa followed next, doing the same as Kiri. Mani stood and bowed her head to Aerin and left.

Kunjae stood up from his chair and noticed the loss in Aerin's eyes. "I guess no one runs with the demon," he said, shaking his head. "You're just a coward, Father." Then he bowed his head and left the hall.

Airian followed with a bow to Aerin.

Only Chenpu sat at the table, seeing the weak demon her father had become. She expected her father to fall slowly but did not expect the extent of it. She sensed her opportunity to take the clan head since her father was losing trust from his family and ranked officials.

"Are you okay, Father?" asked Chenpu. "You know I will keep fighting by your side." She stood to leave.

"Chenpu," Aerin finally said, stopping Chenpu from leaving the hall. "I want you to stay behind tomorrow."

"But it's Indris's funeral," said a confused Chenpu.

"You want to be the clan head. Am I correct?"

Chenpu stayed silent, feeling happiness ringing through her body.

"I want you to stay behind and take care of the palace and the city."

"Do you expect something bad will happen?"

"No, I need you to keep running with the demon," finished Aerin with a blank look on his face.

Chenpu bowed and left the hall with a smirk. Her dream was coming true, but at the expense of her family's downfall. She didn't care as long as she had power in the clan. She wanted the respect that came with power. Only an arrow to the heart could stop her from her goal.

*   *   *

On the day of the funeral, the morning sky was gray over the Forest of Life, waiting for the rain to fall. Every member of the Kimsu clan was at the clan temple. Some had traveled from the southern or eastern kingdom. The Kimsu guards all stood guard outside with Jen-Song guarding the door, making sure no attack will come while the clan grieved.

The temple had black wooden walls around its perimeter. There were several houses on the property. Two golden statues of a lion sat on each side of the steps of the temple. The golden lions were guardians of the gates of heaven. At the back of the temple was a pond full of dragonfish. There were trees with leaves of autumn. The ground was covered in leaves.

Inside the temple sat a giant golden statue of Shenva sitting on a spirit dragon head with both palms opened and facing upward. The left side was meant for death while the right side was meant for life. Around the temple were paintings of stories, such as Chenva and Shenva's conquest over the wing dragons. Resting at the foot of the statue on a bed of black roses was a casket on which rested Indris. His casket was made out of blacktree wood. The wood was dark as night with white paintings of war scenes of victory.

Praying to him was Aerin and Maenellia; behind them were their children, except for Chenpu. Behind the children were all the members of the Kimsu clan. The room was filled, all praying and hoping that Indris entered the heavens and feasted with the ancestors.

Maenellia couldn't contain herself and started to cry loudly. She nearly fainted to the ground but was held up by Kiri. She cried in the arms of Kiri. Her loud cry created a chain reaction. Soon, others joined her in the cry. Even the ones who didn't know Indris cried with her. Seeing a mother crying for her dead son weakened the heart of the demon clan.

Aerin stood and turned to bow to the other clan members to show gratitude. People stood to leave the temple, leaving the family and Akin alone.

Aerin sat back down and faced the casket, now imagining Indris as a kid running around the time when he was pretending to be a phoenix while Iszra pretended to be a dragon. Then he imagined Maenellia with Ausra cradled in her arms and Chenpu by her side as she explained to Chenpu about the story on the wall. The memories of his young children saddened him. He wanted to let out a loud cry but couldn't.

"You always wanted to fly," Aerin whispered to himself. "You can fly now, son." He began to finally cry, hiding his face in the palm of his hand, feeling the failure he had caused on his children. "What have I done!" he cried.

Mani went over to her father to console him, seeing that he was regretting all his decisions, hurt to see the man she thought of as her hero, now weakened. Both of her parents were struck with self-blame, both wishing that it was all just a nightmare.

Akin approached the casket of Indris. He gave Indris a kiss on the forehead. "I should've protected you, nephew," he said with tears in his eyes then turning around and leaving. But first, he took a look at his broken brother. He placed a hand on Aerin's and Maenellia's shoulders and left the room.

One by one, the siblings said their last words to their brother, leaving Aerin and Maenellia alone in the room. Aerin was the first to stand, walking toward the casket of Indris. As he got closer, the more he remembered the life of Indris, from the day he was born to the last day they spoke to each other.

He stared at the stillness of Indris's cold body, ears dropping to the face of Indris. "My boy . . . my beautiful boy. I was supposed to protect you and I failed . . . It's all my fault. I allow my ambition to blind me from my children. I will never knew how you felt." He started to cry, tears flowing down like a waterfall. "Please come back to me! I'm sorry that I failed you!" He looked up to Shenva. "Give me back my son," he begged softly.

He took a final look at Indris then leaned over and kissed the forehead. He stepped aside and waited for Maenellia to say her last word to Indris.

Maenellia stood and walked slowly to the casket, stumbling and limping as she tried to make her way, her stomach turning and her heart aching. All that played in her head was the same as Aerin. When she finally approached, she immediately broke down crying, her tears wetting the face of Indris. "Why!" she cried. "My dear boy! My lovely child! Why am I punished?" She let out a loud cry and wrapped her arms around the head of Indris. "I will always love you, Indris. From the stars and back. Till the day I die, I will always think of you." She turned to Aerin. "I want to be alone with my son!" she demanded.

Aerin agreed and left the temple to allow Maenellia to have her last moment with Indris. As he walked out of the temple, the temple ground was filled with Kimsu clan members. The air felt strange. Aerin tried to look far but was blocked by fog. Then the rain began to fall. People began to look for cover to avoid getting wet. Standing beside Aerin was Akin and Jen-Song on the other side.

Aerin sniffed to stop his crying. "We should prepare to leave," said Aerin.

Akin felt strange about the fog, noticing that it was getting closer and stronger. "Brother, doesn't this fog look strange?" wondered Akin.

"It's just fog," replied Aerin. Aerin also felt weird about the fog. He looked up to the sky and saw seven gray death birds flying over. "Where are my children?" he urgently asked Akin.

"They're at the temple pond," replied Akin.

"Akin, go check on them," ordered Aerin.

Akin nodded, seeing the worry on Aerin's face. He quickly rushed to the back of the temple. Then suddenly, an arrow flew by and hit one of the Kimsu guards in the neck, scaring everyone. Then more arrows rained down and randomly hit either the guards or the clan members, leading to yelling and scrambling.

Then behind the fog, men wearing white armor with the sigil of a blue dahlia on the right shoulder plate rode into the temple with their swords and spears drawn out, slicing and cutting the guards and Kimsu members.

"It's an ambush!" yelled Aerin. He had no weapon on him. Immediately, his hand was submerged with black flames. "Akin, go tend to my kids."

The fog blocked the view of everyone. Aerin could no longer see his guards, clan members, and Jen-Song, trying to figure who would come and attack him, also trying to battle the rain. He fired black flames around him, but each time he fired, the fog just closed. He felt alone in the dark in the fog, listening to the cry and yelling of his clan members. Suddenly, an arrow hit him in the back of the knee, dropping him to one knee. "Cowards! You attack me during my son's funeral!" he mocked angrily.

* * *

Kiri was holding the hands of Isa, trying to see through the fog. She had blue flames dancing in the palm of her hand. Yet it still didn't help her. She held on to Isa's hand tightly, hoping to not lose him. But the rain kept loosening her grip. Hearing the yell of agony around her and the swing of swords, she had no clue to what was going on but knew she had to get out of the fog.

She was standing at the pond with her siblings. Nellina was beside them, and all of a sudden, an arrow came out of nowhere and hit Nellina in the eye. She dropped into the pond, instantly killing her.

Kiri then immediately grabbed Isa's hand and started to run.

"Stay with me, Isa!" she tried to console a fearful Isa.

Isa didn't say anything back to her.

"Say something, Isa," she urged then turned around to see how afraid Isa was. She turned back and continued walking, forcefully pulling Isa, disturbed by the yelling and slashing of swords. "Don't worry, Isa. We'll get out of here."

Suddenly, a crow flew in front of her. She was startled by the crow and had no clue where it came from. The crow wanted her to follow it, so she followed. As she followed, the yells became more distant and the fog became weaker. As she reached the end of the fog, she could see at least five dead soldiers wearing gray armor with a black mamba sigil on the right shoulder plate.

To her surprise, she was greeted by an old lady with Lehue lying by her side. It was the same old lady that spoke with Kunjae. As her first response, Kiri let go of Isa's hand and shot up blue flames in her hand. She quickly charged forward to the old lady, screaming from the top of her lungs in a fit of rage, expecting that the old lady had killed Lehue. The old lady stepped aside and tripped Kiri to the ground then placing her foot on the back of Kiri. Kiri tried to push up but felt something pulling her down.

The old lady turned to Isa with a gentle smile. "Are you going to do something, Isa?" she asked Isa.

Isa stood in fear, not knowing what to do, feeling like a coward for not saving his sister. Then he looked at Lehue's body, who was lying on the ground by Kiri, thinking he was dead but seeing that he was still breathing.

"Leave him alone!" warned Kiri.

"You have a lot of confident, Kiri." The old lady was appalled.

Kiri turned to Lehue and noticed that he was still breathing. "What have you done to my brother!" demanded Kiri.

"Don't worry about him. He's in a sleeping spell," answered the old lady. "It's best we stop talking and leave this forest at once."

. "You expect me to follow you? I don't believe that an old lady like you can kill all these soldiers," argued Kiri.

The old lady sighed in disappointment. "I guess you must sleep," she said then snapped her fingers.

All of a sudden, Kiri felt tired. Every part of her body became numb. She looked at Lehue lying beside her, and her vision became blurry. She tried to fight, but her brain told her to sleep. Slowly, she went into a slumber, fading away from the chaos.

"Now, Isa," said the old lady. "Are you going to listen to me?"

Isa stood in silence and fear, his body trembling by the sight of seeing his siblings on the ground, expecting that he would be next to go. He wanted to let out a loud cry but couldn't, feeling like he was drowning in a river, the water filling his throat and sinking him to the ground.

The old lady smiled. "Don't worry, Isa. I won't kill you," promised the old lady. She turned to leave and pointed her finger in the air. Both Lehue and Kiri floated. "We should get going, Isa. Our journey will be long." She started walking away from the fog.

Isa felt like a coward. He wished he had some kind of confidence to fight the old lady. Instead, all he could do was stare with a dumbfounded look. His body moved by itself, following the lady, preparing for an unknown journey with an old lady that he didn't know, but yet who seemed to know him.

"Isa, my name is Old Lady Prey," introduced the old lady with a smile.

* * *

Back inside the fog, Kunjae was fighting riders off their horse by blasting blue flames to their face, staying close to Airian and Mani as much as possible, blocking the slamming of the rain so he could listen to the stomping of the horse to see if the enemy was near. Both of his hands were submerged with blue flames. Another rider came by, and he blasted the flames at the rider.

Airian had one hand submerged in blue flames and the other hand holding Mani's hand, hindered by only one eye. Both Airian and Mani were afraid, not knowing what was going on. Only Kunjae remained calm, trying to protect his older siblings.

The sound of people yelling and echoing the forest haunted them. They could hear the horror coming from their voices—children crying then stopping after the sound of a blade, mothers calling for their children, and fathers begging for mercy.

"What's going on?" asked a confused Airian.

"Shut your mouth, Airian," said Kunjae. "Just protect Mani."

Then suddenly, Kunjae could hear his uncle calling for him. He yelled back, hoping his uncle could find them. He could see the fog opening for a second by a blast of black flames then closing immediately. They knew right away that it was his uncle.

All three called for Akin, hoping he could follow the sound of their voices. At the same time, Kunjae was shooting blue flames at the fog and at the riders riding by.

"Airian, fire at the fog," ordered Kunjae.

Airian began to fire at the fog, not knowing why Kunjae wanted him to.

Mani opened her palm and started to fire blue flames as well, but she was not as strong as Airian and Kunjae. She kept on trying, hoping they could get out of the fog.

"Keep firing, he'll see us," said Kunjae as he continued to knock riders down.

Kunjae tried to look around for his uncle's flames but couldn't see it anymore. He yelled out for his uncle to no response. Then he thought the worst had happened to Akin. He felt tears dropping from his eyes and sense his uncle no longer with them. "Stop," said Kunjae lowly, the flames on his hands disappearing.

"Why?" questioned Airian.

"He's gone," replied Kunjae.

"What! How do you know?" demanded Airian.

"He's gone," repeated Kunjae then falling to his knees.

Then a giant blast of blue flames came from the temple, exploding it and clearing all the fog in the forest. Slowly, the horror of the scene showed itself, the mayhem it uncovered. There were dead bodies all over the temple ground—monks, children, men, and women alike, all lying dead and wasted on the ground. Some were without heads and some with guts spilling out. There were arrows on the ground and arrows penetrated into people. The autumn leaves were drenched in blood. The air smelled metallic.

Mani quickly vomited after seeing the dead bodies around her. Then the ground began to be covered in white ashes coming from the sky. Mani's eyes widened, recalling her nightmare of her family having died in a forest of snow.

Airian couldn't blink, stunned by the scene of hell. As the fog continued to clear, Kunjae noticed soldiers wearing white armors with a blue dahlia sigil on the right shoulder plate. There were some lying next to him dead.

He looked over to the ground about forty feet from him and spotted the body of Akin with four arrows to his back. Then looking to the temple, he saw the burning of blue flames lighting the forest. His mother had sacrificed herself, sending herself to heaven with Indris.

From a distance, he saw Aerin on both of his knees with Jen-Song standing before him with a moon lion dagger in hand. Aerin had an arrow sticking from the back of his knee and his hand over his stomach. Kunjae turned to Airian and Mani. With sad eyes, they saw what he saw. Then he noticed a passage for them to escape through a damaged opening on the temple walls. "We have to leave," said Kunjae. "We must go south. Our home is no more." He started running without looking back, hurt by the end result of their clan massacre.

Airian took a deep breath, looking at his uncle's body and the burning temple then to Aerin. Again, he was afraid and helpless. He held Mani's hands tightly and forced her to run with him, trailing behind Kunjae.

Mani was in a state of shock. She had never seen so many dead bodies before, the blood and carnage around her now embedded within her. She felt her legs moving by themselves, running with Airian and away from the massacre.

The three siblings disappeared into the forest, not knowing what happened to the younger siblings, their minds now tainted with the image of death. The lives of the innocent were gone. All they knew was to go south and find shelter under the Ma clan or find Ausra and Sukro.

* * *

Jen-Song looked down at Aerin with no emotion in his eyes, the moon lion dagger in his hand dripping with blood.

Aerin had a smile on his face while holding his stomach as blood leaked from it, not expecting Jen-Song to be the traitor. The man Iszra called best friend, the man he saw most loyal to him, snuck behind his back and sided with the Cai clan.

"This is it, Jen-Song?" asked Aerin.

"Yes, Aerin," replied Jen-Song.

Aerin chuckled. "Tell me, what have I done wrong?"

"Nothing. My belief is different from yours," replied Jen-Song.

"Ah, did you do something to Borin? I tried calling for her."

"I paralyze it with the moon lion dagger."

"I guess you stopped running with the demon," said Aerin, feeling his heartbeat slowing down.

Then two men approached Aerin. He looked up to try to get a good look at them and realized they were the two young princes, Lucid and Envio. "Of course. The princes of the east will be the ones to take down the demon of the east," said Aerin, accepting his defeat.

"Aerin Kimsu, you have committed treason. Your clan has become an enemy to the kingdom—"

"Enough talking. Take my life already," Aerin interrupted Lucid.

"Very well then," said Lucid, unsheathing his sword then holding the sword by Aerin's neck.

"Your daughter Chenpu has been taken prisoner by Benyae Smok. The city of Mersane is no more. All the people that follow you are no more. Any last word, demon?" asked Lucid.

Aerin smiled. "I see that the Smok boy is now his clan head. And here I thought giving his cousin the title was a good idea. I guess she couldn't handle the pressure." He then looked Lucid in the eye with a cold and fearless stare. "The Kimsu still lives. My children still live. The Silent Demon, Ausra Kimsu, still lives." He laughed.

Lucid pulled his sword back and quickly stabbed Aerin in the throat, ending the life of the Black Heart Demon. Aerin fell face-first to the ground, his ambition now over, but his children still lived on. But the day of the Kimsu Massacre would be masked by the kingdom of Telamis.

Lucid looked over to Jen-Song. "Should we be worried about Ausra."

Jen-Song kept his eyes on Aerin's body. "Iszra," he mumbled lowly.

Chapter Twenty-Two

Kingdom of Summan

"My king, I have failed you," said Thunder as he stood in the throne room of the Summer Palace before Giovanis. "The bandits had defeated us again. They are growing stronger by the day." He bowed, looking to the ground with a shameful look.

Beside Thunder was Eddis, also with the same look as Thunder. "My king, I believe the bandits have trapped us in our own walls."

Giovanis rubbed his finger on his forehead to relieve the thumping in his head, bothered that every day he was met with a challenge. All he wanted was a day where he could relax and have time to himself. He missed reading books and visiting the city library. He missed painting and visiting the city museum. Ever since becoming king, he hadn't been able to do the hobbies he once loved doing.

"My king, I think it's best we call for the Ma clan," suggested Dada. "The people of the city are starving. I'm getting letters from the lords of nearby villages, and they're starving too. We need to act quickly before everything falls apart." He spoke for the southern people.

"I agree with Lord Dada," agreed Seris. "Our economy is declining. We need a safe passage for the merchants and farmers."

Giovanis wanted to pull his hair out. He hadn't stepped foot outside the palace for a while. He felt like he was being dragged by the same rope as his father, which would lead him to failure. He wanted his small council to stop talking. Every word that came out of their mouths came with bad news.

"My king, if the other kingdoms see that we're struggling, they'll take advantage of us. If the other southern clans see us struggle, they'll rebel. If nothing is done, then we'll be heading into civil war like the north," warned Bente with a smirk as he bowed then peeking to Ocrist and hoping a venomous snake would bite him.

"What should I do?" questioned Giovanis calmly. "Our army has become weak. I'm trapped in my own palace." He looked at each of his council members. "What should I do? I never asked to be king. I never asked to have all this madness to be placed upon me. I never wanted this uncomfortable chair. Yet it is handed to me. What am I supposed to do?" He sighed. "You're all supposed to be advising me, but only come me to with complaints with no suggestions to fix the issues." He looked to Thunder. "Commander Thunder, what has gotten into you? You're the greatest magic user in the southern kingdom. Yet you're struggling against bandits. Do I need a new commander? Someone that can handle weak bandits?"

"I'm sorry, my king." Thunder bowed in disappointment and embarrassment.

"Don't apologize to me. Apologize to the people for your failure. I order you to apologize to every single person that lives in this city. Go knock doors if you must. Show them it's your fault that they're starving," ordered Giovanis with ruthless eyes. "Get out of my face." He dismissed Thunder.

Thunder bowed and left the room without giving Giovanis a look back, embarrassed and irked by Giovanis. He had been serving the Sanila clan for decades and shown them the respect they deserved. He was loyal to them and never thought ill of them. But Giovanis made him angry. He wanted to run to the throne and take Giovanis off it by his throat and slam him to the ground.

Eddis gave Ocrist a concerned look and bowed to Giovanis then followed after Thunder. The other council members were shocked and confused by Giovanis's sudden change in demeanor.

Bente had a vile grin across his face, sensing a downfall brewing in the palace. He then again looked over to Ocrist, only seeing a man that resembled a wall.

Ocrist could see that Giovanis was distressed and incapable of ruling the kingdom. In his own head, he was plotting a plan to find a better ruler for the south. The person he saw suited for the throne was Benavis who had elected to skip the meeting. When Giovanis sat on the throne, all he saw was another Geolana. Weakness in a king only brings downfall to the kingdom. He was thinking of the future not just for the south, but for all of Telamis, afraid that the unknown storm of horror was coming.

"Now all of you," said Giovanis. "How about you advise and help me rule this kingdom? No more complaining."

"With all due respect, my king. What we say is not complaints. It's reports you must decide on," said Seris.

"So you're useless to me?" Giovanis questioned Seris mockingly.

"If that's what you believe, my king." Seris bowed calmly.

"Lord Seris, I have a great deal of respect for you. I looked up to you at one point. But I didn't know that you were useless. All you do is worry about your coins. Is that what you are, a selfish man who cares about his riches?" Giovanis asked Seris.

Seris felt disrespected but kept the same expression. "I don't worry about my own riches, my king. I worry for your riches. If you want to know the truth, then I will tell you." He looked up, and his eyes finally opened, showing a serious cold man's eyes. "In truth, the southern kingdom is falling apart. We're not going to make it to the summer festival. I sneaked behind your back and even tried to ask for loans from the other clans. But they all refused." Seris turned to Dada. "I know you know, Lord Dada. The south will become the north very soon."

Dada shot an angry look at Seris, but couldn't denied Seris's claim since he was the voice of the people of the south. He knew how they felt and what they thought. Ever since Geolana took the throne, the people had been distressed yet everything was kept hidden from the Sanila clan. No one believed in Geolana now; the same feeling was going toward his son.

"Ah, so you went behind my back, Lord Seris." Giovanis was disappointed. "I respect you still so I wouldn't jail you. But you will still be punished for your crime." He gave Seris a hard stare. "You have five daughters. Am I correct?"

Seris nodded in return calmly.

"Each of them will be married off to keep the alliance with the clans of the south. I heard your fourth daughter is the prettiest of them. I want her to be married to my brother."

"I accept the punishment, my king." He bowed and walked out of the room.

Giovanis then turned his attention to Dada, who in return stood straight, waiting for his punishment. "Lord Dada, I'm disappointed that you knew the morale of the people but failed to tell me. Now I have to stop the south from falling like the north. Are you a selfish man, Lord Dada?"

"No, my king. I am a man of the people. I serve for the people," replied Dada.

"You serve me first!" yelled Giovanis. "I am the king—get that through your thick skull."

"I'm sorry, my king," apologized Dada shamefully. "I knew that some of the people were whispering the idea of rebelling. However, the whispers have been happening since your father became king. But you, my king, can put the whispers to rest."

"Again, my father . . . my father was a good man. No one knew how much he cared for this kingdom. Yet they're quick to judge him because he's not my uncles. Now I'm riding the same scorn ship as him. They don't know how hard it is to be king. I sit on this uncomfortable throne and wear this tight crown every day. I wake up every morning already dreading my day. I tried my hardest, and yet no one cares. This throne is a curse."

"King Giovanis, being king comes with hardships. There will be times the people side with you and times they're against you," advised Ocrist, trying to calm Giovanis.

"They were always against me. Ever since I became king, I became their enemy." He looked to Dada. "Lord Dada, I still have to punish you. For your treason—"

"What treason!" argued Dada with a confused look over his face.

"You dare yell at me!" challenged Giovanis.

Dada looked down, trying to hold his rage.

"Your punishment must be severe. The people must know that I'm no king to challenge . . ." He took a while to think. Then an idea popped into his head. A punishment so severe that Dada may not survive. "Lord Dada, you will take the Trial of Pain," ordered Giovanis.

Dada's eyes opened wide, hoping that Giovanis was joking, confused why Giovanis would punish him in such a way. He was ready to fall to his knees and beg, afraid that his life would end. "My king, I'm no warrior or magic user. Please, I was only protecting your clan. There's no way I can do this trial. The result will end in my death."

Giovanis ignored Dada's plea. "If I'm correct, the Trail of Pain is in the name itself. I want you to suffer for treason. You must slay five spirit demons of my choice. You will go to the Forest of Despair and get me the head of a fox demon, wolf demon, monkey demon, hawk demon, and spawn of Chenva."

"My king, please! Think of mercy," pleaded Dada.

"Did you think of mercy when you let the people talk of rebelling?" questioned Giovanis angrily.

"It was only whispered, my king . . .," Dada continued to plead, falling to his knee and bowing to the ground. "Please, give a me thousand lashes if you must. Don't let me go into the Forest of Despair."

"Guards, drag this disgraceful man away. Give him his sword and leave him at the entrance of the forest," ordered Giovanis.

Two guards approached Dada and dragged him away as he screamed, begged, and wailed. Giovanis looked on with disdain on his face, seeing a man that was so prideful quickly changing into a coward. He didn't care about Dada and expected him to die in the forest.

"King Giovanis, I think the punishment was a little too harsh," disagreed Ocrist, clearly seeing Giovanis descending into madness. "Making a man with no skills take trial for warriors and magic users is not right."

"I'm not afraid to punish you too, Lord Ocrist," warned Giovanis. "I'm tired of my advisers pretending to be by my side. There's no one that I could trust in this kingdom but my siblings."

"Apologies, my king." Ocrist bowed.

"Lord Bente, you've been quiet." Giovanis noticed. "Are you not afraid to be punished?"

"I'm always by your side, my king," said Bente confidently.

Giovanis gave Bente a cold and detestable stare. "Do you take me for a fool, Bente?"

Bente was puzzled by the look on Giovanis's face and question. "What are you talking about, my king?" he questioned nervously.

"Just answer me, Bente."

"My king, I never take you for a fool. Why would you think that?"

Giovanis chuckled. "I'm just asking. There's no need for you to be nervous. How long have your ancestors been serving my clan?"

"Since the day your clan became rulers of the south, we have always been loyal."

Giovanis's lips twitched, his fingers tapping the armrest in annoyance. "Don't use that word 'loyal' so lightly, Bente."

"My king, is something wrong?" asked a confused Bente then turning to Ocrist who showed him a devilish smile. Right then, he knew he had lost to Ocrist. He turned back to Giovanis with guilt on his face, but at the same time, he was vexed.

"Bente, your family has been my clan's biggest ally. How come you want to break that bond?" Giovanis asked Bente.

"I'm still loyal, my king," claimed Bente.

"I'm not your king!" snapped Giovanis. "I know you've been acting behind my back, rat!"

"What did this man tell you?" Bente pointed to Ocrist. "He's the one siding against you. Not me."

"You sent horn heads to my clan temple to search for the Book of Shadows. You're trying to use my clan curse so you can have this throne!" exposed Giovanis.

Bente turned to Ocrist with rage in his eyes. "You dare act like you know nothing!" he questioned Ocrist angrily.

"I'm not the one that's sneaking around and trying to uncover the Sanila clan's truth," Ocrist denied calmly.

"Stop with your lies, Ocrist!" shot Bente.

"Enough!" ordered Giovanis. "Lord Ocrist warned me about you. He told me to keep the book safe from you. I wanted it to be a lie, but my spies found your horn heads at my clan temple, Bente. The book is no longer there."

Bente fell to his knees in failure, all his plans dispersed into thin air. The future to build his kingdom was falling apart before it even started. He did not know if Giovanis would send him to the jailhouse or have him executed where he stood. He wasn't an intellectual rival to Ocrist because Ocrist had easily taken him down.

"Bente, for your punishment, you will be banished from the kingdom. Your family will no longer serve my clan. If you're spotted in the south from the Desert of Fire to the Land of Beauty, you'll be executed."

"Where can I go?" Bente asked himself with defeat in his eyes.

"Go wherever you wish but the south. Be grateful that I didn't decide to have you executed, rat."

Giovanis signaled for the guards to take Bente away. Two guards approached Bente and helped him up then led him out of the throne room.

Ocrist bowed to Giovanis and followed the guards out. He walked behind the guards and Bente. When they walked out of the throne room and the giant stone door shut, he made his way in front of the guards and Bente.

Ocrist snapped his finger. The two guards were still. The guard in the hallway were all frozen. Bente looked around and tried to release himself from the hold of the guards, but it was too tight. Ocrist smiled, amused by Bente's struggle.

"There's no use, Bente," said Ocrist with a smile.

"Are you going to kill me?" questioned Bente.

"Of course not. There's no need for me to kill you," assured Ocrist. "I just need you out of the way. You were a rival of mine."

"What now?" asked Bente.

Ocrist reached into his pocket and pulled a sack full of flies. "This right here is all of your horn head servants." He showed Bente. "They are all under a paralyzed spell. Once I snap my finger, they will not be paralyzed anymore."

"What are you planning, Ocrist?"

"Never challenge the gods, Bente." Ocrist dropped the sack to the ground and snapped his finger. There was a sound of flies in the sack trying to escape, and quickly he stomped on the sack, killing all the horn heads that served Bente.

"You monster!" cried Bente.

Ocrist smiled. "Enjoy your life, my friend." Then he turned to leave and snapped his finger.

The guards became unfrozen but had no clue that they froze. Bente started to yell for Ocrist, repeatedly calling him a monster. Ocrist never turned around but had a sinful grin across his face. The Sanila clan and the southern kingdom was in his hand. His plan for the great king was coming near.

* * *

"Do you ever stop talking?" annoyedly Benavis asked to Moon as they walked the halls of the summer palace.

All morning, Moon couldn't stop talking. Slowly, it was making itself comfortable around him. At night, it didn't sleep, floating above Benavis and enjoying itself. Moon was like a fly that didn't know when to give up.

"But I'm bored," complained Moon, floating inside the walls.

"I don't care."

"Can we do something fun? Let's go see that dump again," suggested Moon.

"What dump?" asked Benavis.

"The place where I kill that man for you," reminded Moon.

Benavis stopped walking to recall the moment a man died before him. It still haunted him, but each day, the memory faded away. For the past days, he had been sleeping well even though Moon was an annoyance. He had come to accept Moon's presence. When he woke in the morning and ate his breakfast with his sister and brother, he felt strange but happy. Giovanis seemed to be falling apart mentally but was still hiding his distress with a smile. The day started off normal as it should be for him. Yet he expected that his normal day was only a lie, staying alert for the unexpected to come.

"Enough about that day." Benavis wanted to forget the day he was almost stabbed to death.

"Are you afraid?" questioned Moon. "I think I deserve a thank you."

"You talk too much. Do you ever keep your mouth shut?" asked Benavis.

"I'll keep quiet if I do something fun," replied Moon.

"Leave me alone."

"I can't."

Benavis grunted and continued to walk quickly, not knowing where to go.

Giovanis asked him if he wanted to join in on the meeting at the throne room. But he refused the offer, not wanting to sit and listen to men complaining amongst each other. The advisers needed to be contained, something he noticed Giovanis couldn't do.

He and Moon made their way to the courtyard, Moon still babbling about his boredom. Benavis tried his best to ignore Moon but couldn't. Moon irked him in so many ways. He felt that Moon knew that it was being a nuisance to him and continued its behavior to annoy him.

They finally arrived at the courtyard. Benavis made his way to the bench around the Tree of Sanila to sit, leaning his back against the cool tree and shutting his eyes.

Moon floated inside the tree to avoid the sunlight then sticking its head out beside Benavis. "This is boring," complained Moon.

"I don't care."

"I'm starting to not like you," said Moon, sticking its head back into the tree.

Benavis shut his eyes and tried to listen to the birds chirping from the tree branch. He felt still, listening to the singing of the bird, a feeling he hadn't felt in a while. But living in a world full of darkness and sin made calmness a privilege.

"He's coming?" whispered Moon.

Benavis opened his eyes and returned to reality, seeing Ocrist approaching him with a smile. He wasn't in the mood to see anybody. He wanted to be alone and unbothered. He was bothered and annoyed by the false smiles around him. If everyone just said their truth to him, he would be fine.

"Afternoon, my prince," greeted Ocrist with a gentle head bow.

"Lord Ocrist," Benavis greeted back.

"May I sit?" Ocrist asked politely.

Benavis just shrugged his shoulders; he didn't care if Ocrist wanted to sit or not. Personally, he wanted Ocrist to stop acting polite. He was feeling wary and distrustful toward Ocrist after he admitted to unlocking the shadow in him, having a feeling that he was hiding something and knew more than what he told.

Whenever Ocrist came close to him, Moon would become agitated and wanting to harm him.

"It's a lovely day today," said Ocrist. "Right, Moon?"

Moon poked its head out of the tree between Ocrist and Benavis. "I hate that yellow thing in the sky," said Moon then poking its head back into the tree.

Ocrist just showed a smile in response. "Prince Benavis, do you wish to be king?" he asked suddenly.

Benavis was hit by the question. After standing in the throne room alone with Moon, he pictured himself as king of the south, but hadn't told anybody of his guilty pleasure. "No, why do you ask?" lied Benavis curiously.

"The south is changing, Prince Benavis." Ocrist sighed. "It was smart of you to not attend the meeting. A lot happened. I'm afraid King Giovanis is losing hope."

"What happened?" asked a concerned Benavis.

"He has given up on his advisers. I sense the darkness looming over the south soon."

"My brother is trying his hardest to be king. All his advisers do is complain," Benavis defended Giovanis.

"I agree. He's trying his best, but his best is not enough." Ocrist placed his hand on Benavis's shoulders. "My prince, I know that you want to be king. Your eyes were filled with hunger when you stared at the throne. I believe that you're better fit as a king than your brother."

Benavis slapped Ocrist's hands away and jumped from his seat. Moon floated out of the tree and stood under the protection of the leaves.

Benavis was caught off guard by Ocrist, wanting to know how Ocrist figured that he pictured himself as king.

"Shall we kill him?" asked Moon as shadow daggers appeared in all six hands.

Ocrist stood up with an unbothered smile, acting unafraid of Moon's threat. "Kill me if you want, Moon. But know that I fear nothing but the gods." He then turned to Benavis. "Everybody wants to be king. From beggars to wealthy bankers, they all dream of ruling and sitting on the throne. But not all possessed the mind of a king. But you, Benavis, you have the king in you."

"What are you talking about?" Benavis demanded answers from Ocrist.

"What I want is the south to survive, Prince Benavis. King Giovanis's heart is too kind and weak. He doesn't carry the heart of a king like you. Kindness can hinder the ability to rule. The same problem your father had."

"Don't talk about my father," warned Benavis, debating if he should let Moon have his way with Ocrist.

"I want to let you on a secret, Prince Benavis." Ocrist's smile turned evil. "In this world, we honor the heroes and hate the villains. We are blind to honor and heroism. Sometimes the villains are the hero and the hero is the villain trying to end the world. The villains are always the victim of injustice. Your clan is an example of a villain masked as a hero, Prince Benavis. Look at the immense power you have. That shadow is a curse, but yet it is a gift."

"Enough . . . please stop talking," begged Benavis with a distraught look over his face. He turned to Moon and back to Ocrist. "Don't talk anymore or I'll have you killed."

"Ah, I'm going to make you king, Prince Benavis. The one that possesses the shadow shall sit on the throne."

"Moon, . . . kill him!" ordered Benavis to Moon.

The clouds in the sky blocked the sun momentarily. Moon flew to Ocrist with a dagger pointing out. Ocrist just simply stood still; then as Moon neared, he lifted his arm and opened his hand, creating a portal where Moon flew into. He quickly closed the portal up.

"I can't be killed until the task is done, Prince Benavis."

Benavis couldn't feel the presence of Moon anymore. He was baffled by how easily Moon was defeated by Ocrist, a part of him of wanting Moon back by his side while the other part glad that Moon was gone. But Ocrist still stood before him. "What have you done to Moon?" he asked with fear in his voice.

"I put him in a trap until you understand your destiny, Prince Benavis."

"You're the villain, Ocrist," accused Benavis.

"Correct, I am the villain. I have no shame to admit it." He smiled. "I want to let you on another secret. That morning outside the city walls, when you witnessed the death of your father, I was there too. I saw the pain and fear in our former king's eyes."

Benavis felt like his body was struck by lightning, every nerve in his body trembling. His eyes were wide with confusion and fear. He was standing before the man that killed his father. The only crow that flew back to the city. He felt like he was being suffocated, his chest hurting and beating rapidly, the thoughts in his head all speaking at once.

"We killed King Geolana," admitted Ocrist with no sense of sympathy. "We killed your uncles because they possessed in them a weak king."

Benavis heard enough; his body moved by itself and charged toward Ocrist without thinking. Ocrist lifted his arm up and opened his hand. As Benavis neared, his palm hit the chest of Benavis, dropping him to the ground like he had no bones in his body. But pushing out of the body was Benavis's soul.

Benavis was taken aback, realizing that he could float. He looked to the ground at his slump body. Then looking at his hand, he realized that he could see through them. Not understanding the situation, he thought Ocrist had killed him, wondering if death was supposed to feel empty.

"You're not dead, Prince Benavis," assured Ocrist then opening a portal below the body of Benavis and letting it drop into it. "I simply just took your soul out of the body."

"What are you going to do to me, monster!" angered Benavis. "You will pay for your part in killing my uncles and father!"

Ocrist just smiled. "I'm going to show you the reality of this world, Prince Benavis. Something that your father, brother, and uncles all lacked. I accepted that I am the villain. But I am the villain for the good."

"Don't make yourself the victim, monster!" said Benavis with more rage in his tone.

"Follow me, Prince Benavis." Ocrist turned into a crow and flew up.

Benavis started flying up too. He looked around, baffled as he followed Ocrist to the sky. He looked down and saw the palace from the sky, fascinated by the beauty of it, living in the palace his whole life. He never took the time to admire its beauty. Then looking forward to the city, he was astounded by the view from above. He could see everything from the sky, from the entrance gate of the city to the city center. The people all resembled ants below him. There were some people on clouds floating in the sky. He was much higher than them, feeling like he was on top of the world, forgetting for a moment that he was following Ocrist.

They landed on the rooftop of a shop. Ocrist turned back into himself, and they walked to the edge. Benavis was trying to figure out what Ocrist was trying to show him. When he looked over, he could see a crowd of people all trying to get by each other. The street was tight. People were breathing onto one another. There were vendors set up on the side. The chatter and yelling bounced off the walls of the clay buildings.

"What is this?" asked Benavis.

"Look, see that man?" Ocrist pointed to a man wearing ripped ragged clothing, dirt smudged all over his face. "Watch that man."

"Why should I?" asked Benavis.

Ocrist ignored Benavis and focused on the man.

Benavis grunted and watched the man also. The man had a mischievous look on his face, trying to get by the crowd of people. But his eyes were focused on the waist of the people he passed and pushed by. He walked by an old man and took a pouch hanging from the old man's waist then walked away as if nothing had happened.

"He's a theft!" yelled Benavis, not knowing that he couldn't be heard.

Ocrist turned back into a crow, and they continued to follow the man. The man made his way to the stand and used the old man's coins he had stolen and bought himself seven fried pork sandwiches and left. They continued to follow the man to the Ground, who had turned to the long tight alleyway where there were people of all ages sleeping on the dirty, wet ground.

He finally stopped walking and stopped by a woman with five children. Both Benavis and Ocrist stopped on the roof and looked below. This time, Ocrist stayed in crow form. They watched as the man handed five pork sandwiches to the young children and one to the woman. They all sat around and ate it gracefully as a family.

Benavis's heart sank, seeing the man trying to feed his family. "Why are you showing me this?" asked Benavis with tears gently falling from his eyes.

Ocrist ignored him, and they flew away from the family to let them enjoy their meal.

Flying over the Ground, Benavis couldn't bear to look at the people below, heartbroken on how much they were suffering. There were dead bodies on the streets. There were the sick lying on the dirt ground waiting to be healed. He didn't understand how his own clan could forget about these people.

They returned to the palace and back to the courtyard. The time back, all Benavis could think about was the thief and his family. Even though he had committed a crime and stolen from an old man, he did it for the sake of his family so they could survive for the next day. He saw the smiles on their faces as they ate their food that was just a mere sandwich that wouldn't keep them full for the entire day.

Ocrist opened a portal and floated out Benavis's body. The body of Benavis floated up, and a spirit string coming out of the body connected to his soul and dragged it back in.

Benavis was back in his body, trying to figure out Ocrist's thinking. "Why?" he asked.

"I serve the gods. Our purpose in this world is to defend Telamis from true evil. True evil is coming, Prince Benavis. Your father and uncles were not the kings to rule when evil comes. They don't see the reality of this world like you did. Your brother included." He walked over to Benavis, gently placing his hand on his shoulder. "You saw the reality of this world. You saw your father killed before your eyes, taking your mind into a dark place; but out of your own power, you fought out of it. You were almost killed by a man and saw him die before you by your gift." He took his hand off Benavis's shoulder and sighed. "That man we saw. He was a former guard that was supposed to keep guard of the gates when you and King Geolana sneaked out of the city. For his failure, your brother had to chose to execute him or let him go free. Instead, your brother chose to make this man suffer and turn him into a villain. That man should've been executed instead of walking this world with shame. His family shouldn't suffer because of his failure."

"It was my fault that he lost everything," said a shocked Benavis.

"It's life, Prince Benavis. If you want to change everything, then you must be the one to sit on the throne."

Benavis looked Ocrist in the eyes with a hint of madness in them. "I'm nothing like my father. I am nothing like my brother. It's true . . . I do want to be king. I want to sit on that throne and change the south. But I don't want my brother dead." He clenched his hands into fists. "Ocrist, you will pay for your crime. Your head will sit on a spike in front of the gates of the palace."

Ocrist bowed his head with a smile. "I'll accept my punishment, Prince Benavis. But after you become king." He opened another portal, and it spit out Moon under the tree.

"You will die!" said Moon angrily, lifting his shadow dagger up.

Benavis raised his arms in front of Moon. "Stop, Moon," he ordered. "You will kill him soon." He looked up to Moon. "If we want to become king, he'll help us." Benavis turned around and left.

"You're a lucky man, bald rat!" insulted Moon then he turned around and followed Benavis.

Ocrist watched as the two left him alone in the courtyard. He had a vile smile over his face. He had received a letter from two other members of the God's Hands, reporting that they had finished with their task. There were six members of the God's Hands. Each member was assigned a task to find six greats, which was the great king, the great queen, the great warrior, the great magic, the great darkness, and the strongest of all, the great light. The great magic and the great darkness had been found.

With a wide grin, Ocrist believed he had found the great king in Benavis.

* * *

Still in the afternoon in Sentra, the streets were still full. People were dissatisfied with the direction of the kingdom, some people spreading rumors about Giovanis, saying that he had let power get to his head. Even some of the soldiers didn't believe in Giovanis. They were getting anxious and bitter waiting for Giovanis to feed them. The rich didn't want to be treated like the poor and believed that they deserved to have food first, some fearing that soon the city of Sentra would only have the poor roaming the streets.

Back at their house near the city center was Rain, Yorsenga, and Uesenga. They were fortunate enough to buy a house and live together because of their grandfather. Even though they were no longer a clan under their own banner, Anzoren still managed to have enough money to be considered wealthy.

Yorsenga was sitting at the head of the table with his feet up, leaning back on his chair. Uesenga had his shirt off and was wiping the sweat from his body with a cloth after training in the backyard.

The twelfth day had come. Still, Rain was battling with himself with Janellis's offer. On one side, he wanted to meet Janellis at her clan's crypt while the others reminded him of the hatred toward her clan. For the last few days, he barely saw Janellis, wondering if she had locked herself in her chamber. Some days he wished to see her when he cut the corner in the palace hallways.

"Rain, you look stupid," insulted Yorsenga, leaning forward with his feet still on the table. "Why do you have a book in front of you but staring into thin air?"

"You have been thinking a lot," noticed Uesenga.

Rain shook himself from his thinking and showed his usual straight look. "The both of you should stay quiet," he warned them.

"There's the Rain I know," said Uesenga with a grin.

"Why do you train every day?" Yorsenga asked Uesenga.

"I take pride in becoming the greatest warrior, and I want to restore our clan name," replied Uesenga.

"Stupid . . . but I envy your confidence," said Yorsenga then leaned back on his chair.

"Do you not care about our clan?" Uesenga asked Yorsenga.

"Why should I? If Grandpa doesn't care, then I don't care," replied Yorsenga.

"What do you care about, Yorsenga?" Rain asked Yorsenga.

"Nothing. Maybe sleeping," answered Yorsenga.

"If you want to be useless, then why didn't you tell Grandpa?" Uesenga asked Yorsenga.

Yorsenga leaned forward on his chair. "If I could I would, but Grandpa told me I must honor my father."

"Do you not want to honor your father?" Rain asked Yorsenga.

"Why should I? He lost in battle. You know the saying, 'A Bu shall never die on the battlefield.'"

"My father died alongside him. They never died on the battlefield. They surrendered for the sake of their comrades," argued Uesenga.

"You're going to ask me questions and get angry at my response. Then why ask me questions? Do you think they're telling stories of our father surrendering for the sake of their comrades? They're telling stories of how cowardly they were to give up in battle and have their life tortured and killed," said Yorsenga calmly.

The door flew opened with Ba-Ben entering the house with a loud laugh. He had a fresh coconut drink in his hand and on the other hand a beef stick. "You wouldn't believe who I saw apologizing to everyone on the streets!" He laughed.

"Ba-Ben, shut your mouth," annoyedly said Yorsenga.

"Fine, but do you all want to laugh?" Ba-Ben asked his cousins.

"Tell us," replied Uesenga, wanting to know what was making Ba-Ben laugh so loudly.

"It's Commander Thunder. He's apologizing to all the people in the city, knocking door to door. How pitiful is that? He's being forced to look like a fool!" Ba-Ben laughed again.

His cousin didn't laugh along with him, thinking that someone like Thunder shouldn't apologize to anyone. Even though Thunder was hard on them, he was still a great man with many great feats. What he did for the Sanila clan and southern kingdom could never be matched.

"Ba-Ben, stop laughing," said Uesenga with a stern look.

"Why should I? All that man does is yell at us. He thinks he's better than us," argued Ba-Ben.

"Even though he yells at us, he's a man that deserves all the respect in the world," defended Uesenga.

Ba-Ben downed his drink and threw the wooden cup to the ground, showing disrespect to his cousins. "You know, I hate it when you guys disrespect me. Who made you the leader, Uesenga?" he expressed.

"If we don't stop you, then you'll act like a fool and ruin our clan name," answered Uesenga strictly. "I want to build our clan back, and all you want to do is taint our clan name."

"Taint? I'm tainting our clan name? It's not me tainting the clan name. It's the filthy royal clan that ruins our clan name. If I see that princess again, I'll make sure I put a child in her. Then I'll taint their clan name."

"Enough!" yelled Rain, bothered when he heard Ba-Ben mention Janellis. "If you dare to go near her, you'll die," he warned Ba-Ben.

"What? Do you love her?" mocked Ba-Ben.

"O-of course not. I know my place. They will kill you if you touch her," warned Rain.

"I have enough of you guys. I'm heading to the tavern." Ba-Ben turned to leave and out the door he went with all the rage in his head, hoping the taste of ale could ease his mind.

"Drinking won't solve anything!" Uesenga yelled out to Ba-Ben. He turned to Yorsenga. "Why are you silent? You're supposed to be the oldest."

Yorsenga leaned back on his chair and shut his eyes, acting if nothing had happened. "I'm not his father."

Uesenga stormed out of the room and headed up the stairs to his room. Rain stood and headed to the hallway to his room, leaving Yorsenga alone in the dining room. He heard the upstairs room door slam shut, followed by the one in the hallway.

"Grandpa, why did you leave me these idiots?" he mumbled to himself then he fell asleep.

Rain waited for night to fall lying on his bed and staring at the ceiling. Ba-Ben still hadn't returned from the tavern. Uesenga was at the backyard training, and he thought Yorsenga was in his room upstairs sleeping. He was daydreaming about his mother and father. How life was so simple when the both of them were around.

He got out of bed and grabbed his cloak on the chair, putting the cloak on as he left the room. The house was dark, but he knew his way around. All he had to do was walk the hallway and past the dining room and out the front door. Going through the back would lead him to Uesenga training in the backyard.

He didn't care to sneak his way through. But when he got to the dining room, a chair's legs hit the ground. He turned to look over and was surprised to see Yorsenga still sitting in the dining room. In front of him was a jar full of fireflies. "Yorsenga?" Rain was startled.

"You leaving?" asked Yorsenga out of nowhere.

"Leaving?" Rain wondered if Yorsenga knew.

Yorsenga sighed. "You're a fool, Rain. They will hunt you down," he warned. "But I'm not going to stop you." He leaned back on his chair and crossed his arms to fall back asleep.

"Should I stay?" asked Rain.

"Go," replied Yorsenga. "Escape through the back of the palace."

Rain smiled and bowed to Yorsenga, walking out of the door.

Yorsenga opened his eyes and stared at the ceiling. "Father, when will it be my turn?" he asked himself.

*   *   *

Janellis stood before her parents' statues in her clan's crypt, looking back to see if Rain was behind her. In her hand was her wooden flute. She turned back to her parents' statues and tried to shed a tear, but couldn't.

"Mother, Father. I'll be leaving now. I won't able to come visit anymore. But I promise to keep both of you in my memories. Maybe one day I will shed a tear for the both of you. Don't worry about me, I don't need the two of you to watch over me. But please keep Giovanis and Benavis safe. I'll make sure to take care of myself."

She lifted the flute to her lips and began to play, her eyes shut and imagining the story of the song in her head. She played one final song to her parents, a song called "The Princess and Her Warrior." The story was of a warrior that fell in love with a princess. The ending was met with the death of both of them by the hand of the man who was supposed to marry the princess.

When she finally stopped playing, she moved the flute away from her lips, slowly opening her eyes, showing a single teardrop falling from her left eye. When she played her flute, it felt like she was floating on a bed of white roses. Flying around her were two spirit dragons that danced to her music around her. She wiped the tear from her eyes and bowed to her parents' statues.

"Your playing is beautiful," complimented Rain.

Janellis turned around quickly and was glad that Rain would accompany her in her adventure. "So you have decided," she said with a smile.

"I want to know what freedom is. I can't continue living my father's burden," admitted Rain.

"We should get going." She walked by Rain.

Rain followed her, wondering what she was thinking. "Where will we be heading to?" he asked.

Janellis stopped and took a while to answer. "I do not know. We'll trust the stars to guide us in our travels."

* * *

That night, all was silent in the palace. The guards were getting tired, some nearly falling asleep at their posts. Sitting on the golden throne was Benavis, staring at the giant door. With light coming from the moon through the glass ceiling, he imagined advisers bowing and standing before him. His eyes showed madness.

Moon was floating around the room from wall to wall, to the pillars and up the ceiling.

"I can be king," said Benavis.

"We can be king," corrected Moon.

"Can Ocrist give me my throne?" wondered Benavis.

"I don't trust that, bald rat," said Moon.

"If he can bring my throne, then I must trust him."

"Then we'll kill him after."

"Of course, he must die for his part in killing my father and uncles." Benavis stopped talking for a while, staring hard at the giant door. "My brother is no king. He can't be king. He doesn't have the heart of a king. He's afraid to be the evil to create the good for the kingdom." He showed an evil grin. "I can be the evil of the south."

Moon floated up to the ceiling. "Someone is coming," it warned.

Giovanis came from the side of the entrance of the throne room. He couldn't sleep because of stress. When he turned to look at his throne, to his surprise, he did not expect to see Benavis sitting on the throne.

"Benavis, what are you doing sitting on the throne?" asked a confused Giovanis.

"Brother, I'm just keeping it warm for you," replied Benavis with an eeriness in his voice. Slowly, madness was taking over his innocence.

Giovanis felt an evil aura around Benavis. He became afraid of his own brother and wanted to run out of the throne room. "W-what do you mean?"

"A king should never sit on a cold throne." Benavis chuckled. "You seem to be in distress. How about you go rest?"

Giovanis was speechless. He felt cold sweat dripping down his back. He felt his throat being squeezed. The Benavis sitting on the throne wasn't his brother. He started to back away, feeling something that was beside him. He didn't want to turn and look and quickly turned to the other side and walked out of the throne room in fear.

Moon floated beside Benavis who had a sinister smile over his face. Standing before them, where Giovanis stood, was a shadow figure that stood as tall as Moon. But this figure had four arms. In each of the four hands were black spirit orbs.

"I am you," said the shadow with four arms.

Benavis smiled, eyes wide with madness. "Welcome."

Chapter Twenty-Three

Kingdom of Enstra

"My father, your former king, is no longer with us," claimed George as he stood before the throne in front of all the clan heads of the western kingdom. Below the steps of the throne room was the Wisefool brothers standing by each side. "His mind was broken. Taken by the devil because of our forbidden clan magic. The same magic the God King Chanfer fell victim to. They both asked to see the outcome of the future, but in return, their wisdom is stolen from them."

Chattering began to fill the room. They were concerned for the future of the west. George allowed the clans to discuss their concerns amongst one another, letting them think that the kingdom was going to fall without their king.

"Where is King Euren?" asked Taejin Ro of the Ro clan, a tall man in his midforties with a heroic look, a respected man in the western kingdom. His clan was the most feared, at the same time the most praised. "Even though the gods turned him into a fool, he, who I still claim as my king, should be sitting on his throne."

Everyone in the throne room started to discuss amongst one another again, all wondering where Euren was. George saw the distrust on the faces of the clans' heads. After his mother sent letters requesting them to side with her against him, he couldn't help but feel like a dagger was preparing to stab him in the back. Even though they all rejected Facelia, there were some that doubted him.

He looked to Edsu for guidance. Edsu in return gave him a nod to tell them what had happened to Euren. "My father has escaped the city during sleep. I sent a search party out looking for him, but they returned with nothing."

"Why was it kept a secret?" asked Jilliana Sun of the Sun clan, the former lover of Euren. "I would've come and searched for him myself."

"If I let the kingdom know, then the war would break. I'm no fool to betrayal," explained George as he showed a cold stare to a silent room. "My mother sent letters to all the clan to side with her. Some of them I was able to intercept. She is the poisonous snake that lurks within the darkness. The clans that received her letter all denied her. Even her own clan denied her." He paused. "My father was a man of tradition. For the guards that were to keep watch on him, they have been punished by execution."

"What's the next step?" asked Den Ta-Nore, a short old bald man, his voice frail and tired. "I'm an old man that lived through five kings of the west. I lived through countless wars. I have great-grandchildren. I don't want to see the kingdom fall while I'm still living."

"You don't have to worry about the kingdom falling, Lord Den," assured George. "If you all respect tradition, then allow me to be your king. Let us continue my father's dreams. I promise to bring light into the darkness. I am willing to sacrifice my life for the west." He showed a confident look on his face to let the clans know he was serious. "Let me be the king of Enstra!"

All the clans discussed amongst themselves, some having doubts, some seeing no other choice, and some wanting to see George, as king. Even though he was the prince, little was known about him. He had never fought in wars and had not shown to have any magical power. All they knew about was that he was a prince.

Then Den Ta-Nore stepped forward. As the oldest in the room and the one who saw the most, he had to step up and decide first. "We do not have any other choice. You're the heir to the throne. I am a man that respects tradition. I respect King Euren. But when he returns, I want him back sitting on the throne. But seeing the climate of the western kingdom, it's best we take you as our king." He bowed to acknowledge George as his king.

Soon, all the other clans followed and bowed to George in acknowledgment. George stood with a grin with sinister thoughts in his mind. He didn't respect any of the clans. To him, they were fools and pawns. They allowed him to have power over them. All he could think about was that he had control over the clans in the west.

"I respect all of you," said George. "As your new king, I will surpass all the greats that rule the west. I will add to the greatness of this kingdom." He sat on the throne feeling the power finally absorbing into his body. He felt different than other times he sat on the throne. Now it was true. He had finally become the king of the west.

Suddenly, the great door swung open and coming in furious, storming her way to George, was Facelia, angry that George did a calling for the clans without her knowing. She knew about Euren's disappearance and suspected that George had a hand in it.

For the last few days, she felt like a prisoner to the palace. She was heavily guarded and followed by the guards. The letter to the Cha clan never made it. She had no clue what was going on until Maji told her that Euren was no longer around.

"Get off that throne, boy!" Facelia pointed with rage. "All of you are fools to allow this boy to be king. He did something to Euren!" she accused George. "This boy knows nothing about the kingdom. He's being controlled by those snake brothers." She insulted the Wisefool brothers.

George chuckled. "Mother, you know nothing of this kingdom. Why would I do anything to my own father?" he lied. "While you sat around and conspired against my father, I was taking care of him. I saw the jester he had become. All you did was sit around and drink tea. Everyone knows that you're the thorn to the kingdom. I challenge you. If you want the throne so much, then ask for a voting."

Facelia looked around and realized there was no way she was getting the vote. They were already set on George. The ones that saw her letter couldn't trust her. "I can't believe you all. All of you have become fools to these jesters!" she insulted the clans. She then turned to her father, Dai-Mu Po, with a disappointed look. "Father, you're willing to side against your own daughter?"

"George is the king, and he's my grandson," replied Dai-Mu, an old man with mysterious eyes.

George laughed. "See, Mother? You're fighting a battle you can't win. You know what, since you tried to overthrow your king and making accusations on your new king, I must punish you for your crime. I still see you as my mother. It will be wrong of me to have you executed. But it'll be stupid of me not to let you pay for your crime."

"I'd rather die than call you my king."

"Mother, you don't have to call me king because I'm banishing you from the kingdom," said George, staring coldly into his mom's eyes. "Guards, take this pitiful woman out of the city!" he ordered.

Two guards approached Facelia, each grabbing her arms. Facelia pushed them off and stared back at George with fierceness. "Stupid boy, you should have executed me. I will return and take that throne from you." She then looked at each of the clan heads. "You all will suffer under his rule, fools." She finished then turned to leave with the two guards following her. All she could think about was revenge, planning in her head an army to take the western kingdom.

* * *

The next morning, George sat on his throne watching the decorators decorate the halls for his coronation. Daydreaming about his celebration, he couldn't wait when the crown would finally be placed on his head. All night he couldn't sleep, excited that he was going to be king, thinking that there was no one going to stop him.

Then bursting through the great door with rage was Alexander. He had skipped out on the clan meeting but was more furious when George had been avoiding him and Emmillda. For the past days, he has been searching for his father, asking everyone in the palace if they knew where his father was. He checked every room in the palace, even the ones he didn't know existed. He couldn't ask Facelia because she was blocked by guards. He felt something strange happening in the kingdom. He even went as far as to ask the Wisefool brothers, but they would lie to him.

"Where is he!" Alexander demanded answers from George angrily.

"Is that how you talk to your king?" questioned George.

"My king is Euren. You can never be him," insulted Alexander.

"You're right, I'll be better than him," promised George.

"What delusional world are you living in? Our father is gone. You act as if nothing happened."

"Nothing happens," smirked George.

"Then where is Father!" yelled Alexander.

"Don't worry, little brother. Father is in a safe place."

"So you did something to him?" angered Alexander with a purple energy ball in his hand.

The decorators all left the room in fear. George sat calmly with an ignorant nonchalant smile, not bothered by Alexander's threat. Now that he had the throne, he thought he was untouchable. He felt like the whole world was in his hands.

"I would never do anything to Father," lied George. "You of all people should know what happens if the kingdom has no king. Look at our army . . . Look at them betraying our clan. Now that I'm king, I'll bring stability back to the kingdom. Our army will blossom once again."

"You don't care about the clan. You don't care about the kingdom. All you care about is yourself," accused Alexander.

George was still unbothered. "Wait and see, little brother. I'll show you and Emmillda the perfect world."

"Shut your mouth with the perfect-world bullshit. You're just a pathetic man. I will find Father and expose you," promised Alexander.

"Go ahead, brother, you are free to act in your own free will," allowed George.

Alexander turned to leave. "If I can't find Father, then I will take that throne from you." He stormed out of the throne room in anger. As he walked out of the room, waiting outside were the Wisefool brothers, both with their snakelike smile.

"Prince Alexander." Jensu bowed his head sarcastically.

"Out of my way, snakes!" insulted Alexander, bumping shoulders with Jensu.

"Watch yourself, Prince Alexander," warned Edsu. "It's best you know your place. You don't want to end up like your mother now."

Alexander stopped. "Don't stay too comfortable," finished Alexander as he continued to walk with rage in his mind.

Alexander made his way to the garden where Lumen and Mai were sitting, waiting for Alexander's arrival. He had called for a meeting to discuss his concern about his brother, mother, and father, afraid that the kingdom was going to fall apart. In his pocket, he still held the letter from his father.

He approached with a disappointed look over his face. Mai didn't feel well by how Alexander looked, hoping that he knew where Euren was. Like Alexander, she was afraid that the kingdom was falling apart. Lumen, on the other hand, was trying to hide the fact that he had involvement with Euren's disappearance, acting concerned like Mai and Alexander. At the same time, he was thinking about the other request.

"Do you know what happens to him?" asked a concerned Mai as Alexander approached.

Alexander shook his head in disappointment. "I think my brother did something to him," he claimed.

"What should we do?" asked Mai.

"I don't know," replied Alexander. "I think it's best we escaped." He turned to Lumen. "Lumen, can you guide us out?"

"Where do you plan to go?" wondered Lumen.

"I don't know, but anywhere is better than here."

"Princess Emmillda will be upset," said Lumen.

"She'll understand. I must protect her from my brother. I fear that he'll act out of control and harm her," worried Alexander.

Lumen nodded, but at the same time felt guilty. He wanted to protect Emmillda, but now he was betraying her trust. His heart felt like it was sinking, standing in front of the people he lied to. He carried his honor on his shoulders but slowly feeling it was fading away.

"I will come back to this kingdom and take the throne from my brother," declared Alexander then showing the letter to Mai and Lumen.

* * *

The early afternoon sun shone brightly over the city of Godfree. Decoration filled the streets of the second and first levels of the city while the third was left forgotten. There were lanterns with a light orb floating around the city. There were balloons shaped into butterflies floating all over the sky. People were drinking and dancing, listening to music as they were ready to accept their new king.

At the Fairy Palace, there were tents set up on the grounds of the palace. Tables were nearly decorated. Like the city, there were lanterns floating all over the palace grounds, with butterfly balloons as well. At the center of the palace ground stood all the clan heads and their family, advisers, and wealthy people, waiting for George to come out of the palace and stand from the balcony to accept his crown.

Standing on the balcony were the Wisefool brothers, one standing at each side of the door. Jensu was holding a purple pillow with an emerald crown resting on it. Also standing with them was the Fairy clan monk an old and bald man with frail eyes.

George stood behind the door nervously as he prepared to step out, waiting all his life to finally officially become king of the west. He did not expect to have nerves running through his body. As time got closer, the more his stomach felt like it was twisting. In the morning, he threw up twice out of excitement. He didn't eat breakfast and spent most of the morning preparing and practicing his speech.

"George," called Emmillda, standing behind him, hoping she could bring sense back into him. "We may have our difference, but you're still my brother." She worried. "I think the George of old is still in there."

George grinned, not turning an inch to Emmillda. He stared at the door with malicious eyes like darkness had overtaken him. "My mother betrayed me, and I punished her by banishing her from the kingdom. But my own siblings, I expected them to be by my side. But no, they never believed in me. The George of old is long gone. I am the king." He opened the door to the outside with a sinister smile over his face, leaving Emmillda alone in her own tears.

George stepped out to a crowd of people waiting for him. The monk and Wisefool brothers bowed to him. He continued forward, leaving his past and sanity behind closed doors, gazing at all the clans, advisers, and wealthy people below. He felt like he was a god standing over them.

He turned to his side, then kneeling to one knee with his head bowed down, the monk approached George with Jensu standing beside with the emerald crown. All he was thinking about was having the crown around his head. His family was no more to him. They were pests in his past life that he had left behind on the road to his ruling.

"Prince George of the Fairy clan. Firstborn of King Euren. Under the great sun in the eyes of the seven protectors of heaven. To the four corners of Telamis. I hereby proclaim you as king of the west." He grabbed the emerald crown and placed it over George's head. Then turning to the people below, he announced, "Your new king of Enstra, King George!"

George stood up and faced the crowd. They bowed to one knee to accept their new king. He felt all the power running through his body. Everything he wanted was all coming to him. To him, he had all the ability to control the world. "I am now the king of the west," started George. "I'm not here to continue my father's legacy. I am here to build a world of my vision. A world where Telamis becomes one!" He paused for a second then looked back at the butterfly banner behind him, turning back to the crowd. "If no one follows the butterfly, the butterfly knows all!" he finished then letting the crowd stand with cheers and clapping. He took it all in. "Now, celebrate for your king!"

The festivity was jolly. People danced on the grounds of the palace under the full moon. Musicians played their music, the smell of ale and wine filling the air. Inside the palace in the throne room sat George, watching as the people danced in his hall. Even though the music in the hall was suffocating, he was still able to think of his plan. He looked to the Ta-Nore and Cha clan and saw them as threats. In fact, there was no clan, advisers, or warriors and magic users he trusted. To him, they were not his allies but his soon-to-be enemies.

George saw Dai-Mu approaching him with a sweet gentle smile but suspecting that the smile was a lie, believing that Dai-Mu's heart was tainted. He didn't want Dai-Mu to believe that he had any power in the western kingdom.

"My king . . . my grandson," said Dai-Mu proudly.

"Grandfather," greeted George.

"I am proud of you, you know that. I stuck beside you against my own daughter. I hope you can do the same."

"Of course. You're my grandfather, I'll make sure to repay you."

"What a good grandson you are," Dai-Yu said, looking around the hall for Alexander and Emmillda. "It's a shame that your siblings are not here to support you." He realized.

"My siblings don't see equal as me."

Dai-Yu smiled. "It's such a shame." He nodded in disappointment then bowing to George and leaving. In his mind, he thought he had power in the western kingdom now that his bloodline was on the throne.

George called over Commander Pai-Sen, a tall threatening man who was standing beside the door. He kept a distrustful eye on Dai-Mu as Pai-Sen approached him.

Commander Pai-Sen bowed his head and leaned to him. "In a month, the Po will celebrate the birth of their clan. I want to send a gift to them. It will a great gift, their ancestors will appreciate it," finished George with a menacing intention in mind.

* * *

"Where are we going?" asked Emmillda to Alexander as they walked in the night outside the walls of Godfree. She peeked back to the city, seeing it glowing under the night sky.

Leading them was Lumen with his sword and Yumpy. Behind Emmillda and Alexander was Mai. They were all wearing a hooded black cloak to hide their identity. The group didn't tell Emmillda that they were leaving, expecting that she would rebel against the idea. Instead, they told her that they were going to meet her mother at an abandoned house. Yet she was still confused why her mother wanted to meet at an abandoned house, suspecting that something terrible had happened at the palace. She wondered if her father was at the abandoned house also.

She was still heartbroken after her interaction with George. She wanted to bring him back to reality, believing that in his heart there was a hint of kindness somewhere. But when she heard him talk and watched him walk through the double doors, her heart was shattered into pieces. George was long gone in his own darkness.

"We're going to see Mother," replied Alexander.

"Is Father going to be there? I haven't seen him around the palace. Is he being healed by a witch?" asked Emmillda.

"It's better if you stop asking questions." Alexander turned to Emmillda with a kind smile. "You don't want to ruin the surprise now."

Emmillda became overjoyed with excitement, wondering what the surprise was. For the past months, she had been depressed, dreading every single day, unable to find any sense of happiness after Yumpy admitted that he hated her and wanted to harm her. She thought of herself as a terrible person.

The group continued to walk the path. Emmillda turned around and couldn't see the city anymore. Her legs were getting tired of walking, and she was getting parched. But her excitement about the surprise kept her moving forward.

They continued walking for another hour. Finally, they reached an abandoned village. The houses were nearly falling apart. There was an eerie feeling in the air, making Emmillda feel uncomfortable. She wondered if her surprise was supposed to be in this village.

Lumen led the group to an abandoned house, sensing that they weren't alone. As the group walked into the house, Lumen stood by the door and kept watch. Mai nodded to him in thanks, finally accepting him not as a traitor. He just looked at her then focused back outside, making sure there was no one around.

"We should rest here for a little and continue soon," suggested Alexander. There was a fly flying around his face that was being a nuisance to him. He slapped the fly away.

"Where are we going?" asked Emmillda, suspecting that her surprise was a lie.

"I lied to you," confessed Alexander. "We're running away from the kingdom."

"Why?" Emmillda asked, her emotions coming out of her again.

"Because I don't want our life under George's rule. He banished our own mother from the kingdom. And I suspect that he did something to Father," replied Alexander.

Emmillda pushed Alexander, but it wasn't strong enough to move him. She was overcome with tears and anger. "Why should we run away from our home?" she cried.

"Are you not listening!" Alexander yelled back.

"Princess, it's best you listen to Prince Alexander," urged Mai, trying to console Emmillda.

Emmillda turned to Lumen. "Lumen, say something. You're supposed to be my protector."

Lumen never turned around, keeping his eyes outside. But inside, he wanted to tell Emmillda that he had to do the unthinkable. He was fighting with himself like a storm brewing inside of him.

"I must protect my family," explained Alexander. "And the only family I have is you. Do you know what will happen if we lived under George's rule?"

"No, but we still shouldn't abandon him. Maybe he and mother can be fixed."

"You see, not everything in this world can be fixed, Emmillda. Everyone is consumed by hate in that palace. I'm taking you out of that palace of hate."

Lumen finally turned around and approached Mai, Alexander, and Emmillda with dark and unexpressive eyes as he finally came to his conclusion with his hand gripped tightly on the handle of his sword. "We all suffer by hate. I've been hated my whole life. Everything I do from my accomplishment and to my loyalty. I was hated. All because of my name. Because of my father and brother, I was hated. I'm destroyed because I'm a traitor-to-be."

Alexander sensed danger and opened his palm to show purple energy dancing on his palm. "Lumen . . ."

Emmillda could also see that Lumen was changing to something sinister. "Lumen, I thought you want to break the cycle of hate?" asked Emmillda, hoping everything happening was just a long nightmare.

"Emmillda, Mai. Stay behind me," ordered Alexander.

Mai and Emmillda quickly stood behind Alexander as he prepared for Lumen. Yumpy stood in front of the door, making sure they couldn't escape.

Lumen unsheathed his sword and continued forward. "I can never break the cycle of hate when my family is the definition of evil."

"Stay away, Lumen!" warned Alexander as he fired purple energy toward Lumen. As it hit Lumen, the cloak he wore dispersed quickly, leaving him unscratched. Alexander was shocked that his energy blast didn't do any damage to Lumen. He continued to shoot as Lumen got closer.

Lumen finally came close to Alexander and quickly grabbed the wrist of Alexander. Alexander was frozen, not knowing what to do as Lumen held his wrist. "You're weak, Alexander. You don't have enough energy in your magic to kill me." He quickly sliced off Alexander's wrist.

Alexander yelled in agony as blood splattered out of his severed wrist, leaking to the cracks of the wooden floor.

Both Emmillda and Mai yelled and cried, not expecting Lumen to act in a malicious way.

Mai quickly stood in front of Emmillda as Lumen stepped over Alexander, her arms spread out as she acted as a shield to Emmillda. "To think that I could trust you," she said with fire in her old eyes. "You will not harm the princess."

Lumen ignored Mai's threat and lifted his sword over his head and sliced down to Mai's shoulder, killing her instantly as she kept the fierce eyes on her face on her way down to the floor. Her blood splattered to Emmillda's face.

Emmillda's eyes opened wide. Words could not come out of her mouth. The man she once thought of as her hero had now become her villain. She fell to the ground and looked at the dead body of Mai, not knowing what to do. She looked up to Lumen and didn't see the man she once knew.

"King George has ordered for your death along with your brother for my freedom." He lifted his sword over his head. "I'm sorry."

"Stop!" demanded Alexander, holding a dagger in his good hand as blood continued to spill from the severed wrist. "Leave her alone, . . . traitor!" he insulted weakly.

Lumen turned around, and Alexander charged stupidly forward to him, knowing that his life was over. He stabbed Alexander in the heart and stared him in the eyes.

Blood dripped from the mouth of Alexander. He peeked over to Emmillda and smiled, letting his sister know that he loved her.

Lumen pulled the sword out, and Alexander limped to the ground on his feet.

Emmillda sat frozen as every organ in her body felt like they had stopped, her heart beating slowly with everything around feeling like it was falling apart.

Lumen turned back around, wiping Alexander's blood off his sword.

"Death is such a horrible thing," said a voice.

Lumen turned around and was displeased that he was stopped again. But when he turned, he was faced with five people. A gigantic bald man had his hand over Yumpy's mouth. There was a girl about the same age as Emmillda with her arrow pointing at him. There was a man with a dagger and the bottom half of his face covered with cloth. There was a man with two swords. Lastly, there was a man with wavy long hair, a thin mustache and goatee, and charming eyes.

Lumen looked back and saw a horn head pointing his sword at him, standing behind Emmillda. He was confused about who these people were. But he could sense that they were dangerous.

"Lumen Glasor, it's an honor to meet you," said the man with charming eyes. He had a nonchalant smile over his face.

"Who are you and how do you know me?"

"I'm sorry, how rude of me. I am Chanzo Mosin, leader of the Forgotten Servant." He bowed his head elegantly.

"What?" asked a confused Lumen, wondering how this man was leading his father's old rebelling group. "Are you some kind of fan?"

"We're not fans. We're children of freedom."

Lumen readied himself.

"We do not want to fight, Lumen. We honor your father. It'll be wrong of me to kill his son." Chanzo looked to the ground. "I see that you killed the prince and that poor gentle old lady. I can't let you kill the princess next."

"Stay out of this," warned Lumen.

"Lumen, we'll let you go free. There's no way you could defeat us."

Lumen stood straight and thought about his outcome, not knowing any of their strength. He didn't want to risk his life. He sheathed his sword. He turned back to Emmillda who was still frozen in fear then turned back to the group. "What will you do to her?"

"Don't worry, we will not harm her," said Chanzo.

"Fine, I'll leave," agreed Lumen.

"Very well. But the horn head must die for your sin. You don't sin on the grounds of the dead," said Chanzo, signaling the giant round man to kill Yumpy.

Yumpy felt the hand over his mouth tighten, his eyes opening wide, hoping that Lumen would save him. Instead, Lumen just gave him a cold look. The giant man quickly cracked Yumpy's neck, killing him and letting his body fall to the ground.

Lumen walked toward the door. The group opened a path for him. As he walked by them, he gave each member a cold look. When he walked by the girl with the bow and arrow, she shot him back with a cold stare. For some reason, the girl looked familiar to Lumen. He walked out of the door and away from the carnage and treachery he had caused.

Chanzo walked over to Emmillda and bent over to her. "You poor princess," he said. "Life is supposed to be delighted like a dandelion field, not tragic like a field of black roses." He smiled gently, smoothly running his finger down Emmillda's cheeks and lifting her chin up to see her lost and broken eyes. "I'm not your friend." He snapped his finger.

Emmillda's vision became blurry as she slumbered to the ground. Blinking and seeing the dead body of Mai and Alexander. Her body became numb, and her mind became senseless, wondering if death was supposed to feel like she was sleeping. Then her eyes shut with everything turning to black. But again, she witnessed death before her. But instead, it was the ones she loved by the hand she trusted.

Chapter Twenty-Four

Forest of Despair

Inside the dream of Ausra as he took his nap under a tree, he dreamed of himself lying on a boat in the middle of an ocean with the sun reflecting from the water, his eyes staring at the red sky as clouds passed by him. Life felt peaceful and still alone on the boat, no one to bother and distract him, wishing life to always be boring, tired of all the blood he had spilled.

Then flying above the sky, reflecting his rare eyes, were five white birds. Ausra sat up as he continued to watch the birds fly away into the vast red sky. Then looking back, a giant wave was coming toward him though he wasn't afraid of the incoming waves. In fact, he was accepting the waves to take him away.

Ausra woke from his nap after his mother's blue flame bird landed on his head. As of late, the bird wouldn't leave him alone. At times, he wanted to kill the bird since it was being a pest to him. Wherever he went the bird followed. Even when he needed to urinate, the bird was still lingering around him.

He touched his face and felt a teardrop on his cheeks. He wondered if he was crying while he napped. For the past weeks, he felt strange like something wicked had happened. Not once did he think about his family. But sometimes, memories of them replayed in his head. He would take naps to stop the memories. He shut his eye back and crossed his arms, quickly falling back to sleep.

Watching Ausra from the dock was Daysa. Beside her was Torshen as he tried to fish peacefully.

Torshen was enjoying himself for the past weeks. All day he got to fish and hunt with freedom. Every now and then, Daysa would annoy him with questions, but he found a way to shut her down, which was to stay quiet and act as if she didn't exist.

"Say, Torshen, how can someone like him be so careless?" Daysa asked Torshen about Ausra.

Torshen ignored her and continued to focus on his fishing, enjoying the sound of the river flowing and birds chirping from the trees. If he could, he wouldn't mind the life of a fisherman. He loved catching fish and the patience that came with it. Sometimes if he caught one, he would toss it back into the river.

Daysa felt shunned by the three men. She wanted to know them, wondering why they're so secretive. She remembered asking Torshen about his tribe during Airian and Kunjae's celebration. She didn't mean to cross the line with him. However, the selfishness in her still wanted to know about Torshen and his ice tribe.

She sat next to Torshen and dipped her feet in the river, scaring all the fish away from the bait, making Torshen annoyed and frustrated with her, but kept a straight face.

"I want to know still," said Daysa, being hopeful that Torshen will answer her. "Why is an ice user like you serving the Kimsu clan? It doesn't make sense—ice and fire are enemies."

"Why do you want to know?" Torshen finally talked.

"I'm curious," replied Daysa, surprised that Torshen replied back.

"Are you always curious?" asked Torshen.

"Well yes, my father always told me to always be curious. Because life is full of curiosity."

"Life . . .," mumbled Torshen.

"Are you going to tell me?" wondered Daysa, trying to figure out Torshen's expression.

Torshen stared at the water as the fishes returned to the bait. Even though he was straight with his expression, he was filled with a raging fire. He didn't know his mother or father. All he knew was that he was an ice user and a child that wasn't wanted. "Vesak was my father."

"Vesak? You all talk about him. Is he someone important?"

"He saved me and took me in as his own. His sons treated me like I'm their little brother. His wife, I called her mom. She always made sure I was fed. I never had a family until Vesak came along. He saved me from the wicked witch that was supposed to care for me. She abused me and made all the other kids think I was different." The memories were all coming back to him. The painful memory he tried so hard to oppress. But still, he showed a straight look, talking like he was being forced to. "Because of my hair and eyes, I was a monster. Because I accidentally made ice out of my hands and hit one of the children, I was a monster. Without Ausra and Sukro, I would've been dead. I don't know what you're talking about when mentioning ice tribes." He stared at the fish going for his bait. "I don't know anything about my real parents. All I know is that I was unwanted." As the fish nearly went for his bait, he lightly tugged his fishing pole and scared the fish away.

Daysa's heart just sank. It felt like a shattered glass cup. She didn't expect Torshen to open up to her so deeply. "What happened to Vesak?" she asked.

Torshen gulped, wondering why he was opening up to her. "Lord Aerin ordered for his death. His family was long gone anyway. Every day he was falling apart. He was alone without his wife and sons. He was tired of living without a purpose." He took a while to recall the memory. "Ausra was also like a son to him. I even think Vesak loved Ausra more than his own sons. But on that dreaded day under the purple moon, it was Ausra that stuck the sword to the back of Vesak, gifting Vesak his key to heaven." Torshen felt a tear drop on his cheek.

Daysa held Torshen's hand tightly and turned to Ausra, upset that he didn't look bothered by anything. "Why does he act so careless?" As she was about to stand to march to Ausra, Torshen held her hand tightly, letting her know to not confront Ausra.

"Leave him alone. He's hurting the most," urged Torshen.

Daysa took a while to look at Ausra and turned back to the river, still holding Torshen's hands. She stared at her own reflection in the water and saw a clueless girl.

Sitting on the steps of the house were Srey-Lau and Sukro. Srey-Lau was carving a new wooden flute as Sukro looked on, fascinated by how Srey-Lau could be so peaceful.

"What's wrong, Sukro?" realized Srey-Lau. "You seem bothered."

"I'm fine," lied Sukro.

"No, you're not. None of you are fine," said Srey-Lau as he put his flute aside. "Our heart is always honest."

"You're right," agreed Sukro. "My father murdered my mother and left me parentless. I do not know how he looked like, but I do know I want to kill him. Am I wrong to think in such a way?"

"Ah, revenge." Srey-Lau smiled. "I advise you to not seek revenge, Sukro. It's a path you ought to avoid."

Sukro nodded in understanding. "Is it okay to give up everything?" he asked. "I want to know why did my father gave up everything? Why did he have to kill my mother? Why have a child and leave?" he expressed angrily.

"Sukro, you don't seek revenge. You seek answers. I can tell you who your father is," revealed Srey-Lau.

Sukro's eyes opened wide, wanting to know the name of his father. "Tell me!" he said with urgency.

"Ha, your father's name is Genseng Vilong, Master of Change."

Sukro was glad to know the name of his father. Now it was embedded in his mind forever. Genseng was the man he was going to find and kill.

"I knew him very well. He was a man who always fought with himself . . . a sad man . . . Ah, our greatest enemy is ourselves," he said to himself then stuck his arms out toward Ausra. "I was given a task to teach him the true meaning of fire."

"What are you doing?" asked a confused Sukro.

"You all must leave so I can find my peace again," warned Srey-Lau. Black flames submerged his hand. "I try so hard to avoid violence. But for him to learn, I'll go back to my past." He fired a blast of black flames toward a sleeping Ausra.

Sukro went for a roundhouse kick to Srey-Lau's head. But his leg was trapped in the hands of Srey-Lau. He looked into the eyes of the raging demon. For the third time in his life, he had felt fear.

Srey-Lau sent Sukro crashing to his wooden front door. Then an ice spear flew by him and nearly hit him in the face. With a portal opening behind, coming out of it were daggers. He managed to dodge the daggers and stick his arms out toward Daysa and Torshen and fire a blast of orange flames toward them.

But a giant wall of black flames stopped the blast of orange flames. Srey-Lau looked over to where Ausra was sitting and saw that the tree was still burning. Coming out of the fire was Ausra with blue energy submerged all over his body. Coming out of his back was energy wings and a tail that resembled a phoenix.

"So you mastered the blue flame cloak . . . the phoenix cloak." Srey-Lau was amazed. "You are truly a natural, Ausra. Andrena was correct about you—you are the one. I was told to show you the path of fire. But I see that you made my job easier. You're wondering why I attack you? Well, it's to see your strength and weakness." He looked over to Daysa and Torshen. "Your weakness is your heart, Ausra. When I tell you to find your peace, I mean for you to release all that you love to become a true demon." His body then began to be submerged in orange energy that resembled a tiger. "You see, Andrena sees you as the savior of this world, Ausra. There are stupid people that believe they're serving the gods, thinking of controlling the narrative of this world. There are people that sit on lavish thrones thinking that they stand with the gods. There are people that believe their gods... but you, Ausra Kimsu. You're the demon that was chosen." He got into a tiger stance and stood on his toes.

Ausra ignored Srey-Lau; the energy around him felt like it was controlling him. But he got into a phoenix stance, keeping his foot light on the ground and hands flexible, trying to remember what his grandfather had taught him, recalling the moment his grandpa was telling him to never use the ability unless he has to.

Srey-Lau charged at Ausra, firing orange flames from his elbows and knees.

Ausra managed to reflect all the flames with his own flames coming from his hand. Then a flying knee came from Srey-Lau nearly pushing him back. He recollected himself, feeling the power from Srey-Lau's knee.

Srey-Lau quickly changed into a green energy cloak that resembled a monkey. Then getting into a monkey stance, with the front leg on its toe, he charged at Ausra again with elbows, kicks, and knees. Ausra blocked all the hits but felt his energy draining. He fired a blast of blue flames but missed as Srey-Lau dodged and nearly kicked him in the face.

They faced each other. Ausra was trying to regain energy while Srey-Lau looked as if he could fight all day.

Ausra then let the blue energy return inside his body. Never in his life had he felt defeated. It left a bad taste in his mouth. For the first time, he felt like he had to fight to live. He peeked over to Torshen and Daysa watching the duel in shock, then to Sukro who was recovering from the throw.

"Is that it, Ausra?" mocked Srey-Lau, as purple energy submerged his body. "I know the five stances of flames." He resembled a dragon with two large energy wings coming from his back. "You never knew how it feels to almost die, do you? I want to ask you again, Ausra. What is your peace?"

Ausra picked his head up and showed an eye of a demon to Srey-Lau with an excited smile, finally feeling excited about fighting. "My peace is freedom," he replied. Then in the blink of an eye, he charged toward Srey-Lau and held him by his neck.

Srey-Lau was stunned, wondering what kind of power Ausra was using. Now he was the one afraid. He opened his mouth and fired purple flames out of it. But the flames reflected off Ausra's face. He continued to fire out his mouth. Each time he failed. The grip on his throat tightened and weakened him, the purple energy returning inside his body. He tried chopping down on Ausra's wrist, and still, the grip won't release. "W-what a-are you . . ."

Ausra ignored Srey-Lau. His eyes turned red, including the white of the eye. He looked down at his hand and showed black energy that was shaped into a mask. "I am a demon," he said to himself. Then he put the black energy mask over his face, and looking back at Srey-Lau, he showed a black mask with red eyes and four large fangs from top and bottom.

Srey-Lau was afraid but yet was satisfied. The mask was the face of his father, Chenva, realizing that the gods had chosen their new hero. "We'll meet again, Ausra," Srey-Lau said to himself, shutting his eyes.

Ausra picked him and slammed him to the ground then kicking Srey-Lau back to the steps of his house. He charged over and picked Srey-Lau up by the neck and threw him, sending him crashing into his shack.

Sukro could only watch in fear. It wasn't his cousin that he saw. It was a monster that was living inside his cousin. He was frozen as Ausra walked toward him, not knowing if he was going to live. He sensed that both Daysa and Torshen were also terrified.

The masked on Ausra's face turned back into black energy and returned to his body. He looked as if nothing had happened. The blue flame bird landed on his shoulder, seeing the damage he had done to Srey-Lau's home then seeing the terrified expression on the faces of Sukro, Torshen, and Daysa.

"We should return to the temple," suggested Ausra calmly.

* * *

Kaiso stood before hundreds of fox demons guards with spears in their hands. Beside him was Nisu. For the past weeks, every morning they woke up and ate their breakfast, which was just steamed fish. Then they'd spend the rest of the morning to late afternoon training the fox guards how to fight. Once the training was over, they were brought back into their room and stay locked inside. Their dinner would be brought up to them during the night. The both of them were getting tired of their repetitive life, wondering how long would Queen Aesi wait to order their execution.

Kaiso was annoyed when the guards called themselves warriors but couldn't fight. He listened to their conversation and wanted to strangle them for bragging about their fighting ability. The fox was one of the four protectors of the Forest of Despair, but he wondered how they protect the forest when they couldn't fight.

"Get in your stance, guards," ordered Nisu kindly.

The fox guards get in their fighting stance. Both Kaiso and Nisu were horrified by the clumsiness and weakness of the stance. Something so simple and yet these foxes made it look difficult.

"There's no way we could train these creatures," whispered Nisu.

Kaiso gave Nisu a cold side eye. "It's your fault."

"Come on—"

"Fix your stance!" yelled Kaiso to the guards, cutting off Nisu and focusing on the training.

The guards were all afraid of Kaiso, especially when he yelled at them. Even though they were animals, he resembled more of an animal than them. Kaiso was ruthless to them while Nisu took it easy. Nisu would take the time to talk to them and ask about the city while Kaiso only gave them cold glances and shouting at them.

Kaiso recalled the moment he trained with Vesak. Like the fox, he couldn't get his stance right. Vesak would always hit him in the legs with a wooden stick to fix his foot. He hated when Vesak scolded him in front of the others, but at the same time, it made him train harder. He remembered days where he would just practice his fighting stance, fixing his footwork when no one was around.

The fox guards continued to practice their stance. Still, they looked clumsy and weak. Even though Kaiso tried to act like he didn't care. He was angry that they were disrespecting the art of fighting. Vesak always told him to never focus on the strength when it came to fighting. The technique and knowledge were always the keys in battle.

"You all call yourselves warriors?" questioned Kaiso angrily. "If there was an invasion, I don't think any of you will survive."

"Shut your mouth, human!" shouted one of the guards.

"What!" angered Kaiso.

"You're still a prisoner!" shouted another guard.

Kaiso did forget he was a prisoner for a second. To hold his anger, he clutched his hands and held his breath. His rage was noticeable to the fox demons. But yet they continued to mock him since they knew they were untouchable.

Nisu could feel the situation getting worse for the guards. The more they laughed and mocked Kaiso, the more Kaiso wanted to hurt them. He peeked over to Kaiso and saw the veins exposing from his forehead, the clenching teeth and the pure anger in his eyes. He was praying in his head that Kaiso wouldn't do anything violent toward the guards.

"Enough!" warned Nen as she approached behind Kaiso and Nisu.

All the guards kept their mouths shut and stood straight. Kaiso was jealous that they'd rather listen to Nen than him. Whenever Nen was around watching the guards train, the guards seemed to take their training more seriously. When training was over, he could feel Nen staring at him, but he didn't bother to know why.

"I think that's enough training for today," said Nen.

The guards all sighed in relief. They were glad that Nen had stopped their training with Kaiso and Nisu.

Kaiso and Nisu were also relieved that the training was over.

Nisu was curious why the training was stopped. In the back of his mind, he was skeptical and silently keeping his guard up, hoping that Kaiso was doing the same. They were without their weapons, and both of them didn't have any magic skills. All Nisu had was his speed and Kaiso his strength. And that alone wouldn't be enough against the fox demons.

Two guards approached both Kaiso and Nisu to escort them back to their rooms. But Nen stopped them. "Take the pervert to my mother. She wants to speak to him." She ordered. "Leave the big one with me."

The guards bowed and escorted Nisu to the palace. Nisu had a look of concern over his face. He turned his head back to Kaiso. Showing that he was afraid that something terrible might happened to both of them.

"Why does she want to speak to him only?" asked Kaiso.

"She wants to ask him questions," replied Nen.

"About what?" asked Kaiso in annoyance.

"My mother doesn't tell," answered Nen. She looked up to Kaiso. "I want to apologize." She bowed her head to Kaiso. "It's my fault that you and the pervert are prisoners. My mother was never the same after my brothers died. She still weeps for them." She grabbed Kaiso's hands. "She's afraid of losing me. Have you ever lost anyone before?"

Kaiso ripped his hand away and showed a distant look. "Of course, I'm a warrior. I am bound to see people I know die." He thought of Vesak.

"Are you afraid to lose yourself, Kaiso? All the scars on your body . . . why do you torture yourself?"

Kaiso became angry and exposed by Nen. He did not appreciate that she was reading him and trying to understand him. He wanted to keep all of his sufferings to himself. His thoughts and emotions were all bottled up inside of him. "Mind your business, fox!" angered Kaiso. "You don't need to know me. I know what's going to happen to that weird weakling and me. Your mother is going to have us executed after we train her guards how to kill our comrade. Your enemy is not your friend."

"Why do we have to be enemies?" questioned Nen.

"You don't understand this world because you're protected. Have you ever seen a child murdered before your eyes? Have you ever had to kill a boy that was the same age as you? Want to know about my scars? The scars are symbols of the evil I caused."

Nen just stared at Kaiso with a bit of sympathy toward him. She was holding in her feelings toward him and hiding her sadness for him. She called for the guards to escort Kaiso back to his room. Two of them approached and escorted him away from her. But as he walked by her, she held his wrist. "Don't sleep," she whispered to him as he ripped his hands away.

Kaiso wondered why she told him to not sleep, thinking that he might not live to see the next day. In his head, he had already accepted his fate, ready to die and live freely in the heavens. But in his case, he thought there was no place for him in the heavens. Instead, he believed that when he died, he would roam the earth as a restless soul because he had done more bad than good.

Meanwhile at the palace, Nisu stood in the hall alone, staying on high alert for any attempt to kill him. He was curious and afraid at the same time. It was itching him to know why Queen Aesi only wanted to see him. Thinking that she wanted to split Kaiso and himself from each other, he feared that Kaiso was being murdered by the guards on the training grounds.

The queen finally arrived by the side of the door with two servants beside her. They stopped at the doorway as she made her way to the throne then sat and gave a distasteful glare toward Nisu. She hated humans since her sons all died at the hands of one.

Out of respect, Nisu bowed his head to her with concern over his face. He didn't want to die since there was so much in life he wanted to experience. He wanted to have children, he wanted to travel to Inko Island, he wanted to grow old and tell his story.

"I heard the training process hasn't been going well," said Aesi with disappointment. "Why is that?" she asked strictly.

"Uh, . . . it takes time to learn how to fight, my queen," answered Nisu nervously.

"I don't need time. I need them to learn how to fight so that murderer can pay for my sons' death."

"I have a lot of respect for you, my queen. But your guards are no warriors. They never held a spear or sword before."

"I blamed my valiant husband for that. So much a great fighter he was but his heart was too pure."

"He must be a great man," complimented Nisu.

"Quiet, human!" shot Aesi. "My husband was a great man. It's because of him why all fox demons got along . . . but he struggles with kindness. I know the guards can't fight. I'm not afraid of any invasion coming for my city. I'm afraid of all the freeness and security we have. It was because of my husband that none of them knows how to fight. He promised them a city with no violence, no blood . . . Because of his thinking and kindness, it cost our sons' lives. If only they knew how to fight, then that boy would've never killed them." She began to tear as she thought about her sons. "Why did Chenva took my sons away from me?"

Nisu sensed that he wasn't going to die, seeing that Aesi was suffering because of her sons' death. "My queen, with all due respect, the man that killed your sons, is no human," said Nisu.

"What do you mean?" questioned Aesi.

"The Wild Beast and I could only teach your guards so much. But there's no way any of your guards stand a chance against him. I witnessed him murder a father and mother in front of their children. I truly fear three things in this world—one is the gods, then my dead teacher, Master Vesak, and last is Ausra. I'm sorry for what happened to your sons. But getting revenge for them will result in your death. I like to consider him my friend. What he did still aches your heart. As honorable and loyal as I am, I would give up my life for payment of his doing."

Queen Aesi was displeased. She really wanted her guards to learn to fight and kill Ausra. "Your death is not equal to my sons' death. That boy must die and you dare give up on me? Who do think you're trying to act honorable for?" she yelled. "Guards, remove this idiot out of my palace!" she ordered.

Five guards entered the room and escorted Nisu out of the palace. As he left, he showed a hidden grin, now knowing that Aesi's mind was weak. At the same time, he had to be careful since a weak mind can result in emotional decisions.

Kaiso was waiting for Nisu in their room, curious to know if Nisu was dead or not, keeping his eyes on the door. With his hands balled in a fist, preparing for an attack from the guards, he'd rather put up a fight than die without pride.

The door opened, and Kaiso jumped. But to his luck, it was Nisu. He walked in with a giant smile across his face. Like he had seen a naked woman for the first time. Kaiso settled himself, relieved that Nisu was still alive.

"Why are you happy?" asked Kaiso annoyedly. He wanted to slap the arrogant smile off Nisu's face.

"The queen called me her king," joked Nisu.

"Stop with your jokes!" angered Kaiso.

"Okay . . . you need to smile sometime, Wild Beast. All you do is frown. How can anybody like you?" suggested Nisu.

"I don't care what anybody thinks of me," admitted Kaiso.

"Very well," said Nisu, as he sat across the room. "I don't think we're going to die."

"What makes you think that?" asked Kaiso curiously.

"You know I like the weak ones, Wild Beast. The queen is no different from the women I chased after. Her emotions still hinder her ability to rule. That's why the guards take advantage of her. They don't care as long as they don't have to fight. They know their queen still aches for her sons' death. They're playing her as a fool."

"Stupid observation," insulted Kaiso, but glad that Nisu took the time to observe the situation.

Suddenly, the door opened, and Nen was standing by the doorway. "Do you both want to leave?" she asked.

"Of course," replied Nisu, standing up in excitement.

"Then follow me. The guards are no longer guarding," said Nen.

"Where are they?" asked Kaiso.

"They're off to the tavern or gambling at the main hall," replied Nen.

Kaiso looked at Nisu who had a grin on his face. Nisu was right about the guards not showing respect toward the queen. He felt embarrassed but nodded to Nisu for his observation.

"We should hurry," urged Nen. "The gates is unguarded right now." She tossed them two cloaks and their weapons. "Put them on and put the hood over your head. I'm sneaking the both of you out." She put her hood over her head.

They followed Nen out of the barrack and to the city. They avoided the main street and stayed in the shadows without saying a word to each other. It was hard to not miss Kaiso since he was tall and muscular. He was trying his best to stay low but struggled. To his surprise, he was amazed at how oblivious the fox demons were. Sneaking out was a breeze. The city folks had no clue that the princess was helping two prisoners escape their cave city.

They finally arrived at the entrance where no guards were around. The city folks were all flowing with their lives while the guards were lazy and useless. Kaiso looked around and couldn't find a single guard. He was agitated that they called themselves warriors when they didn't respect the pride of one.

"How are you supposed to protect your city when your guards are useless?" asked Kaiso.

"That's what I worry about. They only become warriors when I leave the city. They're great, but they take safety too kindly," said Nen calmly.

"It's because they sense their queen's weakness," said Nisu. "But they do respect you, Princess."

"So you know. It's all an act to make my mother feel like she was in control. I love her and I want to help her."

"Why are you helping us?" asked Kaiso to Nen.

"Because we're not enemies, Kaiso." She reached into her pockets and pulled the red wooden bead bracelet out. She reached to Kaiso's hands and placed the bracelet in his palm. "My father gave me this bracelet. This proves that we're not enemies."

"I don't need this—"

"Leave before the guards return," Nen cut off Kaiso. "Goodbye forever." She turned to leave with her heart broken.

Kaiso stared at the bracelet in his palm.

Nisu placed his hand on Kaiso's shoulder.

They both turned to leave, Nisu leading the way with enjoyment that he was finally free. Kaiso, on the other hand, was trying to figure out Nen while putting the bracelet around his wrist.

They did not say a word to each other as they walked out of the cave. Nisu was humming a tune he made in his head. When they finally walked out of the cave, smelling the air of freedom, Nisu continued to walk, but Kaiso took one last look at the cave then followed Nisu.

*   *   *

The glowing leaves were nearly fading. Fireflies woke from their sleep. For weeks, Nagen and Leonaris waited for the others to return to the temple. They barely spoke to each other. They sat around the fire with Leonaris reading a book and Nagen staring into the fire thinking about the man that hanged himself in the forest.

All of a sudden, coming out within the darkness of the forest was Sukro, Daysa, and Torshen. All three kept their distance from Ausra as he followed behind. They made their way to the fire and sat quietly. All three looked like they had seen a ghost.

Ausra sat under a tree, acting like he didn't scare the others with the blue flame bird landing on his shoulder.

Then from the other side arrived Kaiso and Nisu. They sat at the fire with the others.

They all sat silently as they tried to recollect their adventure. Their moment away from each other was useful. At the same time, a lot of truth was let out. Torshen still suffered from his childhood, Sukro yearned for revenge and answers, Nisu understood how being comfortable was his weakness, Kaiso suffered from pain inside, Leonaris trying to find happiness, and Nagen searching for his purpose. While Ausra sat alone thinking about his peace and freedom.

Leonaris puts his book aside. "Did everybody find themselves?" he asked.

"We found more than what we asked for," answered Sukro, looking back at Ausra who wasn't paying attention.

"I miss Vesak," admitted Nagen. "Look at us, we're nothing without him."

"He always brought us together," added Nisu.

"I wish his life could've ended better," regretted Kaiso.

"He always told us to find happiness in our lives," said Torshen.

"Are we happy?" questioned Sukro. "We have been warriors our whole lives. He never wanted us to be warriors. We're like his sons, and we can't even stand each other. I don't want him to look down from the heavens and cry seeing us hating each other."

Nagen stood up and took his cloak off, holding it over the fire. "Vesak created us," he said. "When he died, the dragons should have been no more." He looked at each of his comrades. "It's best we separate and find our own path. I want to find my purpose in this life."

Leonaris stood up and took his cloak off and held it over the fire. "I want to find my happiness," confessed Leonaris.

Nisu stood and followed. "I want to be comfortable with my life," sticking his cloak over the fire.

Sukro stood up. "I want to find the answers I'm searching for." He stuck his cloak over the fire.

Kaiso stood up and stuck his cloak over the fire. "I want to end my pain."

Torshen stood up and did the same as the others. "I want to end my sorrow," he said.

Daysa looked around as she felt outcast by the dragons. Not knowing what to do, feeling like her hope in finding the golden phoenix was dwelling. But at the same time, she understood the emotions and struggles each member of the dragons was hindered by.

Torshen looked down at Daysa. "Stand with us," he urged.

She smiled and stood with him, holding on to his cloak, glad that he didn't see her as an outcast. "I want my dream to come true," she said.

Ausra stood up and slowly walked to the fire, taking off his cloak. Torshen, Sukro, and Daysa were still afraid of him. But came to accept that he was not a monster. He looked at each of his comrades and Daysa. "Vesak always said that we're brothers," he said calmly. He stuck his cloak over the fire. "I want my peace," he finished, seeing in the fire his own reflection of a broken demon with his wings clipped.

They all dropped their cloaks into the fire and watched it burn in silence. Signifying that the deadly group, the Seven Demon Dragons was no more. The forest made them all think of Vesak, hoping that he was watching from above and seeing their struggles without him. The first to leave was Leonaris, then Nisu. After, Kaiso and Nagen. All going in separate directions.

Sukro looked at Ausra. "I'm going now, Ausra," he said. "Please watch over yourself." He left his cousin and disappeared into the darkness of the forest.

Torshen sat down along with Daysa. Ausra stayed standing up wondering why the two hasn't left yet. "Are you guys not going?"

"I'm not leaving you alone, Ausra," said Torshen.

"Is that so?" mumbled Ausra. He then looked to Daysa. "We will find that bird of yours." He looked up to the leaves. All of a sudden he felt a raindrop on his cheek.

Somehow a single drop of rain was able to get past the wall of leaves. But to Ausra, the raindrop wasn't just a raindrop. It was the tears of Vesak, telling him that he was upset that his boys were no longer fighting alongside each other. But proud that they were finally searching for their own path.

"How tiresome," Ausra sighed. "The bird is free from his cage, Vesak," he ended.

THE END